HANDS
OF A
STRANGER

Robert Daley

A SIGNET BOOK

NEW AMERICAN LIBRARY

PUBLISHER'S NOTE

This novel is a work of fiction. Names, characters, places, and incidents either are the product of the author's imagination or are used fictitiously, and any resemblance to actual persons, living or dead, events, or locales is entirely coincidental.

NAL BOOKS ARE AVAILABLE AT QUANTITY DISCOUNTS WHEN USED TO PROMOTE PRODUCTS OR SERVICES. FOR INFORMATION PLEASE WRITE TO PREMIUM MARKETING DIVISION. NEW AMERICAN LIBRARY, 1633 BROADWAY. NEW YORK. NEW YORK 10019.

Copyright © 1985 by Riviera Productions Ltd.

This is an authorized reprint of a hardcover edition published by Simon and Schuster.

SIGNET TRADEMARK REG. U.S. PAT. OFF. AND FOREIGN COUNTRIES
REGISTERED TRADEMARK—MARCA REGISTRADA
HECHO EN CHICAGO. U.S.A.

SIGNET, SIGNET CLASSIC, MENTOR, ONYX, PLUME, MERIDIAN AND NAL BOOKS are published by New American Library, 1633 Broadway, New York, New York 10019

First Signet Printing, October, 1986

1 2 3 4 5 6 7 8 9

PRINTED IN THE UNITED STATES OF AMERICA

1

THE FIRST RAPE VICTIM THAT MORNING WAS A NINE-teen-year-old black girl. The second was a thirty-eight-year-old white housewife. Assistant District Attorney Judith Adler could not do much for either.

The black girl was led in by a female detective and directed to the chair across the desk. The detective handed over the girl's case folder and sat down against the wall, a yellow pad on her skirt, her heavy handbag on the floor beside her.

Judith Adler, scanning the folder, saw that the victim, whose name was Bianca, and who had been gang-raped yesterday by six men, had never seen any of her rapists previously. None had been addressed by name in her presence, and she could describe them only as "six black dudes." The description did not make Judith smile.

"How are you this morning, Bianca?" she said to her, looking up. "Are you all right?" There was as much warmth and sympathy in her voice as she could put there because, judging from the case folder, sympathy was all the justice this victim was likely to get.

Bianca said she was fine, thank you, and indeed seemed to be. In her place, a Park Avenue college girl—Judith had dealt with several—would probably be catatonic. Bianca wore jeans, and high heel shoes out of which peeped scarlet toenails. Her face was very young, her complexion very black. She wore scarlet lipstick and a scarlet blouse as well, and by the standards of her own world she was perhaps elegantly dressed. Who was Judith to say? She herself wore a navy blue suit over a silk blouse.

The rape victim waited patiently.

According to the case folder the site of occurrence was a welfare hotel in Harlem. This place was known to Judith Adler. It was her job to know such things. "That's not a nice hotel," she commented, as if the hotel itself was to blame, for the crime against Bianca was otherwise incomprehensible. "Lots of prostitutes there."

Bianca had no job, no fixed address. Last week she had moved from a public shelter to the welfare hotel, and she knew enough to sleep fully dressed even to her shoes lest everything she owned be stolen by morning.

A woman named Maria—no last name—lived there also, and became her girlfriend. But Maria had a husband, whether common law or real made no difference, and this husband bragged one morning about having had sex next door with Bianca in the night.

"He tell Maria I suck his thing."

"And did you, Bianca?" Her role gave Judith Adler the right to ask such questions, and some of those she would ask later would be more personal still.

"I wouldn't have no sex with no man I just met," protested Bianca. "I think too much of myself for that."

This was said with such dignity that Judith, though she only nodded, wished to applaud her. To Judith dignity and courage were the same. Both were rare, admirable, and, in the case of someone whose prospects for life were as grim as Bianca's, totally unexpected.

Maria had gone down and out into the streets of Harlem to collect some men. She had found them lounging on front stoops, loitering on street corners under the lights. She had collected six of the loafers and brought them back upstairs. They ranged in age from the teens to the fifties. "I gonna hurt you because of what you done to my man," she had told Bianca, and she set the men upon her.

Like every other crime, rape fell into categories. This one, Judith Adler saw, was a vengeance rape. Rape to get even. Rape as punishment.

All six men had raped Bianca. They had done so repeatedly and for as long as they could, they had raped her front and back, and when their ability or enthusiasm or whatever kept them going finally flagged they had begun to rape her with objects.

It was lucky, Judith thought, that they didn't inadvertently kill her. Plenty of girls in similar circumstances had bled to death.

Her first job was to get down an accurate description of the acts themselves—what and by whom. Her questions were explicit, and she demanded explicit answers.

But her voice maintained an even tone, for her job did not permit her to display emotion, and sometimes she wondered if she still felt any. She had not wanted to become hardened. I'm a woman, she had reminded herself over and over again. I'm not a man.

The outrages that the poor visited on each other sometimes made the rich seem saintly by comparison. In addition to Maria, who had acted as supervisor, and the rapists themselves, the room had been full of spectators, apparently, and Judith began trying to collect those names Bianca knew, no last names unfortunately. There was Maria, of course, and her husband Willis.

"Did Willis rape you?"

"Willis, he the referee."

Silvia, no last name, described as "two or three tones lighter than me," was weeping as piteously as Bianca, and begging the rapists to let Bianca go. Tiny, described by Bianca as a "humongously fat man with a high perspiration smell," had watched with his thumb in his mouth. This description, Judith realized, would sound funny in the retelling. It would perhaps sound funny even in a courtroom. It did not sound funny to her.

"You stay away from that hotel," Judith advised the girl, looking up from her notes. "Because if they find out you've come to me they may try to harm you." Harm her? They would probably kill her. Judith wrote out phone numbers and handed them across the desk. "These are my home and office numbers both," she explained. "And if you lose them, I'm in the book. If you see any of those people, if anyone bothers you, I want you to call me at once. Do you understand? Call me at any hour night or day."

As the female detective led Bianca out of the office, Assistant District Attorney Adler closed the folder, but not the case. Although there was not much to go on, she decided to pursue it anyway. She would send two black detectives to the hotel. If Maria, Willis, Tiny, or Silvia were still there, and could be identified, and if Bianca acquired an address and remembered to call in, then perhaps a lineup could be arranged, arrests made. Maria and Willis, once arrested, might give up the names of the rapists. If they knew them. Perhaps there could be a trial.

Too many ifs. And where would she get the detectives from? Police commanders did not like to give up men for low priority cases like this one. She would have to do a lot of wheedling.

The next case was little better. The thirty-eight-year-old white housewife took the same chair as Bianca. There was a bruise high up on her cheek and black stitches at the corner of her mouth. She managed a rueful smile, as if embarrassed to be causing so much trouble, and this smile appeared half an inch wider on one side of her face than the other. She doesn't look too bad, Judith thought. Not like some I've seen. The ones the real loonies have had a go at.

The housewife had been accosted while jogging in Central Park. She had been dragged into the bushes and raped. She had screamed, but no one came. She had since viewed the albums of habitual sex offenders, but had been unable to pick out her assailant.

Rapists were recidivists, Judith Adler told her. "The next time he may be caught, and we would ask you to come down and try to pick him out of a lineup."

It seemed pitifully little to give the woman in exchange for what had been done to her.

When the female detective had led her out, Mr. Katz came in with a sheaf of telephone messages. Mr. Katz was her secretary, a man nearing sixty who wore an ill-fitting toupee. He had first come to work in the district attorney's office more than thirty years before. In those days everyone, including the secretaries, had to be men. By the time Judith Adler had got out of law school—scarcely a dozen years ago—there were still only six females on a staff of over two hundred prosecutors and they were not given cases to prosecute. Of course it was not that way now. Applying for a job here, Judith was young, fresh-faced, and eager, and the then district attorney, a courtly old man, did not want to hire her. She still remembered exactly the dress she was wearing that day, how nice she had tried to make herself look for the old man. "Our work is too tawdry for a young woman," he had told her. She had argued, insisted, begged. Finally, against his better judgment it seemed, he had taken her.

The old man was right, Judith reflected now. It is tawdry—more tawdry than anyone on the outside could guess.

One of the phone messages, Mr. Katz said now, seemed peculiar, and he handed it to her: a captain from the New Jersey State Police had called. "He would speak only to you personally. Said it was urgent."

Assistant District Attorney Adler, with a head full of brutalized women, wanted a change from that, any change, however momentary, and so she fingered the "urgent" message and was curious. New Jersey?

"Get him on the phone," she said to Katz, who nodded and went out.

When the button on her telephone lit up she punched it. "Hello," she said.

But she had sent a female voice out along the wire, and the male voice on the other end refused to accept it. He could speak only with the assistant district attorney in charge personally, he insisted.

"This is she," said Judith, already annoyed. That the trooper had expected to talk to a man was obvious. A few years ago he would have said so; now, Judith noted once more, such people merely treated her to a rather prolonged silence.

"This is Captain Sample," the male voice said finally. "Could you come out here? We have something important to talk to you about." And he waited.

"You better brief me," said Judith. Having already lost interest in Captain Sample, she had begun shuffling through her other messages. Lawyers for defendants. The corrections commissioner—trouble with a prisoner, probably. The mayor's office. The chief administrative judge.

"I don't want to go into it over the phone," said Captain Sample.

This remark annoyed Judith also. Cops on a case loved to pretend their every phone line was tapped.

"I'm pretty busy," she said briskly. "If you want to come in here, I can offer you an appointment probably tomorrow or the next day."

Sample tried an assured laugh. "I don't think I could

find your office. You'd have to send a police car to your end of the tunnel to lead me in."

Judith said firmly: "Otherwise—"

There was another silence while her threat sank home. Finally Sample sighed. "Two men are trying to force this young broad into a car," he said. He had a rough voice and a rough accent. "And one of my men happens to drive by, see. We arrest the two perpetrators, see, and in the trunk of their car what do you think we find?"

Judith had decided to call the administrative judge next. A scheduling problem, she guessed. It could be negotiated over the phone. "I don't know," she said to Captain Sample, "what do you find?"

"Forty kilos of hashish," he said triumphantly.

"Interesting," said Judith. She had two courtroom hearings on next, the first of them five minutes from now—and on the fifteenth floor.

Sample, like most small-town cops, was easily intimidated. "I know that don't sound like much in New York."

"Drugs are not my department," Judith said. She didn't want to hurt Sample's feelings but she had best cut this short. "And New Jersey is outside my jurisdiction."

"We get a search warrant on their house," said Sample hurriedly, "and what do you think we find?" This time he did not wait for an answer. "Twenty or more hours of videotapes, that's what. We start playing them, see. They're all live videotapes of actual rapes. Young girls. Models. Playboy Bunnies. Beautiful young girls." He sounded like a barker for a strip show. "But the rapes all took place in New York City. I want you to come out here and look at the tapes. Will you come?"

Judith had stopped shuffling through her phone messages.

"The drug case may lead back there too," Sample said, trying to sweeten the bait.

He's a small-town cop with a big rape case on his hands, thought Judith. He doesn't know what to do with it. He's asking for help.

Then she thought, He's only interested because the victims were attractive. This offended her. As reasons went, it was offensive. Suppose the victims had been old ladies? Old ladies got raped too, she wanted to tell Sample. Grandmothers come in here, she thought. They no longer consider themselves as sexual objects, haven't for years, and their principal emotion as they recount their stories—as they describe what men did to them—is fear that I will laugh.

"So will you come out?" said Sample.

There was a pleading note in his voice. It was very slight because tough guys, tough cops at any rate, did not plead—or so Judith supposed. But it was there and she caught it. I ought to think about this a few minutes before saying no, she told herself. I owe him that much. "Let me see what they have for me here," she said. "I'll get back to you."

As she hurried up to the fifteenth floor, the conversation stayed with her.

The first of her two hearings involved an enormously fat, slow-witted young handyman from a West Side apartment building. Three weeks previously, for no reason anyone could determine, he had decided to rape one of the tenants at knife point. When he failed to maintain an erection, he began stabbing her. The youth then went to visit his mother, to whom he handed over his bloody clothes to be washed. She called the police. Now his lawyer was trying to keep him in the psychiatric ward and out of the general prison population on the grounds that he was as round and soft as any woman and just as physically defenseless. Irony of ironies: in prison he would get raped.

Judith insisted on the proper legal stipulations. Otherwise she had no objections.

The second hearing in an adjacent courtroom involved a stocky, middle-aged black man released from prison only three weeks ago. With no job and no money, with only the clothes he was still wearing in court today, plus his various hungers, he was turned loose on society. In his two weeks at large, knowing no women, without money to pay a prostitute, he had raped two strangers in the vestibules of buildings. Both resembled prison rapes—quick, brutal encounters—no doubt the only kind of sex this man knew or could feel comfortable with. Now the defendant stared impassively at the tabletop while his legal aid lawyer told the judge that his client's civil rights had been violated, his arrest was illegal. The arresting officer had lacked probable cause, and the lineup at which both victims had picked his client out had been improperly arranged.

This was one of the many pending rape cases whose details Judith carried in her head. Before the bench she argued that, on the contrary, this case represented police work of the highest order, and she explained exactly why. She then put the young arresting officer on the stand. First she questioned him, and then the legal aid lawyer subjected him to a withering cross-examination. It was almost a fullscale trial, lacking only a jury and a verdict.

"Your Honor," the legal aid lawyer concluded, "my client was arrested only because he was a black man in a white neighborhood. This arrest stinks to high heaven. I want it thrown out."

The judge reserved decision, meaning he might ultimately decide to order the defendant freed. It happened often enough. Judith would have to sweat this case out too, and she was already sweating out a great many.

Meanwhile, the handcuffs went back on the defendant, who stood less than ten feet from her. If a man is a rapist, she thought, studying him, it ought to be obvious. You ought to be able to tell by looking at him. But nothing shows. Rapists look no different from anybody else. Same with murderers. Evil cannot be recognized at a glance. That's why we have courtrooms. It's the best we can do.

The young cop stood beside her. "That lawyer," the cop said selfconsciously, "he was something, wasn't he?"

It was such lawyers who had poisoned most cops against her profession, and Judith knew this. But she had no intention of denigrating lawyers—any lawyer—in front of policemen, so she gave the cop a smile, and shook hands with him, and he left.

She had one more job to do on this floor, and she moved two doors down the corridor and entered a courtroom where a trial was in progress.

Although the well was crowded—jurors, judge, defense table, prosecutors, stenographer, a number of armed courtroom guards—the spectator section was virtually empty. Rows and rows of chairs for herself and only three others. Trial buffs, probably. In rooms like this all over the country, democracy was defended day after day, and the press and citizenry, except in a handful of spectacular cases, paid no attention. No wonder, she thought, the system worked no better than it did. She took a chair near the door she had come in, and put her two heavy dossiers down on the seat beside her.

The prosecutor was young Benjamin Goldberg. He had a female witness on the stand and was examining her, but when he looked up and saw Judith he shot her a brief smile. He looked pleased that she had come. Benjy was fresh out of law school and only twenty-four years old. He was the youngest of the prosecutors on her staff. But they were all young—the oldest was much younger than Judith. They were underpaid, eager, hardworking, and, compared to the defense attorneys they came up against, woefully inexperienced. Judith was here because, especially in empty courtrooms like this one, it was important to show Benjy and the others that the boss cared—that someone cared.

The case here involved the anal sodomy of a five-year-old boy by the fifty-two-year-old neighborhood degenerate, a man with a twenty-year record of sex offenses. The woman on the stand must be the mother. Benjy handled her beautifully. He was getting better every time out, better nearly every day. Unlike many young prosecutors, he was a natural. He was going to be a great courtroom lawyer. There wasn't much left that she could teach him. His only problem was going to be the child himself. Did the five-year-old even remember what had been done to him? Judith had pushed for trial as early as she could. Still, it had been six months. Would the little boy point out his assailant from the stand, or would the degenerate walk out free? And assault some other little boy tomorrow or next week?

As she stood in the elevator going down to her office, Judith was feeling annoyed. She saw the law only as imperfect, inefficient, and most times totally ineffective, even though it was all civilization had. To love the law, and she did love it, was like being in love with someone who did not love you. Her day was still only half over. Her life was probably half over—she was thirty-seven—and what had she accomplished? What she really needed, she told herself, was some time out of the office and even out of the city. Time away from all of this. A single afternoon in the country began to seem to her the rarest of life's pleasures.

As she came into her anteroom, Mr. Katz handed over more phone messages. None was urgent, he said. Judith, the two case folders under her arm, shuffled through the messages, but her mind was elsewhere. She was thinking about the call from the New Jersey State Police. Why shouldn't she go out there for an hour and help Captain Sample with his rapes? It was a nice drive. There was a shopping mall out on Route 17 on the way. There would be lakes and forests out there, and clean air to breathe. Abruptly she asked Mr. Katz to phone Sample for directions. Today was Tuesday. He was to make an appointment for her for Thursday afternoon.

Should she go alone, she wondered, or ask one of the police commanders to accompany her? If so, who?

By late afternoon trials were being, had been, adjourned. Court had closed for the day. Jurors were straggling out onto the street. Defense attorneys were climbing into their Cadillacs. The judges in their chambers were hanging up their robes. Only the young, underpaid assistant district attorneys were still at work. They had come back downstairs to their offices where they would work further on their cases, some of them far into the night. Cross-examinations had to be prepared, summations polished. They were like inexperienced actors rehearsing between performances. Tomorrow's witnesses had to be contacted and reinterviewed. In some cases detectives had to be sent out to hunt down a witness who was missing, or some final bit of evidence.

It was long after dark when certain of the young prosecutors assigned to Judith trooped into her office. Each night before she went home, she wanted to know how each of their trials was progressing, and they had five on at the moment, plus a sixth on which the jury was still out. All these cases were her responsibility. If problems had come up during the day she wanted to know what they were. Out of her superior experience she could perhaps prevent a case from being lost. At the least she could offer encouragement to the young man or woman prosecuting it.

Judith sat at her desk and they clustered around her, and she was content to have them there. She looked forward to these meetings each night.

These are my children, she thought to herself. Mr. Katz had brought in a cardboard tray of coffee in Styrofoam cups. These were passed around and stirred, and the discussion started. The lights were on. The atmosphere in the room was friendly, but also tense. Trials were emotional. People's lives and careers were at stake. Terrible events were being judged.

Most of the trials seemed to be going well. Only Brian Crawford had a serious problem. He stood with his back against the door, looking glum.

"My chief witness, the victim, that demure little blonde," he burst out, "she just blew my case out of the water."

To these prosecutors trials were like life—totally unpredictable. Courtroom procedure was stylized, but the behavior of witnesses was not. The reactions of jurors were not. Surprises were commonplace. Witnesses forgot their lines or improvised new ones. Some panicked and changed their stories. Some froze. Jurors believed some and disbelieved others for reasons that defied reason. The outcome of trials could never be counted on in advance. The daily adventure of trial work to these young lawyers was an endless fascination, and his colleagues waited to hear whatever courtroom horror Crawford was about to describe.

"I asked her," said Crawford, "to point to the man who raped her." There was a dramatic pause. "This demure little blonde," Crawford said, "points to him while screaming, 'It's that asshole there.'"

There was silence in Judith's office. Then everyone started to laugh.

"I couldn't believe my ears," Crawford said.

The laughter ceased. A jury's sympathy was a fragile thing. Lose it, lawyers said, and you lose the case.

"And wait," Crawford said, "till you hear what she said on cross."

They all knew each other's cases, and now in their minds they paused to review Crawford's. The defendant knocks on the door claiming he's the exterminator. The demure little blonde lets him in. He grabs a knife off the sideboard and rapes her. This had been her story during all her pretrial interviews.

"Unfortunately," said Crawford, "what the exterminator does is he puts the knife down and says to her, can I put my hands on your breasts? She says, what is this, a rape? Because if it is let's get it over with, and she starts to take her clothes off."

Again there was laughter, followed by silence.

"You get another shot at her tomorrow in redirect," Judith soothed him.

"Yes, but what do I say?"

The other prosecutors began giving advice. The story elicited today by the defense counsel was in no way incompatible with terror. Terror takes many forms. Crawford could put a psychiatrist on the stand to so testify. Several names were suggested to him. "But she called the defendant an asshole," said Crawford. "The jury doesn't see her as a demure little blonde anymore."

"The man who raped her is sitting ten feet away," said Judith Adler soothingly. "She's still terrified by him. In her terror she calls him a bad word." Everybody began laughing again. "It's not a demure little blonde using a bad word," said Judith, "it's a terrified rape victim." She glanced around at the others. "Marcy?" she said.

Marcy Miller, the only other woman present, was trying a dentist who had been molesting female patients under anesthetic. This case was going well, she said. And in the sodomy trial of the habitual sex offender, Benjy Goldberg had put the five-year-old boy on the stand late today and had begun his direct examination. The child had an attention span of about sixty seconds. He sat in the witness box sipping Coca-Cola and grinning at his mother at the back of the courtroom. Questions had to be repeated two or three times before he could grasp them and answer. Tomorrow Goldberg would ask him to identify the defendant in open court, and he was worried.

"Have him get up out of the witness chair," suggested Judith. "Have him reenact the crime—how the defendant took him into the alley and—and did what he did. Have him act it out. I've tried that before with small children. It seems to work with them."

The door opened and Mr. Katz stuck his head into the room. "Ligouri has a verdict," he announced. They all knew this case too. Ligouri's jury had been deliberating two days. Katz flashed a big smile. "And he got his conviction."

"In a few minutes," said Crawford, "he'll come in here and brag about how great his summation was."

Everyone was smiling. "I wonder why the jury took so long," mused Judith.

Just then the door was thrown back, and Anthony Ligouri,

twenty-seven years old, stood triumphantly in the doorway beating his chest, Tarzan in a three-piece suit.

The others applauded him.

"I heard the jury wanted to convict you instead," said Benjy Goldberg.

"It was your summation," suggested Crawford.

"As I recall," Benjy Goldberg said, "the defendant is raping her standing up against the back wall of an elevator when the door opens and two cops are waiting to board. Rape with witnesses. So why did the jury take two days?"

Ligouri, sitting down on Judith's windowsill, wiped imaginary sweat off his brow. "I talked to some of the jurors afterward. I nearly lost the case. The victim testifies, the two cops testify, the lab technician and the intern testify. Her vagina is all abraded. There is even semen present, for God's sake. But Juror No. 9 doesn't believe rape took place standing up as described. He holds out for two days. It's not possible, he says. He's a retired postal worker. According to him sexual intercourse standing up is not possible."

"And you ask why the mail is so slow," commented Crawford.

Everybody laughed. "The other jurors argue with him for two days," said Ligouri. "There are four women on that jury, all rather elderly. Finally one of them gets up and tells the postal worker he's wrong, sexual intercourse standing up is very possible. How do you know? he demands. And this gray-haired old grandmother says, Because I've done it standing up myself!"

"That must have cost her," murmured Judith.

"The postal worker won't budge," said Ligouri. "One by one the other grandmothers stand up and admit that they also have done it standing up. Finally the postal worker cracks, and I have my conviction."

Everyone was laughing and applauding.

"I had a case once," remembered Judith. "That jury deliberated two days also. The testimony was that the defendant raped the victim for five hours without losing his erection—"

"Five hours is my record too," said Crawford.

"You should have seen me on my honeymoon," said Ligouri.

"Five hours without having an ejaculation," continued Judith.

"That's another story," said Ligouri.

"You're a sick guy," said Goldberg, "and you got a sick sense of humor."

They were all laughing, but Judith saw that they were ill at ease also. Young though they were, all were married. Even Marcy was married, but Judith was not, and making sexual jokes in her presence made them as uncomfortable as if she were their mother.

This was her brood, and she was very proud of them all. Nonetheless, sometimes they made her feel spinsterish and old.

When she got home she got into the shower at once. She lived in an apartment off Central Park West, and tonight as every night a shower was her first off-duty act. She scrubbed herself down. Was she merely washing the day's dirt and sweat off her body, or trying to wash it off her soul?

Her telephone rang.

Stepping out of the stall, she gave herself a few fast swipes with her big towel, then stepped out into her bedroom and answered it. Her flesh was still faintly steamy, and she clutched the towel in one hand.

"Hello?"

It was still another of her young prosecutors, David Reidy. Her office was staffed around the clock, David had the duty tonight, and a case had just come in—a female lawyer working late raped on her desk by the building's electrician. David wanted her advice, and she gave it, then stepped back into the shower. She stood under the water.

Judith put on pajamas and a dressing gown and went to prepare herself dinner. Afterward she watched television for a while, then lay in bed with *The New York Times* folded open to the crossword puzzle, and the end of a pencil between her teeth. About midnight she turned out the light.

2

A MAN AND A WOMAN, BOTH HALF DRESSED, STOOD IN sunlight in the bedroom. The woman wore a slip and was barefoot. She was tall and well formed, and the carpet came up through her toes. The sun gave a sheen to the slip and another to the sweat that beaded her upper lip, and she confronted the man.

Her name was Mary Hearn—Hearn for nineteen years, Mary for almost forty. She was not a public figure. She had no staff clamoring for her attention. No small, notorious world surrounded her with special duties, special perks, thus arousing the best in her.

The man was Joe Hearn, her husband. She confronted him across an ironing board set up near the bed. Joe was a career policeman who later today would be promoted to inspector. But at the moment he stood in shirttails and skivvy shorts. His uniform blouse hung down over the ironing board, sleeves dangling, like a victim facedown on a slab, and Mary, waving the steam iron, said:

"If you're not satisfied this time, I'm goin to throw this at you."

Earlier she had spent two hours at the hairdresser's. Her hair was three inches shorter than at breakfast and had been restyled too. But her husband had not yet observed any difference in her appearance. Today he was focused on himself and his career. Today he saw her not as his wife but as his laundress.

She curbed her annoyance, or tried to. From now on their lives would be different, Joe had promised. He would be home more, have more time for her and the children.

Inspector was the key rank. "Once I make inspector," he had said, "the pressure's off. I can relax and stop pushing so hard."

Her husband studied the lifeless blouse, and did not smile. "Put a plastic bag over it," he said. "We'll hang it in the backseat. It will still be fresh when we get to the city."

Joe was tall and rather slim. He stood 6 foot 2 but weighed only 180 pounds, unchanged from the year of their courtship. His hair was sandy and very straight—it always seemed to need a combing. He had had a haircut yesterday and as a result looked more boyish than ever. She watched him step into his trousers and buckle on his gun belt. Now he looked like a police commander again, and when he turned and suddenly smiled at her she felt the familiar lurch somewhere near her heart, as if he never smiled at anyone else that way, only at her. She had fallen in love with that smile at nineteen and loved it still, even though she had seen it less and less lately.

"I'll get the car out," said Joe.

"Hey, what about me? Laundresses have to look nice too."

Joe gave her a kiss on the cheek. "You got five minutes," he said, and left her.

Mary had once attended Vassar and then an art school in New York, wanting to become a designer or artist. Instead she had become the wife of a cop and had defied her parents to do it. A new dress hung in her closet, and she put it on carefully over her hair. Its color exactly matched the deep blue of her eyes. Her parents liked Joe now, but they had certainly not approved of him at first. They had told her she would always be poor, was throwing away her future. But they had not known how much Joe was hoping for from life, nor heard him promise her all of it. They had not felt the warmth of that smile. They had not known how good it felt to stand in the circle of his arms—to want to stand there forever.

A final glance in the mirror. I have nice coloring, she told herself, staring. She didn't need makeup, today or any day, and this was lucky. To the New York Police Department heavily made-up women could not be wives, but must be floozies or whores. A need for makeup would have hurt Joe's career. Every human being required a conceit of some kind to get through life, and this was

Mary's: in looks at least she was special. She was better looking than most women; her figure was good too. My hair looks really nice, she thought, patting it.

The car horn sounded outside.

She went down the carpeted stairs, out of her house, and across the lawn to the car.

Joe did not notice the new dress either. He steered down leafy streets toward the grammar school, where they picked up Susie, who was eight. It had taken Mary three days to choose the dress.

"Now the high school," she said.

"I know. I know."

She watched the houses pass. The suburb in which she lived was an old one. Big trees hung over the streets, and she realized how much she and Joe had come up in the world. She remembered Deer Park, where they had started their marriage, row after row of virtually identical tract houses. Although fifty miles from the city, Deer Park had been practically an enclave for New York City cops—probably still was. Four other police families had lived on their street. Sometimes she had thought she was not going to survive Deer Park. Of course a number of police families lived in this town too, but it was twenty miles closer to the city, and they were higher ranking. Chief of Detectives Cirillo lived three blocks away. Mary sometimes ran into his wife in the supermarket. The two couples had not met socially in the past, but might after today, and that could be interesting. But maybe inspector wasn't high enough. The one thing that had never occurred to Mary at the start of her marriage was that cops had almost no friends except other cops.

She had to go into Billy's classroom to get him out. "Will I be back in time for baseball practice?" her fifteen-year-old asked, as she hurried him down the hall.

They swooped up the ramp onto the Long Island Expressway, where Joe Hearn held the Buick to a sedate fifty-five miles per hour, the legal limit.

The expressway sliced through Queens, past the derelict structures of the old World's Fair grounds, past the looming skeletal bulk of Shea Stadium. Then came low, red-brick apartment buildings that were festooned with wrought-iron fire escapes. They dated from World War II, had big rooms probably, and looked cozy. Now the skyscrapers of

Manhattan rose up across the river, and the glare off the chrome and glass facades was almost blinding. Mary began to feel excited. She had been born and raised in New York—so had Joe—and then had been taken away from it, and it seemed to her that people there lived more inter-esting lives than she did. She glanced at Joe as if for confirmation that he was thinking the same thoughts, but he only steered down into the fumes of the Midtown Tunnel. They nosed through the tunnel under the river, under the water and the tugs and barges, and came up on the other side amid the buildings.

Her husband herded them all into the Police Academy. Joe was wearing his blouse now. He was wearing his cap with all the gold braid, too.

This was his day, not hers, and she wanted to make it nice for him. In the elevator she whispered in his ear, "You look very handsome."

The elevator was crowded with cops, and Joe only gave a furtive, embarrassed glance around. He did not acknowl-edge her compliment. Not even a smile.

Upstairs they waited outside the auditorium in a crowded corridor, and Mary said, "Where are you taking us to lunch?"

His answer was Luigi's around the corner on Lexington Avenue, a bar frequented by policemen who worked at the academy. Mary was disappointed—she had hoped he might choose one of the city's better restaurants.

As the ushers—uniformed policemen—began to urge guests inside, Mary put on the felt hat she had carried in from the car, and she moved with her children into the auditorium. Within a few seconds the place was almost full, and a few seconds after that total silence descended, and the auditorium became as hushed as a church.

"What about baseball practice?" demanded Billy.

"Quiet," said Mary who felt, she realized, as reverent as everybody else seemed to. What she was about to witness was only a promotion ceremony, but in the Police Depart-ment this meant prayers would be recited, oaths sworn. The Supreme Court had removed God from the public schools, Mary thought, but had overlooked the New York Police Department. The rite to come would be conducted with almost religious fervor, which made certain kinds of conduct mandatory—silence for instance—and certain kinds of dress virtually mandatory. For wives, it meant hats. For Joe and the other promotees, it meant white gloves. Mary, when she peered around, saw that most of the other wives wore gloves also. She herself did not, her own small act of rebellion. The Police Department, in dress at least, she saw as twenty years or more behind the world.

She glanced up at the stage or altar or whatever it was, which was still vacant, three rows of chairs, no people. In a moment it would fill up with dignitaries, including the mayor and the police commissioner. In a sense these two men were the ones she had shaved her legs for, had got her hair done for, had bought a new dress for. Today she could expect to be introduced to both of them, and she began to consider what she should say.

The corridor doors opened, and in lock step in columns of two the men to be promoted marched into the auditorium, white gloves swinging, Joe and another man leading. To Mary they resembled not the tough cops they imagined themselves to be, but scared schoolchildren being marched into an assembly hall to impress the principal who, in fact, was not even there yet.

When they had taken their places down front, the dignitaries began to trickle from the wings out onto the stage. Mary recognized the mayor, and the PC, and Chief of Detectives Cirillo, but not those deputy commissioners who had bothered to attend, and not the various chaplains either. The Police Department had a lot of chaplains, including even a rabbi, but Monsignor Kelly, who now stepped forward to read the invocation, was the only one with influence and power. Joe and the children were Catholics, but Mary was not. The Police Department in its outlook and rigidity often seemed to her a mirror image of the Catholic Church, which in turn suggested that the rigidity of the clerical mind and the rigidity of the police mind were the same. The department, Mary had come to realize, was a society more rigid than life. Men like her husband adored it, but to her it often seemed frightening, a mindless, implacable monolith, not a person, and not worthy of love because it was only a thing, and things could not be trusted.

Of course the department also had the power to confer success and therefore happiness on those who served it, and was doing so to Joe Hearn today, and therefore to

Mary Hearn also, and so she told herself that her principal emotion at this moment was probably joy.

After Monsignor Kelly's prayer, the spectators all sat down. The promotees remained standing, and were sworn in. Again today, as at each rank in their careers, they swore to uphold the laws of New York, and the Constitution of the United States.

"So help me God," they intoned.

Now the mayor spoke. Holding the microphone like a stand-up comic, he cracked two swift, rather unfunny jokes which set the hall rollicking with mostly nervous laughter. He then made a serious speech about crime in the streets and the efforts of his administration to combat it.

He was followed to the microphone by the four-star chief of operations, Chief Flynn. The liturgy would continue—this was merely a different priest. The first name Flynn read out was Joe's, and Mary beamed with pride to see him onstage saluting Chief Flynn, shaking hands with the PC and the mayor. They were all beaming up there. Joe was beaming. When the PC whispered to him, Joe nodded in a pleased way, but when the mayor did it, he threw his head back and gave a hearty, though brief laugh. Everybody had applauded as Joe climbed up onto the stage and again as he descended the other side and went back to his place, where he turned around and winked at his wife and children. Mary felt an almost overpowering need to hug him at that moment. But the next name had already been called, and the applause ringing out was for someone else's husband.

The ceremony came to seem rather long, and rather boring, so that Mary began to question both its need and its validity. The Police Department was like a giant corporation. It had around thirty thousand employees. Its budget was over a billion dollars a year. Did other corporations of this size promote executives at ceremonies as formal and as quasi-religious at this one? IBM or General Electric, for instance? Mary did not know. Did other corporations think it fruitful, necessary, or even fitting to do so? It did seem somewhat wasteful in terms of man-hours. The officers being promoted, and the policemen-ushers, and the twenty-five or so dignitaries on the stage were all being paid by the city at this moment. Meanwhile, as the mayor had said, there was a lot of crime going on out on the street.

Mary wondered why such irreverent thoughts continued to plague her on such a day. She ought to be feeling as exultant as Joe, and she asked herself if she was jealous of him instead—because he had a career and she did not, because his promotion was being celebrated before so many people while she could only watch and applaud. Then she told herself to stop thinking like a neglected wife. She had a big house in the suburbs, two healthy children, and was the wife of Inspector Hearn. She was a happy woman, and would be even happier after today, because Joe would not have to work as hard. They could begin having fun together again, like in the past.

After the police commissioner's speech, another chaplain stepped forward to read the closing prayer and the ceremony was over.

The dignitaries spilled down off the stage, and the wives and children crowded toward their husbands and fathers. Joe Hearn kissed his wife, shook hands with his son, and picked Susie up in his arms.

Just then the PC came forward, causing Mary to experience a sudden sharp thrill. At last he was about to meet this God figure who controlled her husband's destiny and her own.

He was a small man, about fifty years old, with thin hair and hooded eyes. Mary searched hurriedly for the right thing to say. Yes, she wanted to help Joe's career, but also she experienced a sudden longing to make the PC see her as a person.

She waited for Joe to introduce her. But this did not happen. The PC, who was accompanied by Chief of Detectives Cirillo, stopped two paces away, and called, "May I see you a moment, please, Inspector Hearn."

The PC did not glance at Mary, and Joe did not bring her forward. Her husband merely put Susie down on the floor. The PC and Cirillo drew him off to one side, and Mary could not hear what was said. But she imagined Joe was learning what his next assignment was to be, and she waited for him to come back and tell her.

Joe was learning nothing.

"I wonder if you'd mind stopping by my office about

three o'clock," the PC told him, and Joe could project his future no further than that.

"Yes, sir," he said.

"I've asked Chief Cirillo and some of the other men"—the PC gestured vaguely toward them—"to stop by also."

Joe gave what he hoped was his most engaging grin. "I'll be there, sir."

"Very good. See you later, then." The PC, looking at loose ends, having already forgotten Joe Hearn, turned away.

Chief Cirillo said: "Well, Joe, why don't you and I go get a bite to eat?"

Joe thought of his wife and children waiting for him a few steps away. Then he thought of the job he was hoping to get. He was under consideration for command of the Narcotics Division, six hundred men. The most sensitive job in the department and the one most in the public eye. If he got it he believed he could dramatically increase the seizures, the arrests, for he had new ideas he was certain would work. If he got it, he'd be a deputy chief—his first star—in six months. A year at the outside. But his wife and children were waiting for him. They expected him to take them to lunch.

"If you've got nothing else on," said Cirillo.

Joe glanced back at his wife, his first mistake of the day, because it was a glance Cirillo intercepted. It enabled Cirillo to see the conflict inside him, which put terrific pressure on him to decide quickly. Even to hesitate was to risk offending Cirillo—it would show that he had taken the possibility of refusing under active consideration. To hesitate might damage him in Cirillo's eyes quite as much as an outright refusal. And so he had little time even to think it all out.

"I didn't realize you had your family here," Cirillo said smoothly, giving Mary a nod and a smile—giving Joe the time, possibly, to blow his entire career. "You probably want to go to lunch with your family," Cirillo said.

But the chief of detectives, Joe thought, must have known Mary was here. Even if he had not recognized her—which was unlikely—he knew wives and children always attended these ceremonies. To imagine that Joe might be here alone was illogical, unreasonable, fantastic.

Therefore Cirillo was testing him. How great was his—his what? His devotion to duty? His devotion to his career? Was he a policeman, or was he afraid of his wife?

Joe was an inspector now. They had to put him in a slot that called for inspector's rank. But which one? It could be Narcotics in headquarters or patrol up in the North Bronx. His deputy chief's star could be a million miles away or only a door or two down the hall.

"We've got things to talk over," Cirillo said, "but they can wait."

It was as if Cirillo was holding the Narcotics job out there, saying to Joe, How much do you want it? Joe wasn't even sure Cirillo by himself had the power to give him Narcotics or any other of the plum jobs. But he couldn't take the chance. "I was hoping my family could stay to lunch," he said, "but they can't." As he made the decision, he knew it would infuriate Mary. But he believed he could explain it to her later. He believed she would understand. She might even praise him for having made the correct choice.

"You're sure?" said Cirillo.

Joe, who understood the Police Department game as men like Cirillo played it, believed he had no alternative. "My wife has to get back, and my boy has baseball practice," he said firmly. He knew he wouldn't have time to explain it to Mary now. He'd do it tonight. He'd make it up to her.

"My car's outside," said Cirillo. "We'll look for a place to eat."

"How about Luigi's, Chief," said Joe, after a brief hesitation. If he was going to lunch with Cirillo, then he wanted other cops to see him do it. If they thought him cozy with the chief of detectives, this could be to his advantage. And he had a reservation there already.

Cirillo nodded. "Luigi's would be fine."

"Just let me say good-bye to my wife."

Mary watched Joe and the mayor approaching on converging paths. The mayor was shaking hands again with all the promotees before leaving the hall. He was grinning, talking fast, moving fast. Some of the men held him up long enough to introduce their wives, which Joe was sure to do, and Mary waited her turn. But she was not to meet the mayor either. Joe had not seen him coming. He wrung Joe's hand and wished him luck and then he was gone.

To Mary it was still another of today's disappointments. But this was still a great day for Joe, and she flashed him a big smile. "What did the PC give you?"

"I'm hungry," said Susie.

"I'm to see him at three o'clock."

"We're all hungry," said Mary. "Let's go."

Joe appeared embarrassed. "Listen, honey, kids, I—I'm sorry."

He was down in a crouch at Susie's level, face-to-face with an eight-year-old, cowering like a boxer from punches that had not yet been thrown. "I won't be able to take you to lunch like I promised," he said, refusing to meet his wife's eyes.

Mary could not believe she had heard this. "What?"

"I have to have lunch with the chief of detectives."

"You have to what?" sputtered Mary.

Joe stood upright. "You know how they do things around here."

Mary's lips had compressed into a line. "You just march over there and tell him you're having lunch with us."

Joe dropped his head.

"On the day a man gets made inspector he belongs to his family."

"Mary, please. Please keep your voice down. You know I'm not doing it because I want to."

"You make me—"

Grasping Susie with one hand and Billy with the other Mary stormed out of the hall.

Joe watched her go. Evidently she did not understand at all. She was pretending she didn't anyway, and her reaction bothered him. He liked to please her, not upset her. In any case, this was part of his job, and she would have to get over it. She had always got over it in the past. When she did not look back, he shrugged unhappily, then sauntered over to Cirillo who was lighting a cigar. "Ready, Chief?" he said brightly.

Cirillo was a short, somewhat portly middle-aged man wearing a brown suit. There was only a slight extra bulge under his coat where he packed his .38. He made the announcement Joe was waiting for, hoping for, but not yet expecting, just as they passed through the door into Luigi's. The restaurant was crowded and noisy. Most of the patrons were men, and most, Joe saw, were cops. There was a hot, beery smell in the air.

"I've asked him to gve you Narcotics," Cirillo said. "That's what the three o'clock meeting is about. When he tells you, act surprised." That same afternoon Joe took command of his division. He sat in a high-backed chair behind a big desk in a corner office on the twelfth floor at police headquarters, and his predecessor's chief of staff, a deputy inspector named Pearson, briefed him on major investigations in progress. Italian organized crime. Black organized crime. South American cocaine merchants rich as kings and able therefore to buy almost anyone. The case folders were stacked on Joe's desk. Several were politically sensitive. A diplomat from Thailand and another from Peru. A compromised judge. Two possibly corrupt immigration officials. This was Joe's new domain. He had six hundred detectives to control, to keep from being subverted, to aim like missiles into the nether world of drugs. Millions of dollars were at stake, plus untold human misery. At stake also was the future of Joe's police career. He was not worried. He had served in Narcotics as a sergeant and had been formulating his ideas, his plans, ever since. Now the division had been given to him and he was eager to grasp it.

"Tomorrow I'll go through the folders of the undercover guys," he told Pearson.

"Yes, sir."

"Have them on my desk when I come in."

"Yes, sir."

The undercover detectives were the police buyers. They were like the ball carriers on a football team. The success of the division depended on them and he wanted to know who they were. "Order them all in here on Friday so I can meet them."

"Yes, sir."

A part of Joe's mind now focused on Deputy Inspector Pearson himself, for he represented a problem of a different kind. Pearson had been appointed by another. His loyalty therefore was not necessarily to Joe. He was perhaps even a spy for Cirillo or the PC, and Joe did not want second-guessers peering over his shoulder while he moved the division forward into new positions. Let them judge his ultimate performance, not his preparations for it. Pearson would have to be replaced—it was a high priority. Joe wanted a staff of his own in here anyway. But he couldn't simply fire the guy, creating an enemy who might float through the department for years doing him harm at every opportunity. It was a problem that would have to be worked out.

A phone call came in from some female assistant district attorney—Joe did not catch her name.

"Judith who?"

From her rather pregnant silence Joe gathered that she imagined herself as well known as a film star. She thought he should have recognized her name. This put Joe immediately on his guard. "Oh, Judith Adler," he said. "Of course. It must be this cheap Police Department wiring. I'm sorry. How are you?"

He almost had not taken the call. Now as she hit him with some cock-and-bull case involving Playboy Bunnies in New Jersey, he wished he hadn't. Forty kilos of hashish in the back of a car. Videotapes of rapes. She wanted him to ride out there with her.

"Me?" he said. "What for?"

His tone seemed to give her momentary pause.

"You'd be better able to evaluate the narcotics aspect of the case than I would," she told him, "and we should know each other, shouldn't we?"

Joe was silent. He didn't want to offend her, but he didn't want to drive out to New Jersey either. He didn't know who she was and he didn't have the time.

"That way," she said, "if you ever have any problems with our office, perhaps I can help solve them. And if we should have any problems with yours, vice versa."

Joe did not know what to make of this statement.

"It's a nice ride," said Judith Adler.

"I'm pretty busy," said Joe.

She laughed and said, "Think of it as a lunch date you can't get out of."

Joe pondered. Assistant district attorneys were valuable contacts. Some were anyway. But this case sounded ridiculous. "I just took command here," said Joe. But he agreed to call her back tomorrow.

"Nice ride?" he muttered when he had hung up. "Nice

ride?" He turned to Deputy Inspector Pearson, "Who's
Judith Adler?"

Pearson seemed surprised that he did not know. "Everybody who works Manhattan knows who she is."

"Well, I've been working mostly Brooklyn these last few
years."

"She knows all the top commanders," said Pearson.
"She makes a thing about getting to know them. She's a
one-woman liaison bureau with the PD. That's one of her
jobs over there. She's pretty important."

Joe thought about this for a moment. "Find out about
her for me," he said. "Whatever you can. Be discreet."

Mary by then stood in her kitchen preparing vegetables
for a dinner party in Joe's honor that night. At the counter
she sliced carrots, then mushrooms. She had changed to
jeans and a sweater and her hands were wet. Upstairs the
new dress lay on the bed.

"You have to drive me to baseball practice," said Billy,
and she turned around and looked at him. He stood in the
doorway in his team uniform. The bill of his cap was
pulled low down over his eyes, and he was carrying a gear
satchel with two bats sticking out of it. He's going to be as
tall as his father, Mary thought looking at him, and she
dried her hands, picked up her pocketbook and car keys,
and led him out to the driveway.

At the high-school field Billy did not thank his mother
for the ride. He said, "Come back and get me about five
o'clock," even as he threw the door open and jumped out.

She snapped him a salute: "Yes, sir," and watched him
cross the field toward his teammates and his coach at
home plate. After a moment's hesitation, she turned the
engine off. She sat in the car watching him swing two bats
around his head like a big leaguer. Now the coach divided
his squad into two teams. The coach was a tall, well-
muscled young man with dark eyes and curly black hair.
He was also an algebra teacher, Mary believed. She knew
his name, Martin Loftus, but had never spoken to him,
except hello and goodbye. The kids adored him. As did
some of the mothers, or so she had heard. There had been
rumors.

Loftus was standing at home plate and when he noticed
her in the car he grinned and waved over at her.

Mary gave him a brief nod in return. But the interchange made her uncomfortable. She felt like an intruder. She did not belong here. After a moment she started the engine, put the car in gear, and drove home.

She finished preparing the vegetables. She sautéed the mushrooms and made a sauce to go over them. She made an apple pie. She put all her casseroles on top of the cold burners, ready to go. The apple pie went into the oven on automatic timer.

By then it was time to drive back to the school for Billy. But just as she reached for the car keys he came in the back door.

"Coach drove me," he said, dropping his gear satchel. "I'm hungry. Coach thinks you're beautiful, Mom."

Mary frowned. "What were you saying about me?"

"He asked about you. What is there to eat?"

"What did he ask you?"

"I don't know. Can I have a hunk of bread and jam?"

"What did you tell him?"

"Nothing."

Mary decided to drop the subject. "Don't say hunk of bread."

"Well, can I, Mom?"

"If you clean up after yourself."

She hated the idea of her children talking about her to strangers. She hated to imagine them revealing family things to outsiders.

"Now go up to your room and start your homework," she told Billy.

Finally Mary laid her tablecloth and set the table. She put a bowl of spring flowers from her garden in the center, and took a last look around There was nothing more to do until her guests came, so she went upstairs and ran a bath. She was lying in it when Joe came home. He stood over the tub in his uniform, the new gold eagles shining on his shoulders, a gift-wrapped box in his arms. He began apologizing.

"You're the one I wanted to have lunch with, not Cirillo, but—"

At first she wouldn't look at him. But he was so contrite that her mood began to thaw. She even felt sorry for him standing there pleading, dangling the box over the tu

She wanted to know about his meeting with the PC, and she wanted to know what was in the box.

"What assignment did you get?"

He told her.

She was still lying in the tub. Instead of congratulating him, she said, "What's in the box?"

He would not say. She would have to get out of the tub and open it. "I'll put it on your pillow," he teased.

She stood up, water sluicing off her. She dried herself off, and she took her time about it. With her foot on the tub, she dried between her toes. As she went out to the bedroom she was wrapped in the towel. The package was on the bed, as was Joe's gun belt which he had tossed there. His tie was off and his shirt half undone. She opened the package. Inside was a beige silk blouse. It was not her type of blouse, and from the look of it, wouldn't fit either.

But Joe was feeling pleased with himself. "Put it on," he said.

The towel dropped to the floor, and she put the blouse on. She buttoned it up the front. To her surprise it fit quite well, and in the mirror it looked well, too.

"I got it at Bloomingdale's."

She knew he hated to shop. He did not understand shops, making it an ordeal for him. He had probably spent an hour buying the blouse—for him an hour of misery. She was oddly touched.

"Do you like it?"

He stood behind her, smiling at her in the mirror. She did not smile back. "It's very nice," she said, and took it off.

Joe was ripping his shirt off and ogling her at the same time. "We have a few minutes," he said.

But she evaded his clutching hands. "Try taking a cold shower," she told him. "I have things to do before our guests come." But when he looked at her as crestfallen as a little boy, she said, "Thanks for the blouse."

Wearing a bathrobe, she shuffled downstairs to give supper to her children. She sat at the kitchen table with them and watched them eat it and waited until her husband, having changed to civilian clothes, would come downstairs. She was in no mood to go up there and be mussed or made sweaty by him. It was a nice enough blouse, but she would not be bought off that cheaply.

When Joe came into the kitchen he was wearing a brown tweed sports coat and brown loafers. He did not look like a policeman at all. His hair was damp and freshly combed, and he looked very nice, but she did not tell him so, thinking: I can withhold compliments just as well as you.

She went upstairs and put her new dress back on, penciled on eyeliner, and was ready for her guests. There was still some time before they arrived, so she continued to sit in front of her mirror, looking at herself, wondering what her husband saw when he looked at her, what anyone saw. She realized she was already sick of the new dress, and was wearing it only to get her money's worth. Nobody was going to notice it tonight either except maybe one of the wives. Policemen, when they were with each other, scarcely noticed that their wives existed. Earlier in the marriage Joe had been different from the others. Now he was much the same.

There were ten to dinner, and all the men at the table, though in civilian clothes, were or had been connected with law enforcement, and all sat at her table armed, except perhaps Joe, though of course no guns showed. Her husband, Mary noted, was in a jubilant mood, cracking jokes, making people laugh, pouring out heavy drinks before dinner, and much champagne during dinner, so that everyone became at least tipsy, and the dinner Mary had so carefully prepared passed unnoticed. When she served the apple pie, however, Joe looked up and said, "Let's hear it for Mary," and they all applauded her. She managed a polite smile.

The party ran late. One couple, the Buchanans, seemed to be trying to outlast all the others, and finally did, whereupon Bill Buchanan kicked off his shoes, lounged back on the sofa, and asked for still another Scotch and soda. Mary, who wanted only to get to bed, wore a glass smile. But a moment later, as Bill offered her husband a job, her fatigue vanished, and she listened alertly, the smile on her face a genuine one.

Bill Buchanan had been a police officer for fifteen years, all the while studying law at night. A captain when at last admitted to the bar, he had resigned from the department and had gone to work for a small chain of department stores which by now had become a rather big chain of department stores. He had become the firm's general counsel and a member of the board. Buchanan had been one of Joe's closest friends in the department. Now, after he had gulped down half of the night's final Scotch, he said suddenly, "Mary, I want you to listen to this too." Turning to Joe, he said, "My board has authorized me to offer Inspector Hearn, here, the post of vice-president for security with authority over our three New York area stores."

This dramatic announcement was followed by a dramatic silence. But then Joe gave what sounded to Mary like a scornful laugh.

"Your timing couldn't be worse, Bill. Today I'm an inspector. By this time next year I'll have stars on my shoulders."

"Yeah," snorted Buchanan, "and you'll still be earning only about half what this job pays."

"What's money?" said Joe airily.

Joe had drunk a lot too, Mary realized, and she glanced at him with alarm, afraid he might irritate Buchanan. She did not want Bill's offer withdrawn. She wanted her husband to accept it. With that much money, especially with Joe's police pension on top of it, they would be rich. They could take an apartment in the city. They could keep this house too, live in both places. They could have the excitement of the city whenever they chose. The galleries, the shops, would be just around the corner.

"Well, are you tempted?" asked Buchanan confidently.

"And the year after that," said Joe, "I'll be chief of detectives." He laughed. "Maybe even PC."

"The year after that, if you take this job," said Buchanan, "you'll have stock options. You'll be flying around in the company jet managing security for about thirty stores."

"As police commissioner," said Joe, "I'll have my own helicopter."

Buchanan's confident grin faded. "The board met this morning. I threw your name on the table, and they went for it."

"You want to know how every cop in the city ends up?" demanded Joe. "Shaking door handles in the middle of the night in one of these security jobs."

"That's not what I'm talking about," protested Buchanan.

"Sure it is," said Joe, nodding sagely. "A highly paid door handle shaker. Shall I freshen that for you? A door handle shaker." He shook his head. "But not me."

As Buchanan's face darkened, Mary interjected hurriedly, "I think it's a terrific idea. What don't we all sleep on it and talk again tomorrow?"

"Admit it, Bill," said her husband to Buchanan. "You haven't had a happy day since you quit the department."

"Happy day? Of course I have." He put his empty glass down on the coffee table. Glass slapped glass.

Joe shook his head decisively. "Then why do you still turn up at all the department Communion breakfasts? Why did you keep all your guns? I'll tell you why," Joe said triumphantly. "You walk the streets secretly hoping you'll stumble on a stickup, don't you? So you can intervene and make one final arrest. Save someone's life. Feel like a cop again one last time."

Buchanan, looking angry, stood up. "Think about it, Joe. This is a big job I'm talking about. You owe it to Mary and the kids." Nodding half drunkenly, he moved toward the front door. His wife threw a silent glance at Mary, and followed.

"To be a cop is to be on the barricades," said Joe to their backs. "The adrenaline rushes to your head. Your blood boils. And you're helping people all the time. It's a—it's a holy calling. There's no other job like it. I'm not like you. I couldn't give it up."

"Talk to Mary," said Buchanan thickly. "I'll call you tomorrow."

Mary stood at her front door in the night watching her guests depart. She was smiling brightly, or so she hoped, but tears started to her eyes as soon as the Buchanans' Mercedes had backed out of her driveway. With rage in her heart she turned on her thick-tongued, thick-headed husband, but he was grinning so happily that she said only, "Oh, what's the use?" and stumbled past him.

Upstairs she put on a nightgown and got into bed. Having turned toward the wall, she began silently weeping. Her husband intended to throw away the new life she so ardently coveted, had already done so. He had not even discussed it with her. Presently the mattress sagged heavily. Joe had got into bed, but she ignored him. This however proved impossible to do. He was not wearing pajamas, and he was swarming all over her. "Time to celebrate," he said happily.

She tried to shrug him off, then to fight him. He was laughing. The rage inside her meant nothing to him. He didn't even know it was there. He seemed delighted by her resistance, and was playing a game which, since he was so much bigger, he could not lose. He had her wrists pinned to the pillow, her nightgown up around her waist. With all her strength she tried to hold her legs together but he had got a knee between them and was forcing them apart. She might have screamed at him or coldly ordered him to leave her alone. He was always gentle with her. Most likely he would have subsided on his side of the bed. But she was so upset, so angry, that she was unwilling to speak to him at all. And so she fought him. Her body became slathered with sweat. As the act became inevitable, she found herself imagining that this man on top of her was not her husband at all but a stranger. Which stranger? The image that filled her mind was her son's baseball coach, Loftus. Why him? she asked herself. But she saw his face and imagined his body. She became so fiercely aroused that her husband ceased to exist for her, only Loftus existed. She could feel the stranger's coarse chest against her own, the stranger's weight on her and in her, a man bigger, heavier than Joe. Everything felt different, unexpected, not allowed, an erotic masterpiece, and in her delirium she almost shouted Loftus' name.

Her husband, of course, suspected nothing; to him it had been a splendid romp with his wife, to which she had responded with a passion that had been rare of late. At last he rolled off her.

Why Loftus? Mary thought. Her heart had stopped pounding. I don't even know him.

"I love you, Mary."

This brought tears to her eyes. He probably does, she thought. He gives me all his money and he doesn't chase after other women, and to him that's love.

And she turned toward the wall and tried to sleep.

"This is the best day of my life so far," said Joe happily.

"Is it?" said Mary Hearn.

*   *   *

The second part of this scene was played out the next morning. Mary was awakened when Joe brought her coffee in bed. Outside their bedroom windows, she saw as she sat up, it was still not full daylight, and elsewhere in the house the children still slept, but her husband was already up and dressed. Even his tie was knotted in place.

"My first full day in my new command," he said almost apologetically. "I want to get there early."

Mary, in her nightgown, took the proffered cup and saucer and said nothing.

"Everybody enjoyed dinner last night, didn't they?" Joe said. "It was a delicious dinner. Everybody thought so." He grinned and added, "And afterward was nice too—in bed."

"In bed," said Mary. She thought, He has no notion ever of what I might be feeling.

But she was wrong. Joe most times was extremely sensitive to his wife's moods, and he knew exactly what was bothering her now.

"I'm going to call Buchanan later," Joe said. "I want you to tell me that it's okay."

"You do what you want."

"Mary," Joe said, "please look at me." But she wouldn't.

"I do want you to have more money," he said. "I do want you to have an apartment in New York—if that's what you'd like. All I ask is that you give me a bit more time. Another year or two."

Since Mary still wouldn't look at him, Joe removed the cup and saucer from her grasp, placing them on the bedside table. Then he took one of her hands. "I'm forty-one years old," he told her. "I'm probably the youngest inspector in the job. Don't you want to see how far I can go?"

When this question elicited no response, he said, "I meant to discuss this with you last night, but once we were in bed together all I wanted to do was make love to you."

Mary remained silent.

"Nineteen years, and every time I touch you I want to make love to you."

Again Mary made no reply.

"Admit it," said Joe, and he tried another grin. "You were pretty eager to make love too."

"Was I?"

Her resistance was beginning to put Joe off. "Well, you certainly seemed to be."

Mary looked at him, but said nothing.

"Bill's job will still be there next year," said Joe.

"How do you know?"

"Or another job. And with each promotion from now on it will pay more."

"Suppose you don't get promoted?"

He began trying to explain to his wife how the Police Department functioned, though he was certain she already knew. The slots he was bucking for were wide open. The department was not like private business. The turnover was terrific. With one or two exceptions not a single member of the police hierarchy was older than fifty-two. After thirty years' service their pensions were so generous that these men in their prime executive years simply could not afford to stay. Besides which, the police commissioner changed every time the mayor changed, sometimes more often, and each new PC tended to force his predecessor's staff to resign so as to appoint men loyal only to him. Since the law prohibited bringing in outsiders, this meant promoting young men from below. His wife should see the logic of his decision. So many promotions would be made during the next year or two that he could not fail to land one or several.

"You'll be married to a chief."

But Mary was immune to logic at that moment. She perceived only that her husband's career meant more to him than she did. Now that he was an inspector she would see even less of him than previously, and if he made it as high as deputy or assistant chief, much less chief of detectives, she might not see him at all. It was practically still dark out—she confirmed this by glancing out the window— and he was already dressed and on his way to work.

"It's true my career is important to me," said Joe earnestly. "But I'm doing it for you too. I want you to be proud of me."

"I've aways been proud of you."

"Just let me have another year," he said. "Two at the most. That's all I ask."

Joe's arguments seemed to him so reasonable that he was confident his wife would find them reasonable too—if not now, then later. He did not advance what was to him the strongest argument of all—perhaps he did not recognize it as such. It had something to do with the "holy calling" idea he had somewhat drunkenly articulated last night. As a cop he was on the side of the angels and he was unwilling to give that up just to make money. "Would you like to go out to dinner tonight?" he said. "Come into the city. We'll go to the Four Seasons." To Joe this was the most famous restaurant in New York.

"I don't have a sitter," said Mary. But he could see she was tempted.

"Come to headquarters first," advised Joe, "and see my new office. Come about seven o'clock. Then we'll go uptown to dinner."

After a twelve-hour day, Mary thought. When did we last get a twelve-hour day together?

Joe, who was seated beside her on the edge of the bed, thought, By seven I should be ready to leave. Being a man he could have two loves. He could have it both ways. He leaned down over her. "Now give me a kiss, I've got to go."

I'm being a bitch, Mary thought, feeling repentant. He works hard, he's successful, and being bitchy to him doesn't help either of us. So she fashioned him a smile, kissed him on his shaving lotion, and picked up her cup and saucer again. She watched her husband walk out of their bedroom, and he seemed to her to be hurrying.

3

ABOUT TEN-THIRTY JUDITH ADLER CALLED. INSPEC-
tor Hearn was in a meeting. The captains who commanded
the borough narcotics groups were seated around his conference table, but he decided to accept the call. As Deputy Inspector Pearson handed him the phone, he waved
the men to go on with their discussion.

"Yes, Judith," he said. He had agreed to accompany her
to New Jersey, and today was the day; he had almost
forgotten.

She wanted to leave early, she told him, and stop for
lunch on the way.

By this time Joe knew much more about her which was
why, after putting her off for most of a week, he had
agreed to the trip at all. But he did not have time for
lunch, he told her now, did not have much time at all,
setting the ground rules in advance. She said she understood and hung up. Muttering, "Lunch she wants now,"
Joe handed the phone back to Pearson and returned to the
table.

The purpose of the meeting, he had informed his subor-
dinates as they arrived, was to find ways to free the
detective field groups to move quickly, so as to be able to
mass division strength against clearly identified targets.
For maximum impact, he told them now, sitting down
again, these targets should no longer be individual movers
as in the past. Instead he wanted the division's focus
shifted to the distribution channels themselves.

This was an entirely new concept and the men around
his table stirred with surprise. "Disrupt distribution," In-

41

spector Hearn said firmly, "and you not only make big seizures, you not only cut off the flow of money and drugs, but you also flush the bosses out of hiding. They have to come out to reestablish their businesses. In the open the major guys become vulnerable to arrest, some of them for almost the first time."

The captain in charge of the Bronx Narcotics Group said flatly, "Your intent is to reorganize the entire division."

Joe denied it. He said he hadn't thought of it this way at all, thus calming them down. Change was alarming and he knew better than needlessly to alarm men on whom he must depend. Let them get used to him first. He would serve them up change one dose at a time.

He knew very well his intent was to reorganize the division. He knew exactly how he wished to proceed, too. But since he also understood Police Department politics, he took the trouble to spend the next hour listening to the ideas and contributions of these field commanders. It was worth the extra time, he believed, partly because some of their ideas were good ones, but more importantly because they would accept his plan with more enthusiasm if they believed it, at least in part, their own. One other thing: a plan this big would have to be approved by Chief Cirillo, which might be a tough sell, and he wanted them in agreement behind him when he went in there in about ten days' time and dropped the plan—in writing and in detail—on Cirillo's desk.

It was noon before the meeting ended. "Type up your notes," Joe told Deputy Inspector Pearson, "and let me have them tomorrow."

When Pearson had gone out, a lieutenant who had already been waiting half an hour was shown in. He had a problem, a bad one. One of his men had evidence of a marijuana ring operating in a Catholic prep school in Brooklyn. He wanted to know what to do about it. Did he contact the chancery or what? The lieutenant was followed by two detectives who outlined a case that was about to break. They had their warrants, which Joe looked over; the warrants were in order. The suspects were a pair of trigger-happy Cuban drug lords. They were heavily armed and extremely dangerous, the detectives said.

"Sawed-off shotguns," said one. "It's like Prohibition."

Joe looked up. At the door was one of his clerical

sergeants whom he had sent out to get him a sandwich and a container of milk. "The severed head in the back of the car in Forest Hills last week," the other detective told him, "that was them."

The first detective said, "The three corpses in the basement on Columbus Avenue—that was them too. Blood all over the walls."

The sergeant had come in and put the paper bag down on the desktop, and Joe nodded his thanks. The detectives across his desk stood waiting for orders. Joe told them to make their arrests at 5:00 A.M. the next day. He was peering into the paper bag as he spoke. He had been in his office since seven-thirty that morning and was very hungry. They should kick the door down while the Cubans slept, he said. Did they need extra manpower? He was terrifically hungry. Deciding that it was all right to eat in front of ordinary detectives, he began munching on the sandwich. Five A.M., he said again. He would meet them there and go in with them. As he sent them out, they looked surprised. But to Joe a leader was one who shared the dangers of his men, and the bad hours as well. If you wanted men to follow you, you had to do it. Besides, this was an interesting case and he was curious to see how it came out.

By then it was close to two o'clock and he left his office and went down in the elevator. He walked across Police Plaza toward the Criminal Courts Building. The hot dog stands were open on the plaza. I should have had lunch here, he thought. It's very pleasant here. People stood eating under the awnings. But he hadn't had time lately for lunches of this kind. It was a warm day and he could smell the steaming franks. There were other people eating under umbrellas at tables set out on the square. They were unwrapping sandwiches, pouring coffee out of thermos bottles.

He came out of the plaza onto Centre Street and strode up past the Federal and State courthouses toward Judith's office, for she had suggested they take her car. As he walked he reviewed what he had learned about her. In addition to Pearson's phone calls, he had made others himself. She was the daughter of a department store executive. She had graduated from Harvard Law, which meant she could be working in a big law firm, Joe thought, so what was she doing in the district attorney's office, receiving low pay and dealing with slime? She was the highest-ranking woman in the office and No. 3 overall. She was chief of the trials division and head of the sex crimes unit on the side. And she knew everybody. If the politicians ever decided to run a woman for district attorney of New York County, Joe had been told, it would be Judith Adler. He had asked about and made notes on some of the more important cases she had prosecuted, murders mostly, while making her way up to her present rank. He vaguely remembered a few of them. He had asked—discreetly—about romantic liaisons, particularly if with cops, but no one could tell him very much.

She was worth cultivating, and today he would devote three hours to it, more than he felt he could spare. He expected to be back in his office by five at the latest. He would charm her if he could. He would learn her likes and dislikes, strengths and especially weaknesses, if any, all to be filed away for possible use later. Sometimes it seemed that a police career depended exclusively on contacts, and cops were forever asking each other, "Who's your rabbi?" An officer's career did not really depend on stopping crime, and Joe knew this. Victories over crime were few and far between. They were popfly singles in a game that was already lost. If Joe did still make determined efforts to fight crime, this was due to his Catholic education perhaps, to the idealism of his youth, a good deal of which remained with him even after almost twenty years as a cop. He still believed that a man had to fight against evil every day of his life until he died. He still believed doggedly, despite all evidence to the contrary, that one man could make a difference. However, he was an extremely practical man as well, and an ambitious one, and so he was careful to keep his idealism hidden from the men around him, particularly his superiors. A good many uniformed cops, young ones especially, were highly idealistic, and it showed. But you did not see much idealism at headquarters, a place that Joe now had finally reached. The slogan at headquarters was that crime was like the weather. It could not be stopped. Furthermore, a man who appeared to try too rabidly was often considered a fool.

A commander was rated instead on his ability to get noticed by the right people—and on the image of himself

he showed them. A man like Joe, who had realized this
early, had constructed his image as carefully as one might
construct a house. His contacts were meant to see him as
tough, but reasonable; decisive, but conservative; ambitious,
but not a cutthroat. See, no idealism anywhere. A man of
ideas also, and if the police world resisted nearly all inno-
vations with herculean strength, this was not the point.
The point was to put the ideas in memos. Very often the
department responded enthusiastically to ideas in memos—
Chief Cirillo and the PC were about to receive a lot of
memos from Joe—it just never implemented nearly all of
them. However Joe's memos would be serious presenta-
tions and he would fight hard for some of the ideas they
contained, even after the memos themselves seemed dead.
As for his planned reorganization of the Narcotics Division, he was especially serious about it, had had prelimi-
nary discussions with Cirillo, and believed he could push
it through.

Now waiting to be shown into Miss Adler's office, Joe
was determined to work just as hard during the next three
hours as he had worked earlier this day, and would work
later, probably far into the night.

He had expected a dried-out plain Jane of a lawyer,
probably old. She wasn't old. She was both better looking
and better dressed than other female lawyers he had occasionally dealt with, and seemed far more feminine. He was
no expert on women's clothes, but hers were something
Mary might have worn—a brown-and-beige-striped dress
with, over it, a rather rumpled blazer. The effect was both
sophisticated and casual, soft rather than severe, and in
the height of fashion, he supposed. She stood up and came
around the desk and he saw she was not a tall woman,
about 5 feet 4, with black hair and almost black eyes that
crinkled up as she greeted him. There were pearls at her
throat, he noticed now. She seemed to have a nice figure.
He gave her a warm smile, a handshake as if she were a
man, and his first compliment. Since he knew better than
to praise, in these feminist times, her appearance, her
nice dress, for instance, or her lustrous hair, the compliment he did give was professional.

"You had the Metropolitan Museum case," he told her,
nodding his head up and down in admiration. She had a
strong, no-nonsense chin, but a rather soft mouth. Al-

though the case had held front page in the tabloids for two weeks, he had never noted her name at the time. "Hell of a case. The cops up in the two-one are still talking about it."

Most persons in law enforcement, given such an opportunity, would have discoursed on such a case for an hour. But Judith Adler's reaction surprised him. She only crinkled her eyes a second time, before informing him that she was unfortunately not quite ready to leave for New Jersey just yet. A rape victim had come in who had to be interviewed.

"Not too long an interview, I hope," said Joe. Though annoyed, he was careful to keep his friendly smile in place.

"You could sit in on it if you like," she said, seeming to brighten.

In law enforcement highly placed women were few, and they were a recent phenomenon. Joe Hearn had had almost no business dealings with any of them. But this particular woman seemed already to have confirmed what he had always believed about women in general—they were people to whom time had no strict meaning. Time to Joe was an inexorable, unforgiving master, but they did not see it this way. They did not try to crowd and push time as he did, so as to fit everything in. Women were creatures who were vague about many things, time most of all. Joe saw his allotted three hours stretched to four already, and they had not yet left this office, and he did not like it.

Having no choice, he took the chair against the wall, while a girl was led in and placed in front of Miss Adler's desk. Joe was careful to let his suit coat spill open so that the grip of his revolver showed in his belt. He was aware that this girl was about to make revelations of an extremely private nature, and he wanted her to believe he belonged there, that he was not some sort of pervert hoping to get off on the details of her story, whatever it was.

He had not had much to do with rape in the past. Those few that came his way had usually shunted off to others, usually to one of the few policewomen around at the time. It was a woman's crime. He did not enjoy the company of women who were suffering, and rape was hard to prove. Victims rarely wanted to testify, or even tell him what had happened. Cases fell through. Rape did no one's career any good. He had got rid of rapes whenever he could.

This latest victim gave her name—a Jewish name, Joe didn't quite catch it—and her age which was nineteen, and for a moment he studied her. She wore black slacks and a white blouse and low-heeled shoes. He committed her to memory, like a witness in a case that was important to him, but this was only habit. She looked very much like Judith Adler, though younger, of course. They could have been sisters. Medium-sized, rather pretty. Big black eyes. Black hair that almost concealed her smooth young face. She was very pale, and her eyes were red, presumably from crying. But Joe's interest in the girl was minimal, and from then on he studied Judith, watching her technique, trying to fathom her. Of course he listened to the details of the rape as Judith drew them forth, but the case was not important to him. He was commander of the Narcotics Division, which was a different business entirely. A police executive could not afford to bleed for every victim who crossed his path, not even one as appealing as this girl here.

She was a receptionist in midtown, she said. The perpetrator, if in fact he was a perpetrator, was a salesman who called regularly on her company. The salesman had become infatuated with her, had kept asking for a date, and although she saw him as an older man—he was twenty-seven—she at last accepted.

This was an infatuation rape then—Joe too saw rape in categories.

The young girl's voice was choked with emotion, with an anguish Joe was not anxious to know about. The rape, if it was a rape, took place on this first date.

"He was a nice Jewish professional man," the girl said. "It's not like I picked some guy up in a bar."

Joe began to remember his wife at that age. Of course Mary was taller than this girl, fair instead of dark, and with blue eyes. At nineteen she had seemed just as defenseless. She had needed a man to take care of her, a role that young Joe Hearn had been eager to fill. It was one he still filled and wanted to fill. To Joe Hearn women were frail creatures whom men protected, and he wondered about this Judith Adler. He could see the compassion she pro-

jected toward this girl. She projected warmth and understanding, and never rushed her in any way, giving her all
the time in the world, too much time. But how tough was
she? In law enforcement it was toughness that counted
more often than not, and Joe prided himself on his own
toughness when it was needed. As the girl's story was
spun out at length he wondered how tough, how competent, Judith Adler really was.

The perpetrator had got the girl up into his apartment
on a ruse. Instead of meeting her out in front ready to go,
he had had his dog with him on a leash. Obviously he had
to get rid of the dog before the date could begin, and the
girl went upstairs with him because otherwise, it seemed
to her, she would appear young, or inexperienced, or afraid.
In her place at her age, Mary Hearn might have done the
same. Young girls, Joe Hearn thought, are imbeciles. They
think they can take care of themselves, but they can't.

Upstairs the young man quickly locked the apartment
door behind them. He threw three bolts. "Just habit," he
said. But the girl was a prisoner, knew it at once, and
became frightened. The bed was in the corner on the
floor. The man began mixing drinks. He downed several
while the girl only sipped at her first one. He asked if she
wanted to change into one of his spare sweat suits and get
comfortable. She was wearing what she considered a really
pretty dress, and she asked, no doubt in a tremulous
voice, when they would go out to dinner. "You're not
really your own person yet," he told her, taking the glass
out of her hand.

Joe Hearn, seeing what was coming, became uncomfortable. He began to squirm. "This is my date too," the
young man said. "We're gonna do what I want to do." He
was seated on a hassock in front of her and now he reached
over and removed her shoes. He had a toe fetish, he told
her, as he plucked at the toe of her panty hose. He loved
girls' toes, he said, and he touched his burning cigarette to
the gauzy material he had loosened, which vaporized.
Lifting her now bare toes to his mouth he sucked on them
one by one. The girl had begun quaking. He took his shirt
off, then his pants. There were still three bolts on the
door. The girl began to cry. "We were having a nice
time," she stammered. "Why do we have to take this
course of action?" He pulled her dress off over her head.

"I'm the king, you're the queen, and my dog is the prince," the man explained. "What the king says goes." Her underwear he ripped off, and he began licking her breasts. When the weeping girl resisted being forced down on the bed, the man's eyes filled with rage. He said, "I know this is rape, but this is the way it has to be."

It occurred to Joe Hearn that girls—women—most times did not put up much of a fight. They seemed to have an atavistic reaction to rape. They almost seemed to expect it. For thousands and thousands of years females were dragged by the hair back to the cave and raped. Rape was all they knew. A genetic acceptance of rape was perhaps bred into them at that time. It perhaps existed within them to this day, so that the actual rape itself, however hateful, seemed to them almost normal. Joe entertained such thoughts because his alternative was to share this young girl's pain.

"I begged him not to go off inside me," the girl said, "which he did."

Joe, who saw Mary in this girl's place, was much moved.

But the mood was broken by Judith's next question. "Did he bring your mouth into contact with his penis?"

The girl had not yet looked in Joe's direction. Now she studied her hands. "Yes, he did."

"Did his penis make contact with your anus?"

"No."

"How many times did his penis penetrate your vagina?"

There were many such questions, and they were more and more specific. Judith posed them as if making normal conversation. She went over the same revolting details again and again and again.

More time was lost as Judith walked the girl out into the anteroom where her father sat waiting. The father looked in worse shape than the daughter. Joe stood in the doorway, while Judith tried to soothe them both. She gave them more time than was necessary, Joe thought. She pressed upon them the names of counselors that the girl might want to speak to, especially if her present nightmares continued—every night, she had said, she dreamed that a man was chasing her with a knife. Judith also handed out her home phone number. Joe disapproved of this. Nobody in law enforcement did it, not with all the psychos wandering around this city. He kept glancing at his watch, but Judith Adler was not to be hurried.

Finally she walked father and daughter to the outer door, where she shook hands with both of them.

As soon as they were gone she was all business again, and he heard her say to her male secretary, "Get Ligouri in here for me, please." Joe was surprised that she had a male secretary. To Joe she said pleasantly, "I have just one more short job to do, and then we can go."

So he had no choice but to accompany her back into her office, there to resume his seat against the wall. In a moment a young assistant district attorney entered the office. After handing over the raped girl's dossier, Judith spent at least ten minutes outlining the case to the young man. Joe Hearn, irritated at this additional delay, glanced from Judith's legal diplomas on the wall, to the windowsill crowded with flowering plants, to the neat piles of dossiers on her desk. Obviously a woman's office—he could not have said why. The neatness, maybe. Behind the desk sat Judith Adler herself, wearing her rumpled blazer, her brown-and-beige-striped dress, and her pearl necklace. And in no hurry.

So far she had taken no real notice of Joe at all.

"It's not an easy case," Judith told Ligouri. "It's not a sketch case."

"What's a sketch case?" interrupted Joe, hoping she would hear the impatience, the annoyance in his voice, hoping to break up their dialogue, move this thing along.

"A prosecutor likes to see sketches of himself in the paper," explained Judith with a smile. "But this is just a young girl who got raped on a first date. The press won't take any notice of it. However, Anthony here is not a publicity hound, are you, Anthony?"

Ligouri was thumbing through the case folder.

"No force used," he said.

This was Joe Hearn's thought also.

"The girl believed she was dealing with a psychotic," said Judith firmly. "She believed there was no other way to get out of his apartment alive. You make the jury believe that and it's force."

"No witnesses either, I suppose?" said Ligouri. "No other evidence?"

"No," said Judith smiling. "The law no longer requires corroboration," she said to Joe. "I'm giving Anthony the case because I know he'll do a superb job." To Ligouri she said, "The victim's awfully young, and she's awfully upset. During your pretrial interviews you'll have to handle her gently."

"She's going to want to be hugged a lot. Is she pretty?"

"And you can't hug her."

Ligouri closed the case folder and grinned. "I know. It's hard. I'll send her in to you. You can hug her."

"She may make a superb witness," said Judith. Turning to Joe at last, she said sweetly, "We can go now."

Almost one hour late she steered down into the Holland Tunnel and up the other side, and they headed up toward northern New Jersey. Beside her, Joe was still trying to come to terms with who this Miss Adler might be. He gazed down at her shoes working the pedals. Out of the mouth of this woman had come clinical terms and phrases, discussions about penis, vagina, anus. Joe Hearn had been raised to wince every time he heard four-letter words employed in the presence of a female. Times had changed, but to hear language like that issuing from the mouth of a girl or woman still made him uncomfortable.

"Those questions you asked that girl," he began cautiously.

"Usually I probe even more deeply than that, but you were there. I guess I felt a little self-conscious."

"Some people might object to those questions."

"Like who?"

It was Joe himself who had found them objectionable. "Well," he said, "her father, for instance."

Judith gazed out over the wheel. She may have frowned.

"My job is to force the victim back through every detail of the crime," she said, "even the ones they don't want to talk about."

"Why?"

"To make sure she is telling the truth, for one thing, and to develop evidence against the defendant for another."

Joe Hearn nodded. Age had made him more tolerant, but many old ideas were still imbedded in his psyche. Consciously or unconsciously they still swayed him. Women, to Joe Hearn, were creatures apart. He would have preferred a world in which they sat in party dresses being admired by suitors, and then became housewives and mothers, because life was simpler that way. The modern woman, including, he now believed, the one driving this car, was not a woman at all. She was a business associate.

She demanded constant adjustments from all who did business with her. She kept rewriting the rules. She was hard to deal with. Nearly everything she did threw a man off balance.

"The charges have to be specifically drawn," continued Judith, shaking her head with annoyance. "The law requires it. Rape is a different crime from sodomy, and oral sodomy is apart from anal sodomy. Anthony Ligouri is drawing up the specific charges right now. The man will be arrested as soon as the detectives we send out can find him. When the girl goes before the grand jury tomorrow or the next day, Anthony will ask her the same questions I did. I don't ask such questions because I enjoy it, but because the law says I must."

She was lecturing him, and Joe in turn had become annoyed. "You may very well indict the guy," he said, "but no jury is going to convict him." When Judith did not respond, he added, "Sure the law's been changed. It now favors the victim. But you haven't changed juries. In the absence of corroborating evidence, juries still prefer to believe the woman led the man on. That she wanted to be raped. As you know very well."

This silenced Judith. But several minutes later, as the state police barracks came in sight, she said pensively, "Did you believe the girl's story?"

"With those details she threw in? Sure." He was annoyed with himself by now. Instead of charming her, he was fighting with her—meaning the afternoon was being totally wasted. "The only justice you're likely to get," he muttered, "is if the detectives you send to arrest the guy break both his legs." In the old days, he thought with some satisfaction, this might well have happened.

Judith gave him an odd look. "Would you condone that?"

He turned on her. "Of course not." And in the old days there would be a male district attorney driving this car, not a female one, and he would not be feeling all these conflicting emotions.

She steered off the road onto the gravel in front of the barracks. "We're here," she said. "Let's see what they have for us inside, shall we?"

They went into the barracks. Like most police stations it seemed sparsely furnished, Spartan. There were no carpets. All the men wore guns and the sound of Judith's heels ringing out on the board floor seemed out of place, alien to everybody except perhaps her.

They were led to an office in the back.

Captain Sample was in uniform, a little man wearing an oversized gun—its barrel was as long as a Wyatt Earp six-shooter, and its handle was so thick Joe wondered if the man could possibly grip it.

Sample greeted Joe rather too effusively, as if vastly relieved to find that Miss Adler had not come alone or, even worse, accompanied by other women. As the trooper began to describe his case, he spoke directly to Joe, who was obscurely pleased or perhaps reassured. In the law-enforcement world, his world, men still preferred to deal with other men.

The case, Sample claimed, was half drugs, half rape, or maybe only pornography. He seemed much abashed to find himself in the presence of two high-level big-city officials, and the drug part of his narrative was incomprehensible. Events did not follow in sequence and could not easily be tracked, and when he saw that he was losing his audience he stopped abruptly. There were boxes of video-tapes in the cellar of actual rapes, he offered, as if this would perhaps hold their interest. He thought they were actual rapes. Did they want to see them?

"My interest is hard drugs." In civilian clothes no rank showed on Joe's shoulders so he put it into his voice. "Apart from the forty kilos of hashish found in the trunk of the car, were any other narcotics involved here?" he demanded.

Responding at once to the changed tone, the state trooper became a subordinate in his own office. "No, sir," he said.

"No heroin?"

"No, sir."

"Cocaine?"

"No, sir."

"Even a hint of heroin or cocaine?"

"No, sir." Sample appeared thoroughly deflated. Despite his resolve, Joe shot Judith a hard glance. He was here because this was supposed to be a drug case. Pornographic films, whether or not of actual rapes, did not interest him.

But Judith was repressing a smile, as if in some way Joe

amused her. She was not a bit apologetic. She's very sure of herself, Joe thought.

He watched her turn to Sample, "The videotapes?" she inquired.

So they all moved downstairs, followed by several other troopers who had been waiting outside Sample's office. Joe trailed along, convinced he was about to see only a few simulated rapes—spectacular pornography by the standards of this rural community, perhaps, not by his own. Not by New York's.

Downstairs was a cheaply paneled, windowless recreation room. It contained two rows of chairs in front of a TV console. Sample introduced the other officers, troopers in leather boots. They all took chairs. While Sample fiddled with the videotape machine, Joe glanced around the room. There were rows of sports trophies on shelves. On the walls were framed photos of state police teams in various sports, even a golf team. Being a trooper in New Jersey, Joe reflected, was not the same as being a cop on the streets of New York.

In the dark the screen began to flicker, then lit up. The images coalesced. The scene was somebody's living room. There was a girl, fully dressed, sitting on a sofa. She was clearly high on something. Pot or pills probably. A big bust and pouty lips. Pretty in a vapid way. Crowded brassiere and empty head.

There was some desultory conversation. There were four different men, all clothed. All were much older than the girl. One was the size and shape of a defensive tackle, bald, with tattooed forearms. A fifth man ran the camera, for from time to time his shoe appeared at the bottom of the frame. There was a zoom lens that sometimes closed up on the girl's dazed face, and sometimes opened wide to show the room, including a picture window. Outside this window was only empty air, placing the room high up in a city somewhere. Plainly it was not out here in the woods. However, nothing placed it in New York in Joe's jurisdiction, whatever Captain Sample might think, and there were no drugs in evidence either, except for what showed in the girl's eyes.

"Now we're going to have some fun," said a voice on the screen.

"I'm having fun already," said the girl, slurring every word.

Here it comes, thought Joe, the home porno movie. A whole afternoon shot. For what? He had not even managed to give a favorable impression of himself to Judith Adler, at least so far.

The men moving in and out of the frame became half clothed, then nude. At first the girl did not appear to notice this. When she did, she stood up and began to protest. For a pornographic actress, her performance was quite convincing. Joe sat with his chair propped back against the wall, its forelegs off the floor, his eyes half closed.

"You're not funny," the girl said. "I'm going home."

The pro football type, stark naked, stepped into the frame, "No, you're not," he said. Slabs of muscles bulged. The tattooed forearm was already drawn back and the fist at the end of it delivered a terrific clout to the side of the girl's head. The girl had no time to flinch. She never saw the punch coming. Baldy must have weighed 260, every ounce of it behind the blow.

The girl went down. She lay as unmoving as the rug. When the camera zoomed in close, Joe noted that she did not so much as twitch.

The legs of his chair had come down on the floor with a crash.

"I know," murmured Sample. "Affects me every time the same way.

He sounded pleased with himself, like an impresario whose show was a success. On the screen the four men dragged the girl out into the center of the living room where they started to undress her. At first they undid buttons but this seemed to take too long. Baldy grasped swatches of material at either side of the girl's breastbone and yanked. There was a ripping noise. Now all four of the men began tearing at her clothing. They tore away every remaining stitch of it.

The camera zoomed in close again, as if the machine itself wished to contemplate the girl's body. She lay on the rug surrounded by shreds of cloth, and it surveyed her for some time.

The frame widened again. The four men could be seen staring down at her. She still had not twitched.

"Do you think she's dead?" one of them said.

"I don't know," said Baldy, and he waved his tattooed forearms. "We'll find out after we're done."

"This is where they rape her, Miss Adler," interrupted Captain Sample apologetically. "You don't want to see this." And he put the machine on fast forward.

It was faster than a Charlie Chaplin movie. All four men raped the girl in triple time. When finished, they flipped her over and began to rape her anally.

"No, no," said Judith Adler firmly. "Please back it up and run it through at normal speed."

"It's not something for a woman to see," suggested Sample. He had shut the machine off altogether and the lights had come back on. The troopers in the room were all fidgeting, and they were too embarrassed to look in the direction of Judith Adler.

"I have to know exactly what was done and by whom," said Judith firmly. "The charges must be specific."

If she wants to see it, Joe Hearn thought grimly, let her see it. He said, "Run it through again, Captain, please."

On fast forward, the sound track had offered nothing but a series of squeaks. At normal speed the voices and the noise of bodies slapping together rendered the scene, if possible, even more shocking. The girl lay on the floor, was repeatedly assaulted, and only at the very end showed any sign of life. When they threw a glass of beer on her, she began at last to groan, and her eyes opened and closed several times.

The tape ended. Joe Hearn said to Sample, "Are the other tapes like that?"

"Not as bad," said Sample.

"You mean you saved the best for first," muttered Joe, and so great was the tension in the room that everyone laughed.

"Are all the girls different?" asked Joe.

"Different," said Captain Sample. "There must be twenty of them."

The lights were on. There were seven men and one woman in the room, and no one spoke.

"I'm not sure if you would want to see any more," said Sample.

"There's no proof it happened in New York," said Joe.

"The rapes all take place in the same room," explained Sample.

The room could be anywhere.

"It's New York. In one of the films you can see out the window."

"You better show us that one," said Joe. Judith only watched him, the half smile on her face.

Captain Sample began to shuffle through the box at his feet.

Again the lights went out, and the television screen lit up. This time the victim, a tall, thin redhead, was conscious throughout. She was held pinioned to the rug while the same four men raped her. She was weeping and squirming, which caused the men to make a number of ribald jokes as they worked. When they had finished with her, the girl sat on a chair huddled into herself, still nude, sobbing. The camera, zooming in for a close-up, photographed also the window behind her, and this window framed an easily identifiable New York landmark, the cast-iron stanchions of the Queensboro Bridge.

"That's one of your bridges," said Sample.

"I know very well it's one of our bridges," muttered Joe.

"Do you have the girl?" inquired Judith. "Do you know any of their names?"

"We haven't been able to identify the girls," admitted Captain Sample.

"You'd think the girls would come forward," said Judith.

"Men like that would kill them if they came forward," muttered Joe. Sample ought to be out looking for the girls, not phoning New York for help.

"We would need the girls' testimony before these tapes could even be admitted into evidence," said Judith. Was she trying to organize the investigation in her head or only trying to get over the shock? A woman, Joe thought, should not have to watch tapes like that, should not have to know about animals like the men on those tapes. "They'd have to testify," Judith said, "as to when and where the tapes were made."

The investigation, it seemed to Joe, would be difficult, perhaps impossible. The shock was beginning to wear off. These girls must be somewhere, but where? How did you find them? It would be an interesting investigation. However, his command was the Narcotics Division. His duties and responsibilities were restrictive. This was not his affair.

They were not going to watch any more tapes apparently, which was fine with Joe. Judith did not look very eager either. The lights were on and stayed on, and he watched her.

"The two perpetrators you arrested in the car," inquired Judith, "are they in these films?"

"Negative," said Captain Sample. "The guy, the one who had the films in his basement, claims he was storing them for a friend and didn't know what they were." Sample gave a sheepish smile. "You know how it is."

"They didn't know about the forty kilos of hashish in the trunk of their car either, did they?" said Joe.

Sample did not answer. He was studying his fingernails. "The rapes took place in New York," he said after a time. "It's your case."

"I don't think so," said Joe.

During the first twenty minutes of the ride back to the city, Judith stared out over the steering wheel and did not speak. Joe wanted to ask her about herself. He wanted to know more about her, where she was coming from and where she thought she was going. But her demeanor was too still. She was in a state of such rapt concentration that he hesitated to disturb her, and so he only watched her profile and waited. As for himself, the first hard shock was entirely gone. Although he was still appalled at what he had seen, crime was crime.

But such was not the case with Judith Adler, apparently.

"About those films," she began.

She wants to get involved, Joe told himself. She wants to lock those men up. This impressed him, though it was perhaps not very professional of her. Still, such personal involvement seemed all right for a woman. And it was certainly an interesting case. There were stolen car rings, hijack rings, burglary rings; but this was the first rape ring he had ever heard about. To break a case like this must seem to Judith the summit of her ambitions.

"What do you think we should do?" she asked him.

Joe recognized this as a rhetorical question. She knew very well what she intended to do, he believed.

"If you're smart," he advised, "you'll throw the thing back at the Jersey state police. It's their case, whatever that idiot Sample says. They have the only evidence that any rapes ever took place. They found the tapes, and they have a hook into the guy who had them. It's not much of a hook, but it's something."

For several miles Judith said nothing.

"Those cops are incompetent," she said, and waited for him to reply. When Joe remained silent, she added, "They seemed incompetent to me."

"Most cops are incompetent."

"It's a case we could make."

"We?" said Joe, and he grinned. "Who is we?" He stretched his lanky body in the seat. Then he said gently, "Hey, I can't get involved in this. My job is to run the Narcotics Division. This is not a Narcotics case, and in addition the biggest part of it happens to lie in the state of New Jersey."

"We is the district attorney's office and the New York Police Department together," insisted Judith.

"Do you realize how big an investigation you're looking at? You got four unidentified rapists and an unidentified camera operator. You got an unidentified apartment located somewhere on the East Side, and the East Side is a big place, believe me. You got a dozen or twenty unidentified girls who got raped, and no way to locate any of them."

"It's a sketch case," suggested Judith.

"Maybe. Provided you break it. If you don't break it, which is far more likely, it's a colossal waste of man-hours."

"So, do you want to work it with me?"

"No," said Joe. But she glanced at him with such disappointment that he added quickly, "I'd like to, maybe, but my mission is something else." Now she's going to try and borrow some detectives off me, he thought. She's been working up to it for at least ten miles. How was he going to answer her?

"Will you assign some detectives to the case?" she asked.

"I can't justify that."

"There's evidence of narcotics being involved."

"That's not clear at all."

"It's clear that these people are criminals. I'm sure they're into something else besides rape, probably drugs. Can't you feel it?"

Again, he gave her a smile. "No, I can't feel it. And you can't feel it either."

"I can though," Judith said intently. Her eyes, focused on the highway, turned toward him. "And you could too, if you'd let yourself." For a moment she was almost pleading with him.

"One of the most common rapes we see," she said, watching the road again, "is the woman coming home who finds a burglar in her bedroom. The burglar is already committing one outrage, the burglary, and now he rapes the woman as well. He wants to compound the first outrage with an even worse outrage. There's something in the criminal psyche or maybe the human psyche that makes him want to do that. He has broken something, and when he sees it is broken he wants to smash it to smithereens. Sometimes he kills the woman as well."

Joe had had some of these thoughts himself. "Raping women is just a sideline with them," he mused. "They were already doing something horrible."

She seemed pleased with him. "They're already outlaws, and this is their way of proving to themselves how bad they are." She gave him a smirk. "We're on the same wavelength aren't we?" she said. "I was afraid for a while we weren't but we really are. So will you assign me some detectives?"

She had a somewhat husky voice. And she was very persuasive. "You must be terrific in court," Joe murmured.

"What?"

"Can I call you Judy?"

"It's a sketch case," she said again.

"You've got about fifty detectives down there attached to the district attorney's office," he suggested. "You really should use some of them." The DA's fifty detectives were in constant use bringing in witnesses for trials in progress. They had to be shared among over two hundred prosecutors, and immediate need took precedence over an ongoing investigation. Joe knew this as well as she did. She must be borrowed up to the hilt there already, Joe thought.

She gave him a girlish smile. "So how many detectives are you going to lend me?"

"I'll lend you two." Cirillo would criticize him if he found out.

"Only two?"

"For one week."

"Suppose one week isn't enough?"

"We'll see after that." He could hear Cirillo snarl: That broad—the chief of detectives called all women broads—wants to solve every rape there is. Screw her.

"But if we get something started I can keep them?"

"Who's going to be directing this investigation?"

"I am," said Judith Adler.

"Yes," said Joe, "I thought so. These are pretty vicious guys. Be careful you don't get too close." He was not really worried about her. She was not his to worry about, he reminded himself, and it was too difficult a case. She won't know how to make even a start, he told himself. In a week he'd have his detectives back. And Assistant District Attorney Judith Adler would owe him. Which was all he had wanted in the first place, was it not?

Beside him Judy breathed a sigh that was perhaps relief. But what she said was, "Only a week, eh?"

"Sorry," said Joe.

They were coming to a rest stop. "Why don't I pull off there," Judy said, "and we can toast our partnership over a cup of coffee?"

The afternoon is shot anyway, Inspector Hearn decided. What's another hour? "Good idea," he told her. "I'll buy."

They sat opposite each other in a booth on Naugahyde plastic benches. Joe's was sticky from too many years of spilled food and drink. He could feel it sticking to his trousers. Coffee mugs were placed in front of them on paper napkins that were meant to serve as saucers. They served principally, he noted, as blotting paper.

"Cheers," said Judith, raising her mug in a toast, and this amused Joe, for he had never toasted anyone in coffee before. After drinking, he set his mug down again on its napkin in its wet brown ring, and they smiled at each other across the table.

They talked for over an hour, while one pair of mugs went cold and was replaced by another. Judith's knowledge of the Police Department was both extensive and accurate. Her knowledge of prominent ongoing cases proved as exact as his, and sometimes she knew details he didn't. They talked about judges they had dealt with, about other prosecutors, specific detectives. She knew Chief of Detectives Cirillo quite well and did not trust him. On the other hand the PC impressed her. She was on first-name terms with nearly every member of the police hierarchy.

"In my job I have to be," she said. "Cooperation between the DA's office and the police is important."

He grinned at her. "You mean so you can borrow detectives off somebody whenever you want."

"I heard your name," she confided, "long before you got your present promotion."

Joe was flattered.

"You're the coming star, apparently. That's one of the reasons I wanted to meet you." She added a little shyly, "If you're going to be the PC one day, I want to be able to say I knew you when."

This silenced them both for some time.

"Tell me about your wife," said Judith presently.

"Mary's an artist," said Joe. He counted himself far too sophisticated to drag snapshots out of his wallet, but he was proud of his wife and enjoyed talking about her. "You should see some of the things she's done. Still lifes, landscapes, figure studies. I kid her sometimes, but she's really good. For instance—" Nonetheless, as he described Mary's attributes, her accomplishments, he found himself wishing that she cared more about the police side of his life than she seemed to, that she might understand it as intimately, say, as the woman opposite him. But this notion seemed to him so disloyal to Mary that he not only did not articulate it, but at once tried to suppress it.

"Mary's beautiful," said Joe proudly. "She's a wonderful mother to the kids. What more do you want to know?" But his grin, even as he spoke, turned pensive. Some men were able to bring their wives with them into their other world by inviting them to conventions, sales meetings, business dinners. But law enforcement, at least until recently, was such an all-male preserve that Joe had not been able to do this, and he saw it not as Mary's failing but as his own.

"Does she go with you to all those Communion breakfasts and other police affairs?" inquired Judith.

"Rarely." Joe wrinkled his nose at her. "She finds them rather dull."

Judith laughed. "She's right."

Joe said pensively, "Ideally a husband and wife ought to be in the same business, shouldn't they?"

He was speaking mostly to himself. He didn't expect an answer, and didn't get one. "It's late," he said. "We better pay and leave." He peeled the sodden check from the Formica and rose to his feet.

"Two detectives?" said Judith.

It made Joe smile. "But only for one week," he answered. Despite the smile he meant it. Giving her two detectives for any time at all felt to him like an entanglement—not so much a betrayal of Chief of Detectives Cirillo or of his own mandate, as a betrayal of Mary. The only way he could justify his decision to himself was to assign it a specific limit. One week.

By the time he reached headquarters, it was night. Everyone had gone home except the sergeant who was his secretary. He was still on duty at the desk outside his office. "I need two detectives for a week," Joe told him. "Take them off someplace where they can be spared."

Dinner was another sandwich, this time with a bottle of beer. He stood at his window looking out at the three East River bridges strung with lights, at the moving black river beneath them, at the lights of Brooklyn across the way. He had the beer bottle in one hand and the sandwich in the other, and he munched away, then went back to work—he still had six inches of paper to get through before he could go home.

When the two detectives arrived he came around his desk and shook hands with them. One was named Bracchi, the other Dolan. He did not know them and so, busy as he was, he decided to devote ten minutes or more to what must have seemed to them an idle conversation. He wanted to get a feel for their ability. He was only being careful. What chance was there that they might do something that could embarrass him? But finally he told them to report tomorrow to Judith Adler at the district attorney's office. They would be working for her for about a week.

"What kid of case is it?" said Bracchi.

A sketch case, thought Joe, provided you break it. But what he said was, "I'll let her fill you in. There are two things special about it. The first is, I don't want you talking about it to anyone in this office or in the department. And the second is that you are to phone me every night. I want to know exactly what you're doing at all times."

He went back behind his desk and sat down. "That will be all."

When he got home it was nearly midnight, and his shoulders were stiff. Mary, who had waited up, prepared him a light supper and sat with him while he ate it. "I spent the afternoon with the most remarkable woman," he told his wife, and for the rest of the meal he talked about Judith. In their bedroom later he was still talking about her. They were both getting undressed. The kids were across the hall asleep. "This woman really has it together," said Joe. "Do you know what she said when—"

"No, I don't," Mary interrupted and turned her back on him. "I'm going to take a bath," she muttered over her shoulder, and she went through into the bathroom. He heard the water begin to pound.

Joe gave a shrug, and pulled his tie off. After a moment he hung his tie on the rack behind the closet door.

Joe's alarm clock tweeted once and woke him. He lunged for it. Carefully he got out of bed. It was 4:00 A.M. He crept around in the dark, getting dressed. Behind him Mary slept on, suspecting nothing. In Brooklyn the trigger-happy Cubans slept and they also suspected nothing. So he hoped. His headlights probed the empty highway. Light stabbed into darkness. Detectives made thousands of arrests a year and rarely got shot. The backs of Joe's hands were already tingling. It happened, though. The clean night air bloomed inside the car. It smelt damp, fresh.

Brooklyn: an all-night diner on a street corner. The plate glass was steamed over. Four detectives waited inside. Fresh coffee had just been brewed, the first of the new day. Joe breathed it in. The cup was too hot. It burned his hands, his mouth. The plate glass was so steamed up he could not see out. In whispers his men checked their plans. They joked about getting killed. Their eyes were too bright, their laughter too loud, Joe's too. They opened their guns and counted bullets, then went out and got into the cars and drove the few blocks to the building where the Cubans were holed up. They peered up at the building facade. The night air tasted incredibly sweet to Joe. He savored it as if it was the last he would ever breathe. The hairs on the backs of his hands were standing straight up, a familiar sensation, and as pleasurable as any he knew.

They went into the building with a rush. Two of the detectives had a ram. The door went down with the second hit. The two Cubans in pajamas looked stupefied with sleep. There were two women in the apartment as well. They were screaming. One was stark naked. The handcuffed Cubans were herded out the door by the detectives, one of whom carried a suitcase full of shotguns and handguns. Another had about a kilo of uncut narcotics. In the street Joe watched the Cubans pushed into the cars. The sky had begun to turn gray. As he approached the Brooklyn Bridge the stone of its great Gothic arches suddenly blushed pink. On the other side all of the streetlights winked out. He stood on Police Plaza looking up at headquarters. His hands no longer tingled, but his heart was still beating a bit fast, and he sucked in a lungful of dawn air. The terrible Cubans were out of circulation. Routine arrests had been made.

He loved being a cop, loved everything about it. He could not imagine wanting ever to give it up.

4

Mary, heading from her car toward the baseball field, found that her state of excitement only increased. The thrill was definitely sexual in nature, and accompanying the thrill was guilt. It was as if she were doing something illicit. There were bleachers along the first-base line. Climbing carefully on high heels she stepped up four or five wobbly rows. She noted three schoolgirls at the far end of the bleacher. Nearby but lower down were two younger boys with book bags between their feet. Otherwise the bleachers were empty. The plank wobbled when she sat on it. There were no other mothers present. Sitting there Mary felt conspicuous, even embarrassed. But I have a perfect right to be here, she encouraged herself. The reason I'm here is to watch my son play baseball.

At home plate the boys had surrounded their coach, Loftus, who was giving orders. With her purse in her lap Mary watched him. What am I feeling guilty about? she asked herself. I'm not doing anything. I'm just looking.

Coach Loftus blew on his whistle and practice started. He stood beside home plate hitting fungoes to the outfield. He had a nice swing. Balls sailed high into the sky and boys shagged them and threw them back in. He had the economy of movement of the practiced athlete and she wondered if he had ever played professionally.

Two other mothers came onto the field. They were together. They came toward the bleachers but stopped some distance off. Once, between swings, Loftus glanced over at them, but not at her. The two women nodded

across at Mary and she nodded back. Apart from that she
ignored them. She did not want them climbing up beside
her.

Now Loftus handed the fungo bat to one of the kids,
who began slapping ground balls around the infield. The
first ball hit to Billy at third base struck a stone and
smacked him in the chest. It made Mary jump to her feet,
but when her son pounced on the ball and threw to first,
she sat down again. She watched Billy carefully for a
moment just to be sure. The accident had started her
heart thumping. If anything ever happened to that boy,
she thought, I would die.

"Hello, Mrs. Hearn."

The man loomed over her and his voice gave her a start.
She looked up and it was Loftus. Oh, my God, she thought,
here he is. She wondered how he had got there, and her
first impulse was the same she had experienced often as a
teenager. She wanted to run.

"Thanks for coming by," he said.

But she was not a teenager, and so she continued to
look at him, apparently at ease. She felt as if her dress
were transparent or her mind, and tried to reassure herself. I may imagine I've already made love to him, she
thought, but he has no such illusions about me. Nothing is
transparent.

"And thanks for Billy, too," Loftus said. "He's one of my
best men."

To hear her fifteen-year-old called a man should have
amused Mary. She should have given it the smile it deserved. But she couldn't fashion one. Loftus was a bigger
man than she had thought, and he was standing too close.
He wore a team warm-up jacket that looked too small for
his muscles, and it was open halfway to his navel. He was
like a rock singer, all chest hair and chains. Hanging from
the chains, in his case, was his whistle. In his hands he
carried a fungo bat.

"Mind if I join you?" he asked.

Her eyes crinkled up, but she said nothing. However,
as Loftus moved onto the plank beside her, she placed her
purse between them, keeping him at a distance. If he
noticed this, he gave no sign. I wonder where the rumors
come from? Mary thought. Which mothers has he gone
after? And which ones let him do it? If any.

"I like your new hairdo, Mrs. Hearn."

"Do you?" she said. Several days had gone by. Her new look was no longer all that new.

"Yes. You know why?"

The other mothers had moved up into the bleachers by now, but Loftus sat with her, not them, and she flashed them a smile. "No, Marty, why?"

"Short hair suits you because you have such a lovely neck."

This was so unexpected that Mary began to blush, and had to turn away as if watching the outfielders. The blush passed quickly, replaced by annoyance both at herself and at her husband. Was she so starved for compliments that she had to fish for them from this arrogant baseball coach?

"That's a new dress, too, if I'm not mistaken." She had not worn it since the day of Joe's promotion, and could kick herself for wearing it now. She was definitely wrongly dressed for a baseball field.

After a moment, to see what sort of reply he might make, Mary said, "Do you like it?"

"I like silk dresses."

It wasn't silk, but what did he know? This morning she had put on jeans and a sweater, had gone to the supermarket, had done her housework. For several days she had been thinking about coming to practice. An hour ago she had decided to put this dress on. She had liked herself in it, but then almost had not come anyway.

"Silk feels nice under the hand," Loftus added. She glanced at him sharply, looking for the leer or grin, but found neither. In his eyes was frank appraisal of her, no more, no less. "And the blue in the print exactly matches the blue of your eyes. I guess it took you a while to find exactly the right shade."

Perception of this type in a man was rare. Mary was stirred. All a woman—a wife—really wanted was recognition that she was there. That she had thoughts and desires too; that, for instance, she chose her clothes carefully.

"How did you happen to learn to say such things, Marty?"

"I guess I just appreciate women. I always have."

'Well, you've got a good eye."

This time he smiled. "Thank you Mrs. Hearn."

A silence fell between them. Is it sex this man exudes? Mary asked herself. Or an interest in me, or what? She

should be back in her kitchen preparing dinner. Tonight
Joe was coming home early for a change. The four of them
would have dinner together and she would set the table in
the dining room, not the kitchen. But to play hooky from
all that felt good.

"Your son tells me you're an artist."

What's Billy been saying now? She did not want to get
into this. She could not abide people who questioned her
about art out of politeness, as if she were a child. "I'm not
an artist," she said. "I do watercolors once in a while." But
neither did she want Loftus to think her just another
frustrated housewife painting by the numbers. "I did go to
art school before I was married," she added.

"Which one?"

"Parsons in New York."

"Good school."

"You know Parsons?" Any minute, she told herself, he is
going to say something ridiculous. He is going to turn into
a fool before my eyes.

But not yet. "I know their reputation. I know they
reject hundreds of applications every year."

He had the bat in both hands and was rapping it softly
on the plank between his feet. He had a cleft chin, a long
straight nose, eyelashes as long as a girl, and black curly
hair. When he turned to smile at her he showed small
perfect teeth.

"I may not know much about art, but I know about
competition," he told her. "You must have been good just
to get accepted."

This silenced Mary.

"Do you still take courses?"

She did, and to her surprise found herself talking about
it. She belonged to the Midtown Art League, and every
Wednesday morning went to New York where, from nine
until noon she attended drawing classes from life.

"You mean drawing nudes?"

"Usually," she replied, and looked for the leer again,
but did not find it. "Sometimes we drape the model in
folds of cloth or put her in some outlandish costume."
Mary tried a laugh. "Sometimes the model doesn't show
up and one of us has to sit."

"Have you ever sat?"

"Sure."

This time he did leer at her. "Nude?"

"No, not nude." Mary was again annoyed. Up close
Loftus seemed younger than she had thought, too. How
much younger? she wondered. He might be thirty-five,
more or less. What difference did it make, anyway? "I'm
just an old married woman," she told him.

"I wouldn't say that at all." He looked her up and down.
"Not at all." And then, after a brief pause: "Are the
models always women?"

"Men sometimes. Everything from old men to weight
lifters."

"I don't see how a man could sit around naked in front
of women, if you know what I mean. I know I couldn't."

Mary laughed. Well, there was no mistaking Loftus'
direction now. This was a stupid conversation and even
faintly insulting. Then why had she begun to feel a faint
need to squirm inside her dress?

Having glanced at his watch, Loftus stood up. "We're
going to play an intrasquad game. Will you stay for it?"

There seemed an intent look on his face as he awaited
her reply. But she shook her head. "I have to get home."

Loftus hesitated. "Just let me start the game and I'll be
back."

She watched him stride down the bleachers from plank
to plank to the field. He was about as tall as Joe, but his
shoulders were broader, and his arms more heavily muscled. Loftus had a lithe body. He seemed very physical.
But Joe was better looking, she told herself loyally.

As the boys grouped around Loftus, she was searching
her head for what she had heard about him: whispers,
nothing solid, of an affair with Jane Clancy, whose son
graduated last year. But the Clancys were divorced now,
so maybe there was something to it. There had been some
other housewife before that, and also a teacher in the
junior high, who had been fired. Were these only rumors?
Every suburban town had rumors. You couldn't believe
them. Mary watched Loftus divide his team in two, and as
the game started she asked herself why she had come to
this place today. The answer came back: I just wanted to
have a look at him. Now she had had her look. You should
leave, she told herself. But presently Loftus came striding
up the planks again.

"I only came to watch Billy," she told him. "As soon as he comes to bat I have to go."

"Bad luck for me," said Loftus. "Billy's up second. I should have put him up ninth."

He had brought a glossy magazine for her to sit on. "You could snag that beautiful dress and ruin it."

Loftus had switched to the other side of her now—before she could get her pocketbook between them. As a result he was crowding her, and she did not like it.

When her son came to bat and stroked a double down the thirdbase line, she jumped to her feet grinning and applauding.

Then the inning ended. Mary stood up and said to Loftus, "Please tell my son to catch a ride home with one of his friends. I won't have time to come back for him."

"I'll take care of it, Mrs. Hearn," said Loftus.

She let the Mrs. Hearn pass. As he stepped down the planks with her, he offered his hand, but she ignored it. She did not need him to get down out of a bleacher. "So long, Marty," she said and walked head down to her car.

At home she changed back into jeans and sweater, then worked diligently in her kitchen for some time. But she kept watching the clock.

About 5:00 P.M. she decided she needed a centerpiece for the dining-room table and she went out front into her flower beds to cut one. She was out there about thirty minutes. She took her time about it. Gardening was another of her loves, and her flower beds, each one as carefully composed for color and shape as a still life in a painting, were among the glories of the neighborhood. She was standing with a mass of spring flowers in her arms when what she had expected to happen did happen. A car drew up bringing Billy home from baseball practice, and it was driven by Coach Loftus himself.

Calling, "Thanks a lot, Coach," over his shoulder, Billy ran into the house.

Marty got out of the car and came over to Mary. "So you're a gardener too?" he said. "Those are gorgeous tulips."

"Thanks for bringing Billy home," said Mary. "I didn't mean for you to have to do it. I thought—" She felt herself talking too much, but couldn't stop. "I meant for him to catch a ride with one of his friends."

"No trouble, Mary," said Loftus.

She watched him and said nothing. So it's Mary, now, she thought.

"Could I see your watercolors?" he asked.

"My watercolors?"

"I don't mean to impose on you. If you're too busy—"

She looked back at the house. "Well, I've got to put these flowers in a bowl." But when she started for the door he followed.

"I'll only stay a minute. I really am interested to see your watercolors."

No, you're not, Mary thought. Your interest is me, and I'm taken. Nonetheless, she was both flattered and confused.

At the door, she hesitated and thought to stop him from entering. I'm a grown woman, she chided herself. I can invite a man into my house if I want to. It's all perfectly innocent. What is he going to do, rape me? And so she led him into the living room where, still clutching the cut flowers to her chest, pointing with her elbow, she said somewhat truculently, "Those are two of them there."

Loftus stood reverently in front of the nearest one.

"I have to put these in a bowl," said Mary, and she went into the kitchen and arranged her flowers. This took some minutes, and when on her way back she passed in front of the hall mirror, she stooped slightly to study herself before rejoining him.

In the living room the baseball coach stood now before the second of the watercolors. "It would be presumptuous of me to say whether they are good or bad," he told her. "All I can say is that I like them. This one here is your favorite, isn't it?"

Although he was right, she refused to admit it. "You're guessing," she said. But she was impressed.

"It is, isn't it?"

Their eyes locked. Mary began to imagine Joe walking in through the front door and finding them there in his living room, his wife and a strange man staring at each other.

Maybe it would make him appreciate me more, she thought.

"I like them both," she said.

After a moment she moved toward the door. To her

relief Loftus took the hint and followed, and she showed him out.

When the door had closed behind him she was really quite relieved.

Though it was early evening by then Joe was still in his office. His door was closed. Behind it he had been engaged for the past ten minutes in stretching exercises in an effort to relieve the tension that afflicted his arms and shoulders. His neck ached too. Today had been devoted to solving the problem represented by Deputy Inspector Pearson. Possible replacements had marched through his door one after the other and he had interviewed them, working with extreme care, considering the import of literally each word before he spoke it. A tense day.

Because the candidates, some of whom he had served with before, did not know which particular job they were being interviewed for. Neither did Pearson who, sitting just outside, watched the parade of men go past him, saw that they were the wrong rank, and perhaps imagined himself secure; whatever it was had nothing to do with him. When he woke up in a day or two transferred he would be more than surprised. He would wonder how Joe had managed it.

Providing Joe could push the transfer through.

He was working deviously for a number of reasons. Within the department it was usually impossible to tell who had influence and how much. Not being alarmed in advance, Pearson could not lobby with his rabbi, if he had one, to block any transfer, to keep his prestigious job. The various candidates to replace him, knowing nothing specific, could not lobby either, could not call in an important favor and get themselves rammed down Joe's throat.

Deviousness had not come easily to Joe. It was something he had acquired. His nature was open and forthright. He had had to learn it.

By working in secret he had eliminated to a large extent the risk from below, but not the risk from above.

The ability to move personnel around the department was a jealously guarded prerogative. It was restricted to very few men. One stepped onto such terrain at one's peril, and Joe knew this, but he had no choice. He had to do it. His superiors not only expected him to make changes in his staff, but in fact would judge him on how quickly and forcefully he made them. On the highest levels of the department it was often difficult to judge an officer's performance in any other way. How well has he staffed himself up was a question they often asked about a man. They would be watching him carefully. They couldn't judge him by inventory or sales or profit or loss, but they could measure the excellence of his staff, or thought they could. But when a man was actually trying to form a staff, as Joe was, they not only didn't help, they often opposed his choices, sometimes in order to push a favorite of their own, sometimes just for form's sake. It was no sure thing they would let him get rid of Pearson. The act of transferring the man thus became as risky, as secretive, and as complicated as a military campaign. By using supreme caution Joe cut the risk considerably, but it tended to tie his arm and shoulder muscles into knots by the end of the day.

Joe was lying on the floor now, spread-eagled, his hands grasping the opposing legs of his desk, trying to pull them together.

Ten minutes ago he had decided which candidate he wanted. The problem had become how to get him approved. All personnel requests had to go through the chief of detectives, then the chief of operations and finally the PC, but on Pearson's level others would also be consulted, probably, and all these people had to be both thwarted and dazzled by Joe's choice to replace him. It was for this reason that, after much thought, he had come up with a unique solution. He would choose not another deputy inspector, nor even a captain. He would seek to supplant Pearson with a mere lieutenant—all of the men he had interviewed today were lieutenants.

This was so irregular that at first it would surely be strongly opposed, and his motives would just as surely be suspect. But if ultimately approved by the PC, then all his subsequent choices would be approved routinely and his tactics would be perceived as brilliant even by those superiors who would most oppose him now. He had got around them like a man on ice skates. They hadn't even had time to get in his way, had barely seen him go by. He would be considered not devious but shrewd.

They would see the advantages to Joe as clearly as he

himself did, but would be unable to block him. To bring in a young and inexperienced lieutenant did more than just get rid of Pearson. It also consolidated all power within the division in his own hands; at present many of the older subordinate officers tended to look for their instructions to Pearson. Furthermore, a lieutenant would not have had time to acquire much influence within the department; moving him into a deputy inspector's slot would make him deliriously happy, and he would owe all his loyalty to Joe. Nor in time of crisis, should one arise, would a young lieutenant seem the viable alternative to himself that Pearson perhaps did now.

All this Joe had worked out carefully in his head, brooded over for days, and finally begun to implement.

But could he get away with it?

The lieutenant he intended to select was on the captain's list, would be a captain within sx months probably, and was otherwise highly qualified. As soon as opposition to him surfaced, Joe intended to point this out—he was really choosing a captain, which was certainly acceptable. Captains had often served in the job before. But since the man was actually a lieutenant, Joe's decision was also saving the department a good deal of money. It was actually an economy measure. Most new commanders sought to enhance their own stature by surrounding themselves with more aides, and with aides of ever higher rank, but he was doing the opposite, which was certainly commendable. And he would point this out too. As for Pearson, a man of such talents would be more valuable to the department if used in some important job somewhere else, rather than in a slot a lieutenant could fill. Pearson was overqualified to serve as Joe's chief of staff.

It seemed to Joe that such arguments as these would make opponents, no matter what their rank, back off fast. They would not wish to fly in the face of modern management theory or appear to be spendthrifts. Opposition to him would not seem worth their while.

The only one not convinced would be Pearson. The transfer might blight his career, and Joe realized this. Or else he might land on his feet again. In any case, the day would come when he would have to be told—a thought that made Joe uncomfortable. Over the years he had learned to survive in the Police Department hierarchy, had learned the necessary deviousness. But he had never learned callousness. He was no good at causing other men pain. Most executives could do it without a twinge. Joe could not. He would try to place Pearson somewhere else first. He would work hard at it. He would give him plenty of time. There was no hurry.

Joe's console lit up. Breaking off the stretching exercises, rising from the floor, he punched the button: "Yeah?"

It was Pearson. "May I come in, Inspector?"

"Sure."

Pearson came through the door smiling somewhat unctuously. He was at least ten years older than Joe, and in both manner and appearance seemed to Joe somewhat soft. He was not battle hard. He did not appear tough enough to protect himself. Whatever was to happen to him would always be unexpected. The career and the man might be too easily crushed.

"Bracchi and Dolan," Pearson began, "those two detectives you have on special assignment—" He stopped and hesitated.

He had not mentioned Judith's name, and this was deliberate, Joe believed. His chief of staff was being as circumspect as an Old World servant. If any sentimental relationship existed between Inspector Hearn and the female district attorney in question, he had no wish to obtrude, did not seek to know anything about it.

Joe decided to twit him. "Which detectives did you say?"

"The ones you have working for the Manhattan DA's office."

"Oh, yes, the men I assigned to Judith Adler's office," said Joe repressing a smile. "What about them?"

"Dolan just phoned. An informant in Brooklyn has come forward in a case they were working on. Something about a major sale going down. A possible big seizure. They want permission to go back to work on that case."

Joe thought about it. "How long has Miss Adler had them?" he asked, though he knew.

"About a week, Inspector."

He had promised her no more. This seemed the right time to break the entanglement off. Pearson would no doubt be pleased. Joe himself was tired and wanted to get home to dinner with his wife and children.

"Put them back on the case in Brooklyn," Joe said. "If Miss Adler calls to protest, you handle her, if you can." Feeling somewhat relieved, as if from putting down an unusual burden, he gave a sudden grin. He felt as if he had been carrying a heavy suitcase for a stranger.

Very good, Inspector, said Pearson, and he turned to leave the office.

But Joe stopped him. Preparing Pearson for the transfer had best begin now. For a moment he studied the older man. "Suppose," Joe began, "you could have any job in the department—any job that calls for a deputy inspector, that is. What job would you pick?"

Pearson moistened his lips. He looked immediately threatened. "This one, Inspector."

Joe gave him a false smile. He was suddenly full of confidence; Pearson had no rabbi at all and was no threat to him. Therefore he decided to take preparation a step or two further. "You're just saying that not to hurt my feelings. But I'm serious, man. Surely you must have your eye on something."

Joe's smile seemed to reassure Pearson somewhat. False smiles often did. They seemed more reassuring than real ones, Joe reflected, because they came at times and in situations when no smile at all was called for.

"This is the best job I ever had," Pearson said. His hands were at his throat and he was tightening the knot in his green plaid tie. He was a big man wearing a blue suit to go with the green tie, and thick-soled brown shoes. "Until I came into this office I had been in the bag my whole career."

The bag, to cops, was their uniform.

"You were on patrol your whole career?"

Pearson nodded.

Jesus, Joe thought. I'll never find him a comparable job elsewhere. He'll never find one for himself. He's got no other viable experience. Nobody in the detective division will take him. I'll have to fire the guy, and when I do he'll be back in the bag before he can turn around.

"Think about my question," Joe said, and he gave Pearson another false, amiable smile. "Tell me tomorrow. I'd really like to know the answer." How am I going to fire him? he thought.

Pearson nodded. This time he was not reassured. His eyes were full of fear.

The two men, both worried, went down in the elevator together. When they came out onto Police Plaza they bade each other good night. Joe watched Pearson walk off. He wanted to get rid of him—the situation demanded it—but he had immediately recoiled from the idea of crushing a man who was too weak to put up any defense. Yet no other solution presented itself. But perhaps he could think of one. Otherwise—

He did not want to believe himself the kind of man who would ruin someone else just to advance his own career.

5

THE LAWYER WAS SHOWN IN BY MR. KATZ. HE TOOK the same chair the victims always took. Judith had not recognized the name, and now did not recognize the man either. Not a law-enforcement regular, then. Nor was his appearance reassuring. Nonetheless she smiled pleasantly across the desk. "Well, Mr. Pappenheim, what can I do for you?"

The lawyer was no taller than Judith—about 5 feet 5—but weighed at least 280 pounds. He was not dressed like a lawyer. He did not wear a dark suit. He wore a red-checked sport coat that was neither new nor clean. It stretched across his great girth and was held tight by its one button. Several shades of red were woven into its pattern, but his crimson trousers were a different shade again. He wore brown shoes and black socks. The socks, of the type once called anklets, were very short. The crimson trousers were short also and tended to ride up so that now, as he crossed his legs, almost half of a massive white calf went on display.

"I'm here on behalf of my client, Mr. Ramish Zulfikar," he announced. He had begun to sweat at once, but he seemed sure of himself. "Perhaps you would care to refresh yourself on the facts of the case."

Zulfikar, Judith knew, had been indicted for first-degree rape. The plaintiff was a thirty-two-year-old businesswoman—she owned a small dress shop in the Chelsea section. Zulfikar was accused of raping her in full view of her four-year-old child, and he had blackened both her eyes as well. Judith supposed Mr. Pappenheim was here to plea-bargain, and that he knew the case as well as she did, for he was a lawyer like herself, his unusual appearance notwithstanding. "I'm familiar with the case," she told him. "Please continue."

"Mr. Ramish Zulfikar is a visitor to our shores," Pappenheim said. "He's from Pakistan."

"Yes," said Judith, "He's been here two years, as I recall."

"Hey, there, you do know the case, don't you?"

"And in all that time he hasn't held a job," said Judith dryly. "He's lived off women."

"Objection, Your Honor, comment is irrelevant and should be stricken." The lawyer gave a laugh, although nothing amusing had taken place. He wore big black-rimmed glasses and had a big laugh. "You probably are just not aware of just who my client is. Is my client connected? You should have connections like my client."

"He's at Rikers, I believe," said Judith, "He can't make bail."

"He comes from one of the best families in Pakistan," said the lawyer. "Have you had occasion to look into his family connections as yet?"

"I knew there was something I meant to do," said Judith, and she watched him.

The fat man gave another laugh. "I happen to know he's very well connected. You may recall the name Prime Minister Zia?"

"My knowledge of Pakistan politics is a little weak," said Judith.

"My client's family and the prime minister's family are like that."

"As close as that?"

"Closer. The prime minister—he's like a second father to him."

"Have you checked into all this?" murmured Judith. "You didn't just get it from him?"

"Would you recall who happens to be the minister of defense back there in Pakistan?"

"I used to know," said Judith, "but I forget."

"General Mohamed Mayyim."

"And his relationship to your client is—"

"His uncle."

"Mr. Pappenheim, why don't you tell me why you're here?"

The lawyer had a bald head, and it glistened with sweat. He was pretending to know more about the accused and about the case than Judith did, and she had begun to suspect he did not. Now he removed a handkerchief from his pocket and wiped his pate. The handkerchief, Judith noted, was none too fresh.

"If this thing comes to trial," Pappenheim said confidently, "that's the kind of character witnesses I might have to bring in here."

"The prime minister and cabinet of the government of Pakistan?"

Pappenheim gave a modest shrug. "The charges against this boy—"

"He's thirty-eight years old."

"—are exaggerated. He looks younger."

"The charge against him is first-degree rape."

"I thought you and I might settle this thing between us. It doesn't go any further, who gets hurt?"

"You want to plea-bargain?"

Judith fluttered her eyelashes at him. In a young girl such gestures were usually taken as sexually provocative. With Judith it was a warning signal of which she was scarcely aware. It meant she did not like to be trifled with by lawyers like this one.

"You know what my suggestion would be? My suggestion would be to drop all charges against my client."

"But the indictment says he raped her."

"They used to live together."

This was true, and one of two mitigating factors.

"They had a prior relationship. So how can it be rape?"

"Fifty percent of my cases are prior relationship cases," said Judith.

"They lived together in perfect harmony."

"Except for the times he whacked her around."

"Who'll believe her?"

"Well," said Judith, "I believed her. And the grand jury believed her."

"She may say he beat her up, but there's no proof."

"The neighbors heard the noise through the walls. They saw what she looked like the next day."

He looked surprised. "How do you know this?"

"I have affidavits from the neighbors."

"You do?"

"Yes, I do."

The lawyer paused, but not long.

"You have this alleged rape, right? She goes to the police the next day but the police refuse to lock my client up."

"That's true." This was the second mitigating factor.

"Then two months later she comes forward and charges rape. Two months."

"Not to charge rape immediately is not a crime," murmured Judith. "What he did to her, that's the crime."

"Two months without any formal charges."

"What about the restraint order?" inquired Judith.

"What restraint order?"

"The police made a mistake. They told her it would be better if she went straight to court and got an order of protection, and so that's what she did." Judith waited a beat, then said, "You mean he didn't tell you about the restraint order?"

"I know this boy like my brother. He's never been in trouble before."

"Well," said Judith, "he did beat up his landlord. So there's an assault charge pending against him there. He didn't tell you? And he stole a car from Hertz. There's a civil suit against him on that. And, oh, yes, he's bounced some checks." Her voice got harsh. "And in the case you and I are discussing he beat up the plaintiff and then forced her to have sex with him in front of her four-year-old child."

"So what kind of arrangement can we come to?"

"You say you've known him a long time?"

"Not as long as I usually like."

"I see."

"I've just come from Rikers," Pappenheim conceded.

"And that's where you met him," said Judith. "Would you say you know him—what? Half an hour?"

The lawyer's head was glistening again. Out came the handkerchief. Judith winced to see it.

"There must be some kind of arrangement we can come to."

"Arrangement?" said Judith. "I hadn't really thought about it yet. What kind of charge would you prefer?"

"Something not sexual."

"How about assault, second degree?"

"Is that a felony?"

Is this man a lawyer? Judith asked herself. "It's a Class D felony."

Pappenheim shifted in his chair. The crimson trousers shifted farther up his great bald calf. "What do you really want?" he pleaded.

"Oh," said Judith pleasantly, "I'd like some time."

"You want some time?"

"I think he deserves to do some time, don't you?"

"How much time?"

"A fair amount."

"You're a very ruthless lady."

"Ruthless?" She worried about this constantly. The very word worried her. "I hope not, no."

The unclean handkerchief was working overtime now, brow, pate, back of the neck. The head kept nodding up and down, and the jowls shook.

They stared at each other for a moment, then Pappenheim brought up the subject of bail. He wanted his client's bail reduced. At present it was out of sight.

"He's being held on five-thousand-dollars bail," said Judith.

"That's high, wouldn't you say? I'd say that was extremely high. For a man who's a pillar of the community in Pakistan."

"Why doesn't he have them send him some bail money?"

"I'm looking into that now."

"Have them send your fee at the same time."

Pappenheim gave her a smile and a wink, as if to say: we're all lawyers together, and getting paid is sometimes difficult.

"I'd like to get that bail reduced to, say, one thousand," Pappenheim said.

"For first-degree rape? You're not serious, Mr. Pappenheim."

"To call what happened rape is exaggerated. So how about it?"

"I don't think so, no," said Judith.

"Try not to be so ruthless. Try to have some heart."

"He raped her in front of her four-year-old child."

"Maybe my client got too exuberant in his affections,"

said Pappenheim. "But they used to live together, so it can't be rape."

"Now you've said that about four times," said Judith. "This jury you lose in front of." And she showed him out.

Lawyers, she thought, when he was gone. He's a lawyer just like me. In the public's eye we're both the same. So how can anyone have respect for lawyers?

It was past time to go to lunch—not a lunch she looked forward to. She hated confrontations, and lunch would be another. She went down in an elevator full of young cops, all laughing and socking each other in the arms, as mindless as teenage boys. They made her forget the confrontation to come. They made her feel lonely, as if once long ago she had crashed their all-male world only to find no room in it for a young woman. Worse, by now she had perhaps outgrown it altogether. Although nearly a third of the prosecutors these days were women, she did not have much to say to most of them. They were not really women, they were girls straight out of law school, and younger every year, it seemed. She had seen too much more of life than they, had been part of too many grim cases, had peered into life's dark abyss several times too many. Although her job gave her many satisfactions, companionship was not one of them, and some days she felt she had only her love of the law to sustain her. Is that enough? she asked herself, and she went out the back door of the courthouse and crossed the street. She was walking uptown. Ahead waited Joe Hearn—ten days had gone by since their trip to New Jersey—and today's meeting would be hard. The law is the best and most beautiful thing human beings have yet thought of, she reminded herself. What else is there to save us from each other? Religion?

She was in Little Italy now, and she walked up the narrow sidewalk skirting the garbage cans, the stacks of merchandise, the open trapdoors into cellars. Perhaps the confrontation with Hearn would not be too bad. All the storefronts here had Italian names. She passed a bakery and glanced in at long loaves standing on end. Then came a shop selling espresso machines, pasta makers, and copper pots. There was a coffee bar, and next door to it the funeral parlor in which Mafia dons were sometimes laid out, followed by a store specializing in religious goods; its window contained life-sized statues of saints, some with bleeding hearts painted on their shirt fronts. Judith walked along and was jostled by shoppers and pedestrians, and she found herself smiling. Although not anxious to meet Hearn, she loved her job and she loved New York too. I have two loves, she told herself. Most people don't have any. I'm very rich. The city fascinated her and she saw it from a unique viewpoint. Its crimes took place each day on common sidewalks like this one, on streets lined like this one with parked cars and parking meters, with lamp-posts and "no parking" signs and mailboxes—terrible crimes destined to land within an hour on her desk on the eighth floor of the Criminal Courts Building, becoming part of her, and she of them.

The restaurant she now approached was called Rosario's. It was where she lunched nearly every day, sometimes with other lawyers, often enough alone, and she went in through the door and was greeted by Rosario himself.

"La bella Judith," he said, and gave her an incandescent smile.

Behind the cash desk Rosario's wife flashed her another. "Buon giorno, Judith."

Italians had a gift for making a woman feel not only welcome but gorgeous, Judith reflected. She followed Rosario into the dining room. Hearn, she noted, was already seated.

Waiters bowed and called her by name as she moved through the tables. This was gratifying, and she gave them all a smile. Hearn, aware of her now, had risen to his feet, and he looked surprised at her reception. This was gratifying too, though why? She realized that men sometimes handed out lavish tips in order to be recognized by waiters, but she was not playing men's games by men's rules—some of the things men counted important seemed to her absurd.

She shook hands with Hearn. "They really make a fuss over you here, don't they?" he commented.

"I eat here nearly every day, Inspector," she replied pleasantly, downplaying it, as she took the chair he held out for her. That the waiters remembered her was no miracle. They saw few women at lunch, a detail Hearn might notice in a moment. She glanced around the crowded dining room: nearly all men—judges, defense lawyers, bondsmen, high-ranking policemen. It sometimes seemed inconceivable that she had made a place for herself among them. Sometimes she asked herself why she had wanted to.

Rosario, having left them two menus, had departed.

"He's got a lovely smile, hasn't he?" said Judith, making small talk, delaying the confrontation.

"He's also a big Mafia guy," said Hearn.

"So I've heard."

"One of the kingpins."

"Nearly every restaurant in Little Italy is Mafia-owned, supposedly," she said. Now that the confrontation was upon her, Judith dreaded it less. He is the one who should be feeling the pressure, she thought, not me. "And most of their patrons each day are law enforcement people."

"Yeah. They had any brains, they'd bug every table. They'd know all our plans in advance."

They smiled at each other. Then both fell silent.

The entire opposite wall was a mural of the Bay of Naples, a painting thirty feet long, from Ischia around to Sorrento and Capri. All that scenery rose up out of men's heads and stretched to the ceiling.

"Pretty scene," said Hearn.

She saw he was as anxious to delay it as she was. "Ever been there?" he asked.

"I went to Capri once."

"How was it?"

"Nice," she said, and nodded her head up and down. But it hadn't been. She had gone there with a middle-aged lawyer named Leonard Woolsey who was going through a divorce at the time. They had stayed five days. Capri was not a place she wanted to go back to. Leonard was not entirely out of her life even now.

The bread basket was on Hearn's side of the table. Judith reached into it and plucked a breadstick out from under the rolls.

The breadstick was short, hard, and encrusted with sesame seeds. Judith bit it in half while watching Hearn, who looked thoroughly ill at ease. Let him sweat a bit longer, she thought, and she let the silence build.

"Busy day?" said Hearn.

She decided to give him more of an answer than he had bargained for, and so began to describe that morning's cases, certain of them technically and at length.

Although she saw Hearn begin to squirm, she kept on with it. The raw words abounded. She sensed how offended he was, and this pleased her.

As for Joe, he was having different reactions from the last time they'd met. Yes, it made him uneasy to talk about sex with a woman he hardly knew. And, yes, he hated the clinical words, the too vivid descriptions. Sex, to Joe, was romantic. He did not want to know about it any other way, but she was making him see it as an act of aggression, and this made him unsure of his rights as a man. It was as if man and the male instinct were everywhere and always something ugly, even though somebody had to be the aggressor. But if it turned out bad the woman could call it rape and perhaps make it stick. With the new laws any woman could. But especially Judith, who would know how. For a moment he studied her carefully. The alternative was for the man not to be the aggressor, in which case nothing would ever happen, not rape and not love either.

Then he thought, Whatever made me think about making love to Judith?

"You took your detectives off our case," Judith said suddenly, and the confrontation was upon them.

"You mean that case in New Jersey? Say, why don't we order." Rosario had returned and was standing over their table, ball-point poised, reciting the day's specials.

Judith ordered her usual prosciutto with melon. Hearn asked for spaghetti with clam sauce.

"Say, you don't each much," Joe said to her after Rosario had picked up the menus and left.

His wife probably eats even less lunch than I do, thought Judith. He just never notices.

She said, "You took those detectives off our case, Inspector."

Joe decided to meet her eyes, and she liked him for it. "I'm sorry," he said firmly, "but they weren't getting anywhere. They're supposed to be narcotics detectives, and working on a rape case isn't as it should be, you have to admit."

"The drug part of the case hasn't been developed yet."

"I promised you a week, and I gave you a week."

"They spent the first four days out in New Jersey having blowups made of those tapes."

"Yes, I know that. Would you like another breadstick?" He held the basket up but she ignored it.

"How do you know? Who told you?" She paused, then said, "They reported back to you every night, is that it?" But she felt renewed respect for him.

When Hearn said nothing, her eyes dropped, and she studied his hands. Fine dark hairs curled over the backs of them. She had noted them previously in New Jersey. The fingers were long and the nails short. They were nice hands. Men with hands like that had always exerted a powerful attraction over her. She watched Joe put the bread basket down and felt a slight desire to shiver.

"Anyway," she said, her eyes rising, her voice cross, "that left them only one day to try and find that apartment."

"Well, they didn't find it."

"They didn't have time to find it."

"I doubt a hundred detectives could find it. It's harder than you think."

"I could find it myself in a day."

Suddenly she realized the tension between them was sexual in nature, and she was surprised. It was true she was attracted by him but he could not have discerned this. She had been careful to display no sign of it. Nonetheless, he was giving off a perceptible sexual antagonism. It was in his clipped phrases, the decisive gestures of those hands, his evasive eyes. What could it be then? She knew nothing of Joe's lingering vague notion that to entangle himself with Judith was a betrayal of his wife, a threat to his marriage. Her answer, therefore, was a misdiagnosis: he was prejudiced against her and her case precisely because she was a woman. It made her gloomy. She was tired of fighting this sort of thing and now would have to fight it again. The waiter, reaching their table, put their plates down in front of them, and Judith studied hers. The prosciutto, draped over the melon, was sliced so fine she could see the melon through it. She wasn't a bit hungry.

"If you feel you want to continue the case," Hearn said, twisting spaghetti onto his fork, "there's no reason why you can't get other detectives to do it." The spaghetti went into his mouth.

He had regular, very white teeth, she noted. His lips were rather fleshy, especially the upper one. Did this prove him a sensuous man? She had read somewhere that it did, which didn't mean she believed everything in books.

"That's a bit wasteful, isn't it?" she said. "Your two men have already put in a week. Are we going to just waste that week and start over?" Any new detectives would have to view all the videotapes again, then redo most of the same legwork, and Joe knew this as well as she did. Not to mention the fact that it would take her a while to find any new ones.

"Those two men were taken off an important narcotics case in Brooklyn. I've had to send them back there. I can't risk blowing that case in the hope of developing something in this Jersey business."

"You won't give them back to me?"

"I can't."

It made Judith stubborn. "Suppose I go out and find the apartment building myself? Then can I have them back?"

"How are you going to do that?" said Joe, and he looked stubborn too. Also alarmed.

"I'm not as good a detective as your men, probably, but I know how to walk the streets showing photos to doormen."

"That's incredibly dangerous," said Joe. He too had stopped eating.

"Then give those detectives back to me."

"I can't."

"Give one of them back."

Joe began eating again. Presently he said, "You wouldn't really go out into the streets yourself? Would you?"

"Yes."

"It's more than dangerous. The perpetrators would find out about it and disappear. Or else they would make you disappear. You think doormen don't talk? That's all door-men do, is talk."

They stared at each other.

"That isn't the way to do it," Joe went on. "You don't talk to the doormen until you have found the building; and you find the building by going up on the rooftops. You find the house with the view."

Judith speared a piece of prosciutto. She was smiling slightly because she now sensed she was going to get her detectives. "If it takes more than a day to find the apart-ment," she said, "I'd be surprised. Give me back one of those detectives for one day, and I'll go with him. And we'll find the apartment."

"You mean that?"

Judith, watching him, nodded.

"Those two detectives are needed where they are," he said. He ate another forkful of spaghetti. "But—"

He was struggling with himself, and she saw this and she waited.

He was carrying a great deal of Irish Catholic baggage whose strict sexual morality had been laid down on top of the fierce puritanism that had preceded it to American shores. Nonetheless his professionalism now warred with his resolve to disentangle himself from Judith Adler. Professionalism won out. He could not let her take stupid risks, nor botch a perfectly good case through ignorance. He said, "I'll go with you myself. One day. But on one condition."

"Which is?"

"If we don't find it, you either drop the case, or you find your detectives somewhere else. Understood?"

It was not what she wanted, but it was, Judith saw, the best she was going to get. So she smiled, and thrust her hand out over the food. "Agreed," she said, and they shook on it.

When the check came Judith tried to pay it, or at least pay her share. But Hearn refused, and when she protested, said, "What do you take me for?" But he must have realized how gruff this sounded, for he smiled at once and added, "Can't I buy a beautiful woman lunch if I want to?"

Because he seemed a man to whom gallantry did not come easily, the compliment pleased Judith, and she thought she understood him. Like most cops, he tended to be blunt and even rather clumsy. He was probably a nice man underneath it all. His wife was probably quite a lucky woman. Judith found herself envying her.

They settled the details in the street. Since Joe's calendar was crowded he would not be able to accord her an entire day until the following Wednesday, he said.

"You can wait that long, surely."

Judith nodded. Knowing nothing of his internal struggle with himself, she was confident she could wheedle extra days, even weeks, out of him later. They shook hands again, and she watched him stride off.

That night after work she fished old leotards out of a bottom drawer and went and enrolled in a physical fitness course in a dance studio one flight up over Columbus Avenue. She told herself it was time to firm herself up, lose the five or so pounds she had gained since law school. At the end of an hour she was sopping wet and her muscles were trembling. She did not admit to herself she was doing this for Joe Hearn. She did admit that it was because of him that the idea had come into her head.

The following day she left the office early and went shopping in Bloomingdale's. She bought herself a new raincoat because it might be breezy up on those rooftops, and her old one was looking a bit tattered.

6

MARY'S NEW YORK ART CLASS ENDED PRECISELY AT ten minutes to twelve—figure models, like psychiatrists, worked fifty-minute hours. Today's model stood up and slipped on a transparent peignoir over bare flesh, having turned modestly away from the class to do so. Then she got down from the table. Mary studied these movements as intently as she had studied the girl's body for the last three hours, for she was curious about female nudity, and also about female notions of modesty. She had observed, for instance, that nearly all these models—the women, not the men—turned away from the audience whenever they slipped into or out of their bathrobes or whatever they had brought with them, as if the act of covering or uncovering themselves was a more private thing than their nakedness itself. Why was that?

As the model moved among the forest of easels, her big breasts swaying inside the filmy peignoir, she seemed to Mary even more naked than before, but she chatted with the artists, even studied the way each had depicted her. She was a very friendly girl. Mary herself could never have stood or lounged on that table letting strangers examine her body, or strolled about in that peignoir, not when she was this girl's age, however firm she may have believed herself at the time, and certainly not now. She did not enjoy being nude even in front of Joe, except when teasing him sexually, or when she was angry and punishing him by displaying what he was not at that moment going to get. At other times she was a woman comfortable only inside her clothes.

Today the students had been working in charcoal. The drawing pads on each easel were three feet high, and the artists themselves, though not Mary, had begun to step from easel to easel also, volubly admiring each other's work, making comments that were only occasionally snide. There were about fifteen of them in all, and the pages were lifted and studied, and then dropped again. Mary herself stood studying the topmost drawing on her pad, for she was very proud of it. The likeness seemed to her especially good; one could feel the weight of the girl's breasts, and the legs were well drawn, too.

The instructor, a man of sixty with paint-spattered clothes, a bald head and a dusty white beard, had come up behind her. He reached over her shoulder, and his forefinger traced several of Mary's lines which he praised. The drawing as a whole he called excellent, and she beamed. He carried a can of fixative which he shook as he spoke, and he began spraying the drawing. "That one you should save," he said. "You should take it home and show your husband."

Mary frowned. Joe cared little about art. He would look at this drawing and tell her it was great and then, if she knew her Joe, he'd make witty remarks about the size of the model's boobs. Of course sometimes he especially liked something she did.

The easels were folded and stacked in a closet, the drawing pads were put away on a deep shelf ready for next week, and the students and their instructor stood around sipping from glasses of sherry. The instructor always opened a bottle of sherry after class, which was one of his rituals, after which he usually went into the corner with the model in her peignoir, paying her off, which was another. Mary, glass in hand, watched him pay today's girl, who went out. The next time Mary noticed him, he was slipping a cardboard cylinder under her arm. "I rolled up today's drawings," he told her. "Let me know what your husband says."

Mary thought, What makes you think he'll say anything?

Leaning close, the instructor whispered, "You're my star. There's no one else in this class with half your talent."

So it had been a lovely, lovely morning.

Most of the artists left the building in a group, and several went off to lunch together. Though invited to join them, Mary declined. She intended to skip lunch that day, as she did most days, being worried about her figure, and also because she wanted to go shopping for her children. Macy's had a sale on and her kids, especially Billy who was growing so fast, needed summer clothes. Outside the front door of the Art League she said good-bye to the other women who went off in one direction, and she started in another, walking west along Fortieth Street. When she reached Broadway she would catch a bus downtown. She was walking head down, looking at no one, with what she knew to be a goofy happy smile on her face.

"Well," said a voice that made Mary glance up in surprise. She had walked barely half a block. "Look who's here. I couldn't be more pleased."

It was her son's baseball coach, and Mary was so shocked that at first she could not remember his name.

"What a coincidence to run into you like this," he said enthusiastically.

Loftus' name came to her, together with the realization that this meeting was no coincidence. He's after me, she thought. It made the hairs stand up on her forearms as if she had just had a great fright. It was a sensation connected in her mind not with the thrill of teenage romances but with the time she nearly struck a child with her car. What did Marty imagine that this "coincidence" would lead to? Men, she thought, make plans for women that the women know nothing about, and Marty Loftus presumably had plans for her. She felt threatened. But flattered too.

Buses went by in the street. Yellow cabs went by, while Mary and Loftus stood on the corner chatting. It was lunchtime and the office buildings were emptying out. Throngs of office workers marched past them. There's no reason to get all tingly, Mary thought. So he waited for you in the street, so what? Plenty of guys have waited for you in the street. Yes, she told herself, but that was twenty years ago, and nobody since Joe. She tried to regain control of herself, but to her surprise the tingling continued.

"What's that under your arm?" inquired Loftus.

"Some drawings." Both of them gazed somewhat stupidly at the cardboard cylinder, and Mary told herself, I should break this off and get on with my shopping. But she stayed.

"Why don't we have lunch together?" suggested Loftus.

"I was planning to skip lunch today," said Mary. But he looked so boyish, so unsure of himself, that at once she softened her refusal with a smile. He must have come all this way hoping to have lunch with me, she thought. Where is the famous womanizer I heard so much about? She began to regain some confidence. I'm a mature woman. No one can make me do anything I don't want to do. I'm not some silly girl.

"Well," said Loftus, "you could have just a salad, maybe."

She was flattered to think that she had impressed him this much, enough to take the train into the city to meet her, and the tingling in her hands had stopped. Why shouldn't she have lunch with him?

But someone might see them and tell Joe.

She would tell Joe herself when he got home from work—at whatever hour that might be—and she began to react against the strictures of her life. Why did she have to skip lunch every day? Why did she always have to do what someone else wanted her to do, rather than what she wanted to do? There was nothing between this man and her, which would be obvious across a restaurant to anyone who noticed them. Tongues would not start wagging until the second time she was seen with him, at the earliest, and there would be no second time—she would make that clear at some point. "You're right," she said, "I can order a salad—and as a matter of fact I am rather hungry, now that you mention it." A long, rather nervous speech. Her newfound assurance was gone already, and they had not even sat down yet.

Inspector Hearn had spent the morning on rooftops high above Manhattan's East Side, together with Assistant District Attorney Judith Adler. Also present in each case was the building superintendent, a succession of edgy, surly men who waited in greater or lesser anxiety beside the roof door housing. They waited to be told what this was all about. A car driven by a detective sergeant followed along in the streets below. Except that it was black and bristled with aerials, it was not obviously a police car at all, and therefore all the more ominous.

These were residential neighborhoods, residential roof-tops. From them in the near distance could be seen the office skyscrapers that formed Midtown, the commercial heart of New York, a high, tight mass of towers that pressed one against the other: the Midtown Alps. But Midtown ended ten or more blocks to the south. Up here the tallest buildings rarely exceeded twenty stories. In between stood rows and rows of four-story brownstones and town houses, the abodes of the really rich.

It was the high rises that interested Inspector Hearn.

The procedure at each stop was the same. The unmarked car double-parked in front, and Joe jumped out of the backseat, then held the door for Judith. She was wearing soft leather boots and carrying an attaché case in addition to her pocketbook. On the rooftops her new raincoat remained belted. It was cold up there, and windy.

Out in front of these luxury buildings stood doormen in uniforms and caps. The brass buttons shone. The shoulder boards would have done an admiral proud. In New York these days one could rate a building's affluence or lack of affluence by the amount of gold braid on its doormen.

To each one Joe flashed his shield, but he did it quickly, almost furtively, a trick he had mastered long ago. "Inspector Hearn from the city," he said, slurring his name, but not the word: city. "Get the super up here, please." Most times he was taken for a building inspector, which was what he wanted.

"Building inspectors don't cause comment," he told Judith. "Cops do. Remember that."

When the super arrived, usually looking harried, already frightened, Joe again flashed his shield. "Take us up to the roof."

The dialogue that followed was little changed also.

"What's the matter?"

"I'm taking a look at your roof."

"Has there been a complaint?"

"I don't have to tell you nothing." When role-playing, Joe always switched to his street accent. "I don't have all day neither. So let's go."

Once, while one of the supers rushed to fetch keys, Joe said to Judith, "It's even worse when they know you're a cop. The only ones who talk back are the felons. If somebody talks back, then you know he's a crook. Honest people are always afraid. Why is that?"

"I suspect you're going to tell me."

"In their hearts they imagine they're guilty, that's why. Guilty of something. Whatever it is, they think they've just been caught at it." He gave a laugh, which Judith rewarded with only a faint smile. Joe was not unperceptive. He judged she didn't like to watch him push people around. But if one wanted to work effectively as a cop, there was no other way, and he hoped she would soon realize this. He was working hard to earn her approval, a fact of which he was only half aware.

Mostly, Joe noted, she stood half a step behind him, and said nothing. He became convinced she was like women all over the world, content to let the man do it, and as a result, temporarily at least, he was less impressed with her than he had been.

After riding the elevator up to the penthouse level, the super would unlock the door, and they would stride out onto the roof. The super usually wanted to dog their footsteps. If his building was in violation of the building code, he wanted to be able to plead his case before this goddamn inspector ruined him with management.

"Wait over there," Joe would tell them curtly. "When I want you I'll call you."

While Joe pretended to make a visual inspection of the entire rooftop, Judith always stepped directly to the parapet where she got her pictures out. She seemed completely uninterested in his charades. However he knew them to be necessary; good detective work took time. It could not be hurried. Invariably the super watched Joe, not Judith, and she lined each rooftop up with the Queensboro Bridge and began to search for the intervening landmarks that showed in her photos. After a few minutes Joe would join her, and they would search together, facing into the breeze.

None of these rooftops was really flat. Out of the middle of most of them rose up the elevator housing. Usually it was made of brick, as solid as a turret, as a fort. Most roofs had water towers too, great barrels set on end that stood well above the level of the parapet and sometimes as high as the elevator housing. These were the landmarks one tried to match against the photos, for they were more easily distinguished one from the other than the buildings themselves. However, Joe and Judith were working off photographic enlargements made from a videotape. The photos were large enough but not sharp, and most of their foregrounds were occupied by a naked, recently raped young woman weeping into her hands. The window behind her framed not only the bridge, but a V-shaped wedge of Manhattan whose extreme edge was ten to twelve blocks wide. The girl in the foreground was in perfect focus, the distant rooftops not quite, and most of the water towers and elevator housings resembled each other.

Some buildings they were able to rule out promptly, usually because, once they reached the roof, they saw there was no unobstructed view of the bridge. Another large building was in the way. Then Judith would snap her attaché case closed, and Joe would mutter to the anxious super, "You're in luck, no violations." Leaving him grinning—there would be no fines—or perhaps nearly sick with relief, they would descend to the street and move on to the next prospect.

In this way they visited eight rooftops in the course of three hours, moving gradually uptown, and also farther back from the river. The neighborhoods changed. The storefronts became boutiques, many with European names. There were increasing numbers of antique shops and galleries. By noon they stood on a rooftop above Seventy-eighth Street and Madison Avenue, and Joe was hungry.

"Let's go eat," he said. The wind blew his hair.

Judith seemed to set her stubborn jaw. "Not yet."

Both of them studied the view. "This is not the building," said Joe.

"But the angle seems almost right."

They glanced around them. "It's within two blocks of here," said Judith.

"You're guessing."

"I can feel it."

Joe grinned. "Woman's intuition?"

Judith frowned and closed her briefcase.

The super came forward from the door housing. "So what did you find?"

Joe chose not to relieve his mind. "You'll be informed," he said coldly.

Judith shot Joe a sharp look. To the anxious super she said, "Take it easy. I didn't notice any violations, did you Joe?

Joe was enjoying the day. He enjoyed the fresh air, and

the company of this woman, and it was fun to behave like
a street detective again. He even debated trying to phone
his wife. He knew she was in the city at art class today. He
could invite her to lunch, send the car for her. He could
look across a restaurant table at Judith and his wife both.
For some minutes he imagined that they would enjoy
meeting each other. Then he imagined that perhaps they
wouldn't. He didn't know Judith well enough to calculate
her reactions but he suspected Mary might get into one of
her sullen moods, as if she were jealous—God knows she
had nothing to be jealous about—and if this happened in
front of Judith, he would be embarrassed. In any case,
Judith didn't appear to want to stop for lunch at all. So he
never called Mary.

In her briefcase Judith also carried head shots made
from the videotapes of the four rapists. When they had
climbed back into the car this time, she said, "I keep
thinking we ought to be showing these mug shots to
doormen."

Beside her, Joe said to his driver, "Anything come
over?" He jerked his chin in the direction of the radio.

"It would be quicker than going up on all these rooftops," said Judith.

"Not a thing, Inspector."

"Negative," said Joe to Judith. "I explained all that to
you before. Let's do it my way, shall we?"

"Okay," she said, and sighed.

"And no sighing." He grinned at her. "I'm taking you to
lunch."

And so Joe stepped into a restaurant with Judith Adler.
They were shown to a table even as Mary, in another
restaurant some forty blocks downtown, sat across the
table from her son's baseball coach.

Mary had accompanied Loftus along Fortieth Street as he
searched for a restaurant. They crossed Fifth Avenue whose
smart shops attracted her. She would like to have had the
time to peer into the windows and would another day.
They passed the library, then walked along the edge of
Bryant Park. Trees overhung the sidewalk, big ones about
to bloom. The park was filled with people on their lunch
hour, and with pigeons. It was a lovely spring day.

They found a restaurant across from the park and went

inside, where they waited some time for a table. The wait made Mary nervous again, but Loftus seemed nervous too. He kept apologizing, and Mary liked him for it.

When at last they were seated, Loftus ordered wine.

"What brings you into the city, Marty?" Mary teased.

His face was buried in the menu. "Oh, I get to New York once in a while."

"Don't you have baseball practice this afternoon?" She was flirting, which felt good after so long, and at the same time she was trying to gain control both of herself and of this luncheon.

"Not this afternoon. The kids are taking their SATs." He gave her a sidelong glance across the top of his menu. It was not quite a grin, not quite a leer. He was free if she was. It was definitely the glance of a co-conspirator, but it was rather winning, and Mary found herself grinning back.

With that he put his hand over hers—just a quick touch. He took it away again almost at once.

She had gone all tingly again. It was instantaneous, and not just her hands this time, but her entire body, and she stayed that way almost to the end of the meal. She drank rather too much wine. She kept waiting for him to take her hand again, but he did not do so. She expected to feel his thigh against hers under the table, but this did not happen either. She ate half her salad, then found that her appetite was gone. She did finish the wine, hoping it would relax her, but it did not.

Loftus ate quite well, all the time talking of his third baseman, her son, recounting games Billy had won with a key play, a clutch hit. Some of these games Mary had seen, so that she thought Loftus was overdoing it a bit, though not much.

"I don't know where he got his batting eye from," said Loftus, "but I know where he gets his looks from."

Mary studied the tablecloth. It was nice to hear, but it only confused her more.

"And he's only fifteen," said Loftus. "By the time he's a senior the Yankees will be after him."

This was overdoing it too; nonetheless Mary was thrilled; what mother wouldn't be?

When Loftus stopped talking to eat, Mary's eyes rose. She liked the line of his jaw, his neck. A good face to draw. If this man had been baseball coach when I was in

high school, she thought, I would certainly have had a
crush on him. I would like to draw him, she thought.

"I think I drank too much wine," she said.

Loftus put money down, and they stood up. Then they
were in the street, strolling along. They crossed one street,
and another. The tall buildings rose up to both sides, and
Loftus had her arm, which felt surprisingly good.

"What are you going to do now?" he asked her.

"I don't know. What are you going to do?"

"I know what we can do."

"What's that?"

Loftus pointed in the direction of a building across the
street. "Go over there," he said.

Across the street was a hotel.

The tingling sensation this time was worse than ever.
This is where we've been heading for an hour, Mary
thought. She seemed to herself incapable of any immediate reaction. It must be the wine. Stop him, she thought,
before it's too late. But Loftus' proposition was certainly
flattering, and if she savored it a moment before rejecting
it and him, was that so wrong? A moment's reflection
could not hurt. Then she thought: it's broad daylight, he
might only be teasing me. To decline vigorously would be
to look foolish. Best not to overreact. He can't be serious,
she thought. This can't be happening. Make an amusing
remark. So she ordered herself, but her mouth was dry
and nothing amusing came out.

"They won't let us in," she said. She needed time. The
hotel appeared to be about five stories high, wedged between office buildings that were much higher. Not a big
hotel, then, a small hotel. "We have no luggage."

"They'll let us in," said Loftus. "Come on."

Her arm was bare. Male fingers dug into her flesh, and
she was pulled across the street. They stepped through
the cars. At the curb she stumbled and almost fell. Other
women have affairs, she thought. Her heart was thumping. Loftus moved her across the sidewalk. The hotel was
less than ten feet away. I'm not going in there with this
man, she told herself. Then: I'm nearly forty years old;
this is my last chance. She could feel the male force of him
through her arm. Loftus was herding her toward the hotel.
When she threw frantic glances up and down the street,

she recognized no face she knew. There was no one to save her.

Restaurants on the Upper East Side were unknown territory to Joe Hearn. The one he picked turned out to be too elegant for his comfort. It was occupied principally by middle-aged women with spindly legs, dressed in expensive clothes. It was the type of restaurant Mary's mother probably went to before she and his father-in-law moved to Florida. The coatroom would be full of minks even though it was spring. The dining room was spacious. A captain in a tuxedo led them across to a table. There were tablecloths and heavy silverware, and hardly any men at all, just these obviously rich women with nothing else to do except lunch with each other. No one spoke above a whisper. There was a flowered pattern on the walls and chintz curtains on the windows. The place reeked of perfume. The captain in the tuxedo hovered over each table for a long time. Joe felt distinctly uncomfortable. He felt he had picked the wrong restaurant. This one was going to cost a fortune. Mary would kill him. But she wouldn't find out, of course. He wouldn't tell her.

So thinking, he turned his attention to Judith Adler, who looked impatient, no doubt wanting only to get back onto the street. She must really believe we are about to find that building, he thought, that it will be the next one we check out, or the one after.

Joe himself was in no hurry and he grinned at her. "Do you think the caviar would be good here?" he said. "How about the curried buffalo eggs?"

It made her smile. "Buffalo eggs?"

"Here comes the man now. I'll ask him."

But Judith, after studying the menu, handed it up. "Chef's salad," she told the captain.

"Nothing to start?" inquired Joe.

"We don't have time."

"Plenty of time. Some clams?"

"Chef's salad and coffee," said Judith firmly. Joe couldn't figure her out. Sometimes he could feel that she was attracted to him. She was trying to hide it, but it was there. The boy-girl thing. And he could feel himself respond to it, in a way.

"I'll start with the clams," said Joe. Well what man

wouldn't respond? "And after that the lamb chops with some mint sauce." Turning to Judith, he said, "How about wine?"

"All right, a glass of white wine," said Judith resignedly. Yet at other times he reflected, she seemed completely professional. But it wasn't like working with a man. It wasn't as if they were detectives working on an investigation together. There was no feeling of camaraderie. She was too cool, even distant, and sometimes even seemed annoyed with him.

He saw her glance at her watch. "Don't worry," he promised, "we'll find it."

"This month or next?"

"So what made you want to become a prosecutor?" Joe inquired, leaning toward her across the table.

She looked away from him. "Why do you want to know?"

It was like no hotel Mary had ever stood in before. In the lobby were no chairs or potted plants. No one was sitting around. There was no long counter with many clerks, no furniture of any kind. There was no lobby, only a short narrow corridor with a closed door at the end of it. The front desk was a window in the wall covered with a grille, as if the people here were afraid of robberies. Behind the grille was the face of the desk clerk, who stood like a ticket seller in a train station.

Loftus approached this grille. Although his face was pressed up close to it, nonetheless Mary could hear his voice. He asked the price of a room.

"All night is fifty dollars," the clerk said. "Eighteen fifty for three hours." His voice sounded bored. To engage in such commerce did not embarrass him. It embarrassed Mary just to stand there.

"Three hours," Loftus told him, and Mary cringed. She saw his hand push money under the grille. The same hand, withdrawing, contained a key. As Loftus turned toward her, Mary was conscious of an absence of space, of claustrophobia, and she felt herself begin to sweat. She was sweating into her dress. Behind the grille the clerk was already speaking into the telephone. Brief guarded sentences. One transaction was completed, and he watched her as he started on another. His phone call concerned her, but she did not know this. Loftus' hand on her arm was pulling her toward the door that closed off the corridor. He held it open for her. Ahead were dingy narrow stairs. Loftus, behind her, had his hands on her hips, half pushing her up.

They came out onto another corridor. They walked along a frayed runner down the middle of the floor. Loftus was peering at the numbers on doors. This is not what I want, Mary told herself, and as soon as we get inside the room I'll tell him so. He will understand. I'll pay him back the eighteen fifty.

The door opened inward. Loftus stepped back, letting Mary precede him into the room. She walked past the bed without looking at it, and at the window peered out through curtains that had not been white in a long time. If she shook them, a cloud of dust would rise up. Curtains were something she knew about, unlike the situation in which she now found herself. Across the street were office buildings. She could see workers moving about desks. Loftus' hands cupped her shoulders, and as she turned around to face him, she wished she were somewhere else, anywhere else.

"Marty," she began—

But his mouth came down hard on hers, choking off sound, though not thought. She let the kiss continue for ten seconds, perhaps more, not so much tasting it or testing it as trying to work out a plan. She had, as she saw it, three jobs. The first was to end this kiss, the second was to disentangle herself from Loftus' arms, and the third was to get out of this room.

But even to end the kiss proved exceedingly difficult. Loftus was very strong and he held her tightly with one hand behind her head so that, although she attempted to twist her face this way and that, she could not get away from him. His tongue had forced her lips apart, and was pushing on her teeth, even as she got her hands up against the slabs of muscle over his chest, pushing hard. It was such a fierce kiss she could hardly breathe. Tossing her head with renewed vigor, she at last managed to push him off slightly.

"Marty," she gasped, "we have to talk."

The smile on his face looked sardonic to her—it was not a lover's smile. There may have been passion in it, Mary counted herself not experienced enough to tell, but principally it was the smile of a man who had just achieved, or imagined he had just achieved, some sort of spectacular success. Marty Loftus looked to her like a man gloating.

"Let go of me," she said. "We have to talk."

Evidently Marty did not mind conversation, providing it did not last too long. He went and sat down on the counterpane, and he patted the space beside him. "Sit here," he said.

He looked as handsome as ever to Mary, and as sexy, but not as friendly. She decided she did not like him very much. She certainly did not want to go to bed with him, and she could not understand how he had ever got her into this hotel room in the first place.

She had accomplished two of her objectives—the kiss was over, and she was out of his arms. She was still in this room with him, however. She threw a glance toward the door, which was a simple hotel room door, a single spring lock. Probably she could have dashed toward it, grasped the handle, and been out in the hall before Loftus could react. But this would make him really angry. And suppose he caught her before she could escape? She did not want to have to explain a bruised face or a black eye to her husband. It had not yet occurred to her that, if she made him angry enough, he might rape her. Or that he might rape her simply because, having come this far, she now tried to thwart him. Rape had not yet entered her head. She was not yet afraid of her son's baseball coach. Instead she was determined to be as kind to him as was, under the circumstances, possible. There was no need to run out the door. Loftus did not deserve such treatment. It was her own fault she was in this room. He had not forced her up here, and male pride was a fragile thing, so easily wounded. She was a married woman and knew that well enough. And so she would talk this thing out with him. She would let him down as easily as possible. There was no need to hurt him unnecessarily.

She did not want to sit beside him on the bed, but there was no chair in the room, no other furniture except a television set hanging off the wall. Loftus was still patting the counterpane beside him. After a moment, Mary walked over and sat down.

"I can't believe you have a son fifteen years old," said Loftus, and his voice seemed full of feeling—as if he really meant it. "You are the most beautiful goddamn woman in our whole goddamn town."

"Well, that's very nice," she said. "Thank you very much. Marty, I—"

"To be in this room with you now, Mary—well, I can't believe it. To think that in a moment I'm going to make love to you—I can't believe that either. You are an unbelievably sexy woman, do you know that?"

Mary had time only to frown. Whatever she might have answered was of no interest to Loftus, who was already grappling with her again, trying to force her down on the bed. She was resisting him, but he was too strong for her. "Please, Marty," she cried. "There's something I want to say to you."

"We have time," said Loftus and he let her sit up. He began caressing her hair and at the same time he gave an almost boyish laugh. In it was pride, surprise, and perhaps other emotions that she could not name. "We have three hours. That's what I paid for. I bet you don't think I could last three hours. With a woman like you, believe me I can."

"That's just it, Marty." Mary was searching for the correct words, even as Loftus' fingers sought the zipper down the middle of her back. It made a ripping noise, like material tearing. And it made Mary, her dress half undone, jump to her feet and back away from him. "No," she ordered fiercely. "Stop. I'm terribly sorry, but I have to go home now."

Loftus looked mystified. "But we haven't done anything yet."

"And I don't want to do anything. I made a terrible mistake coming here with you." Trying to be as gentle with him as she could, she said in a much softer voice. "You didn't make a mistake, Marty. I did."

Loftus' mood changed completely, or at least so he pretended. Mary thought it only a change of technique. He opted for gentleness. The man seemed to have several techniques, all tried and true in the past, she supposed. "Calm down, calm down," he said gently, standing up and advancing toward her. "Tell me what's bothering you, little girl."

"I'm not a little girl, Marty. You're a very attractive man." She was still backing away from him, though there was little space. "You're an extremely attractive man. It's just that—"

"It's the hotel, isn't it? I'm sorry. I didn't know it was this kind of hotel."

"It's not the hotel."

"The next time I'll find us a nice one, I promise."

"Marty, stop." Then: "I've changed my mind. I thought I wanted to, but I don't."

The confident smile on his face did not change at all. He had her backed against the wall, and he cupped her shoulders, in a gentle, amorous way. When she tried to shrug off these hands, Loftus only reached behind her on both sides. Grasping the open dress, he yanked the material down off her shoulders. He did this with such suddenness that Mary had no choice but to let the dress fall forward— the alternative would have been a ripped dress. Now she faced him naked to the waist, except for her bra, and she began to be frightened. She had tried to make her position clear, and he ought to have accepted it. He ought to have been able to see how serious she was. She did not want to make love to him. She wanted to get out of this room.

He fondled her. "You've got a beautiful pair, Mary, do you know that?" He was trying to pull her bra up to her throat; she was trying to prevent this, to capture his hands.

In the coldest voice she could manage, Mary said, "Marty, if you touch me one more time I'm going to scream."

This stopped him briefly—long enough for Mary to slip her arms back into her sleeves, to pull her dress back up.

Loftus watched her with disbelief, then with anger. "Do you mean that?"

"Yes, I mean that."

"You're not being fair."

"I don't have to be fair."

They glared truculently at each other. "You led me on," said Loftus.

Mary's arms were behind her, raising the zipper. "I know I did, and I'm sorry. I'm terribly sorry. It's not your fault. It's me. I just can't do it."

"I paid for the room."

"I'll reimburse you." Her purse was on the bed, and she reached for it.

But Loftus slapped the purse out of her hands. "Keep

your fucking money. It's not your money I want." He grasped her shoulders again. "It's you."

"You can't have me."

"Oh, yeah?" And his small cold eyes bored into hers. His voice was full of menace, the most menace Mary had ever heard in a man's voice, and she became very afraid.

"You wouldn't enjoy it," she said. Part of the contents of her handbag had spilled out on the floor. She crouched, and with the side of her hand swept everything back in. She stood up. The cylinder containing her drawings was on the bed behind Loftus, and she wanted it, but would have to leave it behind. The important thing was to get out of the room quickly, and she strode toward the door. She could not show indecision, and especially she could not show fear. She had three paces to go, then two. Without quickening her stride in any way, she was racing for the door.

Behind her, Loftus had sat down heavily on the bed, and he called out her name in a little boy's voice. "Mary—"

Having placed her hand on the doorknob, Mary felt safe enough to accord him the kindness that he had rejected only a few minutes ago.

"An hour in bed with you," Loftus said; "you don't know how long I've dreamed about it, how much it would have meant to me."

She did not know what to say to this.

"You're a beautiful woman, Mary."

"And you're an extremely attractive man, Marty." What idiocies people say to each other, she thought. She held the door ajar. Loftus seated on the bed looked so vulnerable that she was moved to add, "It's not your fault. There's nothing wrong with you, it's just me."

Suddenly the door itself seemed to explode in her fingers. It erupted inward, and knocked her staggering toward the bed. She was dazed by the physical impact of it, and by the surprise as well. At first she was unable to comprehend what had happened. The door had banged backward against the wall, and a black man holding a revolver, the colleague of the desk clerk downstairs, sprang into the room.

Loftus on the bed had jumped to his feet. He stood behind Mary, and again grasped her shoulders. It was not an amorous gesture this time. The gun was enormous. It looked bigger, more dangerous, than her husband's service revolver, a cannon, and it wagged in their faces.

"Over to the wall. Move."

Fear in the face of such a shock was instantaneous. Mary was already trembling. This man only wants to rob us, she told herself. He wouldn't try anything else with two of us here. But instinctively she knew she was in greater danger than Loftus. A man was less vulnerable. However powerless, he retained more defenses than a woman.

The intruder had greenish eyes. The artist in Mary always noticed people's eyes. He was well dressed, pale tan in color, and about twenty-five. These details and others Mary recorded without realizing it. Few blacks had eyes that light. He wore horn-rimmed glasses. He carried an attaché case. He sounded educated. That is, he did not have a black man's accent.

"Face the wall. Make a sound and you're dead."

Mary turned, but not fast enough apparently. The revolver muzzle dug into her dress. It dug into her kidneys and drove her flat against the wall.

"Hands above your heads."

One of Loftus' hands covered hers, and she was grateful.

Her pocketbook was snatched out of her other hand, and its contents dumped onto the bed. See, Mary encouraged herself, it's just a robbery. But she knew it wasn't.

"Thirty dollars. Is this all?"

"Thirty dollars," Mary said, "Yes."

The intruder's hand entered her field of vision. It reached into Marty's clothing and withdrew his wallet. "Are you richer than that, mister? Because killing you won't mean anything to me."

"There's over a hundred dollars in there," said Marty. "Take it—" He swallowed so convulsively that Mary thought: He's even more scared than I am. "Take it," Loftus said, "and let us go."

"Is that all you think your life is worth? A hundred dollars? That's a nice watch."

Marty jerked it off and flung it toward the bed. "You can have my watch. Mary he wants your watch, give him your watch, Mary."

"And that nice gold ring," said the man.

"That's my wedding ring," said Mary.

"Oh," said the man, "and is this dude here your husband?" When Mary remained silent he said, "I'd say you have forfeited any right to wear your husband's ring. Wouldn't you? Throw it on the bed."

Mary, as she did so, was more than terrified. Her knees were trembling, and she was bathed in sweat, but at the same time she was undone by guilt. Whatever happened to her here was only what she deserved.

Behind her she heard the attaché case snap open, followed by odd noises. Strips of adhesive tape were ripped off a roll, and there was a metallic jingling that sounded like handcuffs—any cop's wife knew the sound of handcuffs well enough. Implements being readied for them. She was both mystified and terrorized further. Implements to be used how?

"You," the voice said, and at the periphery of Mary's vision, the gun prodded Marty in the small of the back, "take your clothes off."

"Me?" said Marty.

"Yes, you."

Why Marty? she thought. Why not me? But she knew the answer: Marty first, then me. He only wants to humiliate us, she thought. My turn comes next. If we obey him he won't hurt us.

She caught glimpses of Marty's quick spastic movements. He was shucking clothing as fast as he could. The confident young baseball coach was nowhere in evidence. I'm sorry, Marty, she thought. Her forehead was pressed against the wall, and her eyes were closed, for she did not want to watch Marty's abasement. She heard his jacket and trousers fall to the floor. She listened to the whispery flutter of shirt, tie, underwear. He must be standing now in his shoes, and in a moment it would be her turn. Her eyes were tightly shut, and she was trembling.

"Hands behind your back."

She heard the handcuffs snap shut on Loftus. This was followed by a series of grunts. Curiosity or fear forced Mary's eyes open. Loftus wore a wide strip of adhesive tape across his eyes, another across his mouth. He was pressed against the wall as if trying to force his naked body through it to safety.

"Now you, lady."

"Me?" said Mary.

The gun wagged. "Fast. I'm a busy man."

Fumbling with the zipper, she managed to pull it partway down her back.

"Thirty dollars isn't much," the man commented. "I may have to kill you. But maybe you have some other treasures as yet unrevealed." He laughed.

Mary, still facing the wall, dropped the dress beside her shoes. Stumbling, she stepped out of her half-slip. She stood now in bra and panty hose.

"Everything," the man said in a bored voice.

Mary had begun weeping silently. Reaching behind her, she unhooked her bra and it slid forward down her arms. When she was naked he slapped swatches of tape to her mouth, over her eyes, making her grunt, and cuffed her wrists behind her back. Her helplessness was absolute.

Marty Loftus had had his first complete sexual experience at thirteen, having been seduced by his brother's girl-friend, twenty, who had known exactly what she was doing. Their love affair, if one could call it that, had continued for two months, and afterward Loftus had spent most of each day plotting how to arrange sex with another female. His next affair and first conquest was the mother of one of his schoolmates, a woman about the same age Mary Hearn was now. They were sitting in the woman's kitchen, and she had set before him some cookies and a glass of milk. Ostensibly Loftus was waiting for his friend to come home from school but he had cut his last class and was more than half an hour early.

"What does it mean to lay someone?" he asked the other boy's mother.

"Why do you ask?" the woman said, and she gave a brief, uncomfortable laugh. And then after a pause: "Who do you know who got laid?"

"I did," confessed the thirteen-year-old. Eyes modestly downcast, he told her his story. It was essentially accurate, and it made the color come up in the woman's face. When he saw this, the boy slowed the narrative down and began to add lush detail.

"And did you enjoy it?" asked the flushed housewife.

"Oh, yes," he said, and raised his eyes to hers. Within ten minutes she had led him by the hand into her guest room—he learned it was the guest room only later—where she took his clothes off him. He cut that same class regularly from then on, and for most of the year that particular housewife was always glad to see him.

It was as a result of these experiences, he believed, that he had developed such a tremendous sexual drive. He believed himself more virile than other men. Sex being on his mind almost constantly, he went through a series of fifteen- and sixteen-year-old girls who knew so much less than he that usually they reacted too late to stop him. In college he maintained a C average with difficulty, played varsity baseball, and afterward signed with the Detroit Tigers organization. He was 6 foot 2 and weighed 195 pounds, and he never made it past the Class B league, for his principal interest was not baseball but girls.

After the failure of his baseball career, he had attained a master's degree in physical education, and for the past five years he had coached the high-school team on which Billy Hearn now played third base—he also taught algebra on the side. He had a wife who was a nurse in the local hospital, to whom he was rarely faithful for more than two months at a time. He was thirty-one years old.

About two months ago his eye had fallen on Mary Hearn for the first time—she had come to pick up her son after practice. And he had got her to this room, too, having had to devote to it no more time or attention than he usually did, but the only emotion he felt for her at this moment was hatred. By rights he should be on top of her even now, fucking the daylights out of her. Instead he was handcuffed, blindfolded, gagged, and in the power of a psychotic with a .38 who was about to shoot both of them dead, Mary's fault. To Loftus it was always the woman's fault. All they did was seduce men and steal from them. They stole men's money, their time, even their virility, and gave back nothing. They had stolen Loftus' baseball career, among other things, and now would steal his life.

Even as he pressed his body into the wall he sensed Mary standing naked beside him, but this caused no sexual arousal; there was no lust left in him.

"Over to the bed," the voice ordered Mary. He must have shoved her, for Loftus heard the scuffle of her heels on the linoleum—the floor of this room was not carpeted.

"Lie down."

Now she gets hers, Loftus thought. The sweat was trickling down from his armpits down along his arms, down his sides. For as long as the intruder was occupied with the woman he was safe, he believed. Fuck her, then, he thought. As much as you want. She deserves it. To Mary he silently pleaded, You have to fuck him. Do whatever he tells you to do. It's our only chance.

But to his surprise the hand grasped Loftus' own biceps, and he was pulled off balance. His own shoes scuffed the linoleum. "Lie down," the man commanded and pushed him down on the bed.

The springs creaked. They sagged under his weight. He could feel Mary's lesser weight beside him. He's going to murder us both in this bed, he thought. Our corpses will be found together, making a scandal. He thought briefly of his wife—how would she take it? But he didn't care about his wife any more than he cared about Mary. He only wanted to plead for his life, but couldn't, for the band of adhesive had been pasted tight across his mouth. Underneath it his lips were pulled back into a ghastly grin, and he could utter no sound. Mary's knee touched him. This enraged him. He knew she was reaching out for help, for warmth, but he had no help to give and he jerked his leg away.

Now came a series of clicks whose meaning Loftus was unable to interpret. The intruder was only readying a camera, but Loftus was listening for bullets, so each click lifted him off the bed. As he lay on top of his hands, the handcuffs bit into his buttocks and he waited for one or several bullets to slam into him, and his breath came in gasps.

There came a muffled explosion. It made Loftus jerk spasmodically, certain he had been shot. When he realized it was only a flashbulb going off, he wanted to sob with relief. He was still alive. The next explosion was farther away and did not alarm him as much. The man must be moving about, taking additional photos from other parts of the room.

Now he came close again, for Loftus could hear him breathing. "Knees up, honey, and keep them spread."

The flashbulb exploded from somewhere between Mary's knees, a crotch shot. Loftus, though expecting it, jerked uncontrollably nonetheless.

"Up, mister, on your feet." The hand pulled Loftus into a sitting position. When he tried to walk, his knees would not support him and he staggered in the direction he was pulled. It was a small room. After two steps he was ordered to lie facedown on the floor. He did as he was told. Now comes the bullet in the back, he told himself. The television set went on. The volume went up loud—to mask the sound of the shots, Loftus believed, and this time he did begin to sob. The sound came out his nose, a series of bleats.

But nothing happened, for the intruder had returned to Mary on the bed. It was a while before Loftus realized this. The fellow was not close to Loftus anymore, nor interested in him either. He was working on Mary now, and the baseball coach, still alive, began to take hope.

He was listening hard, as if his life depended on it, which he believed it did. The sounds were all good.

He heard the bed springs creaking. He heard Mary grunt several times. Give it to the bitch, he thought. For as long as the man was occupied with Mary, he was safe. But how much longer would this be, and what would happen afterward?

He heard the voice say, "Smile for the birdie." And then again in a harsher tone, "Smile, I said." This was followed by the explosion of another flashbulb, whose noise sent Loftus into a spasm of twitching.

Mostly the television blared. Although he heard Mary's voice from time to time, he could not tell what she said. Once he thought he heard her crying. But he had no sympathy for her. He could think only of how much he wanted to live. His mouth was full of blood—he had been biting on his tongue, on the insides of his cheeks, and he had partially freed the tape over his lips.

A commercial came on. The bed had stopped creaking.

Mary was thrown down onto the floor beside him. The voice said, "I'm going to watch television while I decide if I should kill you."

"Her, maybe," Loftus babbled from under his tape. He pushed it aside with his tongue. "There's no need to kill me, though. I never got a look at you. You didn't do me any harm."

"Shut up."

"Whatever I had in my wallet I give you as a present. Just don't kill me. Please don't kill me."

The TV sound rose. Loftus lay rigid on the floor.

A few minutes later the voice came close again. "If I decide not to kill you, you'll find the handcuff key on the bed."

This filled the blind Loftus with such sudden hope that he started to cry.

After a short silence, the voice said, "Maybe I'll just take some of your clothes so you can't follow me."

"Anything," blubbered Loftus. He imagined the man standing over him, pointing the gun down at him, deciding whether to pull the trigger or not. Over the television blare Loftus waited to hear the clicks as the trigger was pulled. Weeping, he waited to feel the bullets plunge into his body.

But nothing happened. A few minutes later, he heard Mary whisper, "I think he's gone."

Loftus could hear nothing but the television set.

"I think he's gone," said Mary again, and he realized she was blindfolded too.

"Lie still," he beseeched her, "he'll kill us."

But Mary got to her feet. Then he heard her legs bang against the bed as she felt around for the handcuff key.

"I've got the key," she said, and came back to him.

"Stand up," she commanded.

"Is he gone?" said Loftus.

"He's gone," said Mary with some asperity. "Stand up."

They stood back to back, handcuffs to handcuffs. He felt her hands on his wrists, her fingers searching for the keyhole. As he waited his own fingers came in contact with her buttocks. They were bare and soft, and not the slightest bit stimulating. The key went into the lock, and one of his cuffs fell free. Immediately Loftus tore the tape off his mouth, off his eyes. Seeing that the room was empty, that he was safe, that he was still alive, he began sobbing with relief. Beside him on the floor was his clothing. He stepped into his shorts, his trousers.

Mary was still blindfolded, but not gagged, and she presented her back to him. "Undo my handcuffs," she ordered. He stopped dressing long enough to turn the key in one of the locks. Mary herself ripped the tape off her eyes, and she stood there blinking.

Loftus was searching for his shirt and sports coat, but could not find them. "The sonova bitch stole my clothes," he said. His voice still tended to crack when he spoke.

The fear was still there, but it was dissipating fast. He was becoming very angry.

"He took my dress," said Mary. Looking around for it, she made no attempt to cover herself.

Loftus, having found his tie, rolled it up and shoved it in his back pocket. He was thinking about himself, not Mary, but he realized in a vague way several things about her: that she stood there as naked as a jaybird; that, although her eyes were moist, and her mascara had run, she was not weeping now; and that she had ceased giving him orders.

Her underwear was on the floor. Her toe stirred it around. "What am I going to do? He took my dress."

But Loftus refused to look at her. He did not want to see her. He was as fully dressed as he was going to be: shoes and socks, trousers, T-shirt. And he stepped toward the door.

"I have no dress," said Mary.

"Call someone," suggested Loftus vaguely.

Mary burst into tears. "He did the most awful things to me," she sobbed.

Loftus at the half-open door said, "You'll be better off without me." It was hard to concentrate on her. "If you feel you have to report this, please don't say I was here. Okay? I wasn't here." He went out. Through the door he could hear Mary sobbing. But this did not register on him. He had to get home now. Outside he strode down the street in the direction of Penn Station, a tall, well-built young man, dressed in a T-shirt on a cool spring day. At first no one looked at him twice. He had a train to catch. He was busy preparing one lie for the conductor who would ask for his ticket, and another for his wife about his missing clothes. He was almost out of it. But he had begun to snivel. He couldn't stop. He walked along sniveling. He wanted to stop it, but couldn't. People began to stare. He couldn't catch his breath either. You're going to be okay, he told himself. You're going to be okay.

7

NEW YORK. MIDAFTERNOON. AT THE CORNER OF Fifth Avenue and Forty-second Street the young man waited for a break in the traffic, then crossed toward the block-long Grecian temple, high on its pyramid of steps, that was the public library. He wore a three-piece suit and carried an attaché case. His name was George Lyttle. The library's front steps were guarded at either end by great stone lions. It was a warm day. A dozen or more people sat on the steps in the sun. Some were unwrapping snacks out of brown paper bags. Some stared vacantly. A few held spread-open newspapers between their knees, reading the latest scandals in the *Post*, New York's trashy afternoon newspaper. Although he found an empty spot and sat down among them, George Lyttle had no time for people of such ilk. Opening his attaché case, he lifted out the notebook that served as his journal and read its title approvingly. He had printed this himself in bold capitals on the cover: THE WISDOM OF GEORGE LYTTLE.

George was waiting for someone, but the individual was not yet in sight, giving him time therefore to inscribe in his journal such incisive thoughts as had come to him lately, and from his vest pocket he withdrew his old-fashioned blue fountain pen and unscrewed the cap.

As he gazed at the traffic moving down Fifth Avenue, he spotted a Rolls-Royce. The yellow cabs had it in a sandwich. From halfway up the library steps he could not see inside it but he did not need to. His handwriting, as his pen began to move across the page, was small, meticulous, almost exquisite. "If a Rolls-Royce goes by you with a

brother driving it," he wrote, "you can count on seeing
one of two things: either a white man in the seat behind
him or a cop in the car behind him."

George Lyttle was a man who believed it was best
whenever possible to speak in aphorisms. He favored them.
When he had admired this one for a time, he screwed the
top back on his fountain pen, closed the notebook, and
allowed the currents of the city, its noise and movement,
its grimy odors, to penetrate his consciousness, to collect
in his lungs. He liked to breathe the city, to picture events
occurring even now. In the expensive Midtown restaurants
everyone had left except the waiters, who were laying out
place settings for the dinner service, and the silverware
was clacking in the waiters' hands. Around the library,
north, south, east, and west, rose up tall buildings. In
them George pictured disgruntled office workers now back
at their desks; some, having drunk too much at lunch,
performed their afternoon tasks in slow, dazed ways. In
the executive suites it was even worse, and George Lyttle
pictured this too. The three-martini lunches had taken
their toll. Stunned vice-presidents slept sitting up in tall
chairs and were jolted awake by incoming calls.

Next George cast his eyes upon the Fifth Avenue sidewalks before him. Clogged with office workers an hour
ago, they were relatively clear now. But street traffic was
becoming thicker than ever, and the passenger cars contained predominantly women—George saw them as rich
men's wives in from the suburbs to shop. The side-street
parking garages must be filling up fast. The department
stores too.

All over the city private occurrences would be taking
place as well, and these too George could feel coursing
through his veins. Millions of secrets were being whispered right now, and he was aware of them. Individual
lives had encountered cataclysmic events during this past
hour, and were being rearranged even as he waited on the
library steps for a particular individual to show up. Inspector Hearn was sitting in a restaurant with a woman to
whom he was not married. George Lyttle had never heard
of Inspector Hearn, but he sensed this meeting. Hearn's
frantic wife, meanwhile, was still ransacking a certain hotel
room for her clothing that was not there, and George
Lyttle sensed this too. Marty Loftus, traveling light, strode

into Penn Station, having largely extricated himself from his predicament. George Lyttle was unaware of such details, but believed he sensed them. The city was millions of ants struggling underneath a blanket, with himself looking down on it. His understanding of the city was so great that he believed himself predestined to play a major role in it. His life was to be a historic one. To prepare himself he must seek wisdom. He must embrace every learning experience that came his way. Today had certainly been very educational so far.

But ultimately a leader was known through his writings, and so George Lyttle's fountain pen descended on a fresh page in his journal. "The welfare check," he wrote, "is a salary that the white man pays you so you won't compete with him in the schools and marketplace. He doesn't want you to be educated. He doesn't want you to qualify for high-paying jobs. Brother, you're being underpaid. You're accepting $300 a month to be poor. You're being underpaid to be underprivileged."

When George looked up this time, he spotted Willy Johnson shouldering through the multicolored Fifth Avenue traffic. The cabs were yellow, the buses blue; a police car was caught in the traffic, blue and white. The sun glinted off them and off the windows high up on the buildings as well. Johnson took the library steps two at a time, and George closed his journal. "Have a seat, brother," he said.

But Johnson ignored this greeting, and although George patted the step beside him, Johnson sat down four or five feet away. For a time he only gazed nervously out at Fifth Avenue. He wore black trousers, a white open-necked shirt, and scuffed basketball shoes. When he spoke it was out of the side of his mouth, and without acknowledging George's existence. Like a ventriloquist his lips did not move. "So how did it go?"

George Lyttle laughed. "There is no need for such precautionary tactics," he said. "No active pursuit has been instituted in your behalf. There is no need for trepidation."

It made Johnson more nervous yet, and angry as well. "You're not so smart—just because you speak so good—"

Before one can control men, George thought, a leader must control language. Eloquence is the keynote. He said:

"Do not ridicule yourself with shame that you speak poorly. It is not your language anyway. I wonder how elegant would be the white man's prose should he attempt to express himself in Swahili."

But Johnson remained tense. "You got something for me?"

Spreading his billfold, George Lyttle handed across two twenties and a five.

Johnson eyed the money. "Is that all?"

"As a first installment, it seems to me not insignificant, especially considering the minimal scale of your contribution. Not insignificant indeed."

Johnson's sneakers scuffed the step below him. "Forty-five bucks," he snorted. "You and your big ideas."

"How much remuneration do you earn a day?" inquired George Lyttle. "Forty-five dollars for a single phone call seems to me excellent remuneration indeed."

Johnson thrust the bills into a pocket. "This business sucks."

"Why don't you couch your words for their correct meaning on occasion? You would find on occasion that your words are not adequately couched as to the correct meaning you wish to convey."

"It's too little money."

George tended to agree with this. So far none of their "clients" had proved to be in possession of as much wealth as he had originally projected. But as of today he had decided to compensate for this. The events just ended were not ended at all. In his mind he had altered his original plan. Today's clients, and all future clients, were going to receive follow-up calls, so to speak. But there was no need to say any of this to Johnson.

"And it's too much risk," said Johnson.

"You are a one-third partner. The risk each time is mine, not yours."

"They go to the law, it comes back on me."

"They are miscreants. They are caught where they aren't supposed to be," said George Lyttle patiently. "Miscreants can't go to the law,' as you so crudely opine. They were breaking the law themselves. That's the beauty of it. I explained the beauty of it to you before."

People carrying books moved past them up and down the library steps.

"You said there would be more money," said Johnson stubbornly.

"And so there shall be."

"We haven't made three hundred dollars yet."

"From today onwards I intend to undertake certain beneficial steps."

"What steps?"

"Such information is not required on your behalf."

"See how far you get without me," threatened Johnson.

George Lyttle sighed. "I suggest you console yourself with contemplating the three great virtues. The three great virtues are patience, trust, and faith." But the greatest virtue of all, George Lyttle thought, is eloquence. The gift of tongues. "Consider the forty-five dollars a first installment."

"And the rest of it?"

"In due time."

"When?"

"Today, as already disclosed, I undertook certain beneficial steps in a plan that is, shall we say, foolproof. The word connotes that it is proof even against fools. But the major income from this plan will not be forthcoming until due time."

"Due time?"

"When due time comes, brother, you will understand."

Johnson, staring out at the traffic, muttered, "You gonna wait a long time for the next phone call."

George Lyttle again sighed. "Would you like a watch?"

"Watch?"

"You seem to feel insufficiently remunerated."

"What watch you talking about?"

Lifting his attaché case onto his lap, George cracked it open and fished out a plastic sandwich bag that contained two watches and a gold wedding band.

"Which one?" said Johnson.

"To me it's immaterial," said George.

"The man's watch."

"Certainly. Here."

"What about the ring?"

George took it out and studied it. "I'm keeping the ring. It has, shall we say, sentimental value."

Johnson was admiring his new watch.

"I think that hotel is becoming hot," he said. "I think I should split."

George Lyttle became instantly alert. "Did something untoward occur after I departed the scene?"

"The dude come running down the stairs past me and out the door. They didn't come down together like they usually do. The dude was only half dressed." Johnson chuckled, remembering. "It was like the chick kicked him out halfway through."

"No, the female did not expulse him," said George Lyttle. He fell silent.

"She is still up there—was when I came out to meet you." Johnson studied George Lyttle. "You didn't do her no harm?"

"I may remain in her mind as a salutary experience, but I did her no harm. I left her in good health. Of that you may rest assured."

"You are cool, man, I give you that much."

"You fear an aftermath. Has any aftermath occurred prior to today?"

"No."

"No one has complained to the hotel of occurrences?"

"I'd know about it."

"And not to the police either, you may rest assured. Otherwise they would have dropped in."

"An idea that don't fill me with no joy."

George Lyttle gave another confident laugh. "Return to your employment in perfect ease, brother." Then he added, "You won't hear from me for a while. Next week is my anniversary, and I'm taking my wife on a little trip. I will contact you upon my return, and we can recommence."

Johnson stood up. "You pay the next installment or we don't recommence nothing," he said, and started off down the library steps.

George Lyttle, watching him go, gave small, sad shakes of his head. Johnson was a sad, sad man. He was afraid of everything. Afraid of the police, afraid of losing the demeaning position he held in a hot-bed hotel—a perfect example of a brother intimidated by the white man. Reopening his journal, George penned a new entry: "Some white man has taught you to think you can't do better," he wrote, "and you believed him. Nothing has changed since the Reconstruction Act of 1867. The 1964 Civil Rights Bill was exactly the same bill, and had exactly the same result. It made all you handkerchief-head, always happy, no-trouble Negroes think you had made some progress. But you misread the message. The message was unchanged, because the solution was unchanged. The solution was unchanged because the problem was unchanged, and the problem was unchanged because the enemy was unchanged. If you're not part of the solution, then you're part of the problem."

Glancing through the sandwich bag at the remaining watch, the female's watch, George Lyttle saw that he still had a few minutes in hand, and so continued to brood. He remembered the male and female together, as he had first seen them. Then he considered the male alone for a time while his pen nib hesitated over a fresh page. The male had behaved cravenly. "Whites are the most unstable people on the face of the earth," George wrote. "Confront them with the unexpected and their personalities disintegrate. This must be why so many of them jump off bridges. Even Tarzan was no different. When he came to New York in *Tarzan's New York Adventure*, what was the first thing he wanted to do? Jump off a bridge!"

He glanced briefly into the male's wallet and so learned his name, Loftus. The male's belongings were in one side of the attaché case, the contents of the female's pocket-book in the other, for George Lyttle was a meticulous man. His contact with Loftus had been brief. Loftus interested him less than the female. Having decided to apply his powers of concentration to the matter of Loftus at a later date, George fixed the female in his mind. He remembered how frightened she was, the way her body became covered with sweat, and he reached into his attaché case and stirred her belongings around: five or six credit cards bearing her name, Mary Hearn, plus a make-up kit, sunglasses, the keys to her house, and some snapshots which he picked out and studied. In one she stood with a man who must be her husband, and in another with some kids who were presumably hers. Having studied these things, George believed he knew her as well as any man did, husband or not. He had seen her in her intimity, so to speak. He even knew where she lived, for her address was on her driver's license, which he glanced at. He was familiar with that particular suburb and his fingers fondled her house keys as his mind placed her within it: a rich man's wife, who hired black women to clean her house for her, while she went out to the country club to play golf. He picked out Mary's wedding ring again and worried it between thumb and forefinger.

With Johnson's help he had been working this hotel every ten days or so for about two months. Previously he had only robbed the adulterers. There had been no repercussions of any kind. How could there be—such couples were in no position to go to the police. Today had been an experiment. The best laboratory in which to observe others, George had found, was the laboratory of stress. To expand one's own consciousness and knowledge one pushed others to the limit of theirs. Snapping a rubber band around Mary's cards and photos, he dropped them back into his attaché case. She had handled the fear well. Since he had never had any intention of killing her, whatever she may have thought, he did not see where he had hurt her any, and perhaps had taught her a salutary lesson.

Closing the case, he returned it to an upright position beside his leg, reopened his journal, and prepared to inscribe the day's final entry, devoting several minutes to thought before his fountain pen again descended to the page: "Whatever liberty or justice the white man may seem to give you was rightfully yours at birth," he wrote. "In actual fact he has given you nothing. If I should deny you liberties, if I should rob and disrespect and rape you, are you going to feel you owe me something when finally I set you free? Did I not take everything from you in the first place? Where then is your debt?" George Lyttle paused a moment, then added, "This is the way it is with the white man in America."

The afternoon had begun to wane. George rose to his feet and entered the library behind him, where he procured a book he needed for a course in advanced social theory he had enrolled in at Hunter College.

Later, on the way uptown to his classroom, he stepped into a travel agency and bought two plane tickets to Las Vegas with Marty Loftus' American Express Card. His wife, when he got home tonight and showed her the tickets, would be very pleased with him.

8

MARY'S EMOTION, AS SHE SAT NAKED AND SOBBING ON the bed, was essentially grief. She wept for someone who had died, and it was herself. The proud, self-assured young woman who had walked into this room would not walk out. Almost forty years of life, it seemed, all that she had been, had been taken away from her—her self-respect had been stripped from her at the same time as her nice dress. Her integrity was gone, her inviolability, her normal female arrogance. Such grief was too much to bear, and she sobbed and sobbed. She could not even get out of this room. She would have to call Joe, would be forced to confess everything, and as a result would lose her husband, her children, her house that she had made into a home for the four of them. Grief became despair. The sobs came up from deep inside her chest.

But finally there were no more of them left. There was, she realized, no one to come to her assistance. If she was to save anything of what her life and person had been, then she must stop this useless weeping and start to think. This was the first thought to seep past her anguish into her brain. At first she could not think. All she had was a determination to fight back, to survive. Certainly she would have to lie. Well, then, she would lie as well as she could, and she wiped her eyes on her wrists and forearms and tried to decide what these lies should be. Also, she made a list in her head of what she needed in order to survive at all. She needed a dress, or jeans and a sweater, even a raincoat—anything at all. She needed money with which to get home.

There was a telephone in the room. The rapist had left her that much at least, a lifeline. At this hour, Joe was in his office probably. If she called him he would come in a police car, siren blaring.

But she did not phone Joe, choosing instead her sister Helen, five years younger, who lived in Brooklyn Heights, about thirty minutes away by subway. She knew very well why. She believed she had lost any right to Joe's help, or even his concern, and in addition she was worried about lying to him. She wanted to try the lies out on someone else first. Her sister's number rang eight times, ten. At last she answered. Recognizing Mary's voice, she laughed and apologized for the delay: she had been changing the baby.

"I'm in a bit of a jam," Mary said into the phone. "I ruined my dress. Could you possibly bring me a new dress?"

"I have the baby," said Helen.

"Could you leave her with a neighbor or somebody?"

"How could you ruin your dress?"

"It's ruined," said Mary, who was losing ground and therefore control.

"Can't you fix it? Can't you ask somebody for safety pins or a needle and thread?"

"You've got to come and help me," said Mary.

"But I have the baby."

"Please," said Mary. "Please bring me something to wear. I've been raped. He's taken my dress."

Her resolve was not as strong as she had hoped, and she began to blubber. "Don't tell Joe. Don't tell Joe."

While waiting for Helen, she stepped through into the bathroom, turned the shower on, and stood under the water. She scrubbed and scrubbed. She tried to scrub away the presence of the stranger's hands on her flesh, but could not do it; he was still there. And so she began to sob again. Though she went on scrubbing, it did no good. The man had had long thin fingers with sharp nails. She could feel these fingers on her breasts, on her buttocks, her thighs, her sex. His prints were all over her and could not be scrubbed away.

Having dried herself off, she got dressed in what clothing was left. Her panty hose gave her trouble for she pulled them on standing up—there was no chair in the

HANDS OF A STRANGER   127

room, and she was avoiding the bed. She saw it as her deathbed—there would never be another to rival it. The imprint of her body still showed on the counterpane. The stains were drying there. She couldn't even look at it without revulsion, much less sit down on it. In underwear and shoes she waited at the window, staring out through filthy curtains at the building opposite.

By the time her sister arrived and enfolded her in her arms, Mary had composed both her face and her story. She had been walking along Fortieth Street, she said, and a black man with green eyes had stuck a gun in her back and marched her into the hotel and up to this room and—

"Right past the desk clerk, Mary?"

"You've seen what it's like downstairs."

—Where he stole her money, the contents of her purse, her watch, her dress, even her wedding ring—she waved her naked finger—and then he raped her.

"It was—horrible." She scrutinized her sister's reaction.

But Helen appeared to be waiting for additional details that Mary had no intention of providing. "Horrible, horrible, horrible," she said.

Her sister again embraced her. "We'll call Joe, and he'll come and take you home."

Mary pulled the dress out of the package Helen had brought and held it up. The sisters were about the same size. "I don't think I should tell Joe," Mary said, imagining that as soon as she had put this dress on she could walk out into the street. Once outside in the air, she could perhaps begin breathing again. "If you don't tell him, he won't ever know."

"But, Mary," Helen protested, "you've been raped. You have to tell him."

They argued. It was enough to shatter Mary's fragile control, and she began sobbing again. "I don't want to tell him. Why should I have to?"

Helen took her hands. "You'll have to cancel your credit cards, and change the locks on your house. And your wedding ring is gone. Besides which, you're a wreck. Look at you. Do you think he's not going to notice?"

Tears ran down Mary's face.

"I'm calling Joe," said Helen firmly. And she marched toward the phone.

Mary stood at the dirty curtains sobbing. Behind her she heard Helen's voice, and it kept rising.

"What do you mean he's not in the office? This is an emergency." In a moment she lost all control herself, and she began shouting into the phone.

"Oh, Mary," she said when she had hung up, "they can't find him. They don't know where he is."

He was leaning forward across the table, smiling, and to Judith his interest seemed genuine. But she was unable to determine what kind of interest it was. He wasn't coming on to her exactly, and yet he was. He was sending out signals that she could not read so that she became irritated and began to wonder if he knew he was sending them out at all. "I wanted to do something with my life," she said. But this answer was unsatisfactory to her. Why had she become a prosecutor? "I didn't want to be just a housewife," she said, but this did not satisfy her either. "Lots of young women seek careers now," she said with annoyance. How was she to explain the inexplicable? "Perhaps I was a little ahead of my time."

Up to now Judith had enjoyed the day. Was it playing detective that seemed so delicious, that made her feel so giddy? They were making progress and would find the building before the afternoon was out, she was sure of it. Or was it playing detective with this particular man? She had enjoyed Joe's lanky body leaning toward her in the wind. She had found herself touching his sleeve, touching his coat on any pretext, and had to will herself to stop.

But now in this restaurant he had to ruin everything with his stupid questions.

"Didn't you want to get married and have children?"

This one she had been obliged to answer dozens, perhaps hundreds of times already. "Being a lawyer and being a woman are not imcompatible goals," she retorted. "It's entirely possible to have a career and a family both."

"Well, you haven't done it."

"There's plenty of time for children," Judith said. But she did not have much more time at all, and often she worried about it. What woman wouldn't worry about it? But she did not intend to admit this to Joe Hearn, who sat across the table smiling his big-toothed smile while conducting this relentless interrogation. He seemed to have taken command of this luncheon just as he had taken command of those state troopers in New Jersey. She had resented him then and she resented him now. She resented his wife as well for not teaching him better manners. She saw him as a man with no real understanding of women at all, even though married to one for twenty years, and she interrupted his questions with one of her own. "Where did you go to school, Joe?"

He did not mind talking about himself apparently; he seemed pleased that she was interested, and she led him back over his formative years. They were as she had expected: a Catholic grade school taught by nuns, followed by an all boys Catholic high school taught by Christian Brothers, followed by a Jesuit college that at that time admitted only young men. So he had had little exposure to real life as a youth, and none to females. "How old were you when you got married?"

"Twenty-one."

Judith nodded. He could not have had many girlfriends before that, not in those days. Nor would he have encountered many women in the police department. Until recently there had been hardly any, and an officer's advancement in grade did not require knowing anything about them.

He had lived virtually an all-male life. No wonder he seemed to understand women no better, her no better. Women to him had always been sexual objects, or female victims, or, if the wives of friends, of no interest whatever. It was amazing. Most likely, Judith thought, the only professional women he has encountered before me are the ones with mustaches who work behind the counters at the motor vehicle bureau.

Then she thought: How do I appear to him? What are his feelings about me?

Joe's clams were set down in front of him, and she watched him eat them. Saying, "These are luscious," he speared one and offered it to her on the end of his fork. He had even dipped it in sauce first. It was the gesture a husband might make, and Judith was oddly touched. But, he was someone else's husband, and she almost refused.

Instead she leaned across the table and let him fork the clam into her mouth, a strangely intimate experience, and one that disturbed her more than she was ready for.

"I think we should hurry," she told him. To her surprise her voice came out harsher than she had intended. "We should get back out and find that building."

"You've explained why you became a lawyer," he replied, "but why a prosecutor?"

She decided to try to answer. "Most lawyers write briefs in offices." She gave a short laugh. "They bill clients for their time. But the law is a living thing, or should be. I wanted to live the law, to stand where it was alive and vital—pleading cases in courtrooms."

Joe was nodding his head. "You wanted to be where the action was. Cops feel the same, you know."

"The big law firms don't allow apprentice lawyers to try their murder cases for them."

"But the state does," said Joe.

"The only way a young lawyer can get into a courtroom is as a prosecutor."

Joe's nod indicated that he had long ago seen the irony of it.

"So I became a prosecutor. But for a long time I thought the DA was never going to let me try cases either. I thought I'd never get out of arraignment court. Then he decided to start a sex crimes unit. Probably just wanted a place to put all his women. It was what you did with female prosecutors in those days. He put me in charge. No men. After I won some difficult cases he was under pressure to transfer me to the homicide bureau. That was the elite bureau. But by then I didn't want to go. I told him I'd try big murder cases for him, but only if I could keep sex crimes as well. Finally he agreed."

"How old were you when you tried your first murder case to verdict?"

"Twenty-six."

"Did you win?"

Judith nodded. "There were two defendants. I convicted them both."

"How many other murder cases have you tried?"

"About twenty."

"How many did you win?"

"Most of them."

Joe laughed. "Hey, don't make me drag it out of you." But there was admiration in his eyes—or so she imagined—

and she was pleased. "You want to know one of the most important differences between men and women?"

"What's that, Joe?"

"Men are not quite so modest."

She had not often been able to speak about herself with a man whose experience was such that he could understand what she was talking about. It caused a rush of emotion that she did not expect—pride in her achievements certainly, but also something akin to gratitude. He had given her the opportunity to hold herself out to him like a gift. He had taken this gift and so far seemed to like it. But as she watched him, in effect, looking it over, she became uneasy. Jerking her eyes away from his, she peered at her watch. "We ought to tell them we're in a hurry." She tried to signal a waiter.

But Joe was still leaning toward her. "Women are supposed to be the compassionate sex. So how do you square being a compassionate woman with being a prosecutor?"

Judith frowned. The question sounded almost like an accusation.

The waiter came, took away Joe's clamshells, and put their lunches down in front of them.

"I think of myself," she said, "not so much as a prosecutor, but rather as a defender of women who have been brutalized by men."

"Has it made you hard?"

Another accusation, and not a new one. "I don't know. Has it? That's for someone else to say."

She had bristled. But Joe only smiled.

She began to eat, and she finished her chef's salad quickly. But Joe, she saw, dawdled. "Do you always eat that slowly?"

"You keep eating as fast as that, you're gonna get an ulcer."

"Women rarely get ulcers."

"That was the old-time women. But you're one of the new women, aren't you?" He was teasing her, and she didn't know whether to be angry or not. "That's what you've been trying to tell me, isn't it?"

"I think I've been caught in the middle."

Joe cut into a lamb chop. "So tell me why a woman as appetizing as you isn't married?"

Appetizing? It was such a nice compliment that she was

forced to smile. "Compared to the crises I deal with all day," she joked, "most men seem dull." But once the words were out she was not so sure she was joking. "You can't marry just anybody," she said. She was bouncing all these ideas off him and watching carefully for his reactions. "And the only interesting men I meet are cops."

Joe grinned. "It's true," he said, "we're fascinating."

"But cops all get married so young." Was this supposed to be a joke too? Men of her age, cops or not, were almost always married. If it was a joke it wasn't very funny.

Joe gave her a comical leer. "Being married doesn't stop most of them."

"It does me, though," said Judith firmly. She had no intention, she told herself, of getting involved with a married man, not this one or any other.

After a moment he said seriously, "Nobody's life is as exciting as our lives. In law enforcement we see such fantastic things all the time. We go through doors without knowing what's on the other side." He paused. "The other day somebody offered me a big security job if I would quit the department. My wife wanted me to take it."

"You turned him down?"

"To quit the department," said Joe, "is unthinkable."

"What was your wife's reaction?"

"Well she didn't like it very much." He studied the tabletop. He looked extremely vulnerable at that moment.

"Yes," said Judith. As his eyes rose she glanced hurriedly away and began trying to signal the waiter for the check.

Ten minutes later they stood on another rooftop. The wind had come up harder, blowing in from across the East River into their faces. Judith had one of the photos out. It was lying on the parapet. The wind was trying to lift it and they held it down by its four corners.

"See that projection there?" said Judith, pointing with her chin out into the void. The projection rose out of a roof two blocks away. It was perhaps an air-conditioning unit. She was very excited but trying to hide it. Her forefinger stretched to touch a similar projection in the photo. "That's it, isn't it? I think we've found it. I think this is the building." If she was trying to keep the elation out of her voice, the delighted grin off her face, this was because she was used to concealing her emotions from men. It was automatic with her, a habit dating from her girlhood: if a man knew your feelings it increased his advantages over you, and he already had so many.

"I think you've just broken your case wide open," commented Joe. "Congratulations," and he shook her hand.

She had expected some other reaction entirely, a joke perhaps, a supercilious grin, so that simply having her hand shaken seemed to Judith one of the nicest compliments she had ever received.

"From now on, it's routine," said Joe. "In a week you'll have every one of those guys locked up. Come on."

The superintendent stood out of the wind in the shelter of the door housing, and Joe started toward him. Judith, who had replaced the photos in her attaché case, was two steps behind him. There was an air-conditioning duct to cross. Made of aluminum, it was perhaps eighteen inches square. As Judith stepped over the duct, she felt her right heel puncture the tar paper underfoot, and stick there. She stumbled. Pitching forward, she would have fallen flat on her face except that Joe Hearn caught her.

Her raincoat had flapped open. The length of her dress was pressed against him, and it seemed to her that he held her much too long. Although it took only an instant to regain her balance and look around for her shoe, the heel of which was stuck two paces back, still Joe held her. Having taken a pratfall in front of a man who attracted her, who she did not know very well, and who was married to someone else, she was first of all embarrassed. She was also afraid. A single physical contact of this kind was sometimes enough to alter a male-female relationship completely, and Judith knew this. She feared an overactive imagination on his part. He might suppose she had fallen on him on purpose, and she hadn't. Her shoe back there in the glue was proof, but it was likely to be ignored.

As she disengaged from his embrace she realized she was blushing. Her cheeks felt on fire. Now she was standing on one shoe, her hand still on his shoulder for balance, and when she spoke her annoyance at her situation showed in her voice. "Would you mind getting my shoe for me?"

Leaning down he reached for it, plucked it loose, handed it to her. As she lifted her foot toward her hand, she was still holding his shoulder for balance, a contact that was necessary, however much she resented the need for it. Don't get ideas, she wanted to tell him.

But she said nothing. The blush went away, thank God. They resumed their march toward the door housing, Judith walking head down.

"Well?" asked the super as they reached him.

They stood on the landing inside and listened to the wind beat at the door behind them. The super was a small man wearing a leather Windbreaker.

"You run a good building," Joe told him. "I saw that right away. There are a few questions I have to ask you, though. For instance, how old is the place?"

He had his notebook out. His questions were meaningless and Judith, watching, was mystified. But as Joe wrote the super's answers down, the man visibly relaxed, and when finally Joe asked for a list of the tenants, he rushed to fetch it. "We could've got the list from the Buildings Department," Joe told Judith, as they waited for him in the lobby, "but it's easier this way."

"When are we going to show him my mug shots?"

"Slowly, slowly," Joe advised her. "If you move too fast, you risk blowing the case. I told you that before."

When the super returned and had handed over the list, Joe said conversationally, "There've been some complaints about certain plumbers who work this area. I don't know if they've worked in your building or not. I have some photos I'd like you to look at. Judy, show him those photos, please."

The super hesitated over one of them, the big bald man with the tattooed forearms. "I may have seen him in the building."

"Doing what?"

"I think I have. He never did no work for me."

"Visiting one of the tenants?"

"Maybe one of the doormen would know."

Now we're moving, thought Judith exultantly. But to her surprise, Joe merely thrust the photo back into her attaché case. "We haven't got time," he said. "We're running late today."

When they were on the sidewalk Judith sputtered, "But I don't understand."

Joe grinned at her. "We've got an ally in this super. Let's restrict our contacts to him for as long as we can. It's no good alerting the whole street." The next step, Joe said, was to run name checks on all these tenants. After that they needed two more photos—of the two men arrested in Jersey with the hashish in the back of their car. "It's my guess the apartment we're looking for is rented or owned by one of them. We should have all six photos before we start showing them."

The Narcotics command car was parked beside a fire hydrant halfway down the block. "Call just come over the radio, Inspector," its chauffeur called out when they were still several paces away. "You're supposed to ten-two your command forthwith."

"I have to call the office," explained Joe to Judith, and he peered about for a phone booth. There was one on the opposite corner, and she watched him stride toward it. She stood with the sergeant beside the car, waiting for him.

"Any luck up there?" inquired the sergeant.

"Maybe," answered Judith. "I'm hopeful."

Once in the phone booth Joe made two calls. The first was to his office, the second to his sister-in-law at the hotel. She picked up the phone on the first ring.

"Thank God," he heard her say. "Mary's all right, Joe. Don't worry, she's all right. She's been raped, Joe."

He took the car. He left Judith and the sergeant standing on the sidewalk. No explanations.

"But what's the matter?" said Judith.

"An emergency," he said, and left. When he had turned the corner and was out of sight, he slapped the magnetic red light onto the roof. A block after that, judging he was out of earshot, he turned the siren on and stomped the accelerator into the floor.

The two sisters had come downstairs and outside. They stood on the sidewalk in front of the hotel. Mary heard the siren coming from ten blocks away. The unmarked car squealed into the street, its red light spinning, siren howling. Joe seemed to jump out before it had even stopped, rushing toward her, the car still quivering behind him. His thick arms engulfed her, and she buried her head under his chin, safe for the moment, but for how much longer? She tried to call up tears to forestall his questions, only to find that there were no tears left. She could no longer cry. She could not look at him either.

His first question, "Are you all right?" was repeated many times. He bundled her into the car—Helen too. "Tell me you're all right." He drove with his arm around her, like a teenage boy on a date, and got his information then and later from Helen.

"She's walking along in front of the hotel, and he sticks a gun in her back, and drags her inside."

"Right past the desk clerk? But how did—" Joe cut the question off sharply.

"Then he rapes her. He had green eyes."

Mary stole a glance at Joe's face. He was staring straight over the wheel, trying to come to terms with it. His face was drained of blood.

"But I just don't understand how—" Joe swallowed that question too. He was biting down on his lower lip. Mary, wrapped in his one arm, contemplated her future, which was bleak, and neither moved nor spoke.

"She didn't get a good look at him. He blindfolded her with tape."

"With tape?" said Joe.

"That's right. With tape."

He drove directly to the office of the gynecologist who had delivered both their children, where he created a scene. Other women were waiting, the nurse did not want to make room for Mary, and Joe began shouting.

"Please calm down. I'll tell the doctor it's an emergency."

He would have accompanied her into the consulting room too, except that Mary begged him to wait outside with her sister. By then he was trembling.

The doctor called him in about twenty minutes later. "Your wife is going to live, I think," he said jovially. He was writing out a prescription. "But are you? That's the question. Women have a remarkable resiliency to things like this. Husbands don't. You're probably the one I should have examined, not her."

There was sweat on Joe's upper lip, Mary saw. He drove her home where she sat in the kitchen and stared at the table while Helen made tea. Mary drank it, Joe did not. As soon as Helen, having phoned her husband, had agreed to stay with Mary, Joe jumped up and announced he was going back to the city. Mary knew what this meant.

She knew him. He was going back to that hotel. He was not going to be able to leave it alone. Sooner or later he would find out everything. A few moments later she heard the car leave the driveway in a swirl of gravel.

Mary went upstairs where she took a warm douche and another hot shower. Drawing the shades, for it was still light out, she got into bed. Although it was not a cold day, and the heat was still on in the house, she huddled into herself as if for warmth.

She heard her children come in downstairs. Helen gave them their dinner. They were told Mom wasn't feeling well, an explanation they accepted. In the family room the television set went on. She heard it through the floor.

Night fell. In the bedroom it became very dark. Mary huddled under the blankets and waited for her husband to come home.

9

IT WAS DUSK AS JOE STARTED BACK TO MANHATTAN, night when he got there. He was in traffic and could not get out. He waited, stopped, ten minutes near the entrance to the tunnel. He could see the lights of the skyscrapers across the way, but could not get there.

There was little to distract him. He had the police radio turned up loud. Code numbers only for the most part. The city was calm. Central tonight was a female. He listened to cars responding to her voice from various sections of the city, and some of the responding voices were female too. At the tunnel he flashed his police plate and went through without paying. He was trying to concentrate on such details only. In the tunnel was another slowdown. He sat there inhaling fumes.

He drove west across Thirty-fourth Street, past the Art Deco base of the Empire State Building, past Macy's, which was still open. The street was brightly lighted and still crowded with shoppers. The billboard on Macy's corner rose up higher than most buildings. It read: THE LARGEST STORE IN THE WORLD. He clapped the red light onto his roof and turned it on. He touched the siren once, twice, then he was through and speeding along the length of Macy's. At the corner of Eighth Avenue was another red light. He went through it and turned uptown. Except for one or two second-run movie houses and a number of bars, the city had got darker at once. The buildings were mostly tenements whose fire escapes hung down over the sidewalks.

He turned into Fortieth Street, pulled in next to a fire

hydrant and stuck his police plate in the windshield. The hotel was fifty feet ahead, and he watched it. He was trying to be very careful, to make no mistakes. The first law of his profession was to seal off crime scenes so as to examine evidence minutely. Obviously, he was not going to be able to seal off this one by himself. Years of discipline exerted on him an extremely strong pull, and he struggled with it.

The way to investigate any crime was to bring in ten detectives and line up everyone on the premises, any possible witness—the victim too. Interrogate them over and over again, take statements. Hold them prisoner, browbeat them. Make them eager to cough up whatever bit of information they had. Make the victim answer brutal questions too. In the case of a rape in these modern times you were as nice to the victim as possible. Nonetheless, you made her describe what was done to her in excruciating detail—the victim of the crime was the victim also of the investigation.

Parked across the street from the hotel, Joe made his decision, or perhaps he had made it thirty miles ago. He would protect Mary from that. He was not calling in ten detectives. He did not want anyone to know his wife had been raped. He would do the investigation alone.

He stared across at the hotel. Its facade told him nothing.

He knew the risks. For failing to report the crime, he could be brought up on departmental charges. His career would be destroyed. But if he did report it, how could he protect Mary? He would be taken off the case at once and kept as far away as possible. Thoughts like this were circular in nature. They led nowhere. The decision is made, he told himself, and stepped out of the car. The car door slammed behind him.

He walked toward the hotel. About here, he told himself, Mary had felt the gun in her back. The assailant had marched her through those glass doors there. He could visualize it. To Joe, the idea was not preposterous. To a policeman nothing was preposterous. Cops saw things every day that were bizarre beyond words. A black man with greenish eyes. Joe had too few details—only those furnished by his sister-in-law. It would be tomorrow at least before he could question Mary. The idea of subjecting her to detectives she did not know was unthinkable.

As he went into the hotel he was trying to think as impersonally as possible, but it was difficult. He stood now in the same narrow entrance corridor in which Mary had stood. What kind of hotel was this? How had the corridor looked to her? As he approached a grille window in the wall his mind focused on the idea of the gun. Had the desk clerk seen the gun, seen anything? Was it shoved into Mary's back? And the clerk didn't see it?

Detectives were cynical people. This was among the first questions other detectives would ask, and they might not believe the answer. Detectives might not believe Mary's story altogether, though Joe did. That Mary had no life apart from him and her children was certain, and she did not lie. But detectives might not believe her.

Joe peered through the grille into a small office. A man who sat at a desk stood up and approached him.

"Yes?" he said through the grille.

"How much is a room here?"

"Three hours, or all night?" The man waited.

All right, Joe told himself, so this isn't the Waldorf-Astoria. What's your next question?

"Three hours," Joe said.

A registration card was pushed under the grille. "Eighteen fifty. Sign here."

Joe stared at it for several seconds.

"You gonna sign it or not?"

"I stayed here once before," Joe said. "Could I have the same room? Number twenty-six, I think it was."

"A room's a room."

"But I had good luck in that one."

The man consulted a list. "Late checkout. Hasn't been made up yet."

Joe pushed a twenty-dollar bill under the grille. "Are you the owner?"

"Night manager."

"What's your name?"

"You a cop?"

Joe denied it. Still staring at the registration card, he said, "Do you want to see identification?" Patrons of this hotel would have to be interviewed, but if they all used false names, he would not be able to find them.

"Sign what you want. It's indifferent to me."

Joe scrawled an illegible signature and pushed the card

back. On the other side of the grille the manager dropped the card into a file box. The box looked to be about half full of cards. I want to go through those, Joe thought. His change and the key were thrust at him under the grille.

He went through the door and up the stairs into the hallway. There were only six rooms on each floor, apparently. He looked at the door of the room in which the rape had taken place, then went into the room next to it. He stood there looking around. It was just a cheap, dingy room in a cheap, dingy hotel.

At the door he gazed up and down the hallway. When the rapist came out of the room after he had—had finished with Mary, which way did he run? Probably down the service stairs at the end of the hall. How many maids, maintenance men were on duty who might have seen him? Joe was trying to concentrate on the rapist leaving the hotel, rather than on the shattered state of Mary, left behind him on the bed.

A maintenance man carrying a box of tools came down the stairs from above. He had a ring of keys at his belt. "Can you open my room for me?" said Joe. "The guy downstairs gave me the wrong key."

The maintenance man was black, middle-aged, and seemed amiable. His grin showed all his teeth, and his passkey opened the door Joe pointed out, Mary's room. Joe went in and closed the door.

The room was identical to the one he had just left, and he saw at once that it would tell him nothing. The maid or someone had indeed been in. She had cleaned it up, cleaned it out. The bed was made. It did not remember that his wife had ever lain on it, with the stranger's heavy body on top of her. The counterpane was drawn tight, smooth. The ashtrays were clean, the wastebasket empty. Joe glanced into the closet, pulled open all the drawers. Nothing. He peered under the bed: tendrils of dust. In the bathroom hung threadbare towels that were nonetheless fresh. There was a plastic glass wrapped in cellophane and a strip of paper across the toilet seat. He went out of the bathroom and over to the window. Outside it was dark. The office building across the street was dark. He sat down on the sill and stared at the bed that still bore no trace of his wife. There was nothing of her in the room, not even a wisp of her perfume. His head began to throb.

He went down the service stairs. He found the maintenance man in a small workroom in the basement. He had the evening paper open and was munching his supper.

"I was in my room after lunch," Joe told him, "and I left an important envelope. The maid must have thrown it out when she cleaned—"

"You wasn't alone in there, was you?" said the maintenance man. "I went by there before. I seen the bed."

He had interrupted Joe's lie. "You saw the bed?"

"Willy was in there making up the room."

"Willy who? Don't you have maids here?"

"We all help out."

"I see," said Joe. He shut off thoughts of the bed. "I wonder if I could go through the trash."

"You done had a good time on that bed. Did the lady enjoy it?"

He was a man who wished to share in the age-old sexual complicity of men. Women existed for men's pleasure, and part of the pleasure was to brag about it afterward. He was waiting to hear Joe brag. Man, the rooster. The bragging started in adolescence and never ended. A man's role in life was to brag to his fellows of sated women. Joe saw all this in the maintenance man's grin. He also saw too vividly what the ravaged bed must have looked like, and then he saw his ravaged wife upon it, with the assailant still on top of her, in her.

His eyes began to blink, but he handed across ten dollars. "Willy whatever-his-name is must have taken some trash out. Where would that trash be now?"

"You gonna fish through the garbage?" The maintenance man's grin had faded. No sexual complicity had taken place between him and Joe. Joe had rejected it.

The man led Joe down into a basement corridor where plump plastic garbage bags, their throats tied off, stood in a row against the wall. "You don't have to wait here," Joe said. "I'll clean up after myself."

The maintenance man weighed Joe's ten dollars against the mess the white man might leave. "The last two bags is the ones you is interested in," he said. "The others is from yesterday."

When he had gone, Joe spread the first bag out over the floor: soap wrappers and crumpled tissues, food remnants, cigarette butts, old newspapers, used menstrual pads wrapped in toilet paper. Toward the bottom he came upon what he assumed to be the tape that had blindfolded his wife. He stared at it a moment, then picked it up, a gummy ball with a few hairs attached to it. He wrapped it in newspaper and put it in his pocket. According to his sister-in-law, Mary had been gagged as well, so he spread the trash out further looking for a second gummy ball, but did not find it. After refilling the first bag, he dumped out the second, in which he found three more balls of tape, which he pocketed, four in all. Four was a number he could not comprehend. He started to visualize Mary's terror. Four seemed too many. However, he had no idea in what manner the tape had been applied. Perhaps four was not too many at all.

Farther down in the pile he found an empty spool—the spool the tape had come off, presumably. He wrapped it in newspaper also. He was no expert on fingerprints, but perhaps the lab could find something on this spool. For some minutes longer he continued to comb the trash. Nothing caught his attention. As he began to refill this second plastic bag, the maintenance man came back into the corridor. He was grinning pleasantly and seemed to have regained his good humor. "Did you find what you was looking for?"

Joe choked off the plastic bag, twisted the tie tight. "I must have lost it somewhere else. You didn't notice anything unusual in the room, did you? When this man Willy was making it up?" He stood the bag in the row against the wall.

"You mean apart from the state in which you and the lady left the bed?"

"Not that," said Joe, and he fought to control himself. Helen had seen handcuffs on the floor. He watched the maintenance man closely. "You know, well, unusual."

The grin, though still there, was dimmer. The man had again registered Joe's lack of response. "Sometimes we find some of them, you know, sexual aids. Is that what you talking about?"

"No," said Joe.

"I didn't think so. You still young. Don't need 'em right?"

"No."

The man chuckled. "You wouldn't believe some of the stuff we find in them rooms. I bring it home sometimes and show my wife. She won't have no truck with it." He laughed wholeheartedly.

He's telling the truth, Joe thought. He knows nothing about handcuffs. Somebody else took the handcuffs. Willy, maybe? Holding himself as tightly as possible, he began a long, apparently aimless conversation that was filled with questions about how the hotel was run. He learned that the shift changed at 4:00 P.M., and again at midnight, same as precinct cops. The clerk on duty right now was named Pete. The day clerk was the one named Willy.

"Willy who?"

"Johnson, I think his name is. He only been here a couple of months. I don't see him too often. Usually he's gone when I come on."

"Not today, though. Today he worked late."

"Right you is."

So Joe had a starting place. If he came back tomorrow he could interview this Willy Johnson and the maids and any others. He had the balls of tape and the tape spool in his pocket. He stood looking into the black man's engaging, vacant grin.

He checked out of the hotel.

Outside in the dark street people were hurrying along the sidewalk. He stood in a doorway across from the hotel. He was trying to think, but no thoughts came.

He drove home. His children were alone watching television. Aunt Helen had left about an hour ago, they told him. Mom was sick, they said. He sent them to bed. He had had nothing to eat, but was not hungry. After locking the house, he went upstairs. He looked in on his small daughter. She was already asleep and he sat on the edge of her bed stroking her hair. In the hall bathroom he brushed his teeth. He switched out the hall lights. The house was now completely dark. At last he stepped into his own bedroom.

Mary lay huddled almost in a fetal position. In the dim light from the street she looked asleep. He placed his revolver on top of the dresser, together with his billfold, his watch, his change. He draped his pants over the back of a chair. His pajamas hung on a hook behind his closet door, and he put them on. Approaching his side of the bed, he slipped in to it.

But his wife was not asleep. With what sounded like a

convulsive sob, and with an equally convulsive movement, she rolled on to him. Lying on his chest, she covered him with kisses, his mouth, his chin, his neck. He had heard of this. Some women after being raped sought comfort and reassurance in this way. They wanted their husbands or lovers to make love to them at once. They wanted love desperately. Such a reaction, Joe thought, was perhaps akin to that of a person who had been thrown from a horse; it was necessary to get up onto the horse again as fast and as bravely as possible. Or perhaps, he thought, still cerebrating, a woman imagined that the semen of a man she loved would rinse out the rapist's semen, thus cleansing her. One of Mary's hands slipped inside his pajamas. Although recognizing his wife's need, Joe only intellectualized it. His body did not respond. He exerted all his willpower, but nothing happened.

The manipulations of Mary's hand grew frantic, and before long began to hurt him. "Make love to me, Joe," she groaned. "Please make love to me."

But the image in Joe's head was of his wife naked, the stranger on top of her. Although he tried to dispel this image it kept recurring. It was too vivid. He could not get it out of his head. As he clutched his wife to him ever more tightly, he was trying to do it. He was trying to concentrate on what he perceived to be his duty. He was trying to imprison his wife's hand too, for the level of pain had increased.

"You're hurting me," he murmured.

The hand inside his pajamas became still but remained there. He tried again to concentrate, to will himself into a state of readiness.

"What did someone tell you at the hotel?"

"Nothing." For a time he had thought he noticed the beginning of a response, but he was wrong.

Mary's hand resumed its movement, though more gently. Perhaps if he concentrated on her hand. But this didn't work either. "Don't hate me, Joe. It wasn't my fault."

"I don't hate you. Of course I don't hate you." It was the other man he hated, the one who had befouled her. He had never before had a problem of this kind, and tonight his wife needed him. "I don't know what's the matter."

Hitching himself around, he got his fingers between her thighs.

But this was not what she wanted and she pushed his hand aside. "No," she said.

For a moment they lay side by side, not touching but still within touching distance. Then Mary heaved herself to the far edge of the bed. She lay on her side, curled into the fetal position again, and from then on did not move or speak. Nonetheless, he doubted she slept, for he himself did not. Stiff with tension, he lay there thinking of the rapist, and how he would track him down. He would make him pay for what he had done to Mary, for today's trauma and tonight's, as well as for the worse trauma Joe sensed was coming.

Mary, facing the wall, was consumed by hatred also, but it was for her husband.

And so they lay side by side as the night began to pass, neither of them able to sleep, neither of them moving, speaking, or reaching out to touch the other.

10

IN THE MORNING MARY WENT DOWNSTAIRS IN BATH-
robe and slippers and stood at the stove holding a spatula
over five frying eggs. From time to time she poked at
them. Dressed for school her children sat at the breakfast
table and waited. Susie's upper lip was beaded with orange juice. Billy was buttering toast and talking to his
mother about baseball.

Joe came in. He was dressed too. His shoes pounded on
the linoleum. He stepped across and kissed her on the
cheek. Mary only continued to poke at the skillet; she did
not look at him.

"Coach says he's going to use me at cleanup."

Mary lifted the eggs out, slid them onto plates, one for
Susie, two each for what she had always thought of as her
"boys." Until yesterday they had been the only two males
in her life. Now, like it or not, there were two others.

"So are you coming to the game, Mom?"

"No." She was not going near that baseball field.

"Aw, gee, Mom."

"Your mother's not feeling well," said Joe.

Carrying the plates to the table, Mary put them down in
front of her children, her husband. Joe was wearing his
three-piece gray suit. He didn't look like a cop this morning, he looked like a worried businessman. He had cut
himself shaving, she noted, and slathered on too much
after-shave. Gusts of perfume came wafting off him. He
smelled like a stranger. Mary's coffee was on the countertop
next to the stove. She returned to it, and stood staring out
the window.

"It's against Garden City," pleaded Billy.

"I said your mother's not feeling well."

"You don't have to snap at the children."

"Coach really likes me," said Billy.

Mary said nothing.

She saw her children out the front door, then went back to the kitchen though Joe was still in there. She wanted a second cup of coffee. She did not want to be alone with him, but did not intend to hide from him either.

"Are you all right?" he asked. She could feel him watching her carefully. When she did not answer, he said: "You're going to have to get a new driver's license."

She poured hot coffee into her cup. She watched the spouting column fill the cup.

"I'll call up the department stores and cancel your—"

She turned and stared at him, and he fell silent.

"May I have another cup too?" he said.

She poured it out and carried it to him from the stove. She had nothing to say to him and meant to keep silent but this proved impossible for her. "He has my keys," she said. "He knows where I live."

Joe nodded.

"I never lock the doors in the daytime anyway." Mary gave a frightened laugh. "He doesn't need my keys. He can walk right in."

She heard him behind her. He had got up from the table. A moment later she felt his hands on her shoulders where, she told herself, she did not want them. She did not want him in the house either, or so she believed. "You could stay home today," she said.

"I have to go in."

She spun around. "How many people are you going to tell about me? Are you going to tell the whole department?"

"Can we sit down together?" said Joe, taking her hands. "Can you tell me exactly what happened?"

She in no sense felt like crying, and therefore was surprised to feel her eyes fill up with tears. They spilled down her face. She jerked her hands loose. "You already know what happened."

Joe retreated to the table. She heard him sit back down. "For instance, what did the guy look like?" She heard him fiddle with his coffee cup on its saucer.

He added, his voice on a descending note, "And I need to know his MO, what exactly he did to you."

"He raped me."

"Yes. But how? In what way?"

"I don't remember."

"What were the details of it?"

"Are you enjoying this?"

"I have to know."

"I don't remember."

Joe stood up, but did not approach her. The table was a barrier between them.

"What did he look like?"

"He blindfolded me."

"Was he tall, was he short? How old was he?"

"I don't know."

"Before he blindfolded you, you must have got a look at him."

"Hardly."

"Would you recognize him if you saw him again?"

"No."

"I recovered some evidence."

Joe's attaché case stood beside the back door. He opened it on the table and displayed the four balls of tape, the metal spool.

Mary, peering down, felt herself begin to tremble.

"So is this the tape?"

"How should I know?" She watched him close the attaché case. "What will you do with that?"

"Take it to the lab."

He's going to find out, Mary thought, and tried to will her trembling to stop.

"Mary, you've got to help me."

Despite herself, Mary burst into tears. "Let's just forget about it," she said. "That's what I'm trying to do. Forget about it."

"We can't just forget about it."

"Why?"

"Mary, you've been raped."

She had lived with him nineteen years and knew he would not be able to stop. "What good is an investigation," she sobbed, "when even if you caught him I wouldn't be able to identify him?"

Joe tried to put his arms around her, but she pushed

him away. "Just leave me alone," she shouted. "I can't identify him."

"Maybe someone else can."

This startled her. "Like who?"

When he did not answer she said:

"There was no one in the room but him and me."

"Maybe one of the clerks."

"They're probably in it with him."

"Yes, I've considered that." And after a pause: "You said he had green eyes."

"I said I can't identify him."

"We'll talk about it tonight," said Joe.

"No, we won't," said Mary, and ran upstairs where she sat down on the edge of the bed. "No, we won't," she repeated, and sobbed even harder.

Downstairs she heard Joe making phone calls canceling various charge cards. He stayed until the locksmith came— she heard their blurred conversation and the noise of the man working at the doors. Joe then came upstairs and gave her the new keys.

"You'll be safe here," he said. "The local police will be watching the house. I called them."

Mary, still sitting on the edge of the bed, only twisted the hem of her bathrobe in her fingers.

"I have to go now," said her husband.

"Then go," she shouted.

"Do you want me to stay?"

"No. I want you to go. Will you please go?"

When he tried to embrace her she twisted away from him. Through the window she heard his car start up in the driveway, heard him back out into the street.

The commanding officer of the Scientific Research Division—the police laboratories—was a sixty-one-year-old captain named Lauder. Joe knew him. A few years previously they had gone through captains' school together. They had sat in classrooms at adjoining desks, but one was the rising young star of the department, and the other a superannuated ballistics technician nearing retirement age. Their status was clear to both of them, and their hopes and prospects were so divergent that neither felt any suspicion or animosity toward the other. Since they were not rivals, they had become friends. Or rather, in the upper echelon of the police society they had become what passed as friends.

Lauder's specialty was giving expert testimony in court. He gave this in slow, measured tones that sometimes had jurors dozing. He would set up easels in front of the jury box and on them stand enormous blowups of bullets. Then, using a pointer, he would direct the jurors' attentions to lands and grooves magnified ten thousand times. He seemed a dry, academic kind of man, and a policeman in name only. However, he had worked within the department more than thirty-five years. He knew who everyone was and how high they stood. Although thirty-five years of studying bullets, many with bits of blood and flesh still attached, might have been expected to make him gloomy, or perhaps overly cynical, they had turned him instead into a man who relished gossip and who was one of the chief purveyors of same. Since every notorious crime in the city led eventually to his laboratories, there was much of it to purvey.

He was in his way a dangerous man.

Joe believed it was risky to approach Lauder. Nonetheless, the balls of tape represented the only evidence he had. He drove his car down into the garage underneath the Police Academy, handed the key to the uniformed cop serving as garage attendant that day, and rode the elevator up to Lauder's floor.

"I got something big," he told him, and opened his attaché case. The evidence was in a paper bag which he upended over Lauder's blotter. Although the four balls of tape landed inertly, the metal tape spool rolled. Lauder pinned it to the blotter with a pencil.

"Can't tell you much about it, unfortunately," Joe said, and gave what he realized was an inappropriate grin. "Highly sensitive."

Lauder's pencil poked one of the balls of tape as if it might be alive and begin to move.

"The victim was gagged and blindfolded with that tape," explained Joe.

"Tape like this is hard to do anything with."

"There seem to be a few hairs stuck there. Maybe they can be matched to someone."

"If we know who to match them to."

Joe pointed to the metal spool. "You ought to be able to

prove that the tape came off that spool, right?" He was trying to listen to himself as he spoke, trying not to sound too eager, too intense. "Then if there are prints on the spool—"

"The prints of some detective is what we usually find."

"One more thing, Howard—" Joe chose his words with care. "This case is so sensitive that I'd like you to do the work yourself."

Lauder frowned. "I'm a ballistics man, Inspector." In captains' school they had called each other Joe and Howard. Joe had since advanced two ranks, Lauder none. "I wouldn't know how to process this tape myself. I have only a vague idea of how my lab boys will do it." He looked up.

"Well, keep it as restricted as you can," Joe said.

Lauder's pencil hung poised over a ledger. "You got a case number for this?"

"I'd just as soon there was as little paper attached to this evidence as possible."

"The purpose of evidence is to get a conviction in court," said Lauder patiently. "If you ever want to use this in court, I got to log it in."

"Log it in," said Joe. "Can you do the tests while I wait?"

"Jesus, you don't want much."

"Suppose I come back in an hour," said Joe firmly. He had resumed the posture of command. He outranked Lauder who would do what he was told. "That should be enough, shouldn't it? An hour?"

"I'll see what I can do," muttered Lauder.

With an hour to kill, perhaps more, Joe decided to make social calls on whichever Police Academy commanders were in residence today. He was determined to act as normally as possible, and so got his notebook out and stood at the elevator bank and looked up the names of their wives and children, their hobbies, their past commands. The Police Department was an enormous bureaucracy, and if one wished to move upward within it then political glad-handing was more important by far than combating crime.

The commanding officer was a one-star chief named Devaney, and Joe sat down across the desk from him. "How's Mona?" he asked. "How's Jimmy doing at Cornell?" But his thoughts were with Lauder's technicians several floors below, so that, as he worked down the corridor office by office, he sometimes asked the same questions twice. A number of the men he visited noted this. Certain of them would mention it to each other during the day.

At length Joe entered Lauder's office for the second time.

"The glue matches," Lauder told him. "And we were able to lift a partial print off the inside of the spool."

"Good," said Joe. "You got a name to go with it?" The news was too sudden and too rich. "With the new computers, I understand we can now identify single prints."

"This is only a partial," said Lauder. "I doubt we'll be able to give you a name."

"What about the tape itself?"

"I got nothing on that yet."

It made Joe angry. "Why not, for Christ's sake?"

"Inspector," said Lauder patiently, "the only way to get those balls of tape unstuck is to soak them in a solution. It takes time."

"I'll drop back later, or I'll call you," said Joe, and he strode out of the office.

Behind him Lauder shrugged. Inspector Hearn's conduct seemed curious, and he wondered what this case was all about.

By two o'clock Joe was parked in front of the hotel again, and during the next half hour he watched eight couples stroll up to the door, glance furtively in both directions, then duck inside. Lunchtime quickies. He stuck his police plate in the windshield and got out of the car.

The narrow corridor was empty. At the grille he flashed his shield and said, "Police, open up."

The door beside the window was pulled inward, and he was admitted inside by a man who had become instantly nervous. The room was an office. It contained three men in all, two of whom had been eating lunch across a desk from each other. The third had manned the window. All were middle-aged white men, and all were in shirt-sleeves. So none of them were the rapist, and they did not strike him as likely confederates of any rapist either.

Any good police interrogation was also an intimidation. The intimidation was psychological and physical both. The cop brought power into the room, though it could not be seen. He brought weapons in also, at least one per cop, though these usually could not be seen either. He expected deference the way rich men did; he accepted it as his due. He occupied a great deal of space, and knew it. His mere presence stripped subjects of their rights. Most saw this immediately and became afraid. Whatever the Constitution might say, their rights were in abeyance, had become illusory. Subjects could not exercise them without causing trouble for themselves, and very few, in Joe's experience, failed to realize this.

"Who's in charge here?" It was almost an accusation, and Joe meant it to be.

The three men eyed each other. Then one of them put his sandwich down—it had been hovering in the air for some seconds. "I am."

"You got a place where we can talk?"

The man led Joe through a door into a small, windowless cubicle beyond. The other two men watched them go. The cubicle contained a desk littered with bills and invoices. As if to give himself confidence, the man sat down behind it. But his fingertips began to drum nervously.

Joe sat down opposite and got his notebook out. "Name?"

"Morton Bluestone."

Although Bluestone waited nervously for the next question, Joe merely stared at him.

"We have information about a drug transaction," Joe lied. "Took place in this hotel sometime during the last three days. Tell me about it?"

It made Bluestone stammer. He knew nothing about drugs, never admitted known drug users to his hotel, was careful about who he rented rooms to. His clientele, he said, was "specialized."

"Specialized, Morton?" Another accusation.

"There's no law against it," said Bluestone defensively. If sex was to be the subject of this interview, rather than drugs, then Bluestone was on firm ground, and he knew it. He was a man approaching sixty with thick, hornedrimmed glasses, a potbelly, and a bald head. This was not the first time he had been interrogated by detectives, and he began almost visibly to pump himself up.

"Can I see your identification?"

"No, you can't."

"I got a right to see it," said Bluestone, already less sure of himself.

"You already saw it," snapped Joe. "The transaction I'm talking about was between a white woman and a black man. About this time of day. Yesterday maybe."

"We don't rent rooms to blacks here," said Bluestone. "Our clientele is specialized, like I say."

"Morton, you're not cooperating."

"We offer a place for business persons to relax at lunchtime."

"You mean like a kind of athletic club," said Joe.

But Bluestone was not responding to sarcasm. "If the business clients I'm talking about saw there were blacks in here, it wouldn't be good for business."

"You're a one man Ku Klux Klan, aren't you?" said Joe.

"I don't need to take abuse from you."

"Maybe you'd like to explain yourself at the station house." Joe stared him down. Men like this sometimes showed flashes of courage during police confrontations, but it did not last.

"What is this?" said Bluestone bluntly. "A shakedown?"

"I want to see all the registration cards for the last several days."

"Because you don't have your gang with you."

"Gang?"

"When cops come, they come in a gang. They don't have their gang with them, it's usually a shakedown. How much you want?"

"I want the cards."

Bluestone reached for the telephone. "I'm calling my lawyer."

Joe yanked the telephone away from him. A mass of bills and invoices slid and fluttered to the floor. "After you bring me those cards," Joe said. Bluestone had probably been running places like this all his life, meaning, therefore, that he knew cops. To him this investigation felt strange.

But he was not sure of himself. How could he be? Stepping to the door, he ordered the box of cards brought in. It was set down on the desk. Joe lifted out thirty or more and began shuffling through them. "You verify the identity of any of these people, Morton?"

"I don't take personal checks or credit cards," said Bluestone.

"What would you say was the percentage of these names that are phony?" said Joe. "Would you say it was a hundred percent?"

"Business people like to come in here at lunchtime and relax."

Joe, shuffling, came to the card he was looking for. It was stamped 2:17 P. M. The room number was marked in the upper-left-hand corner. Joe scaled the card across the desk at Bluestone. "This name here, would you say it's phony?"

"I wouldn't know," said Bluestone. His voice had become stolid. He was no longer fighting back.

"Could the man who signed that have been a black man?"

"We don't accept black persons here."

"That puts you in violation of the civil rights laws, doesn't it?"

Bluestone shrugged.

"Take a look at that card. What can you tell me about that particular customer?" Bluestone, Joe noted, eyed him speculatively, so he scaled down a second card, and a third. "Or this customer, or this one?"

Bluestone said nothing.

"Got a rubber band?" said Joe. He squared the cards and snapped the band around them. He was maintaining control of himself, but barely. "I'll take these cards. They'll be returned to you at a later date." He gestured with his chin toward the other room, "Call those other two heroes in here."

"This is very irregular," said Bluestone, but he stepped to the door and called the other two men into the small office. Joe asked most of the same questions a second time. Neither of the other men admitted to having seen a black man enter the hotel with a white woman in recent days.

"Do you notice the people who come in here at all?" demanded Joe.

The younger of the two men gave a grin that was close to a leer. "I notice the broads, if they're good-looking."

It made Joe remember the eight couples he had watched enter this hotel during the previous half hour. He imagined all eight couples, sixteen people, humping furiously on beds just over his head, and it made his eyes blink.

"You got an employee named Willy Johnson?"

"He didn't come to work today," said Bluestone.

"Sick?"

Bluestone shrugged.

"I want the names, addresses, and Social Security numbers of all your employees." When all this had been furnished him, Joe muttered, "I'll be back," and went out of the hotel.

Behind him, one of the clerks said to Bluestone, "What was that all about?"

In the aftermath, Bluestone was feeling onrushes of terror. He took out his handkerchief and swabbed his bald brow. "I don't know," he said, "but maybe I can find out." Invariably, once the police had left him, Bluestone would begin to sweat. He was sweating now. This both embarrassed and infuriated him. Prior to the Knapp Commission corruption hearings, detectives from the precinct had visited Bluestone once a month, and he had paid them. Since then, nothing. It had simply stopped. Now perhaps it was starting again. But Bluestone had lost the habit of paying, and he picked up the telephone. When the police operator came on he asked to be put through to Internal Affairs.

Two detectives appeared the next afternoon. They soothed Bluestone as best they could and left their cards. If there was a repeat visit Bluestone was to phone them at once. Meantime, they would make their report.

When they reached their office they went into immediate conference with their supervisor, a lieutenant. A complaint had been lodged against an officer of higher rank than any of them present. They were worried and did not know what to do. Neither did the lieutenant, who called in a captain for advice. No corruption seemed involved. No bribe had been solicited or paid, apparently. Perhaps they should buck the whole thing across to the Civilian Complaint Review Board. Somebody was merely hassling Bluestone, who probably deserved it. But a man of inspector's rank? It seemed very odd. Then they decided that perhaps it was not the inspector who was under investigation here but themselves; how were they going to respond to this complaint? They had to do something.

Finally they bucked it upward. It was the middle of the

following week before a memo signed by the three-star chief of Inspectional Services, and marked "Personal and Confidential," having moved slowly through department mails, landed heavily on the desk of Chief of Detectives Cirillo.

11

ASSISTANT DISTRICT ATTORNEY JUDITH ADLER STOOD
over Mr. Katz's desk. It was noon and she was on her way
out to lunch. She held her pocketbook in both hands. "Try
Inspector Hearn one more time," she said, and waited.

But Hearn was still—the police euphemism— out in the
field.

"Ask if he got my previous messages."

Katz, after speaking into the phone, looked up at her
and nodded.

"Leave another message."

Judith went down in the elevator and out of the building.
She was heading for Rosario's again. One's orbit seemed to
get more and more restricted, she realized. The world was
a big place, but one's own part of it became smaller and
smaller. She already felt grumpy, and such thoughts as
this only made her mood darker.

Having entered Rosario's, she stood and peered about
for the lawyer with whom she was supposed to have lunch.
He spied her first and waved and she threaded her way
through crowded tables and sat down opposite him.

Though he gave her a big friendly grin, she found it
difficult to smile back. The lawyer was a recruiter for the
White House to whom she had spoken by telephone several times lately. It was his assignment from the president,
he had told her, to induce her to move to Washington to a
job as White House staff counsel. On the phone she had
not encouraged him, but finally she had agreed to meet
him for lunch—a waste of time for both of them, she
believed.

"Sorry I'm late," she told him, and began to describe the case she was working on with Joe Hearn—it was better than small talk, and it had been on her mind all morning. Assuming they had the correct building, she said, probably it would not be difficult now to locate and arrest the perpetrators. After that the legal problems appeared quite interesting. The trial would ride on the videotapes, but the judge might rule them inadmissible. Even if he did admit them, you were looking at a verdict that might be overturned on appeal.

To Judith a fascinating case. But the lawyer across the table, she saw, did not look interested. Crime did not interest him, apparently, nor the legal technicalities that accompanied crime. He was here for a specific purpose only, apparently, and as soon as she had paused he launched into his presentation. The administration, he said, needed Judith in Washington. "We want you on the team."

"And what sort of work would I do on—on the team, as you put it?" The words had not caused him any trouble, but they did her. They seemed almost too pretentious to pronounce.

"Believe me, there's plenty to do."

"Like what?"

"Whatever comes up."

"You mean like preparing the president's income tax for him?"

"If something like that comes up, sure."

In the past this man had offered other people similar jobs dozens of times. His smug smile said so. Most of those he recruited had no doubt leaped at the chance.

"I'm a prosecutor," said Judith.

"This is the White House, right? The president of the United States, right?"

"Yes."

"No prosecutions there."

Judith opened her menu. Looking into it her mind wandered, reverted of its own accord to what she had begun to think of as The Case. Capital letters. To the new photos that had reached her from Captain Sample today. To Joe Hearn who was "out in the field" and had failed to return her calls.

The man across the table brought forth what must have seemed to him the clinching argument. "Bringing qualified women into the administration is one of the president's top priorities."

Which confirmed what Judith had suspected from the start. No one, especially this man, was much interested in any skill, experience, or integrity she might bring to the White House with her. They were interested only that she would bring lots of brassieres and skirts. She would be a political plus. It was a demeaning offer, and this was a demeaning lunch.

Nevertheless, looking up from her menu she managed a pleasant smile. "The district attorney here has much the same problem you have," she said. "My first assignment this afternoon is to pose for a photo with him and his other bureau chiefs for some magazine. The other bureau chiefs are all men, you see, as is the district attorney. He definitely wants me in the picture."

"Yes," nodded the man. "It's a problem. So can I tell the president you're coming aboard?"

"You mean the president is waiting to hear my decision?"

"Indeed he is."

Judith, though trying hard to be charitable, said: "You're putting me on."

The waiter had come up and stood at the table, and she smiled at him. "This is Adriano," she told the lawyer. "He's from Trieste, aren't you, Adriano? Let's order, shall we?"

Her companion wolfed down a plate of lasagna topped by a thick layer of toasted cheese, and she watched him do it. Men had it easy, she thought. Extra girth only made them look more judicious, more substantial. Or so the world pretended. Whereas a woman had to continue to fit into a size 10 dress—size 8 when she was in law school. She had had many job offers recently. In these feminist times everybody seemed to be looking for "qualified" women. Big salaries were mentioned. But she had turned them all down.

Over coffee she informed the recruiter of her decision. Much as she wanted to "join the team," as he put it, she was a courtroom lawyer. She wanted to stay a prosecutor.

"Excuse me?"

"Every day is a challenge."

"I don't understand."

"I want to stay where the action is." The phrase made

her think of Joe Hearn again. Also she realized even as the
words passed her lips that such an argument, though
perfectly acceptable from a man, was simply not acceptable from a woman.

The recruiter didn't accept it. He tried to change her
mind. He was very smooth and confident. The words
"White House" kept reappearing, as if designed to seduce
her all by themselves.

"You argue very well," said Judith pleasantly. She saw
him as a lawyer who had never pleaded a case in a courtroom in his life, poor devil, and she felt sorry for him.
How could any lawyer who cared about the law not want
to practice in court? "I bet you'd be good in front of a
jury."

"I'm sure I would be. Now why not send me back to the
president with the agreement we all want?"

What Judith wanted was only to get back to the office.
Joe Hearn might call back at any moment. Also, she was
very tired of this lawyer. She couldn't go to Washington,
she told him, being obliged to stay in New York because of
"personal reasons."

"Personal reasons?" he said, nodding his head in annoyance. "But you're not married." She fluttered her eyelashes
at him. Personal reasons to him meant some man she was
in love with and could not leave. It was the one impedi-
ment that he would feel forced to accept.

"You could've told me as much over the phone," he said
irritably.

She said nothing.

"You didn't have to make me come all the way up
here."

The accusation was unfair. "You insisted on coming,"
Judith told him pleasantly. "I suggested on the phone that
you would be wasting the trip." But immediately she felt
the need to soothe his wounded pride. "Maybe next year,"
she said.

This only made it worse, apparently. "Next year is an
election year," the lawyer said. "We might not be returned to office."

Again Judith fluttered her eyelashes at him.

"I offered you a job in the White House. If it only lasts a
year, so what? A woman can afford to take a job for only a

year." He stopped. In a moment, Judith thought, he might realize what he's just said. He might even begin to apologize.

But he didn't, which made her angry. To hell with his male pride. "Some women are just as concerned about their careers as some men," she said pleasantly and stood up. "I hate to cut this short, but they're waiting for me to take that group picture."

She went directly up to the district attorney's office and wasted half an hour there. When she got back to her own desk Joe Hearn had still not called. She sat down and picked up the three new photos Captain Sample had sent and spread them out. It was the third photo that was the surprise. The first two were the men arrested in the car containing the forty kilos of hashish, but the third was the owner of the car, whose name had not come into the investigation until now. He was the owner not only of the car but also of an apartment in the building she and Joe had checked out on East Seventy-eighth Street. It was in his apartment, she now assumed, that all those terrible rapes had taken place, and she wanted to tell Joe about it.

Oh, Joe, she thought, why don't you call? And she contemplated the photos with the attention and emotion one usually accorded photos of loved ones.

She was interrupted by the entrance of Mr. Katz, who leaned over the desk close to her ear and whispered that Miss Carlson was outside.

The name made Judith flinch. But she got the case folder out and glanced through it, then buzzed Katz to send the young woman in.

Elaine Carlson claimed to be the victim of rape. For about two weeks Judith had been trying to stall this case. She wanted Miss Carlson to withdraw her complaint, but could not force her to do so and it was not proper even to urge it. Instead she had kept telling the young woman to "think it over, decide what you want to do."

Miss Carlson sat down across the desk. She was twenty-eight years old and wore a severe suit over an equally severe blouse with a small collar. Her hair was pulled back tight. She wore no makeup and she carried a handbag which she put down on the floor.

"I want him arrested," Miss Carlson began.

It meant that the case could be stalled no longer, and Judith sighed. Arrests were easier to order than to undo afterward, and they did great mischief even if the suspect were later exonerated in court. With computers no one could successfully hide the fact that he had once been arrested, and certain professions, the law for one, were simply closed off to any candidate with an arrest on his record. This arrest that Miss Carlson wanted Judith to order might ruin the career and life of a young man who was prhaps not guilty of rape at all, who was guilty of nothing worse than misjudging Miss Carlson.

"Before I order his arrest," said Judith, opening the dossier before her, "I'd like to go over the facts with you again."

"Have you ever been raped?"

The rhetorical question. Judith had heard it many times, always from women like Elaine Carlson. The truly brutalized women, the ones whose noses had been broken, whose teeth were now missing, never asked it.

"Well, I have," said Miss Carlson, "and I want him arrested."

"I just want to make sure that the facts constitute rape under the law."

"We've been over this three times. I didn't want to do it. He forced me, and that's rape."

"Yes, so you say. Did he threaten you with bodily harm?"

"If I didn't do what he wanted, he could have killed me. He's a cop. He had a gun."

And that was the problem. The "rapist" unfortunately was a cop. Judith had not met him or heard his side of the story. According to the dossier, meaning according to Elaine Carlson, he was an unmarried patrolman. He was younger than Miss Carlson, only twenty-four years old.

"Well, did he draw his gun?"

"No, but—"

Judith dreaded rape cases involving cops, and she had reason.

"All right, after the movies you come back to the apartment you share with your mother. Then what happens?"

The story did not change. The mother being away for the weekend, the young couple had had some drinks. They began kissing. The cop, who was also a first-year law student, undressed the young woman, then himself. He was wearing his off-duty revolver in a clip-on holster inside the waistband of his trousers, and he removed this and laid it down on top of his neat pile of clothing.

"And you had intercourse together," said Judith.

"But I didn't want to."

"And after that, what happened?"

"He said he was thirsty. I made some orange juice for him."

"I see, and then what?"

"He wanted to stay the night, but I didn't want him to."

"So he left?" asked Judith pleasantly.

"So he left. But only after he raped me, don't forget."

It was what Judith called a "feeling dirty" case. The next day the cop did not call, nor the day after. On the third day, feeling dirty, Miss Carlson had gone to the station house and charged him with rape. This was not a joke. The young man's future, if the case went any further, could be effectively cut off right here at twenty-four. And further it now would go. Judith was powerless to stop it. If she tried to bury the case or drop it, she could be accused of malfeasance herself and perhaps rightly so. It was not her job to decide guilt or innocence. She was not God.

To charge any man with rape was serious, but to charge a policeman created a special situation. An arrest destroyed him. Once arrested, he could no longer be allowed to function as a cop. He would have to be stripped of his gun and shield, and in addition, most likely he would be suspended without pay pending the outcome of his trial six or eight months from now. And this young cop wanted to be a lawyer as well. With an arrest for rape on his record he would not be admitted to the bar.

"I'll put the case into the grand jury," said Judith brusquely. She was forced into such decisions nearly every day. Why should she be upset over this one? "You'll be sworn. You can tell the same story you've told me." And she stood up to signal that the interview was over. She wanted Elaine Carlson out of her office.

"And then what?" Miss Carlson had remained seated.

"The grand jury decides whether or not to indict him."

"You mean they decide whether or not I was raped?"

"The young man will get a chance to tell his side of the story too." Judith had no idea what he looked like or how he carried himself. It depends what kind of impression he makes, she thought. It depends on how nervous or frightened he sounds, how evasive he seems.

"He'll just lie. He'll say I wanted to. Cops always lie."

"It depends on who the grand jury believes," muttered Judith. It depends on whether or not the jury likes him, she thought, on how good-looking he is, on the right smile, on the right sigh. That is to say, Judith thought bitterly, it could go either way. Because of this woman, a young man's life hangs by a thread.

"But in the meantime, he gets arrested," demanded Elaine Carlson.

It made Judith stubborn. She decided to protect the cop a few days longer. "If the grand jury indicts him, he'll be arrested. Now if you'll excuse me—"

When Miss Carlson had gone out, Judith went to her window and stood there awhile. She could see the roofs of both courthouses and the facade of the Federal Building across the street. Below was part of Centre Street, and she watched pedestrians hurrying along, most of them involved in some way in law enforcement, most likely: lawyers, bondsmen, cops, witnesses, jurors. Many were en route from one courthouse to another, probably. They were part of the system, as she was. But again in the last few minutes the system had let her down. The law had let her down, or at least so it seemed, meaning that she had been in effect once more disappointed in love. The law was an ideal, one of man's most urgent and also his most fanciful. Ideals were always perfect, and therefore it always came as a shock to discover that the law was not. She had to keep continually adjusting her—her what? Her faith, certainly. Her hope. Whatever charity was in her, as well.

Such thoughts brought a wry smile to her lips, and she turned from the window and stared again at Miss Carlson's dossier on her desk. Cases involving cops were always a horror. Judith hated them. In this one a young man would perhaps be sacrificed to the fine print of the law. The trouble with cops was that they all had guns. The presence of that police gun or guns complicated every case. Many, many cops had stood accused of rape, as did Miss Carlson's ex-boyfriend, and some were guilty, but always the issue of lifethreatening force was blurred and many a young man's life was put into a jeopardy he had not sought nor even recognized at the time.

Other cases were even worse. More or less ordinary rapes, if the cop were the victim's father, brother, husband, or lover, turned into revenge murders. Judith remembered a case in which it took twenty-eight stitches to repair the victim's vagina, and all three of her brothers were cops. They went looking for the rapist. They intended to take the law into their own hands, and had the means to do so, and this the law did not permit. Fortunately—or perhaps unfortunately—they never found him. In another case a cop had kept his off-duty gun in his bedside table and the rapist got into the house and found it and rammed its barrel up the wife's vagina and threatened to pull the trigger; he raped the cop's wife with the cop's own gun, and that cop later had to be committed.

Judith, thinking again of Joe Hearn, wanted to describe the Miss Carlson case to him. He would probably be amused to hear her call it a feeling dirty case. She wanted to reveal to him some of her emotions about the law, about crime. She wanted to know if he felt the same. But for some reason Joe chose not even to return her calls, and so she felt rebuffed. I am not his lover, she told herself. I hardly know him. He's a married man, and it sounds like the marriage is a good one. I have no intention, she told herself, of jumping into the middle of something like that.

Then why, she wondered, am I so eager to see him again?

It's entirely professional, she assured herself. I want to see him so that The Case can go forward.

But this was not true, and she knew it. She felt a yearning for him that she could not comprehend, or chase away either. She wanted to tell him what today's strange cases had been like and how they differed from yesterday's. She wanted to know if he thought their lives and interests were as similar as she did. She could understand him better than most women, perhaps did already. Did he realize she had seen rather too often the same seamy side of life he had seen—that all cops had seen—the bloody corpses, the distraught families, the impassive prisoners? Did he perceive that she believed in the random nature of violence just as he probably did—the world was a dangerous place. Probably he believed in the existence of evil and therefore believed, also, in the existence of evil's opposite: good. She did too. Most people didn't really believe in either.

Of course if she said all these things to him he might only make mocking remarks. He might sneer at her, laugh at her. She couldn't be sure how he would react. She didn't know him well enough yet and might never.

She went out of her office and stood over Mr. Katz's desk. It was late, she was tired, and she stood rubbing her neck. "Any messages?" she asked.

But Joe Hearn had still not called back.

That night Judith went to the opening of a new Broadway musical with her friend Leonard Woolsey, a 44-year-old divorced lawyer. Leonard, the father of three teenaged children, was the man she had once accompanied to Capri— that fiasco. Leonard was handsome, rich, successful. He specialized in corporate mergers. He was another of those lawyers who had rarely if ever been inside a courtroom, so that Judith, looking at him, sometimes thought: how can he stand it?

Leonard called her for dinner once a month or so, and invariably she was his guest of choice at bar association functions. She had known him a long time but never felt she could talk freely to him. There were days that boiled up on her, but if she tried to tell him about the people or crimes she had been forced to deal with, he rarely showed much interest.

It happened that Leonard was a friend of this musical's producer, meaning that after the show they found themselves invited to the cast party at Sardi's. The reviews came in around midnight. They were good, and the mood in the restaurant became hilarious. The champagne flowed ever more freely. Judith danced with the mayor, then with the leading man, and for an hour forgot who she was and what she did for a living. Leonard, meanwhile, sat alone at their table studying his glass, looking increasingly glum. Once when Judith returned, he said, "I thought we might go back to my place, have a few drinks."

With Leonard this passed for a romantic remark, and Judith hesitated. She was in the mood for a party as noisy and boisterous as this one. But she was feeling grimy and depressed too. She was like a good many of the victims she dealt with—she needed to be hugged, and to hug someone else, and there was only Leonard around. But did she really want to encourage him? There had to be more to love than Leonard had so far been able to give her—or her him.

Leonard lived in a penthouse on Park Avenue. From his terrace one could see across rooftops all the way to New Jersey. But it was cold outside and Judith came back in and closed the sliding glass door. Leonard had mixed two highballs, and he handed her a glass. Then he moved in closer and gave her a long chaste kiss.

I just have to call my office, said Judith. At the very least it would chase Joe Hearn from her mind.

When she rang the direct night number and got no answer she dialed the switchboard.

The operator said he had been ringing her apartment every fifteen minutes. Assistant District Attorney Reidy, who had the duty that night, had gone up to the 24th Precinct station house. She was to call him there urgently.

David Reidy was twenty-six years old and as inexperienced as most of the rest of her assistants. She phoned him.

"A young nun has been raped," Reidy told her when he came on the line. "They branded her with coat hangers and then shot her. She's in a coma at Roosevelt, and is not expected to make it. The three animals who did it are in the cage upstairs. We've also got about a hundred reporters and TV crews outside." There was a note of urgency in his voice. "I think you better get over here."

Turning from the phone, Judith became aware that during her conversation with Reidy, Leonard had managed to undo the top two buttons of her dress. But now she did them up again.

"I'm sorry, Leonard. Something's come up. I have to go."

"Can't somebody else handle it?" asked Leonard.

He still wore his lawyer's dark three-piece suit, she noted. He had not yet so much as loosened his tie, but when she glanced down she noted with surprise that at some point he had exchanged his shiny black shoes for bedroom slippers.

"It's my responsibility," she said. "It's going to be a big case. It has to be prepared right." She picked up her pocketbook and turned to leave. "You're a lawyer, you understand that."

Leonard understood it so well that he did not even protest, only nodded and shuffled with her to the door.

"I'll go downstairs with you, and put you in a cab," he offered.

She felt sorry for Leonard in his straitjacket, and for herself in hers. "There's no need," she said, "I'm a big girl." She kissed him lightly. "Thank you for tonight."

He waited in the open door until the elevator had risen to his floor. As she stepped into it, Judith said, "I'm sorry, Leonard."

At the station house, after Reidy had briefed her, Judith began taking statements from witnesses, from the arresting officers. The young nun was still alive then.

When the videotape machine had been set up behind the oneway glass, she asked for the first of the prisoners to be led in. To Judith he looked about eighteen. He was just coming down off a high—angel dust, possibly. She asked if he wanted to talk to her on videotape. She gave him a friendly smile. "Do you want to be on television?"

"Yeah," the boy said. He was grinning. He was excited about it. Present, in addition to the prisoner, were only Judith, a court stenographer, and a detective. Judith knew her job. For a while she only chatted with the prisoner, relaxing him, warming him up. She asked which sports he liked, which singers. She treated him like a young friend. Finally, with an almost imperceptible nod of her head, she signaled the operator through the glass to start his machine.

"You understand that anything you say may be used against you in a court of law?" There was a precise legal formula for interrogations of this kind.

The boy said he did. Judith judged that he had no real awareness of what her words meant at all.

"You understand that this interview is being taken down on videotape?"

The youth stopped her there—he asked permission, since he was being filmed, to comb his hair first. Judith gave it. There was a short pause while he did this. He used the one-way glass in the wall as his mirror. Then he went back and sat down and grinned hugely into the camera.

But five minutes later he forgot that the camera was there. He became interested in the crime he was describing. He described it in overrich detail, and without any display of emotion at all, except for an unexpected grin from time to time. It was hard to see him as a rapist and, probably, murderer. He described it like something seen in the movies. It was as if it had never really happened. One could get up and walk out afterward and forget about it.

Judith looked right back at him, as if the details of his story fascinated her. She did not wince or flinch. She did not even blink. The emotions inside her were not permitted to show.

By four o'clock in the morning she had the confessions of all three perpetrators on videotape, after which she asked to be driven in a police car to Roosevelt Hospital. There she rode the elevator up to the operating room. It was on the eighth floor. Five elderly nuns sat in the waiting room saying the Rosary aloud. She went past them and down the corridor, following the policeman who was her guide. When she came to the operating room there was no one in it except for the victim, who had been dead by then for about half an hour. Her body lay naked on the table.

"Wait outside," Judith said to the cop.

She stood looking down at her. All the color had gone out of her. It was as if she had never been alive. Those breasts were not a girl's breasts. That face had never been a girl's face able to talk, able to laugh. The doctors had sewn her up, big loose stitches as if with fishing cord. It looked like a zipper up the middle of her body. They had cleaned all the blood off her too. Her breasts had flattened out to each side of her chest, and her pubic hair was all fluffed up. Her mons was higher than any other part of her body. Looking down at her Judith brooded about virginity, and about idealism again. Most likely this young nun had been a virgin until a few hours ago. The only lovers of her life were those three potheads in the cage uptown. Her virginity had not lasted. She had not been a virgin when she died. She had lived a life devoted to an ideal, and the result of the ideal was this, a female body nude on a slab. Did the nun at any time during her final minutes of consciousness, Judith wondered, wish that she had devoted her life instead to cleaning her house, going to bed with her husband, fixing school lunches for her children?

Were ideals enough to sustain a human being, particularly a female human being, to the end?

Judith's thoughts were becoming more muddled. She was exhausted and knew it. She saw herself occupying much the same role this nun had occupied, her life dedicated not to God but to the law—which was perhaps only God under another name. She was another of society's vestal virgins of only a slightly different type. This was not what she had intended starting out. The law had become her whole life, and at this moment was not sufficient. Ideals were not sufficient. They did not provide enough sustenance. They were too broad in concept, too perfect, and they did not love back.

She went home to bed. The next morning, on three hours' sleep, she returned to her office, where she waited for Joe Hearn to call, but this did not happen that day, nor the following day either, nor the day after that.

12

JOE HAD STARTED AFTER JOHNSON EXPECTING TO break the case quickly. He was convinced Johnson was his wife's assailant. He was equipped with the suspect's last known address, courtesy of the hotel on Fortieth Street, and his date of birth, off the Social Security form he had signed. The date of birth was important. It was a good omen. It should have been enough to separate this Johnson from the hundreds of other Johnsons that Criminal Records had on file downstairs; and as soon as this Johnson's yellow sheet and mug shot came up, Joe would know what kind of man he was dealing with and what he looked like. His confidence would be increased, and he would go to the address and arrest him.

But Criminal Records had sent up nothing, which proved Johnson a virgin, perhaps. Or else that they had him downstairs under some other name.

That made it harder. Joe had started after him anyway, and he was obliged to go alone, which made it emotionally harder still. Detectives were almost always sent out in pairs and the principal reason was that men in pairs provided each other with moral reinforcement. The worst enemy of any investigation was not physical danger but the loss of faith, and Joe knew this. A manhunt was in some ways a religious experience, akin to a search for God, and a detective who did not believe would soon give up in despair. He would find nothing. Two men had a better chance.

But Joe was alone. At that time he believed his wife's story, refusing to question it or examine it closely.

Johnson's address corresponded to a four-story tenement in a row of tenements on a side street in Harlem. Joe drove past it staring. Then he drove past it a second time. There were garbage bags piled up on the sidewalks, and loose garbage was strewn between the parked cars. Finally he drove out onto Lenox Avenue, parked in a bus stop, and put his police plate in the windshield.

Harlem had once been one of the best quarters in New York. Now it was hostile territory, and Joe Hearn, walking in, was more aware of this today than most days. Harlem was part of his job, part of his life, but in the past he had worked there only in groups, and always with the cool detachment of the professional policeman. Today was different. He was alone. He had a ravaged wife at home and his mood was a mixture of pain and rage. He was attempting to redress a blasphemy, a policeman on a crusade.

These Harlem brownstones had started out as stately town houses. Marble steps, oak doors. But he passed steps that were broken off like teeth, doors that were stained with graffiti. Able-bodied men stood on the sidewalks in clumps. Big men, heavily muscled. Men without jobs. Most of them, he saw, were carrying. The ones whose shirts hung outside their pants were carrying. He studied their belt lines, the drape of their shirttails. In three quarters of a block he counted six guns. Black faces watched him, recognizing him instantly as a cop. He knew how they knew. That he stared back at them proved he was not afraid, which meant he must be armed. And a white man armed was a cop. The Supreme Court had ruled he couldn't touch them. Illegal search and seizure. A lack of probable cause. His twenty years' experience counted for nothing. His eyesight was invalid. He roused himself from this line of thought, smothered his anger. He was not here to make gun collars but to find and arrest the man who had raped his wife.

He passed women gossiping back and forth from their windows, from their stoops, for Harlem social life was conducted largely out-of-doors. But as he moved down the sidewalk the women too fell silent. Conversations resumed only after the cop, himself, had passed by. His anger faded. You don't understand these people, he warned himself. They are not going to talk to you. And furthermore, you can't undo what was done. You don't want to know more about Mary's rape than you know already. Arrest Johnson and you will be sorry. But his compulsion to investigate remained. An investigation imposed procedure, and the crusader clung to it because he was in so much pain. He could not stop. There was too much rage in his head, too many questions. An investigation restricted him to one question at a time. It had the effect of holding his emotions at bay, so that he became estranged from Mary's suffering and his own as well. To arrest Johnson became his only thought.

He mounted Johnson's stoop two steps at a time and pushed through a gouged oaken door into a narrow corridor that faced an even narrower staircase. The hallway reeked of a multiplicity of odors—of cooking, of human feces. Mailboxes hung on one wall. None bore a name. Most had been jimmied open many times—people stealing each other's welfare checks most likely. Normally Joe considered himself a tolerant man. Today he hated all these people. He banged on a first-floor door. He heard movement inside, but the door did not open.

"Police, open up."

"What you want?" A woman's voice.

"Willie Johnson. Which apartment?"

The door opened a crack and Joe displayed his shield. The woman was very young, probably not yet twenty, but he counted five toddlers on the cluttered floor behind her. He had no sympathy for her or them. The toddlers were different shades of brown. Different fathers?

"Third floor rear," the young woman said. "He ain't there. Left this morning. Took some boxes out to the car and split."

On the third floor the door looked solid. When Joe rapped, the noise inside sounded hollow.

"You in there, Johnson?"

The door was locked. He shook the handle a second time. The normal procedure now was to petition the court for a warrant, which took time, and the warrant might never be granted. How far are you willing to go? Joe asked himself. If you kick the door in, that's breaking and entering. It's a crime. If you get caught you go to jail.

Taking half a step back, he shouldered forward into the door. He hit the door a second time. On his third try the wood splintered, and the door sprang back and banged against the wall behind it.

Joe stood there breathing a bit hard. Now you've committed a felony, he told himself. You're a criminal. Congratulations.

Inside was a mattress on the floor and a plastic chair. Nude centerfolds hung Scotch-Taped to the walls, and Joe peered at them. Black nudes. The floor was littered with fruit rinds, empty beer cans, old newspapers. There was not much to search, and Joe found all he was going to find on a shelf in the room's one closet: two sets of handcuffs. He picked them up and held them. He had the right man. He was on the right track. But why two sets? The handcuffs raised more questions than they answered, but he shut these questions off at once.

Outside on the sidewalk he peered about for a telephone booth. On the corner stood the newest model, and he made for it. Being open to the winds from the waist down, it could no longer be used by Harlem's legions of junkies as a bedroom or as a latrine. Furthermore, the new-style coin boxes had all been reinforced, and flexible cables now bound the receivers to the boxes. Nonetheless, someone appeared to have taken an ax to this one; it was out of order. Joe gave a choked laugh.

Two blocks away, having found a phone that worked, he dialed his office and ordered Deputy Inspector Pearson to send six detectives and a team of fingerprint technicians up to Harlem at once.

"The chief of detectives has been reaching out for you," said Pearson, who sounded petulant. "And that female assistant district attorney has called you twice."

Joe cut him off. "Just send me those men." And he hung up.

However, the interchange forced him to consider certain realities. He had planned on a small, secret—and quick—investigation. A single detective, himself. With luck the result could be controlled.

But already he needed the fingerprint technicians and the extra men. That was one reality. It would require six detectives just to canvass Johnson's neighborhood, and the trail once picked up no doubt would lead into others. It was going to take time, and six men were not going to be enough. The second reality was that Joe had the Narcotics

Division to run. He had to run it, or at least pretend to run it. If he spent all his time out of the office, he would get fired. His career and this investigation would end simultaneously.

The third reality was Pearson. Although Joe could steal additional detectives off other cases and tell them almost nothing, he was not going to be able to keep Pearson ignorant about the investigation very long, and he could not count on his loyalty. That made Pearson dangerous. He could no longer risk the time it would take to ease Pearson out, place him elsewhere. I've got to get rid of him, he thought, and fast.

He waited for the fingerprint technicians in Johnson's room. They opened their cases, their bottles. There were two of them. They were casual, and took their time about it. Forensic detectives, Joe had noted, were never in any hurry. The evidence was not going to move.

"How'd you get in here?" one of them asked conversationally. He was on his knees working around the door handle. "You get a warrant or what?"

"The door was open."

The technician glanced up at the splintered doorframe, then grinned at Joe. "None of these Harlem doors shut too good, have you ever noticed?"

The two technicians left spatters of dust all over the doors and windows, all over the walls near the light switches, and departed. By then the six investigating detectives were already out on the street. They were looking for a man named Johnson, Joe told them, or for anyone who knew Johnson and could point them in some definite direction. Darkness came. He kept them ringing doorbells, and remained on the scene himself, driving them, communicating little beyond his single-mindedness, his impatience with their lack of progress. It was almost midnight before he let them go—with orders to report to him on the same street corner the next morning. As he drove home he suddenly realized that they would put in overtime vouchers for tonight and this was still another reality—he would be obliged to sign them, and they would have to be further approved by Cirillo. As an ambitious young officer Joe had learned to put his signature to as few pieces of paper as possible. Now he was doing the opposite. But he shrugged the realization off.

The next morning the fingerprint technicians phoned with Johnson's B number, and by noon Joe held his mug shot and yellow sheet in his hands. The name Johnson was an alias, or perhaps these other listed names were the aliases. His arrests dated from age fifteen: shoplifting, criminal receiving, assault, burglary.

When he looked up, Deputy Inspector Pearson stood in the doorway. "That female assistant district attorney just called again."

Joe began pushing things into his attaché case: DD-5 reports, memos from subordinate commanders, a box of bullets, a sap. Johnson's photo and yellow sheet went in there. He shoved all of yesterday's phone messages in too, an afterthought. Pearson, having approached the desk, tried to hold his attention with questions about the planned reorganization of the Narcotics Division. This was supposed to be Joe's number one priority. Chief Cirillo expected him to have a plan ready for presentation to the PC in a week's time. "I have to go out," Joe interrupted. "I don't know where I'll be or when I'll get back."

He increased the number of detectives from six to ten, then to twelve, all stolen off other cases. They left behind them a trail of squawking supervisors, mostly lieutenants. No one knew what the case was about. It became a mystery within a mystery. Officers began to step into Joe's office, to stop him in the hall. To avoid their questions he began to stay away from headquarters altogether. A few traces of Johnson turned up. His mother perhaps lived in South Carolina. He had an aunt somewhere in New Jersey. A girlfriend was said to live in Bedford-Stuyvesant, the black ghetto of Brooklyn. Joe split his force. Six detectives remained in Harlem. Six others went into Brooklyn to talk to the girlfriend, if they could find her. Two additional detectives, stolen off still another case, Joe sent into New Jersey to find the aunt. They were gone less than a day. The aunt, if she was Johnson's aunt, had been dead six months.

It was night when these two men reported back. Joe's desk was again smeared with phone messages he had not returned. Instead of sending them back to their command, Joe gave them new orders. They were to begin interviewing the cleaning women and other personnel of the hotel on Fortieth Street. They were to conduct these interviews after hours wherever the subjects lived. The hotel management was not to be told. Instinctively now Joe was hiding the investigation—trying to hide it—from everyone.

In Bedford-Stuyvesant his detectives located the girl-friend's flat, and one of them phoned excitedly to tell Joe that, according to the neighbors, Johnson was holed up in there right now.

The description matched, more or less. It sounded like Johnson. The detective on the other end of the phone was sure it was Johnson.

"Shall we go in there and get him, Inspector?"

He told them to wait, and rushed across the Brooklyn Bridge. Its net of cables flashed past his eyes. The water below glittered like chrome. The Brooklyn streets were crowded. He kept ordering the detective at the wheel to drive faster. Every time the traffic thickened, he hit the lever that activated the siren. Detectives were often unreliable, he warned himself, trying to stay calm. The information they picked up was often unreliable. Detectives were men who lived on their nerves. They allowed themselves to become excited too easily. Detectives tended to believe every case was going to break in the next five minutes, just as Joe himself did now.

His driver pulled to a stop in a slum street just like Harlem. More hanging fire escapes, more uncollected garbage—at the curbs stood overflowing piles of plastic bags, many of them split open and reeking. Blacks stood around with closed faces that watched him in silence.

His detectives waited in a group. Joe went up to them. "We'll go in now," he said.

He had no warrant. Being in company this time, Joe was obliged to knock. The black man who opened the door, the one who supposedly answered to Johnson's description, was at least fifteen years older than Johnson and fifty pounds heavier. When Joe politely requested permission to look through the apartment, the man granted it. There were only three rooms. Joe's examination took less than thirty seconds. All three rooms were empty.

By then it was late afternoon. From a telephone box on a corner Joe phoned Deputy Inspector Pearson, for in his disappointment he had decided to send men to South Carolina to locate and interview Johnson's mother. Find two more detectives, he ordered. Vouchers would have to be signed, and Joe knew this. It was a big expense, and therefore a risk, but he felt himself forced to take it. The detectives were to meet him in his office two hours from now, he told Pearson. They would need air tickets to South Carolina, and Pearson was to sign the vouchers himself. Joe hung up.

By the time he reached headquarters the two detectives were waiting in the anteroom, and the vouchers lay on Joe's desk prepared but not signed. He stood looking down at them.

It was past 6:00 PM. by then, and Pearson should have been gone for the day. Instead he stood across the desk, and his eyes did not rise from the vouchers. It was as if he were studying them upside down, while waiting for whatever his commander's reaction would be.

"I thought I told you to sign them."

"Yes, sir," Pearson said, and he seemed to cringe.

If he wasn't going to sign them, Joe thought, then why didn't he go home? Why let me catch him here tonight when by tomorrow presumably I would have calmed down?

Pearson said, "I just thought—if you hadn't gotten back in time, naturally I would have signed them."

Joe saw the fear in his face. Fear if he signed them of the ultimate retaliation of the bureaucracy; fear of his commander if he did not.

"I waited around to be sure," Pearson said.

Any other subordinate would have gone home, Joe thought, absolutely anyone. He doesn't know how to protect himself even that much. As he angrily signed the vouchers, he said, "Send those detectives in here." Fire him, Joe ordered himself. Fire him right now. "You wait outside."

Having reached the door, Pearson turned and said hesitantly, "The chief of detectives was reaching out for you most of the afternoon. I stalled him as best I could. He left word for you to phone him at home."

"I thought I told you to wait outside."

The detectives came in then and Joe handed them the vouchers. When he had given instructions and dismissed them, he reached for the phone and dialed Cirillo.

The chief of detectives was chewing on something. Evidently Joe had interrupted his dinner. His voice sounded almost mild. For the moment he was trying to hide his irritation. But there was no mistaking the authority in it. "Every time I ask for you lately, you're out of the office," he began.

Joe said carefully, "Out of the office, perhaps. Not out of touch."

"No one ever seems to know where you are." The mild voice hardened, became an accusation. "So why is that?"

Joe saw a way to throw the blame on Pearson. He could claim his chief of staff had failed to maintain ordinary liaison with him, and ask that he be removed. This would avert Cirillo's displeasure and get rid of Pearson with the same stroke.

"I've been very busy," Joe said, hesitating. He could ask now for the lieutenant he had tentatively selected, who could be relied upon to protect his back until he had got his life in order again.

"You didn't answer my question."

But he could visualize Pearson waiting outside the door for whatever manifestation of Joe's anger might come next, and it made him hesitate longer. "I'll alert my staff so that it doesn't happen again."

"You do that." Cirillo chewed a moment on whatever was in his mouth, then said, "So what's this case you're working on?"

The mild tone of voice had returned. Nonetheless, this line of questioning had to be blocked immediately. "I expect," Joe said firmly, "to be able to give you a full report on that very soon." Even chiefs of detectives could be controlled. If you knew how.

"What's this about you going into a hotel on Fortieth Street?"

Joe thought, How did he know about that? He said, "One of the suspects was seen there."

Cirillo fell silent, no doubt considering his choices. He could demand a full report right now over the telephone or request part of one. He could say the equivalent of: just give me a hint. But if he did either of these things it would seem both to him and to Joe that he was begging a subordinate for information. A loss of face. He would not do it, Joe believed. He was counting on it.

"Let me give you a word of advice," Cirillo said after a moment, and Joe knew he was safe. At least temporarily. "You're supposed to be an administrator. You're not supposed to be out in the field. You're not supposed to be running through the streets chasing people. That's what you've got six hundred detectives for." Although Cirillo seemed to have stopped chewing, his dinner must still be there, almost within reach. "Do you understand?"

Blame Pearson, Joe ordered himself. In a minute it will be too late. You will have lost your chance. But in Pearson's place Joe wouldn't have signed those vouchers either, and he knew this. Admit it, he thought. Furthermore, he did wait around for you. He would have signed them if necessary. He wouldn't have just defied you.

Joe told Cirillo he did understand. The situation had been a "bit unusual" lately, he said.

"Unusual is an understatement." Cirillo's voice became hard again. "The next time I reach out for you, I want you to be there."

At which point the conversation ended, and for a time Joe sat at his desk brooding. He brooded about himself and his suddenly vulnerable career, and he brooded about his failure to denounce Pearson to Cirillo. You can still fire him, he told himself. Fire him now. You won't get another chance.

He went out into his anteroom. Pearson immediately sprang to his feet. This time Joe noted his gray hair, the lines on his face, his fear. Pearson looked back at him with the anguish, Joe thought, of a man who was sure he had just lost his job.

Joe shook his head as if to clear it. "I'm sorry I hollered at you," he said. Just because his own life was in pieces was no excuse to destroy another man. He was not going to do it. "It's late. Go on home. I'll see you in the morning."

A little later Joe himself drove home, where he lay awake most of the night. He lay beside his wife. There was no sexual desire in him, and he believed Mary did not want him to touch her. Tonight, as always lately, she lay on her side facing the wall.

The case was stagnant. He had to find some way to get it moving again. He considered showing certain photos—Johnson's for one—to the men at the hotel on Fortieth Street. Maybe he should show Mary's photo too. He would watch their reactions. It would give him a chance to question them again. Maybe one of them would recognize his wife. Maybe one of them would be able to describe the man she walked in there with. He remained awake gnawing at this idea until Mary's voice suddenly spoke to him out of the darkness:

"Will you please stop moving."

So he tried to remain motionless, went on brooding, and did not sleep.

Judith took an afternoon off and went and had her hair cut and restyled. She sat under a dryer for more than an hour thumbing rapidly through decorating and fashion magazines. Although renowned for their therapeutic value, they did not interest her. She had left the number of the salon with Mr. Katz, and as she was paying her bill she was called to the phone. She felt a rush of pleasure rather than the usual foreboding. It was immediate and very strong. For some reason she imagined the call was from Joe, who was at last trying to reach her, rather than from Katz with the type of office emergency that interrupted her free hours so often. As a result she spoke her hello somewhat breathily into the phone.

But it was indeed Katz, who asked her to return to the office at once, for an important and delicate case had just come in that required her attention.

Two hours earlier, she learned when she got there, a flight attendant for Aer Lingus, the Irish airline, had been raped in the ladies' room next to the cafeteria in the Summit Hotel on Lexington Avenue at Fifty-first Street. The young woman, together with the rest of the plane's crew, had been sitting in the cafeteria after a late lunch. All were in uniform, and they were waiting for the company's minibus to arrive to take them to the plane, when the flight attendant glanced down and noticed a run in her pale green hose. She asked the pilot for permission to go up to her room to change it, but he had already checked them out. "Use the lavatory," he advised her, "there's one right next door." But he urged her to hurry, for the bus would be there any minute. The crew members were all sitting with overnight cases at their feet. The stewardess picked up hers and went along the hall and into the ladies' room, which appeared to be empty. She stepped into the first stall in the row and the assailant, 6 foot 4 inches tall and recently released from prison, was already in there and grabbed her. With one hand he choked off her scream.

With the other he bent her over the toilet bowl and he raped her from behind.

These details and others Judith got from the arresting officer, a young cop named Foley, for the rapist had run out just as a hotel security guard was passing along that corridor. The guard chased him up into the street and almost into the arms of young Foley, who happened to be patrolling that post at that time.

After radioing for help and handing over his prisoner, Foley ran back and found the flight attendant half conscious on the floor. From then on he did everything by the book, picture perfect police work, which in Judith's experience was rare from any cop, much less a young one, and, interviewing him, she was moved to admiration both for his gentleness toward the young woman and his thoroughness with regard to the suspect. He had rushed the young woman to the hospital, had waited with her there, and had come away with statements from the doctors and the victim both. Back at the station house he had strip-searched the prisoner, whose underpants, which seemed to be stained with drying semen, he sent to the lab for analysis. Finally he had brought the victim with him to Judith's office and she was waiting outside now.

"One other thing," said Foley, "the crew flew off and left her. They're already in the air. She's alone here, and she's not in good shape."

Judith had talked to traumatized victims before, though rarely one as broken as this girl, whose name was Bridget McNamara and who was twenty-three years old and quite beautiful. She had red hair, a creamy Irish complexion, and still wore her disheveled green uniform, and she sat down in the chair across the desk and began to sob and could not stop. Time passed. It got dark outside.

Judith sent Officer Foley home but kept Mr. Katz on to answer the phones and fetch coffee, while she tried to soothe Bridget McNamara. But the girl, who had been recently married, was inconsolable. She kept sobbing that her husband would never have anything to do with her again, would never understand. What was she going to do? It was past dinnertime, and still she sobbed. She had never even seen her attacker, nor he her, for he had held her face in the toilet bowl the whole time so that she was sure she was going to drown, and all the time the rape went on she prayed to the Virgin for her life. The rapist wore an enormous signet ring and the ring was in her mouth down in the toilet bowl. It wasn't her fault but her husband would never touch her again. If Judith thought differently, then she did not know Irish men. Judith could believe it. She knew only the ones she had met here, third- and fourth-generation Irish, New Yorkers born and bred. But she had seen many a marriage ruined by rape, Irish or not, for husbands—men in general—were not always in charge of what their bodies would do, or their minds.

The problem became to get this young woman through the night. "Do you have anyone you can go to, anyone you can call?"

Bridget did not. She did have a place to sleep, for the airline had rereserved her regular room at the Summit and had sent a PR man to take her there. For the first hour or two he had waited outside with Mr. Katz. He was gone now, even Mr. Katz was gone, and the Summit had always been out of the question anyway. To Judith it was an outrage that anyone had ever considered sending the girl back there.

"All right," she said, "you'll come home with me."

In her flat Judith fixed supper and tried to force Bridget to eat. She sat up with her most of the night, listening to her broken sobs, sometimes holding her hand, fixing her many cups of tea, finally putting her to bed in the spare room with a night-light burning, and although Judith had been very close to rape for many years, still she had never been as close as this.

She stayed with her all the following day, having phoned in to cancel all appointments, for the girl could not be left alone. Judith took her to the Museum of Natural History across the street from her apartment, where she tried to get her interested in the dinosaurs; and to Bloomingdale's, where she bought her some perfume; and twice she took her to the bathroom, for at the idea of entering a ladies' room alone Bridget began to tremble. She shook like a woman freezing.

Judith kept her car in a garage on Seventy-seventh Street and Broadway. At 2:00 P.M. she got it out and drove Bridget to the airport, for the airline was bringing her husband over on that day's flight to take her home. But in the transit lounge, when the announcement of the plane's arrival was made, Bridget started sobbing again, and she begged Judith to intercede for her with her husband. "Tell him I couldn't help it," she sobbed. "Tell him it wasn't my fault."

The husband, who had no passport, was not permitted outside the customs area. Judith went in there and spoke to him. He was about thirty, a big man, a professional soccer player, and he did not appear to hear a word she said. He kept opening and closing his fists while muttering curses against yesterday's pilot who had flown off, leaving his wife behind.

Finally Judith brought Bridget through into the holding room. She ran sobbing into her husband's arms and he held her. His face was grim and over her shoulder he was still muttering curses.

She left them there together and went out of the terminal and crossed the road to the parking lot and got back into her car and sat behind the wheel and found that she was weeping. She couldn't stop. The more she tried, the harder she wept. She did not even know who she was weeping for. For Bridget and her husband, perhaps. Or perhaps it was for herself. How much longer can I go on suffering this much for other people? she thought. And then: Why do I have to be so alone? At last her weeping stopped. She dried her face on her sleeve and drove home.

She had many friends throughout the city, and that evening she phoned several she thought might be available, for she was in need of company. But they were all married and lacked sitters on such short notice. Her closest friend for years had married only a month ago and moved to Washington—marriage was the natural state, it seemed.

That left Leonard, or her parents who lived in the suburbs and would of course be glad to see her. But Leonard was not what she required tonight, and she was too old to seek solace at her mother's knee. Besides, a good deal of unwanted advice would come with it. So she put her phone back on its cradle and gave up, and went down out of her building and over to Columbus Avenue and then downtown along a sidewalk crowded with strollers and with restaurant tables pushed out almost to the curb. Columbus Avenue in the last few years had become wall-to-wall restaurants serving every type of ethnic food imaginable, and most had terraces and people dining outdoors on warm nights like this one.

She sat down outside a Japanese restaurant at a tiny table in the corner and felt hemmed in by the railing of two-by-fours. She ordered sushi and Japanese tea and watched the people passing by, and they came in all ethnic types as well, all ages, all sexes, including the indeterminate ones. They came on foot, on skateboards, they manacled their bicycles to parking meters, removed the clips from their ankles and the Walkman earphones from their skulls, and went inside to dine more or less elegantly. Men in business suits passed her bearing armloads of bagged groceries; joggers in pairs loped by and homosexuals strolled along, their lacquered hair catching the light just so. A tattooed man in an undershirt walked by very fast, and an old lady with dyed orange hair passed slowly and never ceased muttering to herself. In the street the traffic passed too, the unquenchable one way flood of cars and taxis, of buses, of trailer trucks en route heavily somewhere even at this time of night; and the fumes from their passage rose up all around her, competing in her nostrils with the sweetish soy sauce fumes already lodged there.

She paid and stepped down off the terrace. Walking home, she stopped at an ice-cream bar to buy a vanilla cone, and this she licked at the rest of the way, the icy cold turning warm and creamy in her mouth and somehow this act—the eating of an ice-cream cone—seemed to comfort her as it had sometimes done as a child.

In bed in the dark she began to think of The Case again. Once they had broken it, and she was sure they would, the newspaper headlines would probably refer to it as The Videotape Rapes. There would be lots of headlines, she believed, and she could bribe Joe with that idea, if he ever called. She herself didn't need or want headlines, but they could help Joe's career. But when was he going to call? She had left messages everywhere. Why didn't he call?

Then she began to visualize his hands that she thought so handsome, the fine curls on the backs of the long fingers. Her head filled up with erotic fantasies. She saw herself taking a shower with him. Those hands soaped her all over, and then helped the water rinse the suds down her wet body.

It was very vivid. She became furious with herself and jumped out of bed and went and stood at the window. She looked out at the dark city, and forced herself to think of Bridget and her husband whose plane would be landing at Dublin about now.

Presently her heart stopped pumping. She was calm again, and she got back into bed, keeping a tight control on her mind this time, and at length fell asleep.

13

IT WAS HABIT ALONE THAT GOT MARY OUT OF BED each morning. She put on her most tattered bathrobe, stepped into shapeless mules, and went into her children's rooms and as she woke them it seemed to her that she could not bear to be alive, could not face the coming day.

"Time for school, Billy," she said and shook him.

"Time for school, Susie." Sometimes the small arms came up and encircled her neck, so that she wanted to break down and weep.

Habit got her downstairs, where she prepared their breakfasts, Joe's too if he was there. But some nights he didn't come home and she didn't know where he was or what he was doing.

Emotions beset her that were too numerous, too contradictory, too dark to sort out. She could not cope with them nor see an end to them. They would not leave her, and so she closed up inside herself inside her house. For days she did not get dressed or comb her tangled hair. Bathrobe and mules became her uniform, every day the same. Outside the sun shone on her garden. Flowers bloomed, the earth smelled spring sweet. But she lived inside closed windows behind locked doors. Beds went unmade. Pots piled up in the sink. She did not sweep or clean.

She saw only her own worthlessness, was convinced of it. She loathed her body. She despised herself and believed Joe despised her too, found her repugnant. His deportment in bed proved it. Her shattered ego could see no other explanation. Each night she lay facing the wall, and Joe, if he came to bed at all, made no effort to embrace her. His aversion to her, once he found out what he would find out, would become stronger still. She was not only soiled but guilty and so deserved no better. No one who knew her filthy secret would ever be attracted to her again. She was without hope.

Her other principal emotion was fear. It was of two kinds, one of which was relatively simple—that the green-eyed black man would come to her door, break in on her, and rape her again—or, this time, kill her. This fear came and went, but when it was upon her seemed to strip her of all reason.

On the day following the rape, having been alone in the house for about six hours, she elected to take a shower. But standing in the steamed-up stall with water beating down on her she felt so vulnerable, so without defenses, so truly naked, that panic simply overwhelmed her, and she began to scream. Without even turning off the water, she ran out of the stall, out of the bathroom, and for some minutes stood shivering in the middle of her bedroom rug. She was listening hard for the intruder she believed to be inside the house. Water dripped off her. She was so terrified she was unable to move.

Joe had a spare gun. It was kept in a locked box on a shelf in his closet, and she ran and got it out. Her bedroom door was closed. Naked, holding the gun in both hands, her finger tight on the trigger, she waited for the intruder to come through her door. If any person had in fact come through it, one of her children for instance, the gun would have gone off probably by itself.

But no one did. However, the intruder was perhaps still in the house and Mary went rushing through rooms looking for him, the gun still clutched in both hands. She did not realize she was naked, that her hair was plastered to her skull. Her fear was so overpowering that she could end it only by finding the intruder and killing him, and this she meant to do. But the house was empty.

From then on, if she ceased to bathe, ceased to vacuum her house, it was partly because these activities made too much noise. She would be unable to hear the intruder when he broke in. She would not be warned. She became afraid even to turn on the television—its voices might obscure the sounds of the intruder. The doors to every room had to be open at all times, for she wanted to be able to hear that the house was empty, all of it, no matter where within it she stood. As soon as Joe and the children had left in the morning, she piled furniture in front of the front door and the back, and this furniture remained in place until her family was due home late in the day. Sometimes she forgot to remove it, and there was a delay before her children could get in. As they clambered over obstacles they threw her puzzled looks, but when she avoided their questions, their attention soon went elsewhere. To children almost any conduct seemed normal, even the most bizarre.

She neither saw nor heard from Loftus, and received news of him only obliquely, via Billy. Baseball was not going well apparently. Coach Loftus had begun riding Billy without mercy. He was even threatening to bench him.

Mary was watching her children eat dinner, which she had prepared out of cans. "Has he said anything about me," she interrupted. She was brooding about herself, not her son. "He didn't ask how I was? Anything like that?"

"Coach is on me all the time."

Loftus is having problems too, she thought. Every time he looks at Billy he sees me and he can't bear it. He musn't take it out on my son, she thought.

"Can you talk to him, Mom?"

But Billy's problems were as nothing compared to her own. She patted his hand, stared out the window, and his troubles went past her.

Since she did no food shopping, the larder became depleted, and she was forced out of the house. She dressed herself, dragged a comb through her hair, and bought sixty dollars' worth of groceries at the supermarket. For a time, concentrating on her shopping, she felt almost normal again, but as soon as she had pulled the car into her driveway the old fear returned. The intruder might have got into the house in her absence, might be waiting in there. She got out of the car and circled the house on foot, looking for evidence of forced entry. She found none, and the back door opened normally under her key. At first she could not make herself go inside but stood in the open doorway terrified, listening hard. When she heard nothing suspicious, she called out:

"Anybody here?" and then on a rising inflection that was almost a scream: "Anybody here?"

She had left Joe's gun buried under dish towels in a kitchen drawer. She darted inside and got it, clutched it in both hands, and moved from room to room waving it in the air, calling out, "I know you're there."

She searched every corner, every closet, forced herself to peer under every bed.

Her terror was accompanied by breathlessness, as if she had just run a great distance. Her heart thumped wildly, steel bands constricted her chest, she could not get air into her lungs. But such strong emotion was difficult to sustain. Each bout passed, and for some moments afterward she was at her calmest, her most rational—becoming simultaneously most vulnerable to her second great fear, which was of her husband's investigation. How soon would he see through her lies, find out everything, throw her out of the house? Life had become completely unnerving. She was almost never free of one terror or the other.

The investigation progressed relatively fast, too fast. Each day Joe edged closer to the truth, while she watched it happen and paced the floor and tried to figure a way out, a way to stop him.

He brought home the hotel registration card. "The guy who signed it, that's the guy, I think."

Mary looked down on the card, on Loftus' handwriting. She began to shiver.

"I'll find him," Joe said. "I'll get him."

She saw that he was suffering too.

"The signature is pretty hard to make out," he said. "It seems to be Martin Larkin. It's a phony name, I'm sure it is."

You're a fool, Marty, Mary thought. She was shivering as if with a fever and her face felt flushed.

Joe said, "He wouldn't be stupid enough to sign his own name and then drag a woman in off the street and rape her."

"Joe," Mary pleaded, "let it be over. I'm trying to forget it. Try to forget it, too. Please, Joe."

Her husband declined supper. He had to get back to the office, he said. The investigation was active, there were things to do.

The next time he came home he had found the hand-cuffs. He held them out to her.

"I don't want to see them," she said, and immediately began shaking again. Joe was holding up two pairs. "Put them away," she said. I can't stand much more of this, she thought.

Joe misread her reaction. "There's nothing to be afraid of," he said. "He won't come after you here." He was watching her carefully. "It's lovers who crave the identical woman, the identical experience a second time, not rapists. He didn't make love to you, Mary. You were a target of opportunity. You're as safe here as any other woman in this town."

He was nodding at her, trying to smile. When she refused to look at him, he said, "I better stay."

"I don't want you here. Go."

"You're sure you're okay?"

She was convinced he wanted to get away from her. "I'm fine."

She was as afraid of Joe as of the rapist. At night she lay in bed in the dark and waited for one or the other to destroy her. Her fear was like a toothache that she could contain well enough by day. But it never let up and at night became completely unmanageable. She went to bed earlier and earlier. She swallowed two pills and hoped to become unconscious before Joe came home, if he came home, hoped to be spared tonight's nightmares, both the recurring nightmare in her dreams, and the nightmare confrontation with Joe that was coming, that could not be delayed much longer.

Some nights her husband woke her or tried to.

"Is this the guy?" It was the end of the first week.

She became aware of his voice and swam up toward it. "What?"

Having shaken her awake, lifted her up, he had thrust a photo in front of her face. But her eyes never focused on it. "Leave me alone," she mumbled and tried to fall back down on the pillow. She was heavily sedated and limp in his arms. As he realized this he seemed to become agitated.

"What's the matter, Mary?" he said. "Wake up, Mary."

But she held on to her drugged stupor with all her might and did not answer.

The next morning Joe seemed to wait anxiously for the children to leave for school.

"Is this the guy?" he asked as soon as they were alone. He held the photo up.

They were in the kitchen. He sat at the table, dressed, an empty coffee cup in front of him. Mary in her bathrobe stood ten feet away, rump pressed to the counter. She refused to look at him or the photo. "I don't know. Is it?"

"Where did you get the sleeping pills?"

"The doctor gave them to me for my nightmares."

"Oh, Mary."

"He said they'll stop after a while."

"You have a nightmare, you wake me up."

Mary put her cup and saucer in the sink. They were separated by the width of the kitchen and by an act of darkness, and Joe did not come to embrace her. Instead he again held up the photo.

She said, "That's not him."

"Please come over here and look at this."

"It's not him, I told you." She had an artist's memory for faces and recognized this one from where she stood— the clerk who had taken Loftus' money.

"His name's Willie Johnson," Joe offered.

"Willie Johnson didn't rape me."

In a moment Joe's head began to nod up and down. "Now we're getting somewhere," he said.

Mary watched him.

"At first," Joe explained, "you said you didn't see your— your assailant at all." He tapped the photo with a heavy forefinger. "But if you know this Johnson isn't the one, then maybe you'll recognize the real guy when I find him."

Mary stared at him.

"Johnson's the key to this case," Joe said. "He knows who your—your assailant is. When I find Johnson, I break the case."

Mary believed him. She decided to make one last appeal. It was like an appeal for clemency. "I want you to stop, Joe. I want you to forget it ever happened. I want it to be over."

Her husband came across the room and this time he did embrace her, but she only stood woodenly in his arms. "When I find him is when it will be over," he said, "truly over." And he began to enumerate the benefits that would then accrue. Once the man was in custody Mary would no longer be afraid of him. No more sleeping pills, no more nightmares. They could begin life again. "You'll feel really good, Mary."

"If you arrest him," she said stubbornly, "you'll only have to let him go, because I can't identify him."

"Sure you can. You'll see."

A silence fell between them. Joe studied his shoes. His eyes rose, then fell again. His tension was so extreme that Mary realized he was working himself up to begin interrogating her again.

"Do you," he said carefully, "feel you can talk about it yet?"

He wanted her to name which acts the rapist had forced her to perform and how.

"I don't remember."

"You've got to give me something to go on."

He wanted descriptions of acts she was determined to blot out of her memory, had no intention of ever admitting to anyone, particularly him. She recognized the anguish that had come into his voice. Just to articulate such questions was to imagine another man laying hands on her, and she saw this. The details he wanted would devastate him.

"Well, at least try to remember what he looked like."

"I can't remember."

But Joe pushed doggedly on. "Well, then did you notice any deformities, any scars?"

"You mean," said Mary angrily, "on his private parts? Are you asking if I had a chance to study him?"

Joe said nothing.

Mary said, "I don't want to talk about it."

He nodded. She could see how much he was suffering. "Joe," she said gently, "I was blindfolded."

That was the day she noticed that her picture was missing from its frame on his desk in the room he used as a den, which meant he was showing it to the hotel personnel. There was no other possible explanation. He was trying to find a witness who had seen her—and Loftus—enter the hotel. He was hoping for a description of the man who had taken her into that hotel.

Although Mary had awaited his return with dread, he found no such witness apparently. In any case, when he came home he seemed worn out, filled with despair. To Mary it seemed he was running out of time, running out of possible leads to track down. It was, she decided, his frustration and fatigue that caused him to badger her again for details of what had been done to her. Did she remember nothing at all about the rapist's appearance, weight, size?

"I mean, was he heavy, or what?"

"You mean when he was on top of me? I don't have to answer that." Why did he continue to torture himself with such questions?

"Please, Mary."

"Let's just forget you asked it."

"You act like you don't want him found. Won't you help me find him?" She thought she had never heard such misery in a human voice.

"You have nothing to be jealous about, Joe," she told him. "He hasn't had what you've had. It was rape, Joe. I wasn't making love to him."

With Joe's investigation obviously failing, Mary began to take heart. She was beginning to get over it, was getting stronger. But Joe was going the other way. His obsession, and the degree of his suffering, seemed worse every day.

He came home with albums of habitual sex offenders. He wanted her to try to pick out the rapist's face, if it was in there.

"I was blindfolded. I didn't see him."

Maybe seeing his picture, Joe suggested, she would recognize him.

Finally she sat with him at the kitchen table and he turned the album pages. She knew very well what the man looked like. She remembered him vividly, and in addition had seen his face often in her nightmares—usually he was chasing her through the rooms of her house. She could have drawn his likeness.

As one mug shot followed another she became interested despite herself. A photograph, she realized, could not hurt her, if it was in there, and she might learn more about the man himself: his name, his past record. She realized she wanted to know more about him, and this surprised her. As Joe kept turning pages she noted that rapists came in all shapes and sizes, all hair styles, all shades of color. They had nothing in common except that they were all men. That, and the act itself.

"No," she said. Joe had come to the end of the final album.

"Are you sure?"

"Yes."

"Would you mind going through them again?"

He did not wait for an answer. The faces were already parading past her a second time. Once again she found herself studying them, these faces of sex deviates. She was not the only woman who had been raped, obviously. Gradually this fact seeped into her brain, and it brought some comfort. It was a strange sort of comfort, but it was there. She was not alone in this thing. Other women had suffered it and had survived. Women had been surviving rape for millions of years, and if they could, she could.

"Do any of them resemble him?" inquired her husband.

"No."

"Even slightly?"

"I told you I can't identify him."

Joe closed the albums. There was so much defeat in his face, and in the droop of his shoulders, that Mary grasped eagerly at a new idea—the investigation had come to an end, or nearly so. In a few days Joe would be forced to close it down. He had run out of leads to follow. In a few days she would be safe. She was perhaps safe already. She went and stood beside his chair, and held his head against her abdomen. "You've got to stop, Joe. You need a good meal and a good night's sleep. You need a week off. You can get over this thing. We both can."

Though it was night, Joe stood up and gathered the albums under his arm. "I have to get back to the city."

"Let me fix you dinner first."

"I'll get a hamburger somewhere. I have to get the albums back tonight."

Though the emotions she felt for him—love mixed with pity—were intense at that moment, Mary did not attempt to stop him. She watched him go out of the house. It was almost over for him, too, she thought, and better that he kept going until he admitted this to himself—another day or two. I'll make it up to you, Joe, she told herself. She would never tell him the truth but she would make it up to him, she promised.

Beginning the next day, she began to care about her appearance again. She washed and set her hair. She got dressed—she changed her clothes several times, in fact. She went outside and stood in her garden and felt the sun on her face, on the backs of her hands. The change of mood was at first exaggerated. She would sit for hours in front of her vanity mirror teasing her hair into new shapes, applying careful makeup, then rubbing it all off and starting again. Her home, now enlarged to include the garden, was still her sanctuary, and she rarely left it. But she did make two quick dashes to the supermarket where she piled her cart high with ice cream and boxes of cake mix, for she wanted to spoil her children after so long. She wanted to spoil Joe too, and so bought the double thick lamb chops he liked so much, and she placed these in her freezer for use whenever he began to come home again regularly. During both trips to the supermarket she wore inappropriate clothing, her black cocktail dress the first time, and then the brocaded satin thing she had worn as matron of honor at her sister's wedding; she had forgotten she had it, and it reached almost to her shoes.

But it was her ability to face down Loftus that signaled to Mary her nearly complete recovery. Billy's world had continued to disintegrate. He had been shifted from third base to right field, and then demoted to the number nine spot in the batting order. Two days later Loftus benched him, and two days after that he was told to turn in his uniform—Loftus had cut him from the squad, and as he explained all this to his mother, he burst into tears.

He realizes something's wrong, Mary thought, holding him. He wouldn't ask me to interfere otherwise. His tears wet her neck, and she became angry.

"I'll talk to him."

The boy wiped his eyes. "When?"

"Now," she said grimly.

It was the day she had put on the satin wedding garment, and she was still wearing it. Now she went up to her room, took the dress off, and threw it on the floor of her closet. Staring at her hanging clothes, she debated what to change into. There was a mirror affixed to the back of the door. Her own face caught her eye, and she noted with a start of surprise that she was painted like a harlot. So her first job was to scrub the makeup off. With the scrubbing her cheeks reddened, and her face looked as if she had been making love for an hour. Too bad, she thought. She was sick of thinking only of herself, ashamed that she had wallowed so long in self-pity. She put on pants and a sweater and ran downstairs into the kitchen where she picked up her car keys and handbag. Billy wanted to accompany her, but she stopped him.

"Wait here."

As she drove to the school her anger only increased, and by the time she parked in the lot overlooking the sports field she was furious. She got out of the car, slammed the door, and advanced on home plate.

Practice was just ending. The boys were lapping the track. Loftus, who stood watching them, looked big and strong. He looked cocksure of himself, which she knew he was not. Her strongest desire, she realized, was to knock him down, and this amazed her. But she could not ever in her life remember being this angry.

Loftus heard her coming and spun around. Obviously shocked to see her, he tried a welcoming smile, but it faded fast.

"I want to talk to you."

"Please keep your voice down."

"Oh, yes," she shouted. She was sputtering and had to pause to catch her breath. "I'll keep my voice down," she shouted.

"Did you get home all right that day?" interjected Loftus. His players, as they completed their lap, were straggling off the field, calling out to him. His head was jerking around. He was trying to dismiss them with increasingly jerky waves of his hand.

"I won't have you taking it out on my son."

"Can you just wait?" said Loftus.

"He's my son. What happened between you and me has nothing to do with my son."

"Till the boys are off the field at least?"

"No, I can't wait." And she continued shouting at him.

"I'm sorry about the other day," interrupted Loftus. "You don't know how many times I started to call you up to say how sorry I was that I—that I left you there."

It came as a shock to Mary to hear him apologize. "I don't believe you."

"I behaved badly," said Loftus. "I behaved so badly."

The toe of Mary's shoe pawed the ground. "We're talking about my son. You've been riding him for days—"

"I suppose I have."

"—Trying to get even with me."

"He made an error and we lost a game."

"He belongs on the team."

"Well, I'll think about it, all right?"

"What is there to think about? Did you or did you not tell me he was one of your best players? Or was that just a lot of—of—" Mary sought a word harsh enough to express her feelings. "Of bullshit?" As soon as the awful word had passed her lips Mary, who never used such language, felt ashamed.

Loftus looked off across the empty ball field.

"Oh, I see," muttered Mary. "It was a lie. It was just something you said in an attempt to get into bed with his mother. That makes you a liar in addition to being a—a coward."

Loftus, who had dropped his head, stood there taking it.

"I don't understand you," Mary told him. This was an understatement. Never in her life had she met a man she understood less than Loftus.

"Well," he said, and began to move off from her, "I have to go now."

This infuriated her anew. "You're not going anywhere until I'm finished."

"You're causing a scene," said Loftus, glancing nervously around. Some teachers were walking from the school building toward the parking lot.

"I'll show you a scene," snarled Mary. "I'll show you a real scene."

"You're even more beautiful when you'e angry." Loftus tried another smile. "Do you know that?"

If I told somebody about this man, Mary thought, they wouldn't believe me. She gave an ugly laugh. "We're not talking about me, but about my son. And if you think I'm making a scene now, wait till you see the scene I make in there." And she gave a jerk of her chin toward the principal's office.

"You wouldn't dare go in there."

"Try me."

Loftus' mood too turned ugly. "What would you tell

him? That I screwed you? It was some black guy screwed
you, not me."

Mary slapped him. She slapped him as hard as she
could. Loftus' hand shot to his stung face even as he
glanced hurriedly around to see who might have observed
the slap.

Mary, meanwhile, had started marching toward the office. But Loftus hurried after her. "Stop. Let's talk this
out."

Mary stopped. "I want my son back on the team. When's
the next game?"

"Tomorrow."

"I want him starting at third base, and I'll be there to
see that it happens."

They stared at each other. Mary had no intention of
dropping her eyes. When at length Loftus dropped his,
Mary walked away from him. She was smiling because she
believed she had won, and she strode back to the parking
lot. The confrontation was over. Many things were over,
but she felt strong enough now to start again.

But by then Joe's investigation was over also. By then he
had been sitting surveillance on her for three days. He
was looking for her lover now, not her rapist. He had sat
slouched down in his car at the end of their street for
three days, intending when she came out to follow wherever she led him. He had tailed her both times to the
supermarket wearing the crazy clothes, and now, the third
time, to the high-school sports field, where she had delivered a vicious slap to the face of the baseball coach.
Women do not go around slapping the faces of casual
acquaintances and so Joe, observing this slap, had his
answer at last, the identity of his wife's lover: Loftus.

"Oh, Mary," he said aloud, and put his face down on
the steering wheel and began to cry.

14

ONE DAY A WEEK EARLIER, CARRYING CERTAIN PHOTO albums he had prepared, Joe had gone back to the hotel on Fortieth Street. Peering through the grille he had seen that the same three men in shirtsleeves were at work inside the office, and he had banged on the bars to be let in. Having laid the albums out on top of a desk, he had begun turning the pages, the men standing clustered around him.

The first album contained Johnson's picture. By now the investigation had lasted so long that Joe's soul was in need of confirmation that Johnson was indeed their former clerk, that the man actually existed. However, Joe had a second album with him that had nothing to do with Johnson.

When Johnson's mug shot appeared he saw the three men glance sharply at each other, and this was satisfying, but no one formally identified him.

Joe said harshly, "May I remind you gentlemen of the crime of obstruction of justice?"

Morton Bluestone began to cough. "It looks kinda like somebody used to work here, that fellow—what was his name? Johnson. Was that his name, Charlie?"

Charlie said, "I couldn't swear to it, but it could be him."

Bluestone cleared his throat again. So far as he knew there had been no follow-up to his original complaint to Internal Affairs, and now as he stared at Johnson's mug shot he felt a sudden need to mollify this policeman—the police in general. "What's he wanted for? Drugs, you said."

Joe did not answer. He stared Bluestone down: the policeman as inquisitor. But the role did not last. Joe's triumph ended. That album was now finished, and a different one came next, the one Joe was worried about. An album of female pickpockets with Mary's photo hidden somewhere inside it, with perhaps some answers hidden there as well. Answers he perhaps did not want to hear. He was going to ask if anyone remembered seeing Mary come into the hotel, and if so with whom. He began turning pages.

"Female offenders," he said.

He was turning the pages a bit too fast. Even if they did recognize Mary, probably they would remember nothing else about her. The gunman must have hustled her past them too fast. At this time Joe still believed his wife's story. He told himself he did. As he kept turning pages he remembered nervously how he had borrowed the album that morning from the pickpocket squad, one of the few squads with a big female clientele. Today many dips were women. They worked the department stores. They could get their hands in and out of other women's handbags faster than the eye could follow. This morning he had slid Mary's face in among them. It had felt then like a disloyal act, and he would feel disloyal again in a moment when he came to her.

The three men in shirt-sleeves watched the faces flip by without reaction. Mary's face, the only one smiling, went past them, the photo off his desk at home. No one said anything at all, and presently Joe came to the end of the album.

But you turned the pages too fast, he told himself. You didn't give them time. It wasn't a fair test. You'll have to go through the album again. But the test doesn't have to be fair, he told himself. Why do I have to be fair? But he heard a voice speaking, and it was his own.

He said: "I'll go through it a second time, more slowly. I want you to study each of these women."

Slowly he turned the pages. About halfway through he found himself peering down at his wife; Mary smiled up at him. Although he wanted to flip past her as quickly this time as last, he did not do so. He forced his hands to operate at normal speed—and this proved not quick enough.

The youngest of the three men, he was about fifty, said, "Her I recognize. Well, I think I do."

Joe closed the album. "But you're not sure."

"Let me see her again."

Joe, who had become very tense, reopened the album.

"Nice looking piece of ass," commented the man. He kept staring down at Mary for some time. "Yeah, I saw her within the last few days."

Joe said, "She's the one who checked in here with the black man. Is that what you're telling me?"

"No, no. With a white man."

Joe closed the album with a snap. "What did he look like?"

The clerk thought about it. "Tall guy, I think. Lots of muscles. Him I don't remember. She's the one I remember."

Joe's voice had become a monotone. "Why is that?"

"The guy was taking her upstairs to fuck her."

The most powerful word in the language.

It made Joe shift his weight from one foot to the other. "What was it about her that you remembered?"

"Just that I would like to have fucked her myself."

More powerful than the word God. This time it made Joe flinch. "You couldn't possibly remember this specific woman," he said. A sudden vision assailed him: Mary with her legs spread—and some other man climbing between them.

The hotel clerk shrugged.

"You see dozens of women every day," said Joe. "You're making it up."

Suddenly the clerk remembered something specific. "She was carrying a cardboard cylinder in her arms." For him this clinched the identification. He gave Joe a triumphant grin. "You know, like for a rolled-up poster."

Joe knew nothing about any cardboard cylinder. But Mary might have been carrying one that day. She had just come from art class, after all. She sometimes came home with drawings.

The clerk said triumphantly, "That cardboard cylinder was full of heroin, wasn't it? Is that what you think?"

Joe gave a harsh laugh. "You're a regular Sherlock Holmes, aren't you?"

The clerk said, "I remember she stood off to the side

looking embarrassed, while her boyfriend registered. They all do that—pretend they're embarrassed. As if fucking the guy is the furthest thing from their minds."

Joe headed for the door. "You'll be hearing from me," he muttered, and slammed it behind him.

That night he did not go home, but bedded down on the couch in his office. His stomach was churning and he did not sleep. The next morning he drove to his house to ask Mary about the cardboard cylinder. But she knew nothing about it, she maintained.

"Maybe to carry home some of those drawings you do?"

"No."

"No cylinder?"

She glanced up at him, looking a bit wary. "No," she said.

"Good," Joe said. He went into his den to put her photo back in its frame, then got back in his car. As he drove toward the city, he felt relieved. The hotel clerk's testimony had shaken him, he admitted that. But now he wondered what he had ever been worried about. The man had not remembered Mary at all. It could never have been Mary. Eyewitness testimony was notoriously unreliable. This was proven in court in nearly every trial. Eyewitnesses so-called simply could not be believed.

At the Police Academy, the laboratory analysis of the balls of tape had long since been completed. A report addressed to Inspector Hearn had reposed on Captain Lauder's desk for several days, and he had left phone messages for Joe, but his calls had not been returned.

But Lauder too had heard rumors of Hearn's strange conduct recently, of his mysterious investigation. Obviously the balls of tape were part of this case, and Lauder, being curious to know more, persisted with his calls. At last he got through.

"I thought you were anxious to get this report," Lauder began.

Because his investigation appeared to be over, and because this time Deputy Inspector Pearson happened to be standing beside his desk, Joe had taken Lauder's call. He had to begin taking some of them and returning the rest. The case was totally stalled. He had to try to begin behaving normally again.

"Yes?"

"We finished our tests on that tape."

"I've been busy," Joe said. He was sorting through his other phone messages.

"Four separate pieces of tape," said Lauder. "It's a puzzle."

Joe, the phone at his ear, had turned his chair and was staring out the window.

"You don't have one victim," Lauder said, "you've got two."

"No," said Joe, "one victim."

"Lots of hairs on those tapes, and they belong to two different people. The reason we know that is, they're of opposite sexes. It's all in my report."

Pearson, who had come in with a draft of the reorganization plan, still stood beside Joe's chair. They had been going over the draft paragraph by paragraph. To Pearson the important business was this draft. His job seemed safe for the moment, and this draft was the key to it. He waited beside Joe's chair for the interruption to end so as to get back to it.

"A man and a woman," said Lauder, and he laughed. "Unless," he joked, "one of them was a fag. Lot of fags bleach their hair these days, don't they?"

Joe said nothing.

"The woman had blond-streaked hair," explained Lauder.

Mary's hair, Joe thought. That much he knew already. The rest too, probably.

"The guy's hair was black. Still is black, I suppose."

"A black-haired woman," said Joe.

"His facial hair is black too. His beard. You know, his whiskers. There's a difference between a woman's facial hair and a man's." Lauder tried another heavy joke. "I mean, unless the woman is one of these dykes shaves every day."

Joe said nothing.

"Two blindfolds, two gags," said Lauder. "Two victims, a man and a woman. I'll send over these reports."

When Joe had hung up, Pearson moved in even closer. The draft was on the desk, and in a proprietary way he touched it with his pencil. "Of course, Inspector, I realize you'll want to edit this. Probably rather heavily, in fact."

Joe glanced up at him. Pearson was really very loyal, not at all the dangerous man he had at first imagined.

"You won't hurt my feelings with your editing, Inspector."

Abruptly Joe stood up. "Have it typed up, and I'll sign it."

Pearson looked pleased. "Right, Inspector."

Joe was half out the door.

"Tomorrow you'll have it for presentation to the chief of detectives and the PC," said Pearson to his back.

Joe drove directly to the Midtown Art League. He had met Mary's instructor once, a baldish older man. He did not remember his name: he had to stop in at the office and describe him. After that he had to locate the classroom. The art teacher came out into the hall to talk to him.

He wore overalls spattered with paint. There were drops of paint in his beard and on his bald head as well. He shook Joe's hand with great enthusiasm: "Your wife is quite a talent," he said. "She missed the last couple of meetings though. Nothing wrong, I hope?"

"Nothing wrong," said Joe.

"One of the kids got sick, probably. Something of that nature. Well, how can I help you?"

Joe said he was trying to track down a certain cardboard cylinder. He gave the date of Mary's last appearance at the school. Had she left here carrying some of her drawings in a cardboard cylinder?

The painter was nodding. "They were especially successful drawings. Why do you ask? One was a real beauty."

Five minutes later Joe stood on the sidewalk in the sunlight in front of the building, and there was so much moisture in his eyes that he could not see properly. He stood there blinking. "Oh, Mary," he said, and began walking. He walked uptown. He walked up through Times Square. He walked through crowds past the windows of the sex shops, he passed under the marquees of the porno movies. He walked up Seventh Avenue past the big hotels, past Carnegie Hall to Fifty-ninth Street. Across the street was Central Park. He crossed through the traffic and went into it. He was walking fast under trees, as if intent on getting somewhere. He was breathing hard, but had no destination in mind. At last he had all the proof he had been avoiding. The rapist did not march his wife into the hotel at gunpoint. She was already in there. His Mary.

With another man. But you knew that already, he told himself, didn't you? You must have known it. Sure you did. You knew it from the start. You're a policeman. You've heard all kinds of stories, and you never believed Mary's. You may have wanted to believe it, you tried to delude yourself. But you knew the truth all along.

He walked in dappled sunlight. There was a warm breeze against his face, in his hair. He walked in the park along an alley of trees. There were kids roller skating on the asphalt paths, clackety-clack. Since he knew all along, then why was he suffering this much now? His pain was physical, it was in his chest, in his throbbing skull, but it was intellectual too. He knew the intimacy that existed between husband and wife, between him and Mary, and was trying to understand that Mary had shared this intimacy with another, and it was inconceivable to him. He could not believe that all along she had had a secret life, a life of her own that he didn't know about—three hours a week at the Art League, sure, but not this. He could not accept the idea of her laughing, talking, touching some other man, satisfying another man sexually. A man he did not know. Such conduct was inconsistent with her character as he knew it. A situation confronted him that he could not comprehend. His Mary. His trust in her had been so total. He could not understand how she could have betrayed him so, carried on with another man without telling him, without him knowing anything about it. His Mary.

There were rowboats out on the lake. People, couples mostly, drifted around in the sun. He began to skirt the lake. He passed a pushcart that was surrounded by kids buying ice cream. There was a glare off the water and a glare off what he imagined to be his wife's behavior, and he felt blinded. He could barely see.

A little later he left the park. He started downtown on Sixth Avenue walking against the flow of traffic. He did not know what to do next. He believed he had to do something. He was trying to settle on a course of action. He could not simply do nothing—his own pain was too great. His life up to now had been one of action. Always he had turned to meet fate head-on, and he wanted to do the same now.

A tangle of possibilities began to move through his head. They came in no logical sequence, and some were not logical in themselves. He was suffering so much that he could not think straight. If he confronted Mary, what? She would never tell him her lover's name. He knew her. She wouldn't do it. Furthermore, to confront her would be to drive her into the other man's arms. Is that what he wanted? No. He wanted her back. If he confronted her their marriage was over, and he did not want it to be over. He wanted her more now than he had ever wanted her in these nineteen years, more even than he had wanted her that first night they had ever spent together, in a hotel at the beach with the noise of the surf coming in the window, and mingling with their whispers of love for each other. He had to have her back, but this would be possible only if he remained silent. He would have to remain silent or lose her. If he confronted her she would hate him, especially if her love affair with the other man was over, which perhaps it was. If she thought her husband had caught her in the act so to speak, she would leave him. Her pride would make her leave him. His only chance was not to confront her. She must never know he knew. All he asked was the chance to win her back.

In the meantime he had to learn who her lover was, for the face of every man they knew was running through his head, and in that direction lay madness. He would identify the man. His search for the rapist would now end, and his search for Mary's lover would begin. One investigation would give way to another. He might find that the affair was over. He might even find that there was no man, that he was imagining all this. It was possible. He would do nothing rash until he was sure. To look for the man at the very least would postpone the end of their marriage, his ultimate loss of his wife. It would give him time to make Mary fall in love with him again.

That afternoon he stopped off at the Police Academy where he checked out a voice-activated tape recorder. When darkness came he slipped unseen into his own cellar, opened the junction box, and attached the machine to the telephone wires. From now on it would record any calls Mary made or received.

The tapped phone was one part of his plan, and the surveillance of Mary another. Beginning the next morning he took up his station at the end of his street, and waited to follow wherever she would lead him. He sat there all that day and into the night, and she left the house only once, at noon, wearing a cocktail dress. At noon. He did not recognize it as a cocktail dress. He did think, She's all dressed up, she's going somewhere. And his stomach turned over inside him, and he began to tremble.

But to his intense relief she led him only to the supermarket and back.

The second day she did not leave the house at all, and for Joe that day passed very slowly. As a young detective he had often sat on long surveillances. It was what detectives did. They watched and they waited. It had never bothered him then.

Each night he sneaked into his own cellar and checked the tape recorder. There was nothing on it but the ringing of Mary's unanswered phone.

A dozen detectives, meanwhile, milled around Harlem and Bedford-Stuyvesant, and no one came by to take their reports or give them direction. The Narcotics Division reorganization plan was presented to the police commissioner by Deputy Inspector Pearson who, when asked the whereabouts of his commanding officer, replied that he did not know. With downcast eyes, he modestly accepted congratulations for the plan, and left the PC's office with instructions to begin implementing it—and with the feeling that his own career had just taken a great leap forward. He had instructions too from an angry Chief Cirillo—to find Inspector Hearn wherever he might be and to inform him that he was ordered to report to the chief of detectives' office forthwith.

The third morning Mary came out again, this time wearing a flamboyant orange dress that Joe, who had long since forgotten her sister's wedding, did not recognize at all. Again Mary led him only to the supermarket and back. He sat in his car for most of the rest of the day, calmer now, wanting this surveillance to be over, knowing that any additional information he might obtain would only cause him more suffering. Nonetheless, he was still on post when she backed out of the driveway late in the afternoon and headed for the high-school baseball field.

After watching her park on the first-base side of the field, Joe drove around the school to the faculty lot. He pulled into a slot between two other cars and watched her come in his direction, crossing the field toward home plate. She was dressed in pants and a sweater now, walking purposefully, almost angrily, toward home plate, and it seemed to Joe that this outing by Mary was harmless too, and he was feeling an emotion that was certainly relief, almost happiness. So far there was no indication that Mary had a lover, that any such man existed. Joe was willing to believe it. He was willing to give the whole surveillance up, to put aside his suspicions entirely, to blame his own distraught imagination. In the days following the rape of his wife he had been half out of his mind, and that explained it. So had Mary.

Now he watched her speaking to Loftus, the baseball coach. They stood in the dust at home plate, in plain view of everyone. Clearly this was not any lover's assignation. Now their conference seemed to be coming to an end, for Loftus had walked off several paces. Joe had already turned the key in the ignition. He was preparing to back the car out of the lot so as to be in position to follow Mary home.

And then Mary slapped Loftus. His wife slapped the baseball coach.

Perhaps it was surprise more than anything that made Joe cry. He had not expected to find his proof here and now in bright sunlight on a baseball field.

It was then that he had put his head down on the steering wheel and wept.

15

FOR DAYS JUDITH HAD WAITED FOR JOE HEARN TO
come back, or at least return her many calls, but this did
not happen. For some reason he did not want to call her
or see her. She told herself she only wanted to pursue her
case, The Case, but if this was true, then why did she
simply not commandeer other detectives elsewhere? She
had more than enough stature to do so. Why wait for Joe?
Technically district attorneys did not outrank police commanders, but on a practical level they did. They were
thought to have political power, and sometimes did have,
and they were lawyers, so instinctively cops feared them.
Law enforcement was like a dangerous machine full of
gears and cogs. This machine was run by lawyers. Cops,
who only serviced the machine, sometimes were dragged
in and mangled. This rarely happened to lawyers. Lawyers
were people who put cops in jail, but rarely went to jail
themselves. So Judith could have demanded detectives
from almost any commander. There might have been ini-
tial resistance, depending on how she presented her
case, but if she insisted they would have been accorded
her.

She knew this.

But she hated to throw her weight around. Perhaps it
was because she was a woman among too many men, but
doing so seemed to her the worst sort of ugly behavior. It
was behavior that men resorted to without hesitation everywhere, whether necessary or not, which was part of the
reason the world was in such a mess. She was not a man.
Usually she refused to do it. She would much rather take

the time to make people want to help her, want to do a job her way.

And so she had waited for Joe Hearn and each day she was consumed by emotions more virulent than the ones the day before. Frustration was the first of them, the longest lasting, and the hardest to bear, because it was fueled by the hope without which it could not have existed at all. The next ringing telephone might be Joe. In the meantime she paced and waited and was unable to concentrate on the normal business of her office. Each day's new victims meant little to her and her young assistants seemed like strangers.

Next came terrific disappointment—Joe was not going to call. She had no idea why—some failing on her part surely. She abandoned herself to self-pity.

Lastly came anger. She refused to be treated this way. She would wait no longer for Joe Hearn. She did not need him, nor any other detective either. Gradually she worked herself into a rage, and after that she began acting entirely out of character.

Gathering up her seven photos, she forced them into a manila envelope, then went down into Centre Street and hailed a taxi. She would go up to that building on East Seventy-eighth Street alone. She would show her photos to the doorman, the super, to other tenants perhaps. She would advance the case by herself, and afterwards she would call up Chief Cirillo and complain about the way Hearn had treated her. But as she rode uptown she realized she had no notion of how to proceed when she got there. She was not a detective. She was acting on impulse and emotion only and this was against all her training as a lawyer. Why was she behaving this way? Furthermore, except for her envelope, her glossy blowups, she was unarmed. Not that she imagined she was walking into any danger. What could possibly happen in broad daylight?

At Seventy-eighth Street she got out of the cab. The building's awning came from the door out to the curb. There were similar awnings the length of the street. They made tunnels of shade on an otherwise bright sidewalk. In front of the door stood the building's doorman. His uniform was blue. So was the awning over his head.

She crossed toward him. "Is Mr. Santoro home?" It was

Santoro who owned both the New Jersey car and the apartment here.

"Who should I say is calling?" replied the doorman, who had retreated immediately inside to his switchboard. He had already picked up his handset.

"Wait," said Judith, and she frowned. For some reason she had expected the apartment would be empty. If instead Santoro was home, then this affair became suddenly much more delicate.

"Don't ring," she told the doorman, adding hastily, "Can I ask you to do something for me? Can I ask you to look at some photos for me?"

But the doorman's eyes became evasive. The question was too much for him. His job was only minding the door, and he peered around as if searching for someone else who could answer something so momentous.

Putting her envelope down on the shelf beside him, Judith reached into her purse, for she understood about doormen, and she handed this one ten dollars. She watched the bill disappear and his mood change.

"What you want to know?" he said.

He was a foreigner by his accent. Italian, perhaps. Judith had only three names to go with her seven photos, but all three sounded Italian to her. Maybe all seven would be Italian. Perhaps she was dealing with a Mafia narcotics ring, and now she was trying to interrogate an Italian doorman. She wished that she were not alone. She wished she had stayed in her office where she belonged.

A moment later her anger at Hearn returned. For four photos she had no names at all. That's why she was here—to try to identify these people. She did not need Hearn or anyone else, and she was not afraid of doormen, Italian or otherwise. Give her the names, and she could find addresses to go with them. With addresses she could find out telephone numbers, the plate numbers of cars. Phones could be tapped, cars tailed.

Judith decided to go ahead. From her envelope she withdrew the photo of Santoro. "So who's this?" she asked brightly.

The doorman threw a glance at the photo. "Mr. Santoro."

"Right," Judith said brightly. "Very good." She felt not like a detective but like a grade-school teacher encouraging children to stick up their hands. "Let me ask if you recognize any of these other photos."

The doorman's head began nodding. Already he looked pleased with himself. He recognized them all. He said, "I see them come in here with Mr. Santoro."

"Very good," said Judith again. Her brightness had become forced because she didn't know what to do next. What would Joe Hearn do in her place? If he were here.

"Is Mr. Santoro a big tipper?"

"He tip good."

"How about these other men?"

"They never give nothing."

"Well, good," Judith said. Stupid questions one and all. She was stalling. "Now we're getting somewhere."

"Why you want to know?"

"I'm trying to prepare a surprise for them."

She was stalling for time in which to consider a new line of questioning, one it was perhaps unwise to pursue. At last she said, "I guess they have a lot of girlfriends," she said. "I guess they have good parties up there."

"I only work daytime."

"But a lot of girls do come here to see Mr. Santoro, don't they? You ask their names, don't you? And then you ring upstairs, right?"

"He tell me just send them up."

"Do you know any of the girls' names who go up there?" Judith tried to sound casual. If she could find the name of just one girl she would have her complainant.

"How I going to know their names?"

"I see." She nodded her head several times. "You got me there." She studied her photos. They were laid out on the shelf below the doorman's switchboard. She had become more and more nervous, fearing that if she pressed this thing she might blow the entire investigation. "You're absolutely right, you know that?" This was a job for detectives, not female lawyers. They would know exactly what to do next, whereas she was only guessing.

Then with equal suddenness, she became disgusted with herself. She saw herself as no better than some of the young rape victims who came before her. In the crunch, a female's instinct was to give up too easily. If Judith left now, having asked no further questions, it would change nothing. This doorman was not going to forget that she had given him ten dollars, that she had conducted this strange interview. He was not going to forget viewing the photos. In fact, to continue questioning him might be the most effective way to seal his lips, as it would turn him in effect into her co-conspirator.

She was still not thinking about possible physical danger to herself.

"Let's go over these photos again," Judith said, and she pointed to the first of them. "Do you know this man's name?" It was the brute with the bald head and tattooed arms, the one who looked like a pro football player. Of all the men who had assaulted the girls on videotape this one had seemed the most vicious. In the photo he was wearing a T-shirt and had his arms folded across his chest.

"He don't tell me his name."

"But you see him here a lot?"

"Every time Mr. Santoro come, he come."

And Santoro was there now. This should have been a warning to Judith, but she was listening only for the sound of the man's name. She didn't hear any warning. "How about this next one?"

The doorman, it turned out, could put names to none of the photos except Santoro's.

"Well, can you tell me this?" said Judith. Her bright manner was back, she was pushing hard, forcing the case as far forward as it would go. "Can you tell me which one of these men is the photographer?"

"The girls, they're models. The agency send them."

"Do you know the name of the agency?"

"The girls say to me their name and what agency, but I no remember. I tell them, Mr. Santoro say go right up."

Behind the doorman was the lobby. Antique furniture, potted plants, walls paneled halfway up in old oak like a church. There was an elevator door as well, Judith saw, and at that precise instant it opened, and a man stepped out. He wore a business suit and carried a briefcase.

It was the bald tattooed brute last seen nude in instant replay.

Judith's pictures still lay spread out on the shelf, one of them this man's face, but she could not move. She froze. She failed to scoop them up.

The doorman turned and saw the man also. "You want I ask his name?"

The man had paused to light a cigar, a delay that perhaps saved Judith's life. She lunged for her photos, managed to collect them into a pile more or less, and she flipped them upside down. On his way past her, the man casually looked her over, then continued out the door into the sunshine outside.

Judith had trouble catching her breath. With stiff fingers she shoved her photos back into their manila envelope. To the doorman she said, "Thank you, you've been very helpful." She practically ran past him out onto the sidewalk.

The man had almost reached the corner. Judith was so tense she was having trouble making her knees bend. She had the envelope under her arm, and she followed the man. At the corner he turned and started down Lexington Avenue, and she went after him. He strode quite briskly. His shoulders looked even wider than on videotape, and he seemed to communicate an even greater physical force. He was not really bald. The back and sides of his head, she saw, had been shaved.

Apparently his cigar went out—as he stopped to relight it Judith almost ran into him.

There were huge encumbrances in her brain and she was trying to push her way through them. She had no experience or training at tailing suspects. She felt feverish. It was not simply physical fear, though she knew she felt some—any woman would, she told herself. If he chose to drag her into a doorway or alley he could probably dispose of her quickly with his bare hands. But she was even more afraid of making a mistake that would blow the investigation.

She decided to give him a bit more ground, and as she walked, her eyes began raking the sidewalks, searching for a cop. She could flash her credentials, order him to arrest the man. Would the cop obey her? Would the brute meekly surrender? She passed windows displaying leather goods, designer clothes. The streets were full of shoppers. If there was a shootout someone would get hurt. The windows of one or more of these shops would come crashing down from the bullets. Suppose she got the cop killed? Anyway, she didn't see one. Anyway, she couldn't afford to arrest this man yet. There were three other rapists out there. Arrest this one, and his confederates would disappear. She would not be able to keep him on ice long enough for the other arrests to be made.

The man still strode purposefully down Lexington Avenue. His cigar kept going out; again he stopped to relight it—this time Judith was far enough back that she was able to turn quickly toward a shop window to avoid attracting his attention. She understood why surveillances were rarely conducted by single individuals. An individual had no options; two or more men had many. Judith herself could not even stop at that phone booth there and call for help.

She began to curse herself. Tailing this man was not her job. It was a police job. It was perhaps Joe Hearn's job, but he had rejected it and her. As she marched along behind the bald man she again became very angry.

To hell with Joe Hearn.

At Lexington Avenue and Seventy-fifth Street the bald man entered a parking garage downstairs under a building. From the sidewalk a ramp curved downhill, and he went down it. Judith peered down into the gloom, and hesitated. The man had disappeared around the bend. Taking a deep breath, she went down the ramp after him. It's a public garage, she told herself. Nothing's going to happen.

She came out into a cavernous low-ceilinged room. Five or six cars were parked among the pillars. The place reeked of stale gasoline fumes. To the rear was another ramp that curved farther downhill. It seemed to plunge down into the bowels of the island. Nearby was a cashier's booth with a shabbily dressed attendant standing in it. In front of him stood the bald man who as Judith approached handed across a parking stub. The attendant put the stub into a cylinder which he thrust down a pneumatic tube. The cylinder disappeared with a clap and a whoosh, and the bald man, who had his wallet out, handed across money.

Judith stood directly behind him while this transaction took place, and marveled at how law-abiding the lawless were most times. He was paying his check, just like anyone else. She stared at the middle of his back and felt herself in the presence of genuine evil. He exuded it, or so she thought, and she began almost imperceptibly to shiver as if the emanations of evil came off him like drafts of icy air. Never in a courtroom standing beside the accused had she felt anything like this, and some of them were evil men. But their crimes by the time she met them had been reduced to words in a procedure. This man's crimes, as preserved by modern electronics, she had watched with her own eyes.

The man had stepped off to the side to wait for his car to be brought up. This put Judith in front of the booth searching through her pocketbook. "I can't find my stub," she explained to the attendant, and she went on pretending to look. The shabbily dressed attendant was patient with her. She put her pocketbook down on his chair and began removing objects from it. There was no one else in the garage that she could see, no customer on line behind her, no other workmen, no one to whom she could cry for help.

The bald man, she noted from the corner of her eye, was watching her rather too closely. She was still rummaging through her things, beginning to be frightened, when a new Cadillac came squealing up the ramp. A pimply youth was at the wheel. He came onto the flat much too fast, so that all four tires protested as he jammed on the brakes. Jumping out of the car, he held the door open for its owner.

"Have a little consideration for my fucking car," the bald man told him angrily. "I was going to give you something, but now I'm not going to give you nothing." With the cigar clamped between his teeth, he sat down behind the wheel, pulled the door closed, and drove up the ramp toward Lexington Avenue.

The car had New York plates. Behind him, her hand trembling, Judith noted down the numbers.

She gave the car time to move out into the street. Then more time, until her heart had stopped pounding. Then she walked up the ramp herself. She stood outside in the sunlight: the Cadillac was gone. She had sweated into the pads of her dress, she realized. Her underarms were soaked, her back too. All that fear merely to acquire a few numbers, and she stared down at them in her hand. Then she peered down the avenue. No Cadillac: she was safe.

On the corner was a luncheonette. She went into it and sat down on a plastic stool that turned under her weight. She sat in the steamy heat, still sweating, and ordered a cup of coffee which she did not drink and a leaden doughnut she did not eat. She understood another thing now too: why cops came to care for their partners so deeply. It came from sharing the strongest of all human emotions, which was not love or hate, but fear. Cops experienced shared fear over and over again. Fear was a thicker glue than love. It was shared fear that bonded them so closely, a bonding from which she herself was forever excluded, however much she might feel for cops or claim to understand them. They didn't care for and understand district attorneys, who to them were only lawyers, protected by big desks and big degrees from what cops called "the street," meaning the doubt and danger—the pure, unadulterated fear that went with jobs such as she had done just now.

She sat in the luncheonette until she felt normal again, and tried to decide what to do next. It occurred to her that she could go back to the apartment building, identify herself (truly this time) to the superintendent, and interrogate him. Up on the roof he had seemed a decent man. She could perhaps learn a great deal more from him, perhaps even enough to get a search warrant on Santoro's apartment.

But she knew she did not want to go back there. Admit it to yourself, she thought, you're afraid.

Yes, she thought. I am alone and I am afraid.

Later, when she had got back to the Criminal Courts Building on Centre Street, she sat at her desk and brooded. Think out carefully what you want to do, she cautioned herself. Don't do anything rash.

She went upstairs to see Inspector Davidoff who was the commanding officer of the District Attorney's squad, to whom she briefly outlined the case so far. She suggested he call in whatever sergeant he meant to assign to head the investigation.

"Is that something we have to do right now?" inquired Davidoff. "I'm a little shorthanded, and—"

"Now," said Judith firmly.

He looked at her.

"Now," she said again.

A sergeant was called in, a pleasant-faced young man named Delaney. Judith drilled him until certain he grasped every aspect of the case. She handed over her seven photos, the Cadillac's plate number, the location of the apartment on Seventy-eighth Street, and the phone number of Captain Sample in New Jersey. She outlined the steps Delaney was to take. In an hour, she told him, he should have the bald man's name and address from Motor Vehicles, and by tonight he should have set up his surveillance teams. Within a week he should have all the other suspects identified as well and be able to show their names to modeling agencies. One or more agencies had dealt with one or more of them, had sent girls to Santoro's apartment. When Delaney had found the correct agency, or agencies, he could begin canvassing their models, and this would give him his complainants. With a single complainant he could get a search warrant on Santoro's apartment. He would find further evidence in there, Judith was certain—more tapes or drugs or guns, address books identifying still more complainants. After that, Delaney had only to make his arrests. The case was already broken, she told him. All he had to do was follow through.

"How many detectives will you need?" she asked him. "Six?" Six was a lot, and she saw Inspector Davidoff wince.

But the young man, unaware of his commander's reaction, nodded.

"All right, Inspector Davidoff, see that Sergeant Delaney has six detectives. It's your case," she told Delaney. "When you request your search warrant, your arrest warrants, you come to me. Or if you need a wiretap order, or something. Otherwise I don't want to hear from you until you are ready to lock those four rapists up, and hopefully the other three men also."

Delaney, looking pleased, even eager, shook her hand as she left. She reached her own office feeling both indignant and relieved. As far as she was concerned The Case was over. She had washed her hands of it. She had washed her hands of Joe Hearn too.

16

But Judith remained upset all day, and there was no one to focus this emotion on except the absent Joe Hearn. At dusk she held her regular staff meeting, and although her young prosecutors made their usual jokes the gallows humor did not reach her, and while they laughed, she only stared moodily out over her desk. Later she came out of the building onto the sidewalk in the dark, intending only to head for the subway and home. Instead, with nothing else to occupy her evening, and with the events of the day still churning in her breast, she found herself marching toward Police Headquarters.

Police Plaza seemed to her as vast as a football field as she strode across it. The paths were delineated by rows of lampposts, by rows of small trees. The trees would be glorious things twenty or thirty years from now, if they lived. Her heels rang on the machine-made paving stones underfoot. All the paths converged on the headquarters building, a squat, square fortress in red brick with windows like embrasures. Lights still showed in many of the windows. She did not like the look of the building—the architecture was heavy, oppressive, and too close a match for the public conception of the police mind. Nor did it fit the prevailing architecture of the area, which ran to office towers crowded one upon the other, or else to colonnaded public buildings in imitation Greek.

She went into headquarters, showed her credentials at the security desk, and took the elevator to the twelfth floor, Hearn's floor. She was already cooling down, and even felt rather silly. But since she had come this far she

decided to satisfy herself that Hearn was not in his office—
and why should he be at this hour?

But he was. From the hall, she saw him through his
open door standing at his window, his back to her. In his
anteroom the duty sergeant sat reading a magazine at one
of the desks, his chair tilted back, and Judith, striding past
him, did not slow down.

The tilted chair came down with a crack. The duty
sergeant had time to say only, "Lady, you can't go in
there—" And then Judith was past him, had burst in on
Joe Hearn. Hearn, who had turned from the window,
looked surprised to see her.

The sight of him infuriated Judith. "How dare you not
return my phone calls?" she said. "How dare you?"

Hearn's first action was to step around the desk to close
his door on the duty sergeant, who by then was standing
in it with his mouth open.

"Listen—" Hearn said.

"No, you listen." Her voice began to rise, and with it
the heat of her words. But it was as if a part of her stood
off in the corner watching herself, and she was amazed at
her performance. She was not, under normal circumstances,
a woman even to raise her voice. Why was she behaving
this way? Did The Case mean that much to her, and if so
why? Or was it something else? And as she asked herself
this question her tone became less strident, she turned
down the volume, and she watched Hearn's reactions more
carefully. But he only stood behind his desk and took it,
offering not one word in his own defense.

This was not normal either, or so she judged. "What
possible excuse can you offer for not even returning my
calls?" she demanded.

"I've been busy."

"Not good enough."

"I've been terribly busy."

"On what?"

He stood with his hands resting on the backrest of his
chair. He wore a brown suit. His shirt was pale pink. His
tie was brown with small pink designs in it. He looked
really very nice, except for his face, which showed, she
suddenly realized, an expression of total defeat.

"On what?" she repeated.

His chin seemed to tighten slightly, or perhaps it was

his mouth. "My wife is carrying on with another man," he said and abruptly sat down in the chair.

What was she to say to this? She could not go on berating him. She could not comfort him in any physical way either. She did not know him that well. This was a police office high up in the headquarters building and there was a sergeant on duty just outside the door. But Joe's distress was obvious, and her heart went out to him.

"I just found out for sure a couple of hours ago."

She still did not know what to say. "Have you had dinner yet?"

"No."

"Let's go have dinner together," she said.

He studied her for a moment, then said, "I'm afraid I wouldn't be very good company."

"You have to eat." This seemed to her as asinine a remark as she had heard lately. It was the classic response of all women everywhere in times of crisis, and it seemed to her that a modern woman such as herself living in modern times ought to have thought of something better.

"Come," she said, "we'll have a drink first and we'll talk about it, if you want to. And if you don't, then I'll tell you what I've done with our case in your absence. I think you probably need company." And she gave him a smile. When he did not react, she went around the desk and took his hand. She drew him to his feet and then toward the door. But as she reached to open it, she was careful to let his hand drop. The duty sergeant was not blind. She was not interested in starting rumors.

She took him to a neighborhood restaurant near her apartment. During dinner she plied him with wine, and also with those questions she thought he wanted to answer. The wine loosened his tongue, but so did her sympathetic ear. Obviously his need to talk was strong. And her need to hear him out, she soon discovered, equally so. Gradually her questions became more probing. They were very skillful questions. She had had a great deal of experience probing for details that persons across from her, usually women, were reluctant to divulge.

There was no self-pity in Joe Hearn, or at least none showed. There were, however, a great many rueful pauses, rueful grins. He was like a man who had been in a car crash, his first, and he was trying to figure out how it had happened. His wife's lover was their son's baseball coach, apparently.

"A big muscle-bound jerk," Joe said. "I didn't even know she knew him."

Judith poured more wine into his glass, but he only turned the stem between his fingers, making concentric circles on the tablecloth.

"It was such a shock," he said. "Such a surprise."

"How can you be so sure he's the one? Or even that anyone is the one?" Judith had begun to sense that there was more to this story than she had been told so far. Which was usually the case. Human sexuality seemed to be attached so tightly to the soul that a bruise to the one also bruised the other. People simply could not talk about sexual trauma very well without causing themselves intense pain. However, a sufficient degree of pain seemed to be missing from Joe's narrative up to now. Where was the pain, and why did he not show more of it?

"I still can't believe it." Joe was staring at the table, and his chin seemed to pucker slightly. This was perhaps evidence of the pain Judith was looking for, and yet it seemed both too slight and oddly placed.

"You say you had no reason to distrust your wife?"

"She's just not that kind of woman," Joe insisted. "And we were very happy. At least I thought we were happy. She had everything she wanted."

Judith completed the thought for him. "—Or at least you thought she had everything she wanted."

A silence fell between them. For once Judith could not pour more wine into his glass. It was still full. And so she waited for him to resume speaking.

"When I came to believe there was—somebody—I thought it might be someone from her art class. She goes to art class in New York every Wednesday, did you know that?"

Judith watched him.

"But there are only about three men in that class, and they're all fags."

It seemed to Judith that details like this were being used to cover up other details.

"That jerk of a baseball coach. It's hard to believe, isn't it?"

"I don't know. I've never met the baseball coach."

"I suppose you might say he's good-looking. But Mary's, you know, very artistic. I never thought she'd go for a baseball coach. And he's younger than she is, too."

"Women do strange things sometimes." Judith continued to watch him carefully. The restaurant was rather dimly lit. The candle on their table threw flickering light on the planes of Joe's face. She could see more pain there now than before, which meant they were perhaps getting closer to the rest of the story, the part he had so far not told her.

"So how did you find out about the baseball coach? I mean was it some busybody who told you, or what?"

"I was driving up to the house this afternoon," Joe answered after a moment. "She was just backing out of the driveway. I thought I'd follow her to wherever she was going and come up behind her and give her a big kiss and surprise her."

An outright lie, Judith believed, the first he had offered her. She was sure of it. That married couples sometimes surprised each other in such ways was possible, she supposed. Never having been married she could not be certain. Obviously Joe had been tailing his wife, an unusual step for any husband to take. Why?

"All right, you were tailing your wife and she went where?"

"I didn't tail her, I was just, you know, following her. She went to the baseball field." He broke off.

"And then?"

"She had an argument with him, and she slapped his face."

"She slapped his face?"

"That's when I knew."

Judith studied her plate. She had scarcely touched her food, but Joe had eaten even less. Raising her eyes, she watched him take a long swallow of wine. "Eat something, Joe," she said gently. She did not want him drunk.

But he only shook his head in a disbelieving way and said again, "That's when I knew."

The explanation—one slap—was insufficient. Because Judith was accustomed to thinking in law-enforcement jargon, the words that came to mind now were law-enforcement words. The charge against his wife was adultery, for which he lacked probable cause.

"Joe," she said, "is there something you're not telling me?"

These too were words that she used in her work nearly every day. Legions of wronged women came before her and nearly every one tried to hide whatever details seemed to her most shameful.

"There is, isn't there?" said Judith.

And so the whole story began to spill out: the rape of his wife, his own investigation, and then all the corroborating details that proved his wife's story false. These tumbled forth one upon the other: the two pairs of handcuffs, the four balls of tape, the statement of the desk clerk, the cylinder of drawings that Mary had denied owning.

"She was already in there with the baseball coach when the rapist broke in."

She has well and truly betrayed him, Judith told herself. If some other woman goes after him now, Judith thought, Mary Hearn would be getting only what she deserves.

There was still no self-pity in Joe that she could see. He was not weeping, merely trying to come to terms with what had happened, and it was difficult for him. "Whatever she may have done, she did not deserve to get raped," Joe said.

Judith watched him.

"If she felt she had to have an affair," Joe said, "I guess that's my fault. I guess I didn't give her enough time, or enough love."

"It's not her fault she got raped," Judith said, "any more than it's your fault that she cheated on you."

"I don't like that word," said Joe.

"I'm sorry."

For a time neither spoke. Then Joe asked for and paid the check, and they left the restaurant. At some point during dinner they had ordered a second bottle of wine. Joe Hearn had drunk most of it. In the street he was by no means drunk, but he appeared, under the circumstances, too cheerful. Judith thought about him driving home to Long Island, and the idea caused her concern. They walked along in front of brownstones on a street lined with small trees. The streets of Paris, London and certain other places she had visited were often lined with big trees. Not here. New York trees died young.

They came to Judith's apartment building, and stopped. The doorman stood just inside the glass looking out at them. It was a balmy spring night. A moon hung above the rooftops, and a warm breeze came along the street from the direction of the river. It ruffled Judith's hair, the sleeves of her dress.

"How do you feel, Joe?"

"Fine. I feel real fine."

"Will you drive home now?"

He looked away from her. He peered down the street into the distance. "I don't know. I hadn't thought about it. Home, or back to my office. I've been sleeping in my office a lot lately."

Judith looked up at her building. She could not see much of it. It was red brick and rather old, with decorations in brick and stone over the doorway, and over those lower windows that she could see. "I don't think you should drive a car just yet," she suggested.

"I'm fine. I really am."

She had shared his pain and felt a closeness to him. She knew she did not want the evening to end. Perhaps what she wanted was to feel closer to him still, but her thoughts were not specific. She refused to think about it, and told herself she was merely worried about him driving thirty miles or more in his present condition. She wanted him to come up to her apartment, but did not know how to phrase the invitation. She did not want to sound coy. She did not want to sound too forward either.

They stood there nodding at each other. Finally Judith said, "You should sit down somewhere. You should wait another half hour or so, before you get behind the wheel of a car."

"Well—" said Joe.

"I'll make us both a cup of coffee," she said nervously, "and you can drink it more slowly than you drank that wine, and then you can drive safely home."

"Okay," Joe said.

And so they went in past the doorman and rode the elevator up to the sixteenth floor. Judith stood on one side of the cabin, Joe on the other. He did not leer at her or smirk. Mostly he looked at the floor, as did she.

Once inside she installed him in her living room and handed him a magazine to leaf through, while she went into the kitchen and busied herself making coffee. But when she turned around she found he stood in the kitchen doorway watching her.

They drank their coffee sitting at either end of the new beige sofa which she had bought only the previous week and was very proud of. She was feeling contented and domestic, whatever might happen next, if anything. She was no longer sure what she wanted. Whatever it might be was so awkward. There was no way around the awkwardness. It was awkward in the nature of things, and then afterward sometimes it was more awkward still. She had not had very much experience, and never anything that had felt absolutely right to her. Now she was aware of strange feelings for the man at the other end of the sofa, and was unable to decipher what they were. He was a married man, and she knew better than to get mixed up with a married man. And yet his marriage was over, or appeared to be; he talked as if it were over. During the past two hours he had exposed to her a good part of his soul. She cared for him a great deal, and believed she understood him. Her feelings were intense but confused. What she felt for him now might even be love, or at least the beginning of love. She didn't know. Perhaps it was only pity, mixed with a yearning to mother someone. Up to a certain age everything in one's life is clear-cut, or seems clear-cut, she thought, and after that almost nothing is clear-cut. In a courtroom she knew her way, there were rules, and within the rules she could let her emotions sway her and the jury both. Outside of a courtroom, surrounded by real life, she wasn't sure of herself at all. She knew only that any display of emotion was an invitation to get hurt, badly hurt, sometimes mangled.

Brooding over these thoughts and others, staring into her cup, she suddenly slipped her shoes off and turned to face him, her feet up on the sofa, her skirt pulled down over her knees. Her posture was modest enough, and somehow it was a good deal more comfortable. It was as if she were facing toward where the accident was about to come from; it would no longer take her by surprise.

Joe Hearn then did a strange thing—he kicked his shoes off too, and spun around on the sofa to face her, the soles of his feet pressed against the soles of hers, his toes gently pressuring her toes. She found this rather cute, and it made her smile.

His coffee cup was empty. So was hers.

"A couple of weeks ago," Joe said to her, or perhaps only to himself, "I thought I had everything in the world I wanted." He stopped.

Judith had only to make some benign remark or other to send him out into the night. For instance: do you think you can get home safely now? Almost any remark would do. She knew this. But instead, she opted to continue their dialogue. She said, "And now what do you want?"

In law school she had been taught never to put leading questions to a witness. A lawyer sought responses that were known in advance. Anything else was to invite surprises, and no one functioned very well when surprised. Surprise turned one's knees to jelly which was bad enough. But it turned one's mind to jelly as well.

"And now," said Joe, "I want you."

This was certainly a pleasure to hear. She wanted to grin, but counted herself too old for such a reaction now. Caution was always called for, things were rarely exactly as they seemed. And so she smothered her grin, converted it into a kind of sad smile, and said, "No, you don't. You've been terribly hurt, that's all."

His toes were still pressed against hers, hers against his. It was the oddest form of physical contact imaginable. They were actually touching each other, and yet in such a way that a more intimate touch than this was not even possible without some awkward shifts of position. But neither of them moved, and Joe said nothing, only looked into her eyes, and his mouth worked a bit, but no sound came out.

"You're just looking for a bosom to lay your head on," she suggested.

"Yes," he said, "yours." So he hadn't contradicted her exactly, and the words seemed so stark that she was unable to read into them anything at all, not love or even the possibility of love, not passion either, a curious intimacy perhaps, and possibly, on his part, fatigue. He was tired of running.

Abruptly she stood up. She was more confused than ever, and also she was almost overcome by a feeling of loneliness. She was as alone as she had ever been. When Joe embraced her she felt a stubble of beard against her cheek.

"Oh, Joe," she said, "I'm not sure this is a good idea."

"Neither am I," he answered.

"You should either go, or—"

"I don't want to go." He gave an anguished kind of laugh. "I have nowhere to go to."

She stood in his arms being embraced, and then kissed. During the kiss her soul seemed to go flying out of her into the darkness outside, where it began searching around for his soul. She couldn't tell whether it found it or not. She didn't know whether what she hoped for from the future was even possible, much less likely. Only the present was possible, and she had best take it before the offer was withdrawn.

"All right," she said, "you can stay."

She led him by the hand into her bedroom, which was dark, and then set about arranging things. She switched the light on in her bathroom, leaving the door three inches ajar. She peeled her bedspread down, folded it, and placed it on a chair. When she turned back to look at Joe, he had removed his coat and folded it carefully on a second chair. His hands were pulling at his tie, not in any fevered way, but taking care not to damage it or to communicate haste—exactly, she supposed, the way a man got ready to go to bed with a woman he had loved and known intimately for many years—a wife, perhaps. But she was not his wife. He was standing there in his pink shirt and brown trousers, both hands at his collar, the handle of his revolver visible above his belt. Even as she watched he removed it, placing it on top of his already folded coat. He was very neat, as neat perhaps as the young policeman who had seduced Miss Carlson. Miss Carlson had cried rape, but she herself would not. Judith's brain was racing. She was standing there as if stricken, thinking about guns and cops, guns and mankind, about man's need not only to kill, but to compress the instrument of killing into the tiniest possible package. She was thinking about the bringing of that package into a room dedicated, at least during the next few minutes, to love. So she was thinking about love as well.

Love was man's other need. Woman's too. And if you didn't have it, your need for it became, at times, desperate.

Her policeman had stopped undressing, and he watched her. She was conscious of the awkwardness again. It was always awkward, there was no way around it, though sometimes the man could reduce the awkwardness by embracing the woman, by undoing buttons that her own wooden fingers were having such trouble with. But tonight Joe came no closer to her. He only watched her, his own movements suspended, until she got her dress undone and let it fall forward down her arms. Then she watched him as his undershirt was lifted up and over his head. His shoulders were broad, and there was a tangle of curls on his chest, and the attraction he exerted on her was so powerful it made her feel weak with pleasure. But she looked away quickly, afraid to stare at him lest he stare back. She was no longer a young girl. Her body perhaps would not please him at all.

Then she was in bed with him, but so tense that she sought to warn him, except that it came out sounding like an apology. "I was very romantic as a young girl. I'm not very experienced at this." She might have told him that she had been still a virgin when she became a district attorney, and for several years afterward, that she had always wanted to get married only once, that she had wanted for a long time to be a virgin on her wedding night. She thought he had a right to these explanations, and even started to speak them.

"Hush," he said softly, and kissed her, and after that it was better, and she began to relax and to bask in the heat that came off his body. Presently this was followed by a new awkwardness, but it only lasted a moment, and from then on everything that happened seemed absolutely natural. He was provoking sensations such as she had not known herself capable of, which caused her to think briefly of his wife, on whose body he had had so much practice, this wife whom she was betraying as much as Joe was, so that in the few moments of introspection left her, she sought to justify her own conduct, and her lover's as well, thinking: I'm not breaking up his marriage. No woman can break up a marriage. It was already broken up, or I wouldn't be here now, we wouldn't be here now, these exquisite sensations would not be occurring.

About twenty minutes later, lying up against him, curling his chest hair round and round her forefinger, she thought again of his gun on top of his clothes on her chair. There had never been a gun in her bedroom before. She said, "Joe, did you ever shoot anybody?"

"Once," he replied, and he began to laugh. "I sort of shot him, anyway."

"Is it so funny to shoot somebody?"

"It was this time."

She was totally at ease with him, so that she imagined they would always be at ease with each other now, every time they met for as long as they both would live.

"The case started the night of our fifth wedding anniversary, fourteen years ago. Mary was in the car with me."

"If your wife is in this story, I'm not sure I want to hear it." She could say anything. It was a delicious feeling, there were no taboos.

Joe laughed again. "She's only in it for a minute."

"Fourteen years ago," Judith said, "I was still in law school. I wasn't a district attorney yet." It was, she remembered, the tail end of the era of old-fashioned romanticism—she wore skirts to school every day.

Joe and Mary had been to a restaurant and then to see the musical *Hair*, new that year. About midnight they were leaving a parking garage for the long drive back to Deer Park. The car on the ramp ahead of their Volkswagen was a Cadillac. Its driver turned his head, and Joe recognized a major drug mover named Carlo Tuminaro.

Both cars turned downtown along Broadway. At Forty-seventh Street both cars stopped for the light. The theaters had all let out by then, and the sidewalks were crowded with people. The penny arcades were still open and crowded. So were the shops. The movie marquees were still lit up, flashing on and off. Broadway was one vast flashing billboard as far ahead as anyone could see. This was Times Square at night and Joe, waiting for the light to change, stared at the side of Tuminaro's head and saw none of it.

Beside him on the seat Mary was tired and wanted only to get home. But Joe, operating on impulse, decided he wanted to tail Tuminaro, and he did so. The two cars passed under the face of the Camel billboard that blew huge smoke rings out of a round hole of a mouth. Ahead, the electric bulbs that circled the waist of the Times Tower spelled out the news of the day. It was a while before Mary even realized what Joe was doing, and began to protest.

"I had nothing on Tuminaro except rumor," Joe said as he stroked Judith's hair.

"You were a brave lad."

"Tuminaro didn't know I was tailing him."

"No, but your wife did."

Below Times Square the lights faded out and the sidewalks were empty. The office buildings were empty and dark. Tuminaro turned west toward the river. With Mary sulking in her seat, Joe followed Tuminaro downtown under the West Side Highway. The prows of ships protruded out over the street. Sometimes between the piers Joe caught glimpses of the Hudson, the water glowing like coal under the stars.

Tuminaro parked at a warehouse on West Street opposite the docks and went inside. Though it was nearly one o'clock in the morning lights still showed in there. The warehouse belonged to an importer of pizza ovens. Tuminaro was not, Joe knew, in the pizza business. Joe had turned the ignition off and he waited.

"You can imagine Mary," said Joe to Judith. "This is our anniversary and we still have fifty miles to drive to get home."

At first Joe had pleaded with her to be patient, he said. But later he became angry in his turn. If she wanted to go home so badly, he told her, she should grab a taxi to Penn Station and take the train.

"It cost me a fifteen-dollar bottle of perfume to patch that one up."

"Wives," said Judith. She had begun subtle shiftings of her weight. She wanted him conscious of her, not another woman.

"What would you have done?" Joe asked.

Her leg had moved onto his. "I'd have reloaded your gun for you," she said. This made both of them giggle, for her movements had produced in him a definite physical reaction.

"I think you're doing just that," said Joe.

A little later Judith said, "You certainly do like to make love." But the words came out from between clenched teeth, almost a series of grunts, and there were tears of joy in her eyes.

And a little after that the story resumed. The next day Joe had opened a major investigation into Tuminaro. He had men on the case around the clock. A shipment of pizza ovens reached the warehouse from Sicily. About an hour later three men with suitcases came out and got into a Cadillac.

"We tailed it to an apartment house in Queens. One of those white brick buildings. Looked like a hospital. Tuminaro kept an apartment there under another name." Presently they watched the buyers arrive, two other men who also carried suitcases. These suitcases would be full of money.

"I sent one car racing to the district attorney's office for a search warrant," Joe told Judith. "Not a district attorney like you," he said, giving her bare bosom a friendly pat, so that the words made her smile.

From the back of the other car he watched the building through binoculars. But he could see nothing. "I'm going up for a closer look," he told the detective who was with him; "stay here." And he sauntered down the street. Just then Tuminaro himself came out carrying a Val-pac over his shoulder, plus some hand luggage.

"I saw that my detectives were never going to get back with the warrant in time." But Joe's narrative had begun to slow down, and his voice had gone off slightly.

"If you keep doing that," he said to Judith, "I won't be able to get to the end of the story."

"We can postpone the end of the story."

"Is that what you want to do?"

"Yes. Oh, yes. Oh, Joe, yes."

After a time she laughed and said, "I'm ready for the end of the story now."

"No more interruptions?"

"I promise."

"When Tuminaro went back into the building, I followed him. I was about ten paces behind. The elevator door was just closing."

Joe had raced up the stairs, gun drawn. He hid in the stairwell until he heard the apartment door open for Tuminaro, then rushed forward. Pushing Tuminaro in ahead of him, he sprang into the apartment.

He was face-to-face with seven people, including two women. There were suitcases open on the floor that were full of white powder in plastic bags. There were two other suitcases open on the bed, and they contained bricks of money. It was going to be the biggest seizure both in drugs and money ever made up to that time, if he survived to make it. But there were three revolvers on the bed also, and when Joe waved his single, five-shot, police .38, and ordered everyone up against the wall, nobody moved.

"Now what?" said Judith.

"Right."

"Were you scared?"

"Sure I was scared," he said, "but there were other emotions too." And he tried to describe what they were.

Standing in that apartment alone against five men he was precisely where he wanted to be, scared or not. He had accepted the risk coldly, calculatingly, eagerly. He must care about me, thought Judith, listening. To reveal feelings as intensely personal as these was a more intimate act than any they had engaged in so far, a self-exposure far beyond nudity or sex, and she felt elated and proud that he would do it.

He had realized well enough, he told her, that in ten minutes he might be dead, in less than that maybe, a strange sensation in itself, and definitely to be examined later at leisure, if he lived. Nonetheless he had leaped at this chance. He had been motivated by ambition, not bravery. This was the best opportunity to distinguish himself he was ever likely to get, his chance of a lifetime. He could build a career on it. He was like any young West Point graduate looking for a war. It was important to see action. Risks had to be taken, because those who survived were the ones who advanced quickly in rank.

He had been twenty-six years old. He had a college degree, and was taking courses at John Jay College two nights a week toward a masters' in criminal justice. But he could still talk tough when he had to. Facing five men and two women alone, he had waved his gun muttering, "I got a fuckin' army downstairs in the street. You fuckers try anything, you're fuckin' dead."

But his "army" did not appear. While Joe frantically thought—or tried to think—what to do next, the five men began to mutter among themselves in a language Joe did not recognize.

"They must have been talking Sicilian. I mean, it wasn't Italian. Some dialect or other. I know enough Italian to know that."

This surprised her. But then he had been full of surprises tonight. "Where did you learn Italian?"

"In the streets."

When the conference in dialect ended, all five men seemed to leap in different directions. At least one lunged for one of the guns on the bed. His own gun clutched in both hands, Joe fired.

"I didn't even know who I was shooting at," he told Judith. He began to laugh. "I saw a hand come up with a gun in it and I fired. It was Tuminaro himself. I aimed for his life-support system, like we've been taught. You know: the head, the heart, the spine. I missed all three."

"Look out," said Judith.

"He was moving, I was moving. What it comes down to is—a man's life-support system ain't so easy to hit."

"You missed him completely?"

"Quite the contrary. I shot the gun right out of his hand. The gun slams into the wall on the fly, and Tuminaro jumps back wringing his fingers, screaming. It was a total accident." Joe was laughing. "You should have seen them fade back after that happened. They must have thought they were dealing with the Lone Ranger."

In two strides he had stepped to the window, smashed the glass out, and called for help. "Dial 911," he had shouted into the courtyard.

Less than two minutes later he could hear the sirens coming from every direction, and knew he was safe, he would not die that day.

"And that's the end of that story," said Joe, and he began kissing and caressing her again. "Would you like to begin another?"

"You already have, I think," she said, and there was awe in her voice, not for his performance or her own, but that something this grand could have happened to her.

"You're gorgeous," breathed Joe into her hair.

"No, I'm not." But it was nice to hear.

"You should see yourself," he murmured. "You're gorgeous."

She realized that men in the throes of passion often proclaimed their love for a woman, even if she was someone they had just met, and she waited, but Joe Hearn, though breathing hard, made no such declaration. She realized also that the act of love sometimes adled judgment, men's and women's equally, same as whiskey or drugs. But her heart was thumping, she was covered with sweat, she could hardly breathe. She had never had an experience like this before, so that, even in the face of Joe's silence, certain words seemed called forth from her. They came up out of her chest as if pulled by some force beyond her control, and they were dangerous ones.

"I love you, Joe," she groaned. "I love you."

Later when he had gone, she stood wrapped in a blanket at her window, looking out over the dark city. Below her apartment, rows of brownstones stretched for four or five blocks in all directions. Then the tall buildings resumed. They rose up in cliff faces, their windows as dark as closed eyes, for there were few lights burning anywhere.

She did not know where he had gone, had not asked, perhaps home. He had promised to call her tomorrow. Looking out the window she saw that it was already tomorrow. The sky was beginning to turn gray, and even as she watched the great red letters atop the RCA Building winked out. She thought then of Miss Carlson whose case she would present to the grand jury a few hours from now.

"Please call," she murmured aloud. "I don't want to be a feeling dirty case. Oh, Joe, please call."

17

In Las Vegas George Lyttle was up early. As he knotted his tie, buttoned his vest, he was whistling softly. Today was to be a busy and important day and he was eager to get to it. Leaving his young wife asleep in the bed behind him, he descended to the cafeteria of this small hotel which was located not out on The Strip, but in the center of the city. Its cafeteria was always crowded at breakfast and George, standing in the doorway, saw that there were no free tables. However, opposite a man in clerical dress was an empty chair and George went over there and put his hand on it saying: "Mind if I join you, Reverend?"

"The birds and the bees beeth comfortable, beeth thou likewise," intoned the cleric. "Thus spake the Lord to Isaiah."

George Lyttle grinned as he sat down, because he knew he was going to enjoy breakfast with this man. "Which persuasion do you represent, Reverend? Any particular one?"

"The proper mode of address is Bishop," corrected the cleric. "Let me give you my card." And he fished one out of his waistcoat pocket, and handed it across.

George studied the card. It read: W. Rollo Wilson, Bishop, Church of the Lord. But it bore no address.

"Bishop or Eminence," said the cleric. "Your Honor. Anything of that nature. As you wish."

"I misrecognized you," said George. "Please forgive my seeming ineptitude."

"Have you finished perusing my card there?" inquired

Bishop Wilson. "If so, let me have it back." And he grabbed it and thrust it down into the pocket it had come out of.

At this juncture a waitress appeared at their table. In common with waitresses all over Las Vegas even at breakfast, she wore a very short skirt, and an ultra-low-cut top, which displayed what seemed to be the principal prerequisites for her profession.

"Have you perused your menu sufficiently, brother?" inquired the bishop.

George found it difficult to peruse anything with this young woman's chalk-white bosom hanging over him. She was not to his taste. In fact she repelled him. The girl in the bed upstairs was small-breasted, her skin chocolate brown and smooth all over, and she smelled like a healthy young woman. This waitress reeked of cheap perfume—of cheapness in general.

When both men had ordered and handed the menus back, George's attention returned to his companion. "And what brings you to Las Vegas, Bishop?"

To which the holy man replied, "Sin."

"A lot of it here," commented George. He was happy. He was looking forward to eating his fried eggs, and mopping up with toast, and drinking two cups of coffee, all the while indulging in fascinating conversation with this bishop here. He had met many interesting conversationalists since landing in Las Vegas, and Bishop Wilson, he could tell, was another. "What kind of sin do you find most preeminent?" he asked.

"Whoremongering, wagering and general lasciviousness," responded Wilson. "Las Vegas is replete with them."

"Sounds profitable," suggested George.

"A veritable Sodomy and Gomorrah," conceded Wilson.

"The promised land, eh, Bishop?"

Bishop Wilson, it turned out, was from New York also, and in fact had once conducted a storefront mission in the same neighborhood in which George grew up. But when questioned about possible common acquaintances, the bishop cut George off sharply. "Since my elevation to the bishopric I ain't had no acquaintanceships there at all."

"I just thought—"

"These days I consecrate my missionary work exclusively to the Las Vegas brand of sin, and area."

George had met bishops like this before. Harlem was as replete with such men as Las Vegas was replete with sin. Nearly all did good business. Bishop Wilson's sonorous tones were familiar to George. So was his selection in each case of the precise apt word. He belonged to a tradition George recognized and felt himself a part of. The problem was, men like Wilson employed their eloquence strictly for personal gain. Wilson was in the business of ripping off the brothers. The real sinners, the oppressors of his people, rarely came within sound of his tongue. Furthermore, he was content to apply his gift exclusively in the religious area. To use it to fight political oppression had probably never occurred to him. It had only recently occurred to any of the brothers, for that matter. Malcolm, yes. Martin, yes. And now Jesse. One or two others. A start had been made in a new tradition, and this was the tradition George was preparing himself for, to become a leader in the fight to win back humanity for his people, to get the oppressors off their backs. It will be our turn soon, brothers, he thought.

Because he was a bishop, Wilson said, a cathedral was being envisioned as necessary to keep up with the eminence of his rank. In the meantime he conducted his diocesan affairs out of a groundfloor tabernacle two blocks away. There he preached doctrine to sinners five or six times a day, or whenever enough sinners turned up to make conversion worthwhile, at five dollars a head, and he invited George to drop in at his convenience.

But George was obliged to decline. He was obliged, he explained, to hasten back to New York within hours, to engage in some missionary work of his own.

Wilson took this to mean that George too was a man of the cloth. "Affiliated or free-lance?" he inquired.

"Free-lance you might say."

"That's the best way to go" conceded Wilson. "General practitioner or specialist?"

George said he tended to specialize. "Fornication and fornicators, mostly," he said.

"Very perspicacious of you," said Wilson, "a most pernicious sin. Very difficult to stamp out." And he again invited George to drop by his tabernacle to watch the repenting. "No charge," he said. "Professional courtesy.

On the house so to speak. The first batch of sinners has usually foregathered about ten A.M."

But again George shook his head. He would be very busy that morning.

Nonetheless he lingered for some time over breakfast, for Bishop Wilson had opinions on a variety of subjects, and once started talking did not seem to want to stop. George listened carefully, studying the holy man's oratorical technique, finding him an ace in declamatory phraseology and the use of the rotund word. It would all go into George's journal later in the day.

They shook hands at the door. "Your mode of address is indeed eloquent, Bishop," George complimented him.

"See you around, my man," intoned Bishop Wilson.

George went out into the street and walked along. The desert sun was already hot. As usual there was no breeze at all. He was wearing an open-necked white sport shirt, and the sun baked his bare arms. Again this morning he noted that the traffic of Las Vegas was replete with pickup trucks, too replete. A man's mode of conveyance was important, George believed, as it identified him to his fellow beings from a distance. If this mode of conveyance should be a pickup truck, this marked a man as lacking in sophistication. In straightforward terms, it identified him as being a hillbilly and shitkicker.

When he came to the drugstore where he had left his film, George went inside. Development had been promised for today, but you couldn't trust druggists, and it was with a certain nervousness that he handed over his stub. He was afraid of being disappointed. But when the druggist fished through his drawer, the photos were there. The druggist gave him the thick envelope of prints, and George paid, then went out into the sun again.

He was too eager. He couldn't wait for a secluded spot to examine his handiwork. He went up close to the building wall, out of the way of pedestrians moving by, and shuffled through the postcardsize prints. The results were marvelous. Every single shot had come out, and he paused to congratulate himself on his photographic skill. He was as delighted with himself as with the photos, and he went through them again, this time in reverse order. Here were the three he had taken of his wife outside Caesar's Palace on the Strip. Didn't she look like deliciousness personified? And the one she had taken of him in their room, wearing his dark glasses and pointing his gun straight at the camera. Then came half a dozen scenery shots of the various famous hotels, followed by a portrait of the two of them standing together near the Roman statuary in the garden of the Dunes—it had been taken by one of the waiters who happened to be passing by.

And finally there were the photos of Mary Hearn and Marty Loftus, and as he studied these, George realized how tightly he had put the tape over their eyes, their mouths. They looked like astronauts undergoing G forces. All the flesh was pulled back. But as photos each one had come out perfectly. Since they had been taken with flash, the colors were rather stark, but the limbs and features of the subjects were sharply defined. This was especially true of the closeups. The ones he thought of as portraits. The crotch shots of Mary, for instance: her every pubic hair stood out, and there was a mole on the inside of one of her thighs which he had not noticed at the time.

George was delighted. He had no doubt that the subjects in these photos would be instantly recognizable to anyone who knew them well. Do you think Mary Hearn's husband won't recognize that mole? he thought. As photos they were perfect for his purposes. Grinning with pleasure he thrust them into their envelope and strode back to his hotel.

When he got up to the room his wife was just getting dressed, and he sat on the unmade bed and watched her. They had been married two years, but to watch her get dressed, or better still undressed, created for him an enchantment. He doubted he would ever get used to it.

His wife's name was Maude, and she approached the bed and turned to let him do up the back of her dress. "What shall we do today?" she asked.

George patted her on the rump to signal he had finished. "Got to go back to the Apple, babe," he said.

"So soon?"

He said, "The ugly world of commerce calls me back."

He handed her ten dollars. "Go down and work those slot machines one last time," he advised her. "I have some business to attend to before I join you."

Looking dubiously at the ten-dollar bill, she asked, "Will you be long?"

"Some letters to write. Two only—enclosing a bill for my services, so to speak."

When the door had slammed behind her, George Lyttle cracked open his attaché case, and from it withdrew two pieces of plain bond paper, plus two envelopes he had bought at the post office—the kind with the stamps already printed on them. He next wrote out two identical letters. They read: "I have come into possession of certain incriminating photos of a certain incriminated pair in certain incriminating surroundings. With these items which I will duplicate and distribute among your neighbors, and in-laws, and around the school, I intend to scandal and discredit your character and your family wherever you are now and in the future. But do not despair. Too often I allow my sense of compassion to override my ruthlessness. I have an alternative. Next Tuesday I will phone you to discuss it. Be there, No answer is no."

Because he thought the language particularly succinct, apt, and to the point, George got his journal out and copied this text into it. After locking the journal back into his attaché case, he addressed both envelopes, one to Mary Hearn, the other to Martin Loftus, being careful to copy their exact addresses off their driver's licenses. Finally he sealed the two letters into the two envelopes and went downstairs where there was a mailbox attached to the wall just inside the front door of the hotel. He dropped the letters into it.

His wife was working the slot machines at one side of the lobby. She had a cardboard coffee cup full of coins, and was moving from one machine to the next, yanking handles down, making the fruit rows spin. He watched her for a time. He found her gorgeous and wanted her to have fine clothes and a fine car, and he wanted this for her now. He wanted the same fine things for his mother. He saw no reason why others should have them but not these two women whom he loved. He needed money for himself too, of course. Because, if he was to lead his people out of the wilderness, then he first needed to complete his education; another tuition bill came due soon. He knew exactly how much money he needed immediately, and how much he might reasonably expect to need during a specified amount of time, and he had thought up, he believed, a slick way to get it. Unlike Bishop Wilson, he was not ripping off brothers, he was only ripping off the oppressors, who deserved it.

His wife seemed to have a gift with the levers. She made the ten dollars last most of an hour. He stood watching fondly as she amused herself. Each time the cascade of coins came out of the box, she squealed like a little girl. When at last her cardboard container was empty, he sent her upstairs to pack.

An hour later they went out through the lobby of the hotel. As they passed the mailbox George thought of the two letters he had dropped in there earlier. Perhaps those letters were already on their way. In the hotel parking lot George threw their bags into the back of the Avis car rented on Marty Loftus' credit card, and they drove out of the city into the desert toward the airport.

"Oh, George, I've had such a good time," his wife murmured.

"We'll be back again soon, babe," he promised her. "You can count on it."

When they were in the air George thought again of his letters which perhaps reposed in the belly of this very airplane, or if not, then in the belly of another nearby in the air, speeding along at more or less the same velocity as themselves, letters that were aimed like arrows straight across the country into the hearts of two fornicators who deserved them, who no doubt had been expecting them for some time and who, opening the envelopes, would not even be surprised, might perhaps even feel relieved that the long suspense was over, and that the chance to do penance was at hand.

18

MARY WAS OUTSIDE WORKING IN HER GARDEN. SHE was wearing sneakers, jeans, a sweater, and gardening gloves on a sunny morning. She was on her knees in the flower bed in the front of the house with a growing pile of weeds beside her. Like her garden she felt herself coming back to life, a little more every day.

The mail truck entered her street.

The mailboxes were on posts out in front of the houses. The truck moved down the street under the trees, stopping regularly. Even without looking up, Mary was aware of its progress, for she could hear each flap being pulled open, then banging closed, followed by the surge of engine as the truck advanced.

Rising to her feet she crossed the lawn to the street. She stuffed her gloves in her jeans and the driver handed her a considerable thickness of mail. He smiled, called her by name, and wished her a nice day.

Already sorting through the pile, Mary moved toward her front door. Since this was Tuesday, there were *Time* and *Newsweek*. There were brochures and catalogs from a number of the department stores at which she held charge cards. There were some appeals from charities she had never heard of, a number of bills, and a bank statement. And there was the letter postmarked Las Vegas. It was the only envelope in her hands that did not announce its contents in advance—not even a return address. Who could it be?

In Joe's den, she put the pile down on his desk. For a while she stood flipping one by one through the catalogs.

One by one, she dropped them into the wastebasket.
Squaring the corners she made a neat pile of the bills.
Since she handled the finances in this house, she would
write out the checks later. She would do it in this room.

The possibly interesting letter was still unopened. She
carried it through into the kitchen where she put water on
to boil, intending to make herself tea. Then she ran her
forefinger under the envelope flap, and withdrew and
unfolded the single sheet of paper inside. She scanned the
lines.

Her reaction was visceral. Her entire body became soaked
in sweat, and as her breakfast rose up out of her belly into
her mouth she tottered and almost fell. All this happened
instantaneously. She barely made it to the kitchen sink
where she vomited unendingly.

When at last the retching stopped she read the letter
again. The words had not changed, and another wave of
nausea came over her.

Her next emotion was rage. Ripping up the letter, she
threw the pieces into the garbage pail under the sink, and
for a time convinced herself that this was the proper
response. An extortion note. It was an outrage. No sane
woman was obliged to take it seriously.

This mood too passed, to be followed by one of im-
mense loneliness. Tears came to her eyes. Her life was
about to fly into pieces, and she was alone. There was no
one she could go to for help.

I was getting better, she told herself. She was cleaning
the sink and weeping at the same time. I was nearly
better.

As she fished the note out of the garbage can, her eyes
were so blurred and she could not see clearly what she
was doing. On the countertop she fitted the scraps back
together again. The one word that leaped up at her was
Tuesday—Today was Tuesday. The phone might ring any
moment.

Just then the telephone did ring, and its ringing stiff-
ened her. It rang again and again, imperiously. Don't
answer it, she told herself. He doesn't know you're here.
I'm not ready, she told herself. I haven't decided what to
say. But she wiped her eyes.

The ringing went on. The instrument rang with all its

authority. She stared down at the letter again: *No answer is no*.

He wants money, she told herself. Tell him he'll get it—whatever he wants.

As she unhooked the receiver she was trying to decide where the money was to come from. Not from the house accounts—Joe would notice. The college savings account in Billy's name? But the custodian was Joe. Her father, then. Her parents lived in a retirement village in Florida. But if she asked him for money she'd have to explain why she needed it. But she could lie. He thought she was perfect, same as Joe, and would never guess.

When she tried to speak into the phone no sound came out.

The voice on the other end said, "Hello?" And then, "Hello? Is anybody there?"

It was a cop talking. Mary recognized this at once. He spoke with the New York street accent which had been so common during her youth, but which one rarely heard now except within the Police Department. Cops were like a separate nation within a nation. They had their own accent, almost their own language, and she nearly wept with relief.

"Yes," she said. "Hello."

It was Chief of Detectives Cirillo, but his voice to her sounded nervous—it did not sound normal. "I think we met at one of those department affairs a couple of years back," Cirillo said. "Or some goddamn place."

Mary knew exactly when and where she had met him: on the street in the village once when she was walking with Joe. Cirillo had made a pleasantry and kept walking.

"I'm afraid my husband is not here," she said.

"Yes," said Cirillo. "Look, I'd like to ask you to come by my house tonight. There's something I want to talk over with you."

"What's it about?" said Mary. It was about Joe, obviously, and she was already on her guard.

"It shouldn't take more than ten or fifteen minutes," said Cirillo. "So will you come?"

"You didn't tell me what it was about." Joe and all other cops might snap to attention when Cirillo spoke, but he held no such power over her.

"It's just something you and I ought to talk over." The

chief of detectives was used to ordering people about, and this habit reasserted itself. "What's a good time? Is eight o'clock a good time? Let's say eight o'clock." And he rang off.

What was that all about? Mary wondered. But her glance shifted back to George Lyttle's handiwork, and Cirillo's problem, whatever it was, faded from her mind. The letter was as fragmented as a broken mirror. It stared up at her, promising seven years bad luck, perhaps more.

Just then she heard a car in the driveway. Scooping up the letter in both hands, she ran upstairs and hid the pieces in a drawer underneath her underwear. When she came back down again she was nervously smoothing her hair, and Joe was in the kitchen.

"What are you doing home?" she asked. The phone might ring any moment. How long did he intend to stay?

He asked for a cup of tea, which she fixed him, and they sat at the kitchen table opposite each other. But Mary could not keep from glancing toward the telephone. Presently an idea came to her, and she ran up to her bedroom where she unhooked the extension. Thinking she had bought herself time, she returned triumphantly downstairs.

"Are you going back to work now?" He was taking forever with that tea.

"I thought I'd take the rest of the day off."

Why today? she thought. Of all days?

"I'll go upstairs and change into something more comfortable," Joe said.

Though he was unlikely to rummage through her underwear drawer, she couldn't take the chance, and so went upstairs with him. As they entered the bedroom, Joe noted the phone lying on the pillow. "The phone is off the hook," he said, and replaced it.

"I don't know," Mary said, not so much speaking as babbling, "how that could have happened." She stood halfway across the room, wringing her hands together. At another time Joe might have noticed, but an hour before he had been relieved by Cirillo of his command; he was locked inside himself and not noticing much.

"What are you doing home?" Mary asked. But he pretended not to hear, and did not answer.

Dressed at last, he went downstairs again. Mary remained behind in the bedroom. She stood at the window

until she could see him in the garden, then ran to her
drawer to recover the letter. She dropped the fragments
into the toilet bowl. Waiting on each occasion for the tank
to fill up again, she flushed it four times, making sure that
every fragment was gone, could not be regurgitated.

From behind the bedroom curtain she spied on Joe in
the garden. He was leaning against the trunk of a maple,
sucking on a blade of grass, staring into the distance. If the
phone rings now, she thought, he won't hear it. Why
doesn't it ring? she asked herself. When it does, then
what? How much money would the caller want? But if she
paid him, his demands would only escalate, would they
not? She would be worse off than ever.

Should she talk it over with Loftus? If he had received a
similar letter he would be in a state of hysteria. No, stay
away from Loftus. With Loftus in a panic, she would have
no chance.

Though she kept turning to stare at it, the phone did
not ring. The strain became intolerable. Ring, for God's
sake, she thought. He's doing this on purpose. He's trying
to drive me crazy.

At last it occurred to her that she could go out into the
garden with her husband. Neither would hear the phone.
The caller would have to call back. Never mind that no
answer was no. The caller could not be that unreasonable.
In any case she couldn't answer with Joe at her elbow.

The grass felt soft under her shoes. Her husband was
now looking across the fence into the next yard. "Are you
all right?" she asked.

"Sure." But he gave her that same funny half smile.

"What happened to the investigation?"

"It's over."

"You didn't find him?"

Joe. shook his head.

It was so ironic it made Mary want to cry. She was safe
from the investigation. Today ought to be a day for cheering.

When she put her hand on his back, Joe responded. He
wrapped an arm around her. They were two people in
terrible trouble, neither admitting it to the other. Mary
was thinking about the letter, and she lay her head on
Joe's shoulder. The result was that Joe's thoughts turned
to Judith. To him Mary's head felt no different there from

Judith's, the two heads felt exactly the same, and he did not know what to do about that part of his life either.

Presently he said, "I guess it's lunchtime."

But Mary, trying to keep him out of the house, said, "I don't have anything for you. I didn't expect you."

So they drove to a Chinese restaurant in the village. Joe was not an adventurous eater. Cops, Mary had found, generally were not. But he had discovered Chinese food a few years ago. He had found one or two things he liked. These he now ordered, and they sat over them for a considerable time. But neither Mary nor Joe was very hungry and most of the food remained in the dishes. They drank a bottle of beer each.

When they came out of the restaurant, Mary said, "What do you want to do now?" She was as ill at ease with him as if on a date.

"I don't know. What about you?"

"I was thinking of going to the baseball game." Her presence was perhaps essential if Loftus was to be forced to start Billy at third base. However, she could not afford to let Joe go home alone. Either both would go to the baseball game, or neither.

Beside her Joe thought, She may be going there to watch Billy, or else to meet Loftus. Was the affair over, or not? His career was in ruins, and to some extent his life, but he wanted to hold on to as much as he could, at least until he decided where he went from here.

"I'll go with you," he said.

School let out at two-thirty, and within ten minutes the players were straggling out onto the field. Mary and Joe took seats in the bleachers beside the third-base line, and Billy acknowledged their presence with a wave. There was no sign of any coach at all. The boys milled aimlessly around, tossing balls back and forth. After a time another teacher came out onto the field. It was Mr. Smote, new this year, a tall, gangling young man who taught social studies and also handled some gym classes on the side. He got practice started, and when the other school's bus pulled up, he called his players off the field, and the warm-up session began for the visiting team. Billy came up into the bleachers and sat with his parents.

"I'm starting at third base, Mom. I'm batting second." The boy was beaming, very happy.

"Is Mr. Loftus sick?" said Mary.

"He went home sick this morning. I think it's the first game he ever missed."

He got the same letter I got, Mary thought. Probably he's hysterical. At the idea she became nearly hysterical herself, though she did not move on her plank. I should call him, she thought, before he blows this thing up. Then she thought, He needs help too. Maybe I can help him. Maybe we can help each other.

But how could she meet Loftus, or even phone him, with Joe around her neck?

In the third inning, Billy singled, driving home two runs, which had his mother and father leaping to their feet and hugging each other. It provided a momentary release from the tensions oppressing both of them. Then they sat down again separately, and the game continued. When it ended they sat in their car in silence, waiting for Billy to come out, each imprisoned inside concerns that seemed insurmountable, totally personal, impossible to share.

But as soon as the boy had slung his gear bag into the backseat and climbed in beside it, Joe dredged up energy, animation, from somewhere, which he projected toward his son.

"The pitch you stung," he said, "the one you cleared the bases with—curve ball, wasn't it?"

"On the outside corner, Dad. I saw it coming. I saw it all the way."

Joe was driving. The two of them, Mary noted, were grinning at each other via the rearview mirror. "And the one before that, Bill, the one you missed. Same pitch, right?"

The boy was beaming. "Right."

"You knew he'd come right back with it, and when he did, POW!"

These fine points were of vital importance to Billy, apparently. That his father had noticed delighted him. He was laughing with happiness.

As Joe drove they replayed the game virtually pitch by pitch. To Mary it was as if they were speaking in code, a secret language males had together. Joe was good with his son, she conceded. He never patronized him at times like this or called him slugger or champ like some fathers did.

Instead of mindless praise, he observed and praised specific details.

"The time he walked you—sinkers, weren't they?" said Joe.

"I was waiting for another curve. Or his fast ball. I would have killed his fast ball."

"Your mother certainly was proud of you. You should have heard her."

"That's right, I was."

"We voted to give the game ball to Mr. Loftus, poor guy. He sure missed a big one."

Joe was good with his daughter too, Mary thought. He always put her to bed. When he was home, he did. He read to her in bed, or told her stories. This is my family, she thought, and it is about to disintegrate.

From time to time, as she prepared dinner she threw frightened glances toward the phone on the kitchen wall, as if the instrument were accusing her of having been absent most of the day. She carried the plates to the table in the dinette. Susie refused to eat the stringbeans, said they made her want to vomit. Mary tried to reason with her while listening for the phone. About halfway through the meal the strain simply became too much for her, and she took a deep breath and told herself the phone simply was not going to ring now, not tonight, the hour had grown too late. He must know that her husband would be home. It may have rung earlier when she was out. It may have rung for Loftus, but she herself had nothing to fear now until tomorrow. She began to breathe more easily, she felt her muscles decontract, and she regained a certain appetite for the food on her plate. Across from her sat her ebullient son, all smiles and confidence, everything in his own small world absolutely right. It gave her pleasure to listen to him, even just to look at him. Convulsions were occurring in that world that he didn't know about. Cracks had appeared on its surface resembling the fissures that preceded earthquakes, but he hadn't noticed a thing. That's what parents were for, she supposed. What mothers were for. To get a child through this stage of his life without noticing any of life's traumas, so that when the time came that he did notice he would be old enough and strong enough to survive.

She began to think about her appointment with Cirillo.

She had scarcely thought about him all day. Should she ask Joe what Cirillo wanted to see her for? Perhaps he would not want her to go. After dinner she busied herself with chores. She stacked the dishwasher and turned it on. She scrubbed out pans and left them to drain at the edge of the sink. She decided not to ask Joe anything. She went down into the laundry room, put a load into the washing machine, and set the ironing board up. Her family was elsewhere in the house—in front of the television, most likely. She didn't check to see. A few minutes before eight she slipped out the back door and hurried along suburban streets toward Cirillo's house. She knew where it was.

Cirillo himself opened the door. He had on a cardigan sweater and seemed nervous: Mary was surprised. When Joe and other cops talked about their superiors, they seemed to accord them an almost supernatural aura, as if these men were immune to ordinary human fears and weaknesses. This was normal, Mary supposed—if you went around calling a man Sir and Chief all day, eventually he began to seem special to you—to himself as well. Mary was not in awe of the chief of detectives, and she was beyond nerves. This interview, whatever it was, was so far removed from her concerns of the moment that she wished only to get it over with.

"Come in, come in, thanks for coming," said Cirillo, leading her into the living room. His wife was nowhere to be seen, and Mary's first act was to cast an appraising eye over the decor. The upholstered furniture was covered in transparent plastic slipcovers, and the wall-to-wall carpeting was pink. On the mantelpiece stood the Cirillos' wedding portrait from thirty or more years ago, and the artworks that hung on the walls were reproductions of bucolic scenes such as one bought at Woolworth's. Her own house was far nicer and Joe was only an inspector.

"What did you want to see me about?" said Mary abruptly.

"Would you like a cup of coffee, a drink maybe?" inquired Cirillo nervously.

"I don't have time for that."

Cirillo paced the pink carpet. He seemed unsure how to begin. "I wanted to ask you about your husband."

"My husband?"

"He hasn't seemed himself lately."

"I don't understand."

"Is something bothering him?"

Now Mary felt herself becoming very nervous very fast. "Bothering him?" she said. "Like what?"

"That's what I was hoping you could tell me."

Mary said nothing. After a brief pause, Cirillo said, "For instance, who's Willie Johnson?"

Mary was a cop's wife. She knew how often cops themselves came under investigation. A cop could be guilty of infractions not only of the law itself, but also of department regulations, many more of which existed than any cop could keep in his head at one time. In the course of her marriage Mary had known of many specific cases. A cop's wife had a number of duties at such a time, and the first of them was to say nothing at all, for she had no way of gauging which detail, should she let it slip, might ruin her husband. Innocent details could have effects far beyond their own weight, and a husband subjected even to departmental discipline faced the loss of pay, the loss of vacation days, possibly the loss of his rank, or even the loss of his job itself, together with the accrued pension rights that went with it.

So Mary said nothing, only stared at Cirillo.

The chief of detectives must have recognized all or most of Mary's thoughts. "He's been chasing a guy named Willie Johnson," said Cirillo, and he hesitated. "Let me put my cards on the table." Her husband, Cirillo said, had diverted vast amounts of department man-hours and money to an investigation involving this Willie Johnson. He had done this to the detriment of his other responsibilities and had continued even after being advised by Cirillo to stop. This was not like the Joe Hearn whom Cirillo had known in the past. "Something's going wrong in his life," Cirillo said, watching her carefully, "and I thought you might know what it is."

Mary still said nothing, she simply continued to stare at him.

Cirillo said, "I thought maybe you and I could talk." He watched her. When she still made no reply, he again offered her something to drink. "Why don't you sit down. We could talk for a few minutes."

"About my husband?"

"Sure. About your husband. I'd like to help if I could."

Cirillo was working hard, and Mary recognized this. She believed also that she understood his concern. Cirillo had sponsored Joe's promotion and assignment to Narcotics. Mary knew Police Department politics. If Joe failed, then to some extent Cirillo failed too. His reputation would suffer. His own influence and standing would be diminished. Obviously he did not want this to happen. But Mary did not care about Cirillo. She cared only about Joe, and she realized that by keeping silent she would learn still more. In any case her loyalty to her husband obliged her to keep silent.

"I thought maybe you and I could talk," Cirillo said, "because you're not like most cops' wives."

"You mean most cops'- wives wouldn't tell you anything?"

Cirillo nodded. Then he tried a smile. "That's right. Most of them are just a lot of dumb broads. No education. No sensitivity. But you're different. You've been to college. You come from a higher level of society than most of the others."

"I don't know what you expect me to say," said Mary after a pause.

"For Christ's sake," said Cirillo, "I'm trying to save your husband from ruining his career. I'm asking you to help me. Today I sent him home. I told him he was relieved of his command."

This shocked Mary. "Oh," she said in a small voice. Hasn't enough happened to us? she thought. Can anything else happen to us?

"But I didn't actually do it yet, don't you see?" pleaded Cirillo.

"You didn't actually do it yet?"

"No order has been cut relieving him of his command. I haven't spoken to the PC about it yet. I didn't appoint anybody else in his place yet. You can save his job for him. But I've got to know what this case is he's been working on. I've got to know what's eating him."

Mary and Cirillo were standing close enough to shake hands. She could have stepped on his brown loafers. His shirt was open at the neck and chest hair stuck out. He was a short, stocky man, only a little taller than she was, and the tension he was under was as nothing compared to hers. She did not entirely believe him, and certainly did not trust him. No street cop ever trusted the headquarters brass. Headquarters had betrayed the men in the street too many times. Those who staffed headquarters had made too many compromises in order to reach there in the first place. Their loyalty now was toward the men above them, not below. This was the traditional outlook of the entire department, an article of faith, part of a religion, almost a commandment. It had been spoken aloud by cops at so many police gatherings over so many years that their wives believed it too, including now Mary. She needed time to think, time to decide. Perhaps she needed to talk to Joe first. But she couldn't talk to Joe. They hadn't talked to each other since this awful thing happened to her. Joe had refused to explain himself to Cirillo; therefore he would never permit her to do the explaining in his place. Mary's ears seemed to be pressing in on her brain. She had to get out of this room, away from its deplorable plastic slipcovers and Woolworth art. She needed air.

"I'll try to find out," she said and plodded toward the door. Cirillo moved to intercept her, and for a few minutes longer continued to plead for her help. He considered himself her husband's friend, he declared, and wished to be her friend too. He wanted her to do the right thing for her family. He wanted to know what Joe's investigation was all about, and why he was pursuing it to the detriment of his career. Only when he knew these things could he take steps to save her husband from himself.

But at last Mary was outside in the night drawing deep, cooling breaths into her chest. She walked down the street away from Cirillo's house, but once at the corner she stood there under the streetlight for some time. A dog walker strolled by her wishing her good evening, and she replied in kind. A few minutes later two joggers ran by, a middle-aged man and his middle-aged wife, and the streetlight shone on the fluorescent fuchsia panels on their backs.

Abruptly Mary spun on her heel and returned to Cirillo's door. Cirillo, opening to her, nodded his head. A slight smile came to his lips, but he must have realized something of the strain Mary was under, for the smile immediately vanished. He said only, "Please come in."

As she marched past him into the living room she neither liked him better nor trusted him more. There had always seemed to her something slimy about him, and the idea of describing to such a man what had been done to her was no more attractive now than before. But she had decided that his arguments were substantially true ones: that her husband was about to throw his career away on her account—his career that meant so much to him—and this she could not permit. She stood in the center of the living room and stared at her hands.

Cirillo said, "How about that cup of tea after all?"

"He's been trying to find the man who raped me," said Mary in a low voice.

"I think you better sit down," said Cirillo. "You better tell me all about it."

When she came in the door, Joe was standing in the laundry room. "You left the iron on."

"Oh, did I?"

He said, "Where were you?"

She tried a smile. "I went for a walk." She knew she sounded caught in the act. The act of what? But she could hope Joe would not notice her guilt, for he had no reason to suspect her of anything, it seemed to her. "I walked as far as Cirillo's house. It's not a very attractive house, is it?"

Her head was too full of fears, plans, options, to think of a better explanation. Her head was churning.

"Do you often go for walks alone at this time of night?"

Now she felt badgered. Her love and sympathy for her husband faded, and with it her compassion. She was under such tension herself that the remark that came to her lips was a cutting one. "You haven't been home enough lately to know what I do after supper."

Joe nodded and left the laundry room. Presently Mary resumed her ironing. I'm sorry I said that, she told herself. He's suffering. I mustn't be mean to him.

Later, when the children were in bed, when their own bedroom door was closed and they were alone with each other, Mary tried to decide what to say about her conversation with Cirillo. Her husband's vulnerability at this time must be intense, but she felt estranged from him. She could not talk to him when the mood between them was as distant as this. She had to get closer to him first, and the way to do that, she believed, was through sex.

And so she got undressed in front of him. Of course she had done this nearly every night of their marriage, but rarely with as much artifice as now. Moving about the room she was half dressed, and then undressed. She turned the bedspread down, found a fresh nightgown, put her slippers out, giving him an eyeful if he cared to look, a wife's inviting gestures, the signal that she was available, if he cared to make use of her. Then they were in bed together in the dark. It was good to have him there close to her, breathing nearby, though he made no move to embrace her. When she snuggled backward against him, his arm came over the top of her, but after that it simply lay there. Nothing else happened. She lay in the enveloping heat of his body and for a time her love for him only grew. He is like some wounded animal, she thought. He is lying up. For the moment it's all he can do.

But this mood passed. She was wounded herself, and could have used more comfort than an arm draped over her that became increasingly heavy. What about me? she asked herself. She began to be angry, and after a time moved away from him to her side of the bed. She forgot his problems and began to concentrate on the extortionist's phone call that doubtless would come tomorrow, would come soon. How should she respond? Loftus would be no help. She did not see how she was going to get out of this thing. Her body became increasingly tense, and the night began to pass, and she did not sleep.

At last it was morning. Having dozed only fitfully, she prepared breakfast, and the children left for school. Joe got dressed and left for the city. Except that he was more than an hour behind schedule, it was the same as any other working day. He gave her arm a squeeze and went out the door to the garage. A squeezed arm was not the same as a kiss, but at least it was not hostile. Nothing had been said on either side. Mary stood in the doorway in her bathrobe and watched her husband back out into the street. Then he was gone. She did not know where he was going. Not to headquarters to his office, certainly. Where then?

She went back into the house and began waiting for the phone to ring.

19

    IN THE GRAND JURY ROOM JUDITH STOOD ON THE topmost tier looking down over the jurors' heads at the young man seated in the chair in the well. Off to one side sat the court stenographer at his machine. The twenty-three jurors seemed to Judith interested in the case. They were paying attention, leaning forward in their chairs. But she could not tell where their sympathies lay.

She said over their heads, "And did there come a time when you took Miss Carlson back to her mother's apartment."

The jury had already heard Miss Carlson's side of the story. "Yes, there did," said the young man. He sounded scared which, under the circumstances, was both normal and proper. More importantly, he sounded honest.

"Please tell us in your own words what happened next."

The jurors were aware that the young man before them was a policeman. However, he was dressed in a gray suit and a red polka-dot tie. His hair was cut fairly short. He looked clean-cut, and younger than twenty-four. As he spoke, his eyes rose, and his voice became firmer. Some of the jurors from time to time nodded their heads, and Judith noted this and wondered what it meant.

"You say you put your gun down on top of your clothes," Judith said. "Did you threaten Miss Carlson in any way?"

"Oh, no, I kept telling her how much I liked her."

"That you liked her, but not that you loved her?"

A stupid question, Judith thought, even as she asked it. That's romantic me talking. Then she thought: it ought always to be done with love. Otherwise it ought not to be

manipulate the jury, manipulate the law to conform to her own prior belief in the young man's innocence? He was probbly not totally innocent, men seldom were. Perhaps she had decided in his favor only because she so heartily disliked Miss Carlson. If that was the case, then she had betrayed her oath of office. A prosecutor normally could make a grand jury vote any way he or she wished, and Judith had done this, she believed, today. She had emphasized the orange juice, the transparent nightgown. She had leaned heavily on the issue of life-threatening force. She could just as easily have indicted the young man, she believed. Suppress the orange juice, suppress the nightgown, accentuate the heavy threat that the cop's gun represented—that's all it would have taken.

Within a few minutes Judith had half convinced herself that she had perverted the law. At that point the buzzer sounded and the warden, looking startled, jumped up from his desk and went into the grand jury room. He was out a moment later holding the slip of charges in his hand, and grinning from ear to ear. He gave the cop the thumbs-up sign.

Judith took the charge slip and glanced at it. The cop was leaning forward tensely. He was accepting his verdict from Judith, not the warden. She let him wait a moment longer. At the bottom now the slip was marked with two red checks—a single check would have signaled an indictment. Judith turned to him. He was staring at her absolutely frozen with fear. "Case dismissed," she said curtly.

"Well, well," said the cop's lawyer to his client, and he grabbed the young man's hand. "Congratulations."

But the cop was looking at Judith. Rushing forward he embraced her, gave her a resounding kiss, and said:

"What a nice lady."

Judith watched him go dancing out into the hall. She could still feel his kiss, and she heard him whooping down the corridor.

After collecting her papers, she went downstairs to her office where she informed Miss Carlson. To her surprise she felt sorry for her.

Miss Carlson said, "Thank you for—for giving me my day in court." She moved toward the door. As her hand grasped the handle she turned and said, "I'm sure you did everything just right." Then she started to cry. "The only

thing is, he did rape me. He really did. He raped me."
Sobbing, she ran out of the office.

Once again assailed by doubts, Judith began to drum a
pencil on her desk. Did I do the right thing? she asked
herself. Why has it become so hard to do this job? Why
does it seem to become harder every day?

"He did rape me. He really did."

The words seemed trapped inside Judith's skull. It was
as if they were loose in there and could not get out.
Probably she would go on hearing them from time to time
for several days, after which, presumably, she would have
forgotten Miss Carlson, and her doubts would fix on some
newer case, some other decision also made on very little
evidence that affected people's lives, affected their ability
to get through one day after another.

Mr. Katz buzzed her from outside. "There are a lot of
people out here to see you."

Judith stood up and went out. In her anteroom waited
Inspector Hearn, and this delighted her. Sergeant Delaney
was there too, together with an unknown young woman.
Judith's eyes darted from one face to another. Delaney's
presence was puzzling—surely a development in the videotape case, something she needed to know about. And
who was the young woman who wore the tight clothes and
flamboyant makeup? A showgirl or model most likely. She
sat close beside Delaney as if for protection, which identified her perhaps as one of the rape victims.

But Joe was the one Judith wanted to see. She was
suffused with pleasure to see him there, a pleasure so
intense she feared it showed. She wanted to draw him
inside her office, close the door, and not come out for a
while. Since leaving her in the night he had made no
effort to contact her. She had waited for calls that did not
come, and a while ago in the grand jury room she had
understood Miss Carlson much better. But now Joe was
here at last.

Delaney had jumped up, and it was he who spoke first.
"If I could see you a moment right away, Miss Adler—"
He looked anxious.

She could make Delaney wait. Protocol was on her side.
A sergeant would defer to an inspector anytime—for as
long as necessary.

Her need to make physical contact with Joe was urgent,

and her hand shot out before she could stop it. "Inspector Hearn," she said, "so good to see you again." But she wrung his hand only briefly. She had to let go of him at once or perhaps be unable to do so at all. Stepping back she turned toward Delaney. "Sergeant Delaney, do you know Inspector Hearn?"

"It's extremely important, Miss Adler."

Her eyes were still riveted to Joe's face, and the woman in her wanted to be with him immediately. But her prosecutor side wanted to know why Delaney was here, and also who the actress or model might be.

"Excuse me a moment, Inspector Hearn. I'll be right with you," she said. Placing duty before personal feelings, she motioned Sergeant Delaney into her office.

Having opened a briefcase, Delaney began tossing photos down onto her desk, each clipped to a yellow rap sheet. "I've got all four of these yo-yos made," he said. "Intelligence identifies them as low-ranking members of the Persico family. A bunch of morons is what they are, according to the people I've talked to."

Judith picked up the photos and shuffled through them. When she came to the bald man she had tailed through the street she stopped and studied the attached sheet.

"His name is Vito Fillocchio," said Delaney. "A strongarm guy. He once did ten years for murder. He killed the guy by lowering the wheel of a truck onto his head. He was trying to get the guy to talk and he wouldn't, so he jacked up the truck and stuck his head under the wheel. As soon as he talked, Vito lowered the jack the rest of the way. The skull exploded like a melon, I'm told. He's out on life parole."

Cops, Judith reflected, sometimes sought to increase their importance or even to justify their presence by recounting horror stories. They were like nightclub performers—it was their way of warming up audiences. It was a routine designed to win people over. In Delaney's case the horror story proved mostly that he was ill at ease. He had stepped in front of an inspector and now was having second thoughts.

She smiled and said, "That's not the story you came in here to tell me, is it?"

"The girl outside is a complainant," Delaney said hurriedly, "I mean a possible complainant. She's on one of

those videotapes. She said she won't testify. She didn't
want to come even this far. If you don't talk to her right
away I'm afraid we'll lose her, and she's the only potential
complainant we have."

"What's her name?" Judith had stood up and come
around the desk.

"Are you ready?" said Delaney. "She calls herself Peaches
Tree."

When Judith grinned, so did Delaney. He was feeling
better. "Do you want to sit in while I talk to her?" asked
Judith.

He shook his head. "To me she won't admit a thing. It's
better you talk to her alone."

As she stepped outside into her anteroom, Judith was
afraid Peaches Tree would have fled—and Joe Hearn as
well. Especially Joe Hearn. But they were both still there.
She put Delaney and Joe together in her conference room.
"Sergeant Delaney will brief you on the investigation,
Inspector," she said formally. "I'll be with you as soon as I
can." And she waited to make sure he would accept this
second delay. To her relief he nodded and docilely followed Delaney into the adjoining room.

Miss Tree's real name turned out to be Charlotte Bell.
She was twenty-one years old. She sat across the desk
from Judith and wanted to know what her rights were. She
was here strictly to obtain information, she said. She wasn't
admitting she had ever been raped. On the other hand,
she wasn't saying she hadn't been either. She wished
there was a lawyer present, as she had questions about
this alleged rape which may or may not have taken place,
and as to what her legal rights might be.

"Well, I'm a lawyer," said Judith gently. "What would
you like to know?"

"Well, whatever I might have said to Sergeant Delaney,
I might want to deny that if you put me in court."

Judith said, "What shall I call you? Shall I call you
Charlotte?"

"My professional name is Peaches. Everyone calls me
Peaches now."

"I see," said Judith, and she talked to her about herself
and her "career" for some minutes, trying to win her
confidence. The girl was wearing a rather lacy blouse and
pants so tight there was an indentation line along the

crotch. Those pants must be difficult to get on, Judith thought, and almost impossible to get off, and most likely they chafed her severely in sensitive places. She appeared to have a splendid figure, and her face was truly beautiful.

Which was perhaps a lucky thing for her, Judith thought, for her beauty might help her to get through life. To Judith it seemed clear already that the girl—it was impossible to think of her as a woman—was not going to go far on her brains.

Judith began to speak of the rape, but Peaches continued to deny it had ever happened.

"Those four men hurt you," Judith insisted gently, "and they raped you."

"I'm not saying they did and I'm not saying they didn't."

"Come now, Peaches, we know the rape took place. We've seen it on videotape."

Suddenly Peaches burst into tears.

Judith went around the desk, knelt beside her chair, and took her hand. "You can say anything you want to me," Judith told her, stroking her hand. "I promise it won't leave this room without your permission. You don't have to sign a complaint. You can help us put those men in jail for a long time, but you don't have to do it."

Peaches only bawled louder, but when these tears at last stopped she began to blurt out her story. She worked for the Eager Beaver Modeling Agency, she said. (Judith thought, Peaches Tree, eager beaver; at another time it might have made her laugh.) Peaches had been sent on a job up to Santoro's apartment. Her agency understood Santoro to be an importer of Italian bicycles, and she expected to be photographed riding one. An apartment on the twentieth floor of an East Side apartment building did seem an odd place to ride a bicycle, but stranger things than this happened in the modeling game, she said. Peaches duly rang the doorbell and was invited in, and one of the men—from his photo Peaches now identified Santoro himself—told her that the slogan of the advertising campaign was going to be, "Nice seats for nice seats."

Recounting this line, Peaches wiped the tears from her eyes and attempted to smile.

They gave her something to drink, either tea or coffee, she couldn't remember which. After that she didn't feel good. Then they thrust a piece of paper in front of her face. She read, YOU'RE ABOUT TO TAKE PART IN A PORNO-GRAPHIC MOVIE. IF YOU SCREAM OR RESIST YOU WILL BE KILLED.

Peaches began weeping again.

"All right," said Judith soothingly, "you don't have to talk about it anymore. But all this happened weeks ago, and you didn't come forward. Why was that?"

Peaches wiped her eyes with a tissue that came away black with mascara. "They said they'd make stills," she said.

"Stills?"

"They said they'd send the stills to my father. He'd throw me out of the house."

"More likely," Judith said, "your father would have come straight to me." Or if he had a gun, Judith thought, he'd go after them. "A father doesn't throw his daughter out of the house because she got raped," she said.

"You don't know my father." Peaches began to wail again. "And what about my career? They were going to send a second set to my agency. I'd never work again."

"So you decided to just forget about it," said Judith.

"Yes."

"How successful were you?" she asked conversationally.

Not very, apparently. Peaches had since been awakened by nightmares every night. She sat up in her bed in terror and after that couldn't sleep. Her appetite was gone.

"Look at me," Peaches said thrusting out her bosom. "I'm skin and bones."

Judith let that pass. "Don't you think," she said carefully, "it would be best all around if you helped us put these men in jail?"

"Everyone would find out."

"Well," said Judith carefully, "grand jury testimony is secret. If you testified in the grand jury, no one would find out."

"My father would. You don't know my father."

Peaches had stopped crying. She seemed able to turn her tears on and off at will. As Judith continued talking, she looked wary again, though interested, for perhaps she saw herself in a starring role in court. However, she continued to make objections, and finally it seemed clear to Judith that she was not going to agree to sign any complaint today. She would eventually, Judith believed, and she decided to cut this interview short before Peaches became imbued with a sense of her own importance, decided that the entire criminal justice system hinged on her decision, and became impossible to deal with.

Assistant District Attorney Adler terminated the interview by standing up. "Well," she said, "if you change your mind and want to talk to me again, just give me a call." She handed across her office and home telephone numbers.

Peaches looked disappointed. "Is that all?"

"That's all for now. Call me up if you want to talk. In the meantime, we have some other girls willing to sign complaints. You weren't the only one raped, you know."

"Oh," said Peaches, and she thrust Judith's phone numbers into her pocketbook. "I'll think it over," she said. "I may give you a call."

She'll call tomorrow, Judith thought. "You do that," she said, and showed the girl out.

It was by now late afternoon and Judith moved past Mr. Katz's desk into the conference room. Joe and Sergeant Delaney, who were sitting on opposite sides of the table, looked pleased with each other. Judith took the chair next to Joe.

"Is she going to testify?" said Delaney.

"I think so," said Judith. "What else do you have?"

The photos of the rapists were scattered across the table. Judith picked up Vito Fillocchio's picture and stared at it a moment.

"They're button men gradually moving into more sophisticated work," said Delaney. "My information is that they deal in Mexican grass, a little hashish oil, maybe ludes—they're small-time narcotics dealers hoping for better. The brains of the group is Paulie Santoro. A real genius. He's the one who thought up the idea. You photograph actual rapes. You can get relatively big money for films like that. You make a lot of copies and sell them in South America, Europe maybe. The only problem is deciding which girls to rape. One of their solutions was to hire models from agencies for the day. Santoro has a bicycle distributorship and that made a good front. They could hire models supposedly to model his bicycle."

"They must have been pretty careful which girls they picked," said Judith. "It's been going on for months, I gather, and not one girl came in here about it."

"Santoro did a lot of bragging," said Delaney. "You'd

think the silly bastard would keep his mouth shut. But no, he had to tell all his friends. According to one of my informants not all the girls were professional models. Some they hired off the street or out of the key clubs, and those we'll never find. That's why I thought it was so important that you talk to Peaches right away."

A silence fell over the table. Judith picked up another of the photos and looked at it a moment. Rocco Frula, former resident of Greenhaven Penitentiary. Low forehead, dull expression. Were evil and stupidity the same? Sometimes, she decided.

"I'll have to dig out the videotape Peaches stars in," said Delaney. "She's a knockout, isn't she? I'd like to rate her performance."

Judith, who did not think this remark funny, studied another of the photos, and for a time no one spoke. She was mulling over her options. What should be her next move? "What else do you have?" she asked Delaney.

"I interviewed the super of Santoro's building," said Delaney. "He was up in the apartment yesterday to fix the plumbing. He says they have a videotape machine in the back bedroom. He noticed stacks of videotapes in boxes against the walls. Is that enough for a search warrant?"

Judith thought it was, provided they served the warrant almost immediately—within twenty-four hours. "The question becomes, do we want to serve it tonight?" she asked.

"Pick up Santoro," commented Joe, "and the others run."

"Possibly."

"We could wait a couple of days, couldn't we?" said Delaney.

It was amazing how little most cops knew about warrants, even though they dealt in them all the time. Judith shook her head. "The key things any judge looks for before signing a search warrant is specificity and staleness," she explained. "Specificity you have. Your informant, the super, specifies that the evidence is in the back bedroom. And your information is quite fresh. By tomorrow most judges would probably decline to sign a warrant on the grounds that your information was stale."

"Then it's tonight or never. Is that what you're saying?" said Delaney.

Judith nodded. She looked across at Joe, who had said

very little. He was watching her, a half smile on his face. So far he had offered no word or gesture to reassure her of his affection, and she was suddenly fearful to be alone with him.

"What about arrest warrants?" inquired Delaney. "If we could arrest all of them at once—"

"Without a complainant," said Judith, "no judge would sign one."

Arrest warrants represented a special problem, and all three fell silent while pondering it. A warrant gave a cop the right to go into a man's house and arrest him. Without a warrant such an arrest was illegal—under the Constitution every man was supposed to be safe inside his castle; he could be legally arrested only on the street or some other public place. This legal distinction was one cops often ignored. They would drag a suspect out of his house and afterward swear in court that they had arrested him after he followed them out into the hall. It was an explanation Judith had heard dozens of times and had usually not attempted to refute. To some extent law enforcement was like politics. To get along you went along. However, this particular case was too close to her, and she wanted every legal right accorded to the defendants.

"There are ways to get around not having arrest warrants," murmured Joe.

"No," said Judith. "Absolutely not. The difference between them and us is that we obey the law."

"Nobody's going to break the law." Joe grinned at her. "Say the word, and we'll arrest all of them and we'll do it legally."

"How are you going to do that?"

"You'll see."

"I'll see about the Santoro search warrant," said Judith, and she glanced at her watch. The hour was so late that the secretaries would all have gone home. Sh was going to have to do the clerical work herself. "It should be ready about seven o'clock," she said. "What time do you want to serve it?"

"We'll serve it with dinner," said Joe, and he grinned again. "We'll serve them something that will give them a stomachache. Santoro first, then the others."

"We'll obey the law," stipulated Judith.

"Right," said Joe.

Judith spent the next hour with the manual open on her knees, writing out the search warrant and also the affidavit accompanying it. Joe and Sergeant Delaney meanwhile went out for coffee and a sandwich in a diner on Canal Street. After typing out the forms, Judith carried them upstairs and walked along the hall looking for any judge still in his chambers. There were always one or two on hand at this hour killing time before meeting their wives uptown for dinner or the theater. A judge named Eisenfarb read her affidavit. He was new and she didn't know him. He was drinking a Scotch and soda. His robe hung from the peg in the corner, his coat was off and his tie undone. She was ready to answer any questions he might have. Some of these judges were self-styled civil libertarians and had to be begged. But Eisenfarb merely scrawled his name and pushed the warrant back across the desk. He offered her a drink, but she declined with a smile and went back downstairs.

Joe and Sergeant Delaney were back from supper and sitting in her office. "I'll relieve you of that search warrant, if I may," said Joe, and he took it out of her hands, scanned it, and put it in his pocket.

"What's the plan?" she asked.

"Sergeant Delaney and I will serve your search warrant on Santoro," said Joe. "And if the videotapes are there we'll arrest him." He looked enthusiastic. "We've added a pair of detectives to Delaney's group, and we've assigned one pair to arrest each of the others."

"I don't want cops making arrests in anybody's house or apartment without an arrest warrant."

"You worry too much," Joe told her, but there seemed to her a fond note in his voice. "I promise it will all be done legally. Now stop worrying."

He turned away from Judith. "Are you ready, Sergeant Delaney?"

Delaney was in a good mood too. "Ready when you are, Inspector."

"See you later," said Joe to Judith.

"I'm coming with you," she announced stubbornly.

Joe and Delaney looked at each other. After a moment Joe said, "Sure, why not."

They drove uptown in Joe's car. Delaney sat beside him and Judith rode in the back, like somebody's wife. Which she wasn't. In her own mind at least, she was the director of this operation but she had been relegated to the rear, the standard role and place for women all down through the ages. This annoyed her, made her wish to assert herself, and yet Delaney and Joe seemed so boyish and happy at the prospect of action that instead Judith kept silent.

Having double-parked in front of Santoro's building, Joe tossed his police plate in the windshield. Then, before getting out of the car, both Joe and Delaney took their guns out and flipped the cylinders open. After counting bullets, then spinning the cylinders like Western sheriffs, they rammed the guns back in their pants. The only difference between today and 1860, thought Judith, was that the gun barrels were snub-nosed, rather than ten inches long.

This was the first she realized that tonight's arrest was no lark, that cops got shot at and sometimes killed. Earlier she had been too preoccupied even to consider the danger.

Nonetheless, she coolly followed the two men into the building.

"You stay down here in the lobby," Joe ordered her at the elevator. He looked surprised to see she had come this far.

Her stubbornness again surfaced. "No."

As she got into the elevator with them, it seemed to her that Joe was trying to puzzle out where to put her, what to do with her, and when all three had disembarked on Santoro's floor, he began searching for the stairwell door.

"Santoro's apartment is at the end of the hall," whispered Delaney.

Joe had found the doorway he was looking for. In it he placed Judith. "You stand there."

But she had no intention of standing there. As soon as he had turned away from her and was advancing on Santoro's apartment, she left the stairwell and moved up close behind him. She saw him withdraw the search warrant from his breast pocket, and with the other hand draw out his gun. The gun went into the side pocket of his suit coat, and his hand went in there with it. He and Delaney had crept silently up to the door. As Joe rang the bell, both men flattened themselves against the wall. They were so totally concentrated on the door that Judith was able to move up even closer. Just before the door opened, Joe turned and noticed her there, scarcely an arm's length away. "Get back," he hissed. "Back, back."

But she ignored him. She had intended to ignore him all along. Did she, like some of those young cops she met, actually want to be in danger? Or did she only want to go where Joe went, be with him in danger too? Was she already a fair way along toward loving danger for its own sake (just like a man) or did she only accept it as part of something bigger?

Just then the door opened. Joe and Delaney pushed immediately into the apartment. They pushed Santoro backward. For Judith there was finally no danger whatever, nor even any closeness. Joe wasn't thinking of her at all. He was flashing his search warrant in Santoro's face and reciting the legal formula at the same time. He had probably forgotten she was even there. She followed the two cops into the apartment and quietly closed the door.

20

SANTORO WAS A SMALLER MAN THAN SHE HAD EX-
pected, no bigger than a jockey. Was that why he had not
taken part in the rapes personally—because he did not
want to display himself in front of the others? He was
wearing a black pinstripe suit and black tassel shoes on
tiny feet.

The two detectives pushed him into the living room.
They pushed him onto a couch and stood over him with
guns in his face. They could have explained this conduct if
asked: cow him first and have no trouble later. They had
their backs to Judith. Santoro's face was visible between
them. It had turned red, and he was beginning to sputter.
He looked to Judith like a man ferociously blushing, and
she herself moved past the living room and down the hall
into the back bedroom, the supposed location of the cartons full of tapes.

They were there as promised. This was a great relief.
Had they not been, it would have been legally impossible
to search the apartment at all, and of course impossible to
arrest Santoro. They were ranged along the wall beside
the bed, eight or ten cartons stacked in three piles. She
opened the top ones. The videotapes were packed as
neatly as books. She drew out two thick cassettes, turning
them over in her hands. Although they bore no labels,
each was marked with numbers in grease pencil—presumably a code of some kind. The sides of the cartons were
marked in grease pencil, too.

There was a television console in the room over by the
closet door. On top of it sat a videotape player into which

she inserted one of the cassettes. She began fiddling with buttons. Eventually the screen lit up, and she backed off a few steps to see what she had.

The start of this tape was similar to those she had already viewed in New Jersey: the same four men, and this same apartment, though a different girl. Judith pushed fast forward, holding the button down a few seconds. When the picture reappeared, the girl was nude on the floor being assaulted by the bald-headed man with the tattoos, whose name, Judith now knew, was Vito Fillocchio.

She removed that cassette and replaced it with the other. After a short time she realized this was the same film. In any case, it was the same girl. She shut off the machine and walked over and replaced the two cassettes in their carton.

Having done this, she stood indecisively in the bedroom and tried to think out where she stood legally. As far as she knew Santoro himself did not actually appear in any of these films. Perhaps he did, but it would take hours of viewing to find out. She could and would order him arrested right now, even without an arrest warrant, but once they got him back to the station house, what would she charge him with? The charges would have to be specific.

She went out into the living room. "You better call for a department truck to cart the evidence away," she said to Delaney. To Joe, she said, "Read him his rights, Inspector, please."

Santoro's suit, Judith noted, was shot silk. It must have set him back at least a thousand, she thought. He was about thirty years old, olive-skinned, with jet black, blow-dried hair. He had begun sputtering again. "I want to call my lawyer."

"What's his name?" inquired Joe amiably.

Delaney was on the phone requesting the truck.

"Mr. Weinglass," said Santoro.

Judith nodded. So did Joe. They both knew this name. But Joe winked at her, and he stepped to the phone that Delaney had just hung up. "You get your call in a minute," he assured Santoro. "I have to make some calls of my own first," and from his pocket he withdrew a list of phone numbers.

As he began dialing, Judith's mind was still fixed on Weinglass: a very skilled lawyer who devoted much of his energy to indigent defenders. He also defended nearly every Mafia hoodlum who got indicted these days, and furthermore he got most of them off. Santoro would be easy for him, unless more evidence developed. It would be difficult to prove Santoro knew what was on the tapes, even though they had been found in his bedroom. Electronic impulses could not be seen with the naked eye. Videotapes were not glossy photos or even cinema film. He could claim he didn't know, no one told him. In some ways modern technology was a great aid to law enforcement, but at other times it rendered prosecutions difficult or even impossible.

The four actual rapists were the ones Judith wanted, anyway. But without arrest warrants they could not be touched tonight—or for as long as they stayed in their homes. The detectives would have to wait outside. Meanwhile, the subjects would learn of Santoro's arrest by telephone, at which point they would likely go out the fire escape or over the rooftops. After that they would be hard to find. She looked over at Joe at the telephone, and wondered who he was calling.

"Mr. Fillocchio?" Joe said into the receiver. "Mr. Vito Fillocchio? I'm calling on behalf of Mr. Weinglass." There was a pause, then Joe said impatiently, "Weinglass. That's right, Weinglass. Your lawyer, you asshole."

After another pause Joe said, "The cops just locked up Santoro. Our information is they're coming after you now. You better come over here as fast as you can."

Joe's finger pressed the lever down. "There are two detectives waiting in his lobby," he said. As he turned to Judith he was chortling. "In about ten seconds he'll come busting down the stairs right into their arms." He began dialing again.

Santoro had again jumped to his feet. "Wait a minute, you can't do that—"

"Mr. Ritti?" Joe said into the phone. "The cops just locked up Santoro and Fillocchio. You're next. Beat it." After depressing the lever, Joe dialed the next number on his list. "Two down, two to go," he said to Judith, and grinned.

The prisoners, all five of them, were brought to the 19th Precinct station house and locked into the cage in the corner of the squad room on the second floor. Judith stood a few paces off staring in at them. Beside her were rows of desks. Except that the desks were so scarred and stained this might have been a newsroom, even a schoolroom. Some of the desks were occupied. Detectives sat at them or on them punching typewriters, sipping coffee, dialing telephones.

This was not the first time Judith had seen men locked in cages, but it was a sight she never got used to. Each time it made her realize that men were animals too, as lethargic as lions at times, but at others more dangerous than all the wild beasts in the world combined.

Fillocchio said to her through the wire, "Who are you?"

Judith chose not to answer, but from behind her one of Delaney's detectives spoke her name and rank adding, "She's the one gonna put you bastards away for twenty-five big ones."

"I seen you before," Fillocchio said, studying her.

"That may be," said Judith.

"I seen you the other day in the street. You followed me into the garage."

With a nod, Judith acquiesced.

"I owe you one," muttered Fillocchio.

Judith turned away.

Each prisoner in turn was brought out to be processed. They sat on one side of the detective's desk, while Judith stood on the other, holding the penal code open, sometimes leaning over the typewriter to read out the specific charges she wanted listed. The prisoners were not handcuffed, were under no restraint, and the last of them to be processed was Fillocchio. He sat in the chair a few feet away and looked only at Judith. His eyes never left her face. She herself, when forced to glance in his direction, focused on the top of his big bald head. She could feel the power of his fists, could feel the punch that had knocked one girl cold on videotape. She imagined she could feel violence coming off him like an odor. She felt intimidated by him, and this made her angry so that, to the long list of rape and sodomy charges, she added, "Put down first-degree assault as well."

"Where'd you get that from?" said Fillocchio.

"You're lucky I didn't charge you with attempted murder," snapped Judith. She turned away from him.

"You'll get yours, honey," Fillocchio muttered.

"Not from you. You're going to be held on bail so high you'll never get out."

The prisoner attempted to stand, was pushed back into his chair by Joe, and only glowered at her.

All the prisoners were taken downtown to night court to be arraigned. The rotunda there was full of cops and handcuffed prisoners. In the courtroom waited more cops with prisoners, together with lawyers, witnesses, bondsmen. All these people seemed to be in constant motion. They stood up, moved forward, moved back, sat down again. They came and went. This was not a trial courtroom. Trial courtrooms were places of quiet and decorum; they were given over to careful deliberation. Arraignment court was a room bubbling in the aftermath of recently committed crimes.

As she pushed her way down the aisle, Judith saw that the judge on the bench was Justice Forester. For eight hours he would deal with this raucous flood of humanity, with prisoners and victims who were sometimes equally bloody, with arresting officers who were sometimes bloody and disheveled as well, for the most part devoting only a few seconds to each case. It was his job to decide which prisoners were instantly remanded, which ones went free, which ones would be obliged to post bail, and in which amounts. And it was Judith's job, as she neared the bench, to convince him to set impossibly high bail for Fillocchio, and the others. She wanted them to stay in jail until trial.

Forester was normally a trial judge and tonight was filling in for someone. Greeting her, he looked harried. In his own courtroom, Judith knew, he presented a different picture. He was somewhere between fifty and sixty, a big man with peppery hair, manicured hands, and impeccable tailoring. He lived alone, and was rarely seen in public without some young beauty on his arm, models, actresses, or perhaps call girls for all anyone knew. In his own courtroom he liked to talk tough. Also, sometimes he liked to talk dirty. Such language, coming from a judge in black robes sitting high up on the bench, was both shocking and disturbing. Sometimes he looked sexually aroused while doing it.

Judith, as she prepared to present her arguments, remembered the last time she had stood before Justice Forester. She was prosecuting a man who had raped seven

women over a period of two months, but the defendant
had agreed to plead guilty in a single case in exchange for
having all other charges dropped. He had stood before
Forester with Judith on one side of him, and the defense
lawyer on the other, while Forester scanned the papers
that Judith had just placed before him. The only spectators
present in the courtroom were the parents and several
friends of the defendant. Judith had waited nervously, and
she had reason. She was afraid the defendant might withdraw his plea, and she was afraid of Forester.

Guilty pleas in a rape case were never a sure thing,
whatever the defendant may have agreed to beforehand.
To plead guilty to a crime like, say, armed robbery was
cool, most defendants seemed to feel. They would admit
to crimes of violence, then turn around and grin proudly
at any spectators present, as if looking for applause. But
admitting to rape in open court was not cool at all. In fact,
numerous defendants had withdrawn their pleas at the last
moment rather than do it. After scanning the papers Judge
Forester had peered down upon the defendant.

"You're here to plead guilty, right?" he demanded in his
roughest street accent. "Then a month from now you'll try
to withdraw your plea claiming you didn't know what the
charges meant. So I'm going to go over them with you
now, one by one, and you're going to plead guilty to each
and every charge."

And he had taken the charges and translated them from
legalese into four-letter words. He had described the rapist's actions in the harshest street language possible. The
terrible words abounded: cock, cunt, fuck, asshole—all
this from a red-faced, black-robed judge seated high up on
the bench. "And then you fucked her up the mustard trail,
right? Did you come? Answer me. Did you come? Did
you get it off?"

Judith could not believe her ears or her eyes. Judge
Forester looked like a man about to have an orgasm. She
peered across at the court stenographer, who was taking it
all down word for word. It went on so long that Judith
cringed. She thought, This is an act of sexual perversion
too. This judge is as bad as the defendant.

Forester had come to the end of his description of anal
sodomy. "Do you plead guilty to that?"

Except for the noise of the stenographer's machine, the

courtroom was absolutely silent. The young man nodded his head. "Speak up," commanded Judge Forester.

"You fucked her up the asshole," said Forester, bringing his gavel down. "Guilty as charged."

This was the man that Judith now approached. Stepping up onto the platform, she explained to him that five defendants would stand before him as soon as their lawyer appeared. Briefly she outlined her case. She explained about the cartons of videotapes and described the several tapes she had viewed personally. She explained how vicious the defendants were and the difficulty of convincing frightened young victims to come forward for as long as they were on the street. She asked Forester to hold the defendants on $250,000 bail each.

Forester commented that this was more money than they would be able to raise. It would have the effect of holding them without bail.

Good, said Judith. In jail they would be unable to threaten potential witnesses or to rape and videotape any additional young women.

"I see your point," said Forester. Having made a few notes, he promised to fix the high bail requested as soon as the case came up. He even thanked her for bringing this information to his attention. He then turned toward the next defendant and she stepped down from the bench.

Joe and Delaney were waiting for her outside the courtroom.

"Just one or two things more to do," Judith told them. "Then we can go." It was a message directed to Joe, assuming he wished to receive it, but her smile was directed toward Delaney, and her words seemed to be also. So far this day and night she had not had a moment alone with Joe. He was being as careful as she, apparently. He too had given no hint of any intimacy between them. There had been no secret look, no secret touch. He was being so careful that it worried her when she thought about it. The casual acquaintanceship to which both pretended seemed entirely too real to her, more real than any other. The extravagant emotions of the other night had become overlaid by too many normal hours. Time appeared to have erased them so completely that Judith suddenly felt frustrated and upset.

"Fine," Sergeant Delaney said. "We'll wait for you,

then we'll go out and celebrate. I'm hungry. Are you hungry?"

"Famished. How about you, Joe?"

"I could certainly use something to eat," said Joe.

She looked at him for a moment. Well, what did you expect him to say, she asked herself. Did you expect him to answer with some sort of endearment?

She went down the hall to the complaint room and found the young assistant district attorney who would present the case to Judge Forester in an hour or two. The judge had been advised, she told him, and would set high bail. It should be routine from here on. The prisoners should be arriving shortly. She herself would be going out for a bite to eat. After that she would be home. He should call her if there were any difficulties.

By the time she got back into the corridor, Delaney's detectives were there together with their prisoners. They would have to wait for lawyer Weinglass to appear, she told them. They would no doubt be here for a while.

The defendants already knew she had asked for high bail. The handcuffed Santoro was on his feet, armless, his jaw thrust out. "A quarter of a million dollars?" he demanded. "For what? That's not legal. That's unconstitutional."

Judith was watching Fillocchio. "Now you won't be able to knock any girls cold with one punch, will you?" she said. "Not for a while, anyway."

His hands too were manacled behind him, but his face was contorted, his voice menacing. He had risen to his feet. "Whenever I get out, baby, I'm looking you up."

Joe pushed him back down again. Judith was not afraid of him. He wasn't going anywhere. But he continued to glare at her, and after a moment she looked away.

She went out into the street with Joe and Sergeant Delaney. Centre Street was empty of traffic, but the lot across the street was full of police cars. There were blue and whites parked and double-parked in front of the courthouse as well. The criminal justice system was in operation around the clock, but had its peak periods just like any other business, and most of its customers came in at night. Cops and prisoners approached the doors even now, as Judith turned up Centre Street toward Canal. Delaney was on one side of her, Joe on the other. Neither took her arm.

"This is your neighborhood, not mine," Joe told her. "So where are you taking us?"

"There s a restaurant on Canal that stays open all night," she replied. "I've gone there plenty of times."

As they got farther from the courthouse, the streets became absolutely empty and silent. There were pools of lamplight on the sidewalks, with darkness in between each pool, and the city made no sound except for the noise of a police siren a long way off.

"It's been a fun day, hasn't it?" said Delaney, once they were seated in the restaurant. Judith smiled at him. He would go home eventually and then she would be alone with Joe. In any case, she was close to Joe now. Across the table he was smiling at her in a fond way, and she was feeling relaxed and very pleased.

"It's the best case I've ever been on," Delaney said. That a memo about it would go into his personnel folder was certain. More importantly, he believed he now had two rabbis to back his career, one of them a highly placed prosecutor and the other the inspector who commanded the Narcotics Division, and who, about the time Delaney could expect to make captain, might be chief of detectives or even police commissioner. Delaney saw his entire career assured with this one day's work. Contrary to Judith's hopes he was not anxious to go home. These two people were part of today's triumph—and part of tomorrow's future too. Tonight he was sticking close to them for as long as he could.

The dinners they had ordered were set down, and they lingered over them. To Delaney they were like a football team after winning the championship game. The victory would last only as long as they remained together. Once they separated, it would become a thing of the past.

Judith began to long for the meal to end, but Delaney did not know this. After dinner he wanted to order another round of drinks.

"I'm so tired," Joe murmured, "that one more is liable to knock me on my you know what."

Judith said, "Me too." Fatigue had made her want to giggle.

At last Delaney got his timetable out. "What time is it?"

he said, sounding a bit drunk, and he glanced at his watch. "Oh, Christ, I've missed the last train." He turned toward Joe. "Can you give me a ride home, Inspector? I live near you."

This request sobered Judith instantly. Delaney, she realized, must have been planning it for some time. It made her eyes drop, and she stared into her drink. It was a request Joe would not be able to refuse. Delaney could not even be blamed. How could he know of her longing to be alone with Joe? He had seen no signals pass between them all day—they had sent none. They had been too careful, and there was no way to undo such care except overtly, which was out of the question.

She felt trapped and almost overpoweringly resentful. But as she rose from the table she realized how tired she was. She could see Joe tomorrow. They had had a big triumph today, after all.

The three of them went outside onto Canal Street and Delaney hailed a taxi. They rode uptown together, for Joe had left his car outside the 19th Precinct station house. Their cab stopped first at Judith's apartment house where the night doorman was staring out through the glass. He opened the door for her even as she got out of the cab. She said good night to the two men. Joe did not offer to walk her across the sidewalk and into the building, and for a moment she was bitterly disappointed.

Her alarm woke her three hours later. The sun was streaming in her windows, and she stumbled groggily into the shower, where she turned the water on hard and began to wash her hair. Her thoughts were fixed on Joe Hearn. She was not sure of herself. She was not even sure he would call her today. If he did not call, then how long should she wait before calling him? She was kneading her skull, eyes tightly closed. She felt all of the urgent desires of a young girl, but was not a young girl. It was a peculiar situation. She could not even be sure about Joe's feelings toward his wife, his family. How available was he? She felt frustrated, impatient. She did not know how to behave at all.

She became conscious of the telephone. Water streamed down her face and she opened her eyes. It had already rung several times, and she turned the faucets off and stepped out of the stall. She moved out into her bedroom where she grasped the receiver. Her flesh was still faintly steamy, and she clutched the towel in her other hand.

The voice in her ear was full of menace. It said, "You shouldn't have put your name in the book. It makes you too easy to find."

At first Judith thought someone was playing a joke.

"I've been watching you," the voice said. "In fact, I am watching you right now."

It made Judith clutch the towel to her bosom, though the statement was absurd. She was alone in her own bedroom on the sixteenth floor, and the nearest building that rose to her level was five blocks away.

The voice laughed harshly. "Don't try to hide from me. You can't do it." And then, "I'm waiting for my chance."

Judith had stepped into the corner. He's got binoculars or a telescope over there, she thought. He's just a peeping Tom, she told herself, trying to fight down fear. It was a voice she had heard before. Someone she had prosecuted probably. Perhaps one of the psychos. Someone now out of jail. Who?

"How are you?" she said. "I've been thinking about you a lot lately." She had begun to sweat. Her armpits had become sticky, the insides of her thighs. I'll have to take another shower, she told herself.

"You got a nice cunt, I see," the voice said.

"The jury convicted you," Judith told him. "Not me." She was trying to think this out but was groggy from too little sleep.

"I'll be waiting downstairs for you when you come out. You look for me."

Suddenly she placed the voice. Fillocchio.

"I'm going to open it up to your navel. You'll have the biggest one in the world."

Judith hung up. When the phone rang again a moment later, she lifted it and set it back crossways on the cradle.

Once before she had received a similar phone call. It had come at night during a trial from a defendant free on bail. The next morning she had sought to have his bail revoked, but the judge said she was imagining things and refused. So she had phoned police headquarters. She had asked for and got two detectives to guard her around the clock until the trial ended.

She turned the shower back on and stepped into it, and

she was trembling. Fillocchio. When she closed her eyes his bald head and meaty tattooed forearms flashed onto the screen of her mind. Though she blinked several times trying to chase it, the image remained.

Judith was scrubbing herself with a washcloth, but didn't realize it. It can't be him, she told herself. His bond is $250,000, Judge Forester promised. He couldn't raise it. He's in jail.

She had to wait for the dial tone to come back on. Standing dripping wet beside the phone, she dialed her office which was staffed around the clock. Walter Rooney, another of her young prosecutors, came on the line. "Find out the whereabouts of Vito Fillocchio for me, will you?" she asked Rooney. She had to spell the name for him. Her voice was steady, or so she told herself. "He was supposed to be held last night on a quarter of a million dollars' bail. I'd appreciate it if you'd make sure he's still inside."

Rooney laughed. "What's the matter? Are you getting phone calls again?"

"Just find out for me, please."

"Get your number changed. And get out of the phone book."

"I asked you to do something for me."

After drying herself off, she sat naked on the rumpled sheets of her bed, waiting.

After about five minutes Rooney called back.

"He's out all right. I'm sorry."

"I got a call from him."

"They were just about to notify you."

"Weinglass," said Judith.

"He's a good lawyer," agreed Rooney.

There was silence.

"Forester set bail at twenty-five thousand per man," Rooney said. "Weinglass had a bondsman there who posted it immediately."

Judith put on a dressing gown and went out into the foyer to see that the chain was on her door, then went into her kitchen to prepare herself breakfast. She brewed a pot of coffee and sat over it while it cooled, and did not drink it.

She could visualize Weinglass arriving in court just as dawn was breaking. Despite the hour he would have been immaculately groomed, manicured, perfumed. He always was. He would have persuaded Judge Forester that the high bail demanded by the district attorney was not necessary, and in fact was even unconstitutional. It would have been easy for him. Weinglass would have lectured Forester. She could hear his arguments. The purpose of bail, Your Honor, under the Constitution, is to assure the defendants' appearance at trial. It is not, Your Honor, to punish them or put them in preventive detention. They can be punished only after trial and conviction, and preventive detention in a case like this is unconstitutional. These defendants have roots in the community, Your Honor, and are not going to flee. They are men of influence. You, Your Honor, might be—badly hurt—if you insist on such high bail.

There, the kicker, the thinly veiled threat that was part physical, part professional.

And now, Judith brooded, Fillocchio is on the street.

After a time she got up and went to the phone and dialed Joe's number on Long Island. He would not yet have left the house and might still be asleep. The phone might be picked up by his wife. Judith disregarded all these possibilities. She told herself Joe would want to know about this development in the case. She refused to admit to herself how much she wanted to see him, to feel protected by him, to feel the weight of his arms around her. She refused to admit to herself how frightened she was.

It was Mary who answered the ringing phone. "Who's calling?" she said, and then, holding the receiver out to her husband, "For you."

On the stove bacon was frying. The kitchen was full of the odor of it. Mary cracked the first of Joe's two eggs into the pan and watched the liquid spreading, turning white. But she was listening hard. Behind her she heard Joe say, "They're out? I don't believe it." After a pause he said, "You're the only person in law enforcement whose phone number is in the book. Now you know why the rest of us don't do it." But something in her husband's voice ought not to have been there.

Mary's spatula lifted the eggs onto a plate, which she carried toward Joe's place at the table. She heard him say,

"I'm leaving now. I'll be there as fast as I can. Call Delaney and have him meet me there."

"What happened?" inquired Mary when he had hung up.

"I'll eat the eggs," he said, "but I don't have time for the coffee. She's had a threatening phone call from one of those hoods we locked up yesterday."

"What hoods? Are you going to her apartment?" said Mary.

Joe was wolfing down the eggs. He had not even sat down. In response to Mary's question he nodded, and for the first time since her marriage, jealousy entered her life. She felt its first sharp bite and sensed, or perhaps knew, that there was more to this relationship than her husband admitted to. We don't talk to each other anymore, she thought. We barely see each other anymore. I'm suspicious of him and he's suspicious of me.

When Joe hurried out the door to the car without kissing her good-bye she wanted to cry. She heard him back out of the driveway at such speed that his tires showered gravel onto the lawn. He wants to get to her in a hurry, Mary thought.

She had not even had time to talk to him about Cirillo.

Just then the phone rang again, making her jump. But it was only her sister to ask how she was.

"I'm fine," Mary told her. But what she thought was, my husband's lost his job, he may have a girlfriend, our marriage is a shambles, and I sit home all day waiting for a telephone call from the man who raped me who wants money.

"Oh, yes, fine," she told her sister. "How are you, how's the baby?"

21

EVEN BEFORE JOE ARRIVED, JUDITH HAD GOT OVER
her fear. Vicious men were not new to her. Fillocchio was
just another psychotic such as she dealt with every day.
She would take ordinary precautions and beyond that she
could rely for protection on the system.

The system. It did most of the work, and with reasonable care it worked well, if not perfectly. Systems worked
well enough, she thought, if you were careful. She was
trying to buck herself up, and was succeeding more or
less.

By the time Joe came in the door and embraced her,
she was ashamed of having called him in the first place.
She sat him down and made him a cup of coffee, as if he
were her husband. He was not her husband, but there was
no more sexual urgency between them than if he had
been. Perhaps he would have carried a fluttery helpless
woman straight into the bedroom. Not having found one,
he sat calmly at her table sipping from his cup while they
discussed what to do next. She was not afraid of Fillocchio,
Judith said. If she wanted him in custody as soon as
possible—and she did—this was for professional reasons,
not personal ones. Because for as long as he and the others
were on the street, the young women they had brutalized
were not likely to sign any complaints, even assuming
Sergeant Delaney could find them. Nor was Peaches Tree
going to testify alone. She was dumb, not brave, Judith
said, and not *that* dumb. Therefore, all five men had to be
got back into jail as soon as possible—today if possible.

"I'd be satisfied just with Fillocchio," Joe said.

"All of them."

"He's the dangerous one."

Judith shrugged.

"I just don't understand," said Joe, "why you would put your name in the phone book."

The question annoyed Judith. It was one she was tired of answering. Joe annoyed her, and she wondered why. Because he had not carried her immediately into the bedroom? Because he was nonetheless smiling at her across the table with such apparent fondness? Or simply because he already had a life and wife quite apart from her? An embrace lasting no more than a few seconds, a single kiss—it was not enough under the circumstances, or else it was too much.

She would go to Judge Forester and get him to revoke bail, Judith said. She would get him to set new bail at a quarter of a million dollars each. She would go to his house. Right now. She would wake him up.

"What you're proposing is very difficult to do." Joe was shaking his head. "Judges don't like to do it. They almost never do it."

"For me, Forester will do it," said Judith grimly. "I know how to make him do it."

"How?"

"You'll see."

Joe's face wore the same warm smile. It was as if he believed her capable of any miracle she set her mind on. After a moment he said, "If you're sure you can get bail revoked, then we ought to rearrest Fillocchio right away— he's a convicted murderer, for God's sake—while we know where he is."

"We don't know where he is," said Judith.

"Of course we do."

"He could be lurking around outside this building, he could be anywhere."

"You are afraid of him, aren't you?"

"No."

"Well, he's not lurking outside your building. He's home in bed."

"You can't be sure."

"He's sound asleep. For a smart lady, you overlook some pretty basic facts."

"Such as?"

"Criminals have to sleep too. And this one was up all night in court. That's why I say we should pick him up fast—while he's still snoring, if possible. That's the safest way."

"Maybe he didn't go home."

"Why shouldn't he go home? That's where people usually sleep. As far as he's concerned, he's got nothing to fear from us. He's out on bail."

"More coffee?" said Judith, and she refilled both their cups. "On what grounds would you rearrest him?" she said thoughtfully.

"He threatened to kill you, didn't he? That's the crime of aggravated harassment."

"It's a misdemeanor."

"So what? It's grounds for arrest. You sign a complaint and swear out a warrant and off we go. But we should do it fast—within the next hour. Once he finds out you're trying to revoke his bail, and Weinglass will tell him, he'll disappear. Where's Delaney? Is he on his way here?"

He wasn't, and Judith found herself unable to meet Joe's eyes. "I told him to meet us at my office."

"I see."

Judith gazed at him, and he gazed back. Perhaps a slight smile played about his lips, but he said nothing else.

"He'll be there by now," said Judith hurriedly. She was embarrassed. "We'd better leave," she said.

"Okay."

They rode downtown in Joe's car and made small talk all the way. He seemed totally at ease with her. She was not at all at ease. She didn't know where she stood with him. Furthermore, she was worried about the various confrontations that this day would bring, especially the one with Judge Forester.

About an hour later she was in possession of the misdemeanor warrant, which she handed to Joe. He and Delaney went off together, looking cheerful. She wondered only briefly how Joe was able to spend so much time out of his own office.

When they had gone she fished through a filing cabinet and, when she had found the folder she was looking for, caught a taxi back uptown toward the building in which Judge Forester lived.

After talking her way past the doorman, she rose to

Forester's floor and leaned on his bell. As she waited, she was half afraid that some blowzy young woman in a see-through nightgown would come to the door rubbing sleep from her eyes. But this did not happen. It was Judge Forester himself, wearing a bathrobe over pajamas and slippers, who stood in the doorway. He was so surprised that he could think of nothing to say except, "What time is it?" When Judith, carrying her folder, marched past him into the apartment, he first closed the door behind her, then sputtered, "What's the meaning of this?"

Judith began to argue her case: she wanted bail revoked and new bail imposed in the amount of $250,000. She explained, as she had last night, that these men were dangerous and constituted a threat to the lives of their victims, who were also the principal witnesses in the case. She decided not to mention Fillocchio's phone call nor to argue on a personal basis—she had done that the other time and had been refused. Instead she argued calmly, forcefully, logically, professionally, but before she was half finished Judge Forester began shaking his head in a negative way.

"You've forgotten just one thing," he told her. He no longer looked half asleep. "The Constitution forbids preventive detention." He then began to regurgitate the same arguments Weinglass must have advanced in his courtroom a few hours previously, and these were not unreasonable just because they were secondhand.

"I'm not leaving here," Judith told him, "until you see it my way."

"That's preposterous," said Forester.

For a time the discussion remained on an even-voiced, civilized plane. His decision, Forester said, had been made on the basis of judicious reflection and more years of legal experience than Judith had been alive.

Judith interrupted him. "That's an exaggeration, Judge, wouldn't you say?" She certainly couldn't mention Fillocchio's threats now. "Put your clothes on. You're wasting time, mine and yours."

Forester lost his temper. He charged that the executive branch of the government, namely the district attorney's office, was attempting to exert undue pressure on the independent judicial branch, namely himself. Which brought, he said, still another constitutional issue into play, and he began to expound on it. He expounded on it with such ringing anger that Judith felt relieved of all normal restraints on her conduct, and she opened the folder she had fished out of her files and removed the documents it contained. These she thrust into the hands of Judge Forester, saying, "Read this."

As the jurist scanned them his jowls began to quiver. His entire body began to shake, and he demanded, "What's the meaning of this?"

He was holding the minutes of his sentencing of the rapist a month ago. "You translated all the charges into the vernacular, Judge," said Judith with mock sweetness. "Would you like me to read those minutes to you aloud, Judge?" She leaned over his shoulder as if to read from the topmost page, but he yanked it away from her.

"You can't get away with this," he cried.

"I want you to get dressed," said Judith. "I want you to come down to the courthouse with me right now and revoke that bail. I want you to sign the order and give it to me. Otherwise I can't be responsible for what happens to those sentencing minutes you're holding. They could fall into the wrong hands."

"This is the crime of extortion. You're trying to blackmail me."

Judith shrugged. "They're the official courtroom minutes of a sentencing presided over by you. They are public documents. Anybody has the right to read them. Reporters can read them. Politicians who nominate judges for election can read them. Anyone at all. Anyone who knows that they're there and chooses to look for them."

For some seconds Forester only stared at her. His mouth worked, but no sound came out.

Fillocchio lived on President Street in Brooklyn. Joe and Delaney, leaving two other detectives in a car two blocks away, went to look the building over. They strolled on by. This street was Mafia territory and it paid to be careful. The building was old and run down, but was not quite a tenement. Out front was a stoop with three steps and wrought-iron banisters and railings. The two front doors were wood with mullioned glass panels. Strolling around to the rear, they noted the twin fire escapes that zigzagged like great iron shoelaces down from the roof. The eyelets were the windows. Fillocchio's flat was on the left on the third floor. From the courtyard they could see that his shades were down.

"He's in there," said Delaney.

Joe, peering up at the window, said nothing.

"If he comes out that window onto the fire escape," said Delaney, "he can go up or down."

When Joe did not answer, Delaney said, "In my view we put one man on the roof, one down here in the courtyard, and the other two hit his door."

"No," said Joe, "if he comes out the fire escape, I'm going to be sitting there."

Delaney gave him a sharp look. "We'll both be sitting there."

"Not enough room," said Joe.

"That's a sergeant's job," said Delaney, attempting a smile.

"Get the other two men. Give me time to get down from the roof, then hit the door."

"Fillocchio's dangerous." If an inspector got shot while Delaney was supposed to be serving as backup, his career would be over.

"He'll be half asleep. I want to see the surprised look on his face. Get the other men. Now go."

"Please don't do anything till we get back," said Delaney anxiously.

Joe went in through the front door and up the stairs to the roof. The roof door was locked, but he shouldered into it and the jamb split, leaving the lock dangling from its hasp. I've been spending an awful lot of time on rooftops lately, he told himself as he came out into the sunlight. He ducked under hanging laundry and moved to the parapet. Delaney's right, he told himself as he went down the steel ladder, this is harebrained. But his life was a mess and he seemed to be returning to a simpler, more reckless past. He was a young cop again, an ex-collegian, danger was fun, and he was looking to commit an act that would be talked about. He was showing off for Judith Adler. When she heard, she would applaud him, and her eyes would shine.

He crouched in the corner of the fire escape. The window was open about three inches, but it was better not to peer inside. He heard his men begin pounding at the front door, followed almost immediately by heavy movement behind the window. Delaney was below him in the courtyard now, but Joe did not know this. The sergeant had run around into the courtyard, gun drawn. He stood gazing upward, and he was full of anxiety because he was too far below to help if needed.

Joe never looked down. He heard one of his men shout through the door: "Open up, police," and about thirty seconds later the shade snapped up, the window was raised as high as it would go, and a leg came out onto the fire escape. The rest of the bald-headed man clambered out after it. He was still zipping up his fly. When he turned and saw Joe his jaw dropped open. The expression on his face was one of pure surprise, and seemed so funny that Joe began laughing at once. He could not help himself. Fillocchio looked astounded and bewildered at the same time. Laughing, Joe pushed him back inside the apartment and made him open the door to the detectives. By then Joe's laughter was out of control. Tears were streaming down his face and he was experiencing spasms of pain in his chest. Delaney, having left the courtyard, came running up the stairs and into the apartment gun still drawn, and this struck Joe as funny too. The laughter choked him. It doubled him over, and he had to sit down. It was a long time before he could make himself stop.

The revocation order was signed late that afternoon. As soon as Forester had handed it to Judith, Delaney's arrest teams went out. They picked up all the remaining defendants except Santoro. One of the arrests took place in a bar. It was the barman who phoned Santoro, warning him they were coming. Carrying a small suitcase, Santoro too went out his back window onto the fire escape. But in his case Joe Hearn was not sitting there waiting. No one was sitting there waiting. Santoro went down the fire escape with enormous haste, lost his grip, and fell off the ladder. He fell fifteen feet to the concrete. He landed on his coccyx on top of his suitcase, which he crushed. He got up holding the suitcase in one hand, his ass in the other. His ass felt like it was broken. There was an intervening fence which he limped to and attempted to climb but he lost his grip there too and, trying to save himself, let go of the suitcase. It landed on the pavement on the inside of the fence, and Santoro crashed down on the outside. Abandoning the suitcase, he got up and moved off at a fast limp. He was sure he had broken all the bones in his ass, but he had got away from them, and he fast-limped out through the building that gave on to the next street.

Such precautions were unnecessary. The detectives sent to arrest him did not arrive for another ten minutes. They found his apartment empty and in the courtyard below they found the crushed suitcase. They then spent considerable time driving up and down neighborhood streets looking for him. Once they caught a glimpse of him, or thought they did, a short man fast-limping through the crowd two blocks away. But it was rush hour by then, and the streets and sidewalks were clogged with traffic. One of them got out of the car to run, but there was a subway entrance up there, and too many pedestrians hurrying toward it. And so they lost him again.

It was nine o'clock at night before they reported back to Judith Adler.

The two detectives were embarrassed. Sergeant Delaney was embarrassed also. "We'll get him," he assured Judith, and he began to make the necessary dispositions—teams of men to stake out Santoro's flat around the clock, other teams to search for him in the various bars and social clubs he was known to frequent. "We'll get him," repeated Delaney apologetically.

Joe said, "You're worrying about nothing. Three days from now he'll come in here with Weinglass looking to make a deal."

They were all seated in Judith's office. Joe looked across at her with that same fond, half-whimsical expression on his face. He said finally, "Come on, I'll take you home," and smiled. "That is, if you think you'll be safe with me."

It made Delaney laugh. Judith began to gather her briefcase, her pocketbook. Her face was deadpan. She said nothing, and the unsuspecting Delaney bade them good night. Looking at him, Judith thought, what is there to suspect? It seemed to her that it had all gone wrong someplace, Joe's feelings for her, hers for him. In Joe's car she remained ill at ease and so began to describe the Miss Carlson case. She did not refer to it as a feeling dirty case. She told how the young cop had embraced her outside the grand jury room, saying, "What a nice lady."

"Hey," said Joe, "that's a very sweet story."

Otherwise they drove uptown in almost total silence.

When he had double-parked in front of her building, Joe tossed his police plate into the windshield, and said, "I think I better come up with you just to be sure." He grinned. "Maybe Santoro's laying for you. Maybe the little guy took a contract from Fillocchio."

Now is the time, Judith told herself, to say something light, perhaps even witty. But nothing came to mind. Her principal emotion was fear. She was stiff with it, and it had nothing to do with the fugitive Santoro.

Upstairs he left her standing in the hall while he checked out each of her rooms. When he came back to her he said, "In the morning, when you're ready to go to work, call the precinct and ask them to send a radio car for you."

"Santoro's not going to try anything."

"I know, but it's cheaper than taking a taxi. You might as well milk this case for something."

It made Judith smile. But when she realized how closely Joe was watching her, her eyes dropped to the floor.

"Well," Joe said, "I guess I better go."

Judith stepped forward and laid her forehead on his chest. "I wish you'd stay," she said.

His arms came around her. He tugged on the hair at the nape of her neck pulling her head up, then his mouth came down on hers.

When Joe got home it was after midnight but Mary was waiting up for him. She was pacing the living room which was full of smoke. The ashtrays, he noted, were full too.

Mary said, "Would you mind telling me where you've been?"

"Working."

Mary shook her head. "No, you weren't, I've seen Cirillo."

Joe said, "Oh."

"So what other interests do you have?"

When Joe did not answer, his wife said, "You better sit down. We've got to have a talk."

22

"Mary's coming to see you."

It was too early in the working day. These were not the words Judith was prepared for. Joe had stepped into her office and blurted them out. Having risen from her chair, she had gone to meet him, had closed the door behind him. Then, as expectantly as a girl, she had turned toward his arms. Deliberately she was not wearing lipstick. He must see that a kiss would be safe enough. But there had been no endearments, no embrace.

Instead: *Mary's coming to see you*.

The effect was overly brutal. The sun was still low and slanting in across the case folders on her desk. She peered down at them, willing her face not to move, not to change expression, while her mind jumped about. It jumped in one direction only. It reached the obvious conclusion. Joe had already, it seemed, confronted his wife, or she had wormed it out of him. And it was Mary who had demanded the right to confront her husband's lover, namely Judith. It didn't make sense, but it had apparently happened. Judith was annoyed. Although this indicated that his feelings toward her must be stronger than she had dared hope—which pleased her—yet he had not asked her permission first. He had simply put her in an uncomfortable spot. No promises had been exchanged between them, no plans made. He had not considered her feelings at all. She had no desire to meet Joe's wife, not now, not ever.

But the words still hung there. *Mary's coming to see you*.

"That's nice," Judith said dryly. "I'm sure we have lots

to talk about." To give herself time she moved a pile of folders from one side of her desk to the other. "What have you told her about me? About us? And why?"

That Joe was feeling pressure was clear. His agitation now as he tried to explain only increased. "You don't understand," he said. And to her embarrassment she learned that she didn't. "It's to report the crime. It's got nothing to do with you."

As Joe continued talking, Judith felt the blush rise from her neck up to her ears. Mary would be at her door any minute, apparently. To report the crime only. Though at this late date why? And why to her personally when the woman was married to a cop who might have arranged it another way? These were only some of Judith's unanswered questions. But she was unable to give them her strict attention, being chiefly concerned with the cursed blush. She was trying to get rid of it. She had turned her back to him and was hiding her face in the window. She felt she had been made to make a fool of herself, and it was Joe's fault. *What have you told her about me? About us? And why?* How could she have said such a thing? How could she possibly have exposed her own yearnings, her total vulnerability to this extent?

Joe was still trying to explain but he was doing it badly, or else he was concealing something, and with this realization her antennae went up, and she turned around and began to scrutinize him, his face and statements both. The chief of detectives had ordered Mary to report the crime, he said, had sent her right down to the district attorney's office to report it. Joe had barely got here in time to warn her. "I wanted to warn you."

Judith said, "She told Cirillo she had been raped? Why him? Is he her father? Is he her husband?"

"She went to see him about something else."

Joe's head was nodding up and down, which added up to a surplus of affirmation. Furthermore, he was having such difficulty meeting her eyes that Judith knew he was lying. This brought forth all her professionalism, plus those emotions and attitudes which by now were so closely allied to it that they scarcely existed alone, and the principal of these was pity—pity not only for what each victim had already suffered but also for being forced in this office to talk about it. Her pity now was for Joe.

"Joe," she said gently, "I think you better tell me."

His mouth began to work, but some seconds passed before words came out. "Mary went over there," he began, and stopped. After a moment he started again. "—To try and save my job."

"Oh, Joe."

As he told the story he was grinning. It was not a successful grin. "One of us had to report it," he said. "Her or me." He was clearly not looking for pity. Tough cops did not look for pity, or at least Joe did not. "She didn't want to report it to a man. She thought of you."

"Why me?"

"I guess I've mentioned you around the house a few times."

This was nice to hear certainly. "You did? What did you say?" Now she was fishing for compliments, she realized, and felt immediately humiliated.

"Just that I was impressed by you, that you seemed to have your act together."

Hearing this, Judith was warmed, and her pity for him rose up, and she came around the desk and embraced him. But his arms remained at his side, so she let go of him and returned to her own side of the desk and sat down.

Just then the phone buzzed beside her hand. Joe's eyes, she noted, flicked to the phone and remained fixed there.

After listening to Mr. Katz, Judith pushed the hold button and said to Joe, "I think you'd better go. I'll call you later. Where will you be?"

"Who is it?"

Judith laid the phone down on her desk. "Your wife is downstairs, Joe. You can go down the back elevator if you like."

Joe's manner became anguished. He said, "Everything she's going to tell you, you know already."

"So?"

There was anguish in his voice as well. "So how will you act?"

"Surprised, Joe. I'll act surprised."

"If she talks about the baseball coach, you'll ask—"

She studied him. "I'll ask what?"

"How long it's been going on, what they—" The next phrase Joe choked on: "What they did together."

At first Judith saw Joe's emotion as very strong and not particularly pretty. Male proprietorship violated. Male sexual jealousy to the fore. Then she realized with a sinking feeling that there was much more to it, that Joe was suffering, that his were not the emotions of a man ready to shed his erring wife in order to love someone else.

But she couldn't be sure. Perhaps she was misreading the signs. "Don't tell her I know about the baseball coach," Joe begged. "She doesn't know I know. I haven't told her I know."

She was listening, it seemed to Judith, to a man still in love with his wife, and the ache beside her heart began to spread until it seemed to occupy the entire middle of her body, and she nearly burst into tears.

But she knew how to conceal her feelings. She had had much practice, and as she lifted the phone to her ear, she gave Joe a half smile and a wave, as if casually waving him out of her life. But she waited until he had left the office before pushing down the telephone button a second time.

Katz placed Mary Hearn in the usual chair across the desk, and Judith tried for the usual welcoming smile, the one she used every day. But she felt it dry up on her. Mary's answering smile appeared equally weak. She seemed very nervous, and her hands in her lap would not keep still. She was much better-looking than Judith had expected. She's better looking than I am, Judith thought, and immediately felt on the defensive. Women always tended to rate other women on their looks or at least Judith did; she measured them carefully, and if the news were bad, as it was here, sentiments of inferiority, of inadequacy, rose up and had to be coped with before any other transaction could even be begun. Mary Hearn, Judith saw, must have had boys and men after her all her life. This would have made her into a certain type of personality—the type Joe Hearn had sought out and married—a different type from Judith Adler. What chance even now do I have against her? Judith asked herself.

Mary was also better dressed than Judith had expected. She wore a pale blue spring suit, with a navy blue scarf knotted loosely around her neck. She's not dressed like a cop's wife, Judith thought.

Remembering that she was not supposed to know about

Mary in advance, Judith got out a rape report form and began to fill it in.

"Name please. And your age? What was the date of the incident?"

The answers came in a voice so low that Judith had to listen hard to hear. She found herself leaning too far forward, listening too intently.

"You're the wife of Inspector Hearn, commander of the Narcotics Division, isn't that right?" she interrupted lightly.

Mary nodded. She acted like a woman who knew the hard questions were coming, questions she dreaded in advance.

Judith's tongue wanted to say more but her head stopped her in time. "All right," she said briskly. "Let's talk about the incident."

For a little while longer—time measured in seconds—they would be able to talk of it like civilized people as the "incident." After that both would have to confront it as the trauma it had been and still was. A good deal of emotion would be expanded in this room during the next thirty minutes, much of it by Judith, for she felt herself responding to this woman. She knew very well why. Admit it to yourself, she thought. Say why. Be blunt. Because we've both experienced the same man, she more than I. Does that make us sisters? How could she not want him as much as I do?

Abruptly Judith became angry both with herself and with Mary. "Please tell me in your own words exactly what happened," she said, and during the telling she watched her.

Mary stuck by her original fairy tale. She was only walking down the street when a man stuck a gun in her back and marched her into that hotel. Once upstairs in the room he had stripped and raped her. Her story to her was finished, and she stopped.

"All right," said Judith, "now let's go back over it in more detail. I have to know everything."

Mary tried a thin smile. "There's not much more to tell."

A woman raped undergoes many emotions, Judith thought, and loss of dignity is one of them. After that, whenever she is obliged to retell the experience, she also relives it. She loses her dignity still again. And if she reports the crime to the police she will retell it many, many times. The strongest desire of women like Mary seemed to be simply not to talk about it, a reaction Judith tended to admire—even as she marshaled questions designed to break the reaction down.

"Well," said Judith, "why don't we try this time to begin at the end, and work our way back to the beginning? For instance, did he sodomize you, or force you to sodomize him?"

"I don't really know what that word means."

Mary was a cop's wife; she must have heard the word used in the legal sense many times. Judith gave the woman a half smile. "Well, there is oral sodomy and there is anal sodomy." Then she said bluntly, "Did his mouth come in contact with your vagina?"

Mary's too bright smile was still in place. "Yes, it did."

"Did he force your mouth into contact with his penis?"

"Yes."

"Did his penis make contact with your anus?"

"Yes." She's been fidgeting since she came in here, Judith noted; this fidgeting had become more extreme, and she no longer met Judith's eyes. In a moment, Judith thought, if I keep the pressure on, it's all going to come gushing out. And her job required her to keep the pressure on. She was not being arbitrary or impolite or unfeeling. She was not satisfying mere prurient curiosity. She could not be blamed. Indeed, she would be praised. "All right," she said, "which occurred first?"

"I don't understand. Which what occurred first?"

"Anal sodomy or oral sodomy."

"Do we really have to go into that?"

"I'm afraid we do," said Judith, and she watched Mary carefully. If interviewed soon enough, rape victims had little trouble divulging the lurid details. But Mary had revealed nothing to anyone for a long time. With such women it was another story. These were women whose entire effort, once the rape was over, went toward willing themselves into a state in which it seemed to them that no rape had ever taken place. They caked this willpower over their emotions like a layer of thick paint. You could only pick at the different paint layers, not peel it off all at one time.

"And did his penis penetrate your vagina?"

"Yes it did."

"And did he ejaculate?"

"You mean inside me?"

With these questions Judith was stripping Mary naked, figuratively speaking. She did the same to other victims every day, but that was impersonal, whereas this victim was Joe Hearn's wife.

"You haven't answered my question."

"I'm sorry. I've forgotten what the question was."

Ejaculation, penetration—obviously the terms were too strong for her, Judith said, "How many times did this happen?"

Mary's eyes were darting about, never still. "Did what happen?"

Judith insisted. "How many times did his penis penetrate your vagina?"

"At least twice."

"All right, let's go over the sequence. Which of these acts took place first?"

"First?"

"I'm sorry to put you through this," Judith said. But was she really? "I do have to ask these questions. I have to know exactly what happened."

Across the desk a glazed look had come over Mary's eyes and her head kept nodding.

"Nothing you can say will shock me," Judith encouraged her. "I've heard it all before."

"I'm sure you have," said Mary, and she gnawed for a moment on her lower lip. "First he forced me to take all my clothes off. Then he blindfolded me with tape. Then he gagged me with tape and handcuffed my hands behind my back. Then he jabbed one of my breasts with the muzzle of his gun and made me go over to the bed and lie down on top of my hands."

As she enumerated these acts her voice seemed to glaze over too, as if to match her eyes. It was as if she were reading a roster of events or describing something she had read in a newspaper—an accident that had happened to someone else. However, she was speaking much too fast, and it was this above all that betrayed the tension she was under.

"Then he got between my legs and tried to rape me. But he couldn't." She gave a mirthless laugh.

"Yes, they often lose their erections," said Judith. "What else?" she said curtly.

"He kept losing it and losing it." This time Mary's laugh sounded even closer to hysteria. "At another time I would have ben embarrassed. I would have asked myself what was wrong with me."

"I thought you were blindfolded."

"I didn't see it, I felt it. I felt him go soft. I was awfully tight, you see. Because I was so scared. I was so tight you couldn't have got a tampon in there."

"Then what happened?"

"That's when he—started that other stuff."

"He sodomized you?"

"He sodomized me."

"From the back?"

"He tried. I've never done that even with my husband," Mary said.

"I see," said Judith. Spare me your marital confidences, she thought angrily.

"I was horrified. On top of everything else I was horrified at what he was trying."

"Please continue."

"He would do that for a while, then get between my legs again and push hard, and it didn't work in either place, and he would get soft."

"Where was the gun all this time?"

"Mostly he had it lying on my chest. The muzzle was between my breasts. I didn't want to feel him pick that gun up. I realized nothing could help me, I knew I was totally trapped."

"You said he did penetrate you."

"Here he is trying to rape me, and he doesn't even want to really. Why did he bother? He kept going soft. Finally he ripped the tape off my mouth and made me—"

Her voice broke, and Judith waited.

"He wanted me to put it in my mouth. He grabbed up the gun. He said, 'If you want to get out of here alive, you better make me come,' and he put the gun against my ear, and—and—and so I did what he wanted. He pulled the hammer back and the gun was against my ear. It was so loud. I sucked him for a long time. He wanted me to make him wet, you see, so he could get in. But I had no saliva. My mouth was completely dry."

Tears had come to Mary's eyes, Judith noted. Her own emotions kept bouncing back and forth between anger and sympathy, and she could not control them. "Do you want to take a break?" she asked gently. "Would you like a cup of coffee or something?"

But Mary only went on with her narrative. It was as if she hadn't heard the offer. She was caught up in the memory now and wanted to get to the end of it. "He made me lick him all over. He said, 'Lick my balls.' He said, 'Lick my asshole.' He said, 'Smells funky, doesn't it?' and he laughed. I was so scared. I hope you're never that scared. He put it in my mouth and he started to get hard and I thought he was going to go off in my mouth. If he did I was afraid I would vomit all over him and he would kill me for it. Finally he was hard, and he pushed me back down on the bed. There's your penetration, Miss Adler. He—he raped me for the longest time. My knees were shaking so. He said, 'Stop those knees shaking or I'll kill you.' I tried to make them stop, but they wouldn't. I couldn't make them."

Most people, Judith reflected, imagine that the worst part of rape is the sexual indignity, the physical violation of one's body. They are wrong. The worst part is the fear.

"He stopped and got off me and for a while he watched television, I guess," Mary said, and she paused to wipe her eyes with a Kleenex. "I had with me a cylinder of drawings I had made that day. He asked me what it was and I told him. I heard him throw it in the corner. Then he came back to the bed where I was still lying on top of the handcuffs, and he began raping me again. At the last second I felt him pull out. The next thing I felt was a wet face. He came all over my face. He said, 'Wipe that off with your hot-shit lady artist card.'"

Mary stopped. For a time neither woman spoke, and the office was silent. At last Mary gave another odd laugh. She said, "When we were first married Joe got sent to the FBI school in Virginia for two months. I didn't see him for two whole months and when he came back we went right to bed and we made love and Joe pulled out too, because we didn't have enough money to have children yet, and he was all so pent up after two months that he shot me right in the eye." Mary was laughing and crying both. "Same thing, don't you see? Whether it's love or rape, the act is the same, isn't it? I never realized that before. No difference. It's the same act exactly."

"The central act of human existence," said Judith.

"The only part that's different is the part you can't see. When Joe did it, we lay there and laughed and laughed. He wiped it off and kissed me over and over again and told me how much he loved me, and then we made love some more."

Judith's mood had reverted to anger, and she knew why. It was on such tremendous intimacies that lives were based, and in a good marriage there were many of them. Mary and Joe had had many. She herself would never be able to catch up, and it was painful for her to realize this.

"This time there were no love words," continued Mary. "As he climbed off me I heard him cock that gun again, and I thought, Now he's going to kill me. He made me lie down on the floor, and I thought he was going to put a bullet into the back of my head, and I waited for it to happen for I don't know how long. Then I realized he was gone. I got out of the handcuffs and phoned my sister."

"Not your husband?" said Judith.

Mary's eyes were on the floor. She merely shook her head.

"Why didn't you call your husband?"

"I don't know," said Mary, and her voice had dropped almost to a whisper.

"All right," said Judith, "let's go back to the beginning again. There's something there that puzzles me."

"I've told you everything."

"Yes, but I have a question about the handcuffs."

Mary looked suddenly wary. "What about them?"

"Something you said puzzles me. For instance, you were lying on them, right?"

"Yes."

"You were cuffed behind your back."

"I told you that."

"Show me how it was."

Mary stood up with her wrists touching behind her back.

"Yes," said Judith, "and in that position you were able to get the key into the lock. That's what puzzles me. It must have been very difficult for you."

Mary stared at her.

"Are you sure," said Judith, "you didn't have help?"

"From whom?"

"From somebody else in the room, maybe."

"There was no one," said Mary in a whisper, but her eyes filled with tears.

"Do you want to tell me about it?"

And so Judith heard the whole tearful story about Loftus.

"I didn't even decide to go to the hotel with him. I don't think I did. I just let him push me along. I was mad at Joe. I was trying to punish Joe. And like most times when I try to punish him he wouldn't even know about it."

"So you went upstairs with this man and had sex with him?"

Mary denied it, explaining exactly what happened in a voice with no energy left in it, as if hardly aware Judith was present. In any case, Mary said, it made no difference whether she had had sex with Loftus or not. She had gone up to that room with him, which in itself constituted adultery in the world's eyes. The fact that no sexual act had taken place between them was neither here nor there. No one would believe her.

Judith said, "Had you ever been unfaithful to your husband before?" This was prying. The answer was of no legal importance whatever. But she wanted to ask the question—had to ask it—and she had done so.

"Oh, no," said Mary, and she sounded shocked. "Never." Then she gave a wry laugh. "I'm the one who got caught the first time."

"Has he ever been unfaithful to you?"

"I don't think so. I'd be very surprised."

"Don't be," said Judith grimly.

But Mary, ignoring this remark, said, "It's inconceivable to Joe that I could be unfaithful to him. He thinks I'm perfect, you see." She turned beseeching eyes on Judith. "My husband believes the story I told him," she said. "He mustn't find out about Loftus. It would devastate him. You don't know him. He wouldn't be able to take it. He doesn't deserve suffering like that. Promise me you won't tell him."

The plea hung in the air while the two women gazed at each other; on Mary's face was an expression of such raw need that Judith was obliged to drop her eyes. "Tell him?" she said. "Why should I tell him?"

When Mary had departed, Judith stood at her window looking down on Centre Street, and her thoughts were bleak. This was not a failed marriage. These two people were going through an awful time and their only thoughts were to try to protect each other. As for herself, she now had enough facts on hand to destroy the marriage if she so chose. It was perhaps about to self-destruct anyway; she would only be hastening things along. Joe would come out of a divorce so distraught that to snare him on the rebound would probably be no great trick.

Was this something she could live with for the rest of her life?

23

AT THIS POINT IN HER BROODING, HER DOOR BURST
open and in stepped Joe. Mary had departed only a
minute or two before. She was almost certainly still in the
building. She was possibly still in the elevator. Turning
from the window, Judith looked at him and thought, He
must have been watching my door from the end of the
corridor. We have long corridors here.

"What did she tell you?"

Judith thought, During all the time his wife was with
me he must have been hiding down the corridor in a
doorway, wondering what she was saying.

The rape report form, together with notes Judith had
made on a legal pad, lay on top of her desk. She picked
them up and glanced through them as if to refresh her
memory. She did not need to do this. She remembered
every word. She put these papers into a folder and printed
MARY HEARN on the tab. She placed the folder on top of
similar folders at the side of her desk.

"Please tell me what she said."

Judith was thinking of Mr. Katz seated outside her door.
What did he make of this frantic coming and going of the
Hearn family? For a man supposedly so careful about
appearances, Joe had certainly forgotten himself this morning. This is how rumors start, she told herself.

"I have a right to know."

Judith reached for Mary's folder. She glanced again at
the pages it contained and wondered what to answer. She
thought, Your wife begged me not to tell you about Loftus.
She was trying to keep you from being hurt. She said that

310

if you found out it would devastate you. She was trying to protect you.

But Judith said none of this to Joe. "According to your wife," she said, as if reading from the folder, "she did not have sex with Loftus that day. She was still fully dressed when the assailant came in the door."

"Can I see that?" said Joe.

"No you can't."

Joe's head was nodding up and down, but his eyes had dropped to the floor. "How long," he said, "had the affair been going on? Did she tell you that?"

Your wife was in that hotel room because she was trying to punish you, Judith thought. "According to her," Judith said grudgingly, "it was the first time." She was watching Joe's reaction.

The expression on his face was—what? Relief? The beginning of joy? "And you?" he said eagerly, and his gaze rose. "Did you believe her?"

There was a row of wooden cabinets along one wall of her office. Judith carried the pile of folders to the cabinet and locked them inside. A one-word answer was coming up, but it was a crucial one, yes or no, and her life, her whole world seemed to be riding on it.

"No," she said.

"You didn't believe her?"

To Judith the pain in his voice was unmistakable. "I said no. Didn't you hear me?" She spun around and faced him. He looked as absolutely crushed as she had expected. "How can you ask such a question?" she demanded. "How am I supposed to know if she's telling the truth or not?"

"Will I see you tonight?" Joe mumbled after a moment.

"Sure, why not?"

He was again studying the floor.

"Now I think you'd better go," said Judith crisply. "I'm due in court in ten minutes, and there are some things I have to do here first." And she showed him out of her office.

Mary drove directly home. So did Joe, who was only a few miles behind her. She hurried into her kitchen, put her pocketbook down on the countertop, and stared immediately in the direction of the telephone. Had it rung in her absence? It must have. NO ANSWER IS NO. But he would call back. If he wanted money he had to. She changed her clothes, made herself tea, and resumed waiting. It was as if her vigil had never been interrupted. The interview with Judith Adler had left her trembling, but it was over, she was home now. But home was not home until that phone rang. She did not know how much more she would be able to stand. Where was her tormentor, and why did he not get it over with?

The telephone bell suddenly sounded. She grabbed at the receiver, nearly ripping the entire instrument off the wall. But it was not George Lyttle. It was Loftus.

"I've got to see you."

"Are you crazy? Calling me here? Suppose my husband was home?"

"You don't understand." But from the panic in his voice she understood perfectly. "I've got to see you."

He has called Loftus, Mary thought. "Where?" she said.

They decided on the town beach—or rather Mary did. Loftus seemed almost catatonic, and even this decision he left to her. She picked up her pocketbook and keys again and went out the back door.

When Joe, ten minutes later, found the house empty, he went down into the cellar. He went straight to the voice-activated tape recorder which he had attached to their telephone. He had not checked this machine in days: he had almost forgotten it was there. In his head he was still replaying lines—two particular lines—from this morning, one his, one Judith's.

"Did you believe her?"

"No."

He pushed the reverse button and the machine screechingly rewound itself. Then he pushed play, and the tape began to come forward again. He put the earphones on.

A considerable length of tape had been used up. There must be something on it. He was listening for male voices only. He kept pushing fast forward, skipping entire conversations. Lately Mary had talked to her mother, her sister, Billy, other housewives.

Finally he came to the most recent conversation on the tape, and as he listened he rammed his knuckles into his eyes. It was to him the most damning conversation imaginable.

"I've got to see you."

"Are you crazy? Calling me here? Suppose my husband was home?"

Joe listened until they had agreed to meet at the town beach, then shut off the machine. He went out and got into his car. At the beach he parked off the road in the scrub forest that grew behind the dunes, taking care that his car should not be seen, then crept forward through the trees. There was a concession stand boarded up now in the off-season. He reached it and peered around its side.

Mary stood at the water's edge looking across at the Connecticut shore. A warm breeze blew into her face, and the wavelets came up almost as far as her shoes. There was no one else on the beach. She heard Loftus' car come into the lot, and when she turned around he was crossing the sand toward her.

She did not greet him, nor did he greet her. He said, "He called me. He wants money."

Mary nodded. It was what she had expected. With her head down and her hands thrust into the back pockets of her jeans, she trudged along close to the lapping water. Loftus walked at her side. The sand was wet and hard packed.

"He wants ten thousand dollars."

Mary, studying the sand, thought, If I were alone here, if I didn't have this on my mind, probably I'd kick my shoes off and walk barefoot, and the wet sand would feel nice between my toes. Instead she said, "What else did he say to you?"

"He threatened me. He said he'd make those photos public."

Mary stopped and looked at him. The breeze blew her hair. She said nothing, and in a moment resumed walking.

"I'd lose my job," Loftus said. He gave a sick laugh. "I wouldn't be able to get another one either. A teacher involved in a sex scandal? No school would hire me."

"Not to mention how your wife would react," said Mary.

Loftus was not thinking about his wife. "They'd fire me so fast. You have no idea how straitlaced this town is."

The sky was very blue. "Yes, I do," said Mary. There were a few big, billowy clouds high up and far off. She walked along. "Ten thousand dollars," she said. Having reached the end of the beach, she turned around and started back, reversing the two pairs of footprints that came toward her. The imprint of Loftus' shoes, she saw, went in much deeper than her own. It was a clear day. The breeze was blowing. The Connecticut shore looked close enough to swim to. Mary wanted to plunge into the water. She wanted to swim all the way to the other side, to put Long Island Sound between herself and all this. When she got across she would start running. She would keep running until no one would ever find her.

"What do you want to do?" she asked.

"I have no money. I'm a teacher. Do you know how much teachers get paid?"

"You're telling me you don't want to pay?"

Loftus was gnawing on the end of his thumb. He had the nail under his teeth. He was in a state of such obvious panic that Mary felt calm by comparison. She almost felt sorry for him.

"Let's discuss it calmly," she said. "Can you do that? Can you try to think about it calmly?"

They walked back and forth along the edge of the beach. Loftus, it turned out, had about twenty-five hundred dollars saved. It was something. Not much, but a start.

"You want me to put up the other seventy-five hundred dollars, is that it?"

Loftus grabbed her arm and spun her around. "If those pictures become public, it won't do you any good either. Your husband will probably shoot you."

Mary jerked her arm loose and resumed walking. She resumed her intense study of the wet sand, the breathing holes of clams, the bits of shells. "No," she said, "he won't shoot me."

They walked a little way in silence. "I don't have any money either," Mary said. "Where am I supposed to get money like that?"

Evidently Loftus had thought it out. "You come from a rich family." He was almost pleading.

Such pressure as this, Mary realized, forced a woman to consider courses of action that were despicable. She laughed brokenly. Yes, she could ask her father. It was a possible way out. She had thought about it. She could lie to him, and then—

Such pressure as this forced a woman to contemplate her own weaknesses, recognize the depths to which she was perhaps willing to stoop. "My father's seventy-two years old," she said. "He lives in Florida and has heart trouble." Being near tears, she shook her head doggedly. "Asking my father is out of the question."

"Then what are we going to do? We have to pay. There's no way out."

"Calm down," said Mary. "Calm down and let's talk about this a bit longer." And so she learned that Loftus had been contacted at the school, not at home. There had been a number of calls into the faculty lounge while he was in class. No name had been left. Finally the caller had left a number. Loftus was to call back at a certain hour and ask for George. He had done so, and George, if that was the man's name, had demanded ten thousand dollars.

"He left a callback number?"

"Yes."

He's not afraid of us, Mary thought. He leaves his phone number. He knows we can't do anything.

"Do you still have that number?"

"He's given us until tomorrow to raise the money."

"I wonder why he never called me," Mary said. But she thought she knew why and felt somewhat proud. He thinks I'm tougher than Loftus, she told herself. To make sure he gets what he wants, he attacks us where we are weakest.

They were still walking back and forth along the water's edge. In many places the lines of footprints overlapped. Joe was peering out at them through the gap between the concession stand and the phone booth next to it. He was invisible to them, and they were not looking around for him anyway.

"I have to call him again this afternoon with our answer."

To Mary the beach seemed to be getting smaller, shrinking, closing in on her, as if it had walls. She could not decide what their answer would be. It was as if there were a band around her skull and thumbs pressing into her eyeballs. She could not see clearly, could barely think at all, and yet it was up to her to decide for both of them.

The conclusion she came to was imperfect, but no other suggested itself. They would offer this George half what he had demanded, five thousand dollars only, all they could raise. Loftus would meet with him, hand over the money, and receive the prints and negatives in return. Loftus would warn the man that any further demands would be refused.

"It's worth five thousand to us if that's the end of it," Mary said. "If that's not enough, then let him do whatever he likes with those pictures." She spoke with extreme forcefulness. She had to convince Loftus first, if Loftus was to convince the extortionist, that there would be no additional payments. One payment. They would not agree to another. "I'll have the money for you this afternoon."

She continued to talk to Loftus in a low forceful voice, pumping him up.

"You can do it, Marty. You're a tough guy. In the hotel room he took you by surprise. This time you'll be on your guard. He won't dare mess with you." She put her hands on his shoulders and even lifted up his chin so that their eyes met. Her watching husband took this as an affectionate gesture. He expected her to kiss him lovingly, and was almost surprised when she did not.

"You can do it, Marty."

They had reached the near end of the beach again. Without another word, Mary turned away from Loftus and slogged through the soft sand to the parking lot. As she did so, Joe Hearn faded backward toward the wooded area where he had hidden his car.

Driving home, Mary felt almost relieved. That problem was over. She could do no more with it. It was up to Loftus now. This left her mind free to range over her other problems.

This morning Judith Adler had broken her down, made her blab. She had put potentially damaging information into the woman's hands, and was aware that this could haunt her later. But it was too late to change anything. It was no good worrying about Judith Adler. As for Chief Cirillo, she would have to see him or phone him, describe her visit to the district attorney's office, and beg him to give her husband his job back. She was not sure he would do it. Maybe he would. She would work on him, work hard. Finally she had to find some way to sit down with Joe. She would win him back—if that was the correct way to phrase it. She would find some way to win him back.

Having parked in her driveway, she went into her house. She knew exactly what she had to do. About five minutes later she came out carrying the chest containing her grandmother's silver which she placed in the trunk of her car. She drove straight to Garden City, the biggest of the nearby towns, which contained, according to the Yellow Pages, two pawn shops. She carried the silver chest into each in turn, accepting the better of the two offers, $3200, from which the first year's interest was deducted in advance.

She was being tailed throughout by her husband, who understood up to a point what was happening. He had recognized the silver chest, and when Mary exited from the second shop without it, he realized it had been exchanged for money. But what does she need money for? He asked himself miserably. I give her all my money. There was to Joe in his present state only one conceivable explanation. She's leaving me, he thought. She's going to run away with him. That's what the money is for.

He tailed Mary from the second pawnshop to the supermarket nearest their house, where she began to fill a shopping cart with groceries. She's going to leave as much food as possible for the kids, Joe thought. As soon as she joined the checkout line, he drove home, parked his car around the corner, and got into the house before her. He went directly down into the basement, where he put earphones on and sat down next to the tape recorder to wait.

He waited there two hours before the phone rang. The caller did not have to announce himself. By now Joe recognized the voice.

"He won't go for it," Loftus said.

"He won't go for it?" Joe thought he had never heard so much despair in Mary's voice, and a feeling of incomprehension began to come over him.

"He wants the full amount."

"I don't have the full amount," said Mary. "I've only got twenty-seven hundred. It's the most I can raise."

"He said all or nothing," said Loftus.

This was followed by silence. Joe could hear both of them breathing.

Mary sounded close to tears. "Why am I being punished like this? I didn't even do anything."

"Don't try to lay it on me," cried Loftus. "You were willing enough to come up to that hotel room."

"I was there about a minute," Mary said. "I was just leaving."

There was more silence, more sustained breathing. Joe could feel Mary trying to control herself. "All that is past," she said. "The question now is, what is our next move to be?"

"He gave us until four P.M. to make contact with him. Or else."

"Or else?"

"Tomorrow he mails the photos to your husband and to the school."

"Talk to him again, Marty. Tell him we don't have the money. Tell him we need time. Talk to him, Marty. You can do it. You're a very persuasive guy. You've got strength, integrity."

Joe's emotions, as he listened, were in such a turmoil that he scarcely comprehended what he was hearing.

"I can't convince him," protested Loftus. "I already tried. It's not going to work."

Joe was sitting in the dark on a wooden box next to the boiler. The earphones were clamped to his head.

"You talk to him, Mary. Maybe he'll listen to you. Here's the number to call." Loftus read the number out. He read it twice, and then Mary read it back to him. Joe had no pencil and no paper in the basement, but did not need any.

Loftus said: "Call at precisely four P.M. That's what he said, four P.M. We don't want to make him mad."

"All right," said Mary. Her voice had become almost a whisper. There was no energy left in it.

When she had hung up, Joe removed the earphones and set them down on top of the machine. There were two doors out of the basement. One went up through the kitchen, the other directly out into the driveway. He listened at the kitchen door until he heard Mary going up the stairs toward their bedroom. Then he crossed the cellar and went out through the rear door. He went through the hedge into the next yard, and from there made his way back to his car.

24

THE POLICE DEPARTMENT OWNED SPECIAL PHONE directories arranged by number. Every station house in the city had a set, and Joe knew this. They were called Coles books. At the precinct closest to home, the 111th in Queens, Joe found and flopped open the Manhattan Coles. He moistened his thumb several times turning pages. After a moment his fingernail drew a line under a number that corresponded, he saw, to a phone booth located in the waiting room of the old New York Central Railroad Station at 125th Street in Harlem.

A railroad station, Joe thought, how brilliant. He gives a number he imagines can't be traced back to him. Maybe he imagines it can't be traced at all. He doesn't know about our Coles books. The idea that we might stake out a railroad station phone booth never occurs to him either. Criminals, he thought, are all about as brilliant as this guy. Then he thought, The ones we catch are, anyway.

We. Us. The vast police brotherhood. It wasn't us this time, it was Joe only, Joe personally. Back in his car, he checked his watch, then his gun. He had time, about an hour, and he threw open the cylinder and counted bullets. As he rammed the gun back into place, he was still reasoning coldly and accurately. Or so he believed. He started driving.

The waiting room was vast. Its roof was the four tracks and two platforms that ran overhead. It was one of the oldest rooms in the city, as old as some station houses. It dated from 1900 or before, a time when the railroads dominated the imagination of the world. Joe glanced around

319

as if he had never stood in this place before. How elegant it must have seemed in its day, all wood and heavily decorated. Now it only looked old-fashioned. It was as ornate as the inside of a Victorian mansion, and its thick moldings, its windows and doors, were caked with layers of paint.

At this time of day the waiting room was nearly empty. The ticket windows were behind brass grilles. There were six of them but only one was open, and a man moved about behind it. A newsstand occupied one corner, and next to it stood a row of chrome food and drink machines—accretions of a more recent age. Then came a raised shoeshine platform supporting three leather chairs that must have been part of the original decor. No shoeshine boy. No customers either. A middle-aged businessman sat high up in one of the chairs reading a paper. He looked prosperous. Once Pullman trains stopped here en route to Chicago and the West. Now the station served principally the commuter towns of Westchester and Connecticut, richer suburbs by far than the one Joe lived in, than most cops lived in.

The phone booths were all the way to the rear near the rest room doors. There were three of them. Joe stepped into the middle one—his intention was to check out the number while pretending to make a call, this booth first, then the others, but as he grasped the receiver the dial seemed to reach up and slap him in the face. This was the booth. He had guessed right the first time, and his hand began to shake and his coin would not fit in the slot. Pulling closed the folding door, he read the dial again, and thought for a moment he might suffocate or vomit or faint. He was absolutely certain that the next man to enter this booth would be the man who had raped his wife.

He went out of the booth. The ornate waiting room was still virtually empty. The middle-aged businessman, idly turning pages, still sat high up on his throne. He was oblivious to Joe, oblivious to Joe's turmoil. The rapist was not present.

Opposite the phone booths was a wooden bench against the wall. From there a man could see into whichever phone booth he chose. Joe went over and sat down on the bench, trying it out.

Just then a train went by overhead. The whole room

shook, and the noise was deafening. This made Joe brood. He sat waiting until a second train went through as loudly as the first. It was as he had thought. You could shoot a gun off underneath one of these trains. No one would hear. You could fire shots into that phone booth, and heads would not turn.

A careful man could afford no mistakes now; Joe checked the waiting room for alternate exits. He looked into the men's room. He even peered under the row of stalls, but noted no shoes, no bunched-up pants legs. Two staircases led to the platforms above, and he climbed the nearest one, coming out into the afternoon air above the south-bound tracks. He was alone there. About a dozen people waited for trains on the opposite side, and some stared at him curiously. He turned and looked out across 125th Street, Harlem's Broadway. He saw movie marquees, shops, storefront churches, hair-dressing establishments whose specialty was straightening hair. All this represented a world and culture that were part of his country, part of his city, even part of his life, but which, nonetheless, he did not understand. Which white cop could ever understand it? He looked down on crowded sidewalks, sluggish traffic. He watched a police radio car come toward him, pass underneath the tracks, and continue on. There were two white cops inside. It reminded him that he could call on such men for help at any time, though not today. Today's work could not be shared.

He went down the stairs and out through the waiting room onto crowded 125th Street. At the corner he turned and started uptown. Overhead were the tracks. He walked in lacy sunlight, and he passed abandoned tenements and he scrutinized each one of them. The Buildings Department had condemned them by nailing up sheets of aluminum, had stoppered each mouth, blinded each eye. Alleys—they were virtually tunnels—used to run under some of these buildings. Joe remembered such alleys from his childhood. They started three steps down from the street. A different neighborhood, but similar buildings. Men used to carry sacks of coal down the steps on their backs. Halfway along the alley would be the boiler room door. At the far end would be daylight—a tiny garden. The Buildings Department, when condemning all these buildings, had closed off their alleys as well, though less successfully. In neighborhoods like this they were too useful to stay shut long—useful as latrines, as shooting galleries for junkies.

As expected, Joe came to one whose aluminum sheeting had been torn down. It lay half crumpled on top of rubble at the entrance to the tunnel. Joe went down the steps and walked across, and the metal protested all the way. By the time he reached the ex-boiler room door, he was holding his nose—the stench of urine, of human feces, was that strong, and he stopped and looked back the way he had come. He was virtually invisible from the street and this was also as expected. More importantly, he had found a second place where shots could be fired that no one would hear, a better place than the last one.

Suddenly he thought about time. This panicked him. How much time had gone by? How much had he used up, how much was left in which to complete his preparations? The hands on his watch were too close to the hour. Disconcerted, he ran down the alley, up the three steps and back to the railroad station. After passing through the front entrance, he stopped at the newsstand and bought a paper, which gave him a moment to glance around, but the hall was still virtually empty, no rapists present. The paper was that morning's *New York Times*, four thick sections, though he needed only one. He carried it into the men's room where he again satisfied himself that he was alone—once more peering under the toilet stalls. This done, he pushed three-quarters of his unread paper down into the overflowing trash basket, then opened the remaining section over a sink and punched a hole through the centerfold with his ball-point pen. After refolding it he stepped into a toilet stall and drew his gun. He flipped open its cylinder and counted its bullets one last time. But he did not reholster. He dropped the gun instead into his suitcoat pocket. He was not a Western sheriff. In modern times fast-draw artists avoided holsters. The side pocket was more accessible, and if need be one could fire through the cloth.

Some of these preparations Joe had enacted many times before. At the climactic moment all cases resembled each other. The arrest had to be made, and this was potentially dangerous. A cop with any brains prepared carefully. He checked out the site, and its environs, and his gun, and possible lines of fire. For a moment the ordinariness of the situation occurred to Joe, and this brought with it a return to sanity. He would do nothing rash until he was sure he had the right man. He would conduct his own interrogation. The rapist—if it was the rapist and not a messenger—would be armed. Joe must be very very careful. If force was used, if a gun showed, he would fire. He was within his rights. The law would applaud him. He was not going to kill anyone, but was ready to do so if necessary.

There were no other preparations Joe could think of. He was as ready as he would ever be. It was now five minutes to the hour and he went out of the men's room and crossed toward the bench opposite the phone booths. It was an odd bench for a railroad waiting room: it looked like a pew. It looked like it belonged not here but in a church, and his rage turned inward again. His head filled with notions that were basically religious in nature. His profession was a religious one or it was nothing at all. He had sworn an oath under God, had sworn to a strict interpretation of the law. He was a religious man. He had gone through Catholic schools, had married in the Church, was raising his children as Catholics. But he was also a policeman who believed in an Old Testament God. The Old Testament God was the one who suited cops. It was their job to mete out God's punishments, or so it often seemed, to enforce God's will. The biblical God did exist, the God of wrath, and in earthly matters the policeman was more than God's agent, he was His stand-in. Joe sat down on the pew. In the case of the rape of Mary Hearn an arrest was about to be made, or else judgment was to be rendered. Biblical retribution was perhaps at hand.

The rapist by now might have entered the waiting room. Joe could not risk peering about for him. The man's suspicions must not be aroused. Looking neither right nor left, Joe only opened his newspaper. He put his head in it, then peered into the phone booth through the hole in the centerfold. He could see very little, and moved the hole around trying to see more. He could see the seat, which was empty, then the telephone box, which was silent, but not both at once. He could see the receiver hanging from its hook, and about half its limp cord, and he left his focus there, the most restricted focus of his life, the narrowest vision. He framed the receiver and waited until the bell would ring. He waited to see a hand insert itself into his frame. Any moment it would happen.

Though his nerves were tight and his rage approached the boil, he forced himself to sit still. His vision was fixed on the approximate center of the bell inside the telephone box—the bell that in a few moments might or might not ring—he had begun to suffer doubts. Its ringing depended on Mary, and he could not know what state of mind she was in. She might make the call, she might not. Either decision would be painful for her, an additional ordeal he wished he could have spared her.

Suppose she did not call?

Then this peephole view of the world, this focus on half a telephone box, became counterproductive. The rapist would enter the waiting room, would approach these telephone booths, and would then slip out again, unseen by him.

Additional scenarios suggested themselves. Suppose the phone did ring, but the rapist, having noted Joe's unmoving newspaper, became alarmed and chose not to answer it? He could be out the side door and gone before the bell stopped ringing, before Joe even looked up.

What time was it now? He could not even look without dropping his newspaper, dropping his mask, his shield. But he believed the phone ought to have rung by now. He became sure of it. Four o'clock had come and gone. Time was a prison. Time was more restrictive than handcuffs. It was time that imprisoned a man, not bars, time that imprisoned him here. He longed to know the exact time. Though a single glance at his watch could have removed this strain, or at least lessened it, he did not move.

Mary was not going to call. He could picture her pacing her kitchen, picking her phone up, putting it back down again, pacing some more, not knowing which way to turn.

Soon he became convinced that the rapist was not even in the hall, had had second thoughts, had realized his peril, and decided to contact his victiins some other way.

Or perhaps he was in fact nearby, eyeing the phone booths. How long should Joe wait before throwing the paper down and scrutinizing every face in the waiting room? He was not going to be able to wait long, it seemed, for his tension was so severe that his entire body had begun to twitch.

The phone rang.

It rang about ten times. The paper became so heavy Joe could barely hold up his arms. Overhead a train roared through. When it was gone, the phone was still ringing. No one's going to answer, Joe thought. He was miserably disappointed. His thoughts went to Mary. She would be more frightened than ever. He decided he would step into the phone booth, stop the infernal ringing. He would also talk to Mary, soothe and reassure her as best he could.

The receiver disappeared from the hook. Simultaneously the ringing stopped. A hand had reached into Joe's frame and out again. It had happened so fast he never even saw it. A hand had unhooked the receiver and withdrawn. Joe jerked his peephole all around trying to find the hand again, then thought to raise his frame to eye level. He found the hand there.

He could not see the face. It was turned into the booth and blocked by the receiver. A black man, which in Harlem was to be expected. In itself it proved nothing.

Folding his newspaper, Joe placed it carefully on the bench. He did this slowly. He had more than enough time now. All the time in the world. An almost stoical calm had taken possession of him, and he stepped across the two paces of intervening hallway and into the phone booth and he rammed his gun into the individual's kidneys.

The crinkly head spun around in astonishment, the eyes dropped to the gun, and the man—he was quite young—recoiled as far into the booth as he could fit. Joe was in there with him. They were chest to chest. Joe tore the receiver out of his hand, and put it to his ear.

"Hello?"

It was Mary's voice. Joe was listening to it.

"Hello?" she said again. Perhaps he hoped to take strength from that beloved voice. Perhaps he hoped only to hear it one last time before something irrevocable occurred. But something irrevocable had occurred already.

"Hello?" said Mary's voice a third time.

Joe hung up.

The two men, one of them carrying an attaché case, were still jammed into the phone booth. Their faces were so close they might have been kissing. Their bodies were as close as lovers. Nothing separated them but the two-inch barrel of Joe's off-duty gun.

A prisoner could not be searched or handcuffed in a phone booth, lacking enough room, nor out in a public railroad station either—the arrest process, being dramatic, tended to draw a crowd, and crowds to cops could be dangerous. Crowds sometimes attempted to free the prisoner. Or a crowd might contain an accomplice, who might be armed. One hustled a prisoner into a vestibule, an alley, and did the job before the crowd gathered. To a cop, handcuffing a man was private.

Joe moved them both toward the nearby men's room, a more fitting place. They marched in locked step, no air between them, the gun pressed so tightly into the individual's clothing it could not even be seen. Joe at that moment was reacting to years of training, was hardly thinking at all.

He bent him over the urinals. "Hands up on the wall. Spread your legs." The brown face was terrified. "Reach your hands higher. Higher, I said."

Joe patted him down. Working one-handed, he grabbed the wallet on the way by and tossed it into the sink, and went on. He checked for ankle holsters, snaking his hands up the inside of the pants legs to the crotch, and he was rough about it. He made him grunt. He lifted him six inches off the floor.

Reaching behind him, Joe retrieved the wallet, which he flipped open and glanced at. "George Lyttle. Is that your name?" For the first time Joe took a long look at the prisoner's face. He saw it in the mirror above the sinks. Their eyes met in the mirror, and Joe recognized that the prisoner's eyes could perhaps be called green. Joe would not have called them green himself, but he could see why Mary might.

They were the eyes of a badly frightened young man.

Joe said, "Who was on the phone?"

"It sounded like some lady with whom I am unacquainted."

"You came here to take that call."

"I heard the phone ringing."

Joe had himself barely under control. "Do you often answer phones that ring in railroad stations?"

"It's a hobby with me."

"Who was on the phone?"

"Usually it's a wrong number."

Lyttle's attaché case lay across two sinks where Joe had set it down. He was trying and failing to get it open with one hand.

"You and I had best converse," suggested George Lyttle. He had half turned and was talking over his shoulder.

"Hands on the wall," Joe snapped.

Instantly George Lyttle jerked back into his previous pose. After licking his lips, he talked to Joe in the mirror. "I fail to comprehend," he said, "which matters might be at issue here."

There was some sort of combination lock on the attaché case. Joe was trying to watch George Lyttle and work the lock at the same time. The photos would be in there. Once he had them he could act.

Footsteps approached the men's room door. George Lyttle heard them. He turned from the wall and his hands came down. He tightened his tie, and with this gesture seemed to regain some confidence.

Joe heard them too. His gun went into his pocket, his hand with it, and it remained there. His eyes remained locked on Lyttle's, and his expression read: try something, and I'll put one right through you.

The men's room door opened. The middle-aged businessman had climbed down from his shoeshine throne. His hands were already at his fly which was half unzipped. He looked with surprise from one face to the other, and became instantly nervous. He noted one man with his hand in his pocket, perhaps concealing a gun, and a second man who looked scared. He knew he had interrupted something private. He stepped up to the urinal, but was unable to concentrate on it. Over his shoulder his eyes flicked from one of them to the other. It made him hurry. Hurriedly he shook himself dry, zipped up, and went out.

Ten seconds later Joe and George Lyttle left the men's room also. Lyttle led the way. Joe was less than two paces behind him, the gun still in his pocket. He was carrying the attaché case in his free hand, and muttering directions out of the side of his mouth. Whatever came next, he had decided, that men's room was not the spot for it. Joe knew a better place, and that's where they were going.

They stepped out the side door into the sunlight and fresh air, and marched uptown on the sidewalk opposite the track stanchions. In a block and a half they came to the alley where the aluminum sheeting had been torn away. Joe pushed George Lyttle down the three steps and over it. He moved him along the alley toward the light at the other end, moved him stumbling over the rubble and garbage underfoot. Again the latrine odor made Joe want to retch. When they reached the depth of the boiler room door, Joe stopped him, saying, "That's far enough."

His voice sounded ominous even to himself, and it seemed to magnify Lyttle's fear—his head was swiveling about as if his shirt collar was too tight for his neck. Or perhaps he was looking for a direction in which to run. But in this alley there was no escape. Joe said, "Now open that case."

When George Lyttle did not immediately comply, Joe slugged him with the side of his gun. The blow was aimed at his ear, but Lyttle saw it coming and ducked. The gun caught him on the shoulder. Immediately he straightened up again. "Take it easy, man," he pleaded. "Easy."

"Open it, I said."

"I don't possess the combination," said George Lyttle. "I'm carrying that case for somebody. That particular case is not my particular case."

Joe brought his gun muzzle flush against Lyttle's forehead, pressing his head back against the wall. The green eyes, if in fact they were green, got very wide indeed, and Joe felt a rush of intense pleasure. "I'm going to count to ten," he said.

"What's coming over you, man?" Lyttle stammered. "You want to arrest me, you put handcuffs on me, you take me to the station house. You read me my rights, and you give me my phone call." His long red tongue darted in and out and he licked dry lips. "That's my advice to you."

It was good advice, and Joe, though half crazed, was still sane enough to realize it. A cop was obliged by law and department regulations to work by the book. Correct procedure was his legal safeguard, and often his physical safeguard too. The book had all the answers and to step out from under its protection was professional suicide; when he tried to get back he would face charges. But for Joe it was too late. Like most cops who have departed from the book, he was no longer in command of his own actions.

Hysterical behavior only encouraged other hysterical behavior.

He said, "Open it. You have about four seconds left," and he pulled off a shot into the wall.

The shot must have seemed like a crack of lightning to George Lyttle, and the muzzle blast turned his face greener than his eyes. Before the sound had ceased reverberating he was on his knees, scrabbling to open the case. He had to tilt the lid toward the light to see the numbers. His hands were shaking.

As the case broke open, a pair of handcuffs slid out.

"Well," said Joe picking them up, and he studied them. "Well, well, well." They were not police handcuffs. They were cheap imitations, almost toys. They were the type of handcuffs one bought in an S and M shop, along with a mink glove. Joe had seen them often enough at crime scenes.

Lyttle's handcuffs sat on his palm. As idly as a baseball Joe tossed them into the air and caught them again. Though flimsy they could immobilize a man well enough. Or a woman. One could put such cuffs on a woman and rape her to one's heart content.

Above Lyttle's head ran a pipe fastened to the ceiling. Joe handcuffed him to the pipe by the right wrist. He did it as viciously as he could, squeezing the cuff tight, pinching flesh.

"Hey, man, am I under arrest or not? What about my rights?"

"Who was the woman on the phone?" said Joe. "Did the woman on the phone have rights?"

25

Now Joe in turn went down on his knees beside the attaché case. It was as if it had become an altar. Its tabernacle contained the Word. Joe plucked out a notebook and flicked through its pages. A journal apparently. He read its title aloud: "The Wisdom of George Lyttle."

He gave a choked laugh.

He drew forth the two plastic sandwich bags, one containing Loftus' credit cards, the other Mary's—there was just enough light to discern the names, and an icy cold came down upon him, as if a wind blew along the alley. An instant later he was sweating. In a vague way he realized this. His body was not working properly. He found and examined a ring of keys: Mary's. The attaché case had sleeves and pockets, in which he found other papers unrelated to Mary, classroom notes of some kind. He strewed them onto the rubble and went on searching.

He found and withdrew the photos. His fingers had encountered a gun in there too, but for the moment he ignored it. The photos, in color, were postcard size. The top one was of Loftus. It showed his head and part of his chest. His eyes and mouth were taped shut. Joe yanked off the encircling rubber band. The next photo down was a similar close-up, this time of Mary. The flesh of her face had been strapped back toward her ears. Her neck and bare shoulders were stiff with terror.

Both photos indicated nudity and ought to have warned him about what came next. The fourth picture down showed Mary and Loftus together. They lay side by side on top of their hands on the bed. Both were stark naked.

"I want you to tell me about this photo," he said. He did not know what the following photos would show. For the moment he could not bear to look further. "All right," he said, "you bust into the hotel room. The man and the woman are in there. What are they doing? Do they already have their clothes off?"

Joe was in anguish. These tremendous details, it seemed to him, were at the root of his pain. He could perhaps live with Mary whatever the answer would be, but he had to know for sure. "Are they both naked, or only the woman?" He had snapped the rubber band around the photos again. His hand dug into the attaché case and wrapped itself around George Lyttle's gun, a Saturday night special from the feel of it. "Are they in bed together? Is he on top of her, or what? You give me the right answers, and I'll let you go." Unseen by George Lyttle, his finger slipped inside the trigger guard.

George Lyttle, hanging from his chain, considered his state. In recent minutes his state had improved. Having recognized his previous terror as unprepossessing, he had mastered it. He was still manacled to this pipe, which was indeed a predicament, but he had resumed cerebrating and a solution had come to mind. Alternate solutions in fact. His predicament was certainly solutionizable.

First of all, he had worked out who this dude was. Or rather, he had worked out who he was not. He was not the police. The police did not chain citizens to pipes in alleys using that citizen's own handcuffs. They used their own. In addition, this man was in quite as much of a state as George had been. According to George's experience, states were quite common to the police mind. In their contacts with citizens they often worked themselves into states. But this man's state was not your everyday cop state. George Lyttle, therefore, was by no means in the clutches of the law.

To confirm these conjectures, he went back over his original hypothesis. Mary Hearn and Loftus—he thought of them by name, almost as friends—had been caught indulging in the crime of fornication and adultery. George Lyttle knew nothing about the New York State penal code. To him fornication and adultery were crimes punishable with the utmost severity, namely a severe jail term.

Mary Hearn and Loftus therefore were felons. Such people could not have recourse to the police. George's original hypothesis was sound. Being criminals, furthermore, they were responsible for all logical consequences of their acts. The woman especially had gone to that hotel determined to subject herself to fornication. She was guilty of provoking whatever fornication occurred there, under whatever form.

No, George had nothing to fear from the police.

But he was indeed in the clutches of this nut case who had chained him to the pipe, and he reasoned that this must be her husband or other close relative who had somehow intercepted one of his missives or phone messages. He must have traced the phone number back to the railroad station. This was a surprise to George, inasmuch as only lawmen had access to such top-secret telephone lists, he believed.

George's mind seemed to him to be working like lightning. His thoughts were as fluid and as powerful as a river surging between its banks to the sea. If this man were a husband instead of a policeman, it made George's predicament no less urgent, merely different. Jealousy was an evil empire and to all appearances it had encroached upon the man's demeanor. It had corroded his breast with the most virulent poison to which mankind was subject. The man was obviously not thinking at all, only emotionating, and an emotionating man could be swayed through eloquence. Eloquence was the keynote here. George believed that the way to extricate himself was through the power of the spoken word—failing which he had noted a certain weakness in the pipe to which he was attached. He was a strong and athletic young man. He could rip the pipe from the wall without too much difficulty, he believed. George's plan therefore was to commence with elocutionary techniques. If this failed he would still be in a position to break loose. A struggle would ensue in which surprise would give him the advantage. The pipe would become a club. He would club the gun hand first, then the dude's head. He would dent his cranium a few times, making further thought difficult for him, and then amble out of here.

Eloquence first. George began a speech about his friend Zorro, whose briefcase that was on the floor there. Zorro had asked him to intercede in the case of a lady who owed

Zorro money. Having ascertained that Zorro preyed upon couples in hotel rooms, George had garnered the evidence—that briefcase there—and had made the determination that the legal authorities ought to be informed at once. He had been on his way to inform them. In the matter of Zorro the law would take its course and deal with him in good time. However, George had first stopped off in that phone booth back there in the railroad station in order to accept the phone call from the lady so as to relieve any incipient preoccupations that her mind might have harbored on the matter.

But partway through this speech George saw that he had lost his audience. Eloquence was not going to work. The man was not listening. Instead his hand had come out of the briefcase and he had begun to fumble through the photographs once again. This was alarming. In a moment he would come to the one which, to George Lyttle, represented the supreme subjugation of the tyrant. Symbolically speaking it showed mastery by the former slaves of the slave masters—not by George himself, but by his people. But he was afraid such symbolism might be lost on this man, who did not seem to have too subtle a turn of mind.

George said, "I don't think you care to peruse those things too closely, my man."

Joe's brain was feverish, and this made his fingers clumsy. He dealt off photos of Loftus. Loftus did not interest him.

It was the first of George's crotch shots that stopped him. Joe recognized the crotch in question: Mary's. He could have identified Mary among all the other females in the world just from this view of her, could have sworn to her identity in court. The core of life isolated and disembodied, as if belonging to no particular woman. It was the type photo deviates collected, that teenage boys stared at with lust, but to Joe it represented love itself. He remembered the first time he had ever seen Mary's legs spread that way, how he had reached up to throw on the light, saying, "I want to see you." A moment later, also for the first time, he had added a new word to their lexicon of love: "I want to see your cunt."

Mary too had lifted up, trying to see the place where they were joined together. "Do you see it?"

"There seems to be something in it."

"Leave the light on," Mary had said, and her arms had pulled him down again.

Joe was still staring at the photo. This time Mary had been unable to reach for anyone. She was lying on her handcuffed wrists, and the tips of her fingers could be seen peeking out from beneath her buttocks.

The next photo down was another in the same series. The angle had changed slightly. The flash threw different highlights. Joe stared fixedly at this beloved part of this beloved woman and the effect was cumulative. Mary's face could not be seen. Most of her body could not be seen. On display was pubic hair and vulva only. Nothing identified Mary. But to Joe the identification was as positive as her signature or her fingerprints. He could see all of her that was not in the photo, her knees, her feet, her arms and breasts, her mouth and hair and eyes. She must have been so afraid. Her suffering must have passed beyond all reckoning, and his own rose up now to match hers.

He dealt on. The final photo showed Mary on her back on the bed, her gag gone now, but still lying on her handcuffed hands. Between her knees, buried deep inside her, was George Lyttle. Having reared up over her torso, he had photographed the actual rape in the mirror on the wall. He wore sunglasses, and the camera hid much of his face, but there could be no mistake. Joe began to scream. He screamed on and on, and was not aware he was doing it.

"Easy, man, easy," said George Lyttle.

Though his screaming soon stopped, Joe did not hear him. He heard nothing. These photos were proof, but as evidence in court they could well be suppressed, for they had been seized without a warrant—despite his consternation Joe's mind tried to work it out. The arrest was irregular—indeed, it hadn't even occurred yet, though the prisoner was manacled to a pipe. George Lyttle might go free. The courts might release him. He had a good chance. The photos meanwhile would become public property. Mary would be destroyed by them, and by the trial.

There must be no trial. The trial would take place now. It was no good wishing he had never looked at these photos, that George Lyttle had not made them, or at least had left them home. There was a chimpanzee hanging by one arm from a pipe, an animal to be exterminated. I'm going to kill him, Joe told himself. Mary had suffered enough pain already. Her suffering ended here. Once more reaching into the attaché case, Joe pulled out the gun. I'm going to kill him with his own gun and drop it on the corpse, he told himself. It would all be over in a second, a modern rite of purification. Mary would be purified. Joe would be purified. Even George Lyttle, hanging half crucified from the pipe, would be purified, his crime expiated in a single incandescent flash.

"Read me my rights," demanded George Lyttle in alarm.

Joe muttered, "You don't have any rights." He raised the gun and thumbed the hammer back. His finger nestled itself on the trigger.

"The woman should have remained home in the kitchen," cried George Lyttle, "performing everyday tasks." He stood on the rubble, one arm manacled above his head, the other gesticulating wildly. "Blame the woman."

But the gunsight would not stay on target. Lyttle wore a white open-necked shirt and tan trousers. The sight kept moving up and down the shirt. It would not stand still.

"You might call it an accident of copulation," said George Lyttle. "There is a commonality in occurrences of this kind."

Joe steadied the gun by holding it in both hands. The front sight was fixed now where he wanted it. The problem was elsewhere. His finger refused to tighten on the trigger. It would not obey the order from his brain. In addition his eyes were full of moisture and he could not see very well. At first he thought it was sweat, then he realized it was tears—tears of rage, or perhaps despair. I want to kill him, he thought, and I can't do it.

"She came to that hotel to copulate," said George Lyttle. "And she copulated. She got what she wanted."

Even then Joe did not pull the trigger. Instead his chest was racked with dry sobs.

"Shoot her," said George Lyttle, "not me."

The gun went off.

The first bullet went into the rubble beside Joe's leg. The report in that confined space was magnified a hundred times. After that Joe found himself firing shots one after another. Frustration and rage demanded action of some kind, some kind of release, and no other was available. He

fired into the wall all around George Lyttle. He had fixed
on a single thought, one that would return to haunt him
later. If he could not execute this creature, then at least he
would terrify him. He would introduce him to fear on the
level of Mary's fear. It would not be the same, would not
purify anything, but at least Lyttle would know something
of what it had been like for her.

"You deserve to die." he sobbed. "You hurt Mary."

The shots continued. Perhaps he hoped a ricochet would
catch Lyttle between the eyes, and this thought too would
return to haunt him—because then he would have killed
him without killing him. He did not know what the shots
might sound like from the street. He was not thinking
about the street. He did not know what kind of gun this
was in his hand either, only that the bullets kept coming
There seemed an endless supply of them. He noted the
whites of George Lyttle's eyes. He saw the fear there that
he had hoped for, perhaps even absolute terror, and then
in an instant—an instant for which he was simply not
prepared—something totally unexpected occurred. George
Lyttle somehow broke the handcuff chain or pulled the
pipe down—in any case, he was loose, and tried to dive
past him. Instead he dived headfirst into the last bullet
leaving the gun. This bullet was aimed as wildly as the
others. That is, it was not aimed at all. It should have gone
into the ceiling or the wall and Joe did not realize at first
that it hadn't.

Instead, the autopsy would later determine, it went in
one ear and came out just behind the other. Even then,
Lyttle's charge continued. His shoulder, or perhaps his
exploded skull, struck Joe in the chest. The policeman
went down under him.

His prisoner was loose and Joe was, he believed, fighting for his life. He meant to hold onto his prisoner if he
could, but his first job was to save himself from this
unexpected assault, from hands that in a moment would
be reaching for his throat.

The unregistered gun had gone flying. Joe was trying to
get his own gun out of his pocket while fending George
Lyttle off. Lyttle was Joe's size, much younger of course,
and he seemed to Joe as dangerous a threat to his life as
any he had ever faced.

In less than a second all these thoughts had collided in Joe's head, with more coming. The weight on top of him was entirely inert, which made no sense. In addition, a slippery mess was spreading itself across his chest. Had George Lyttle somehow thrown up on him? Joe, wriggling out from under, pushed the corpse off him and stood up. As he did so, he realized that's what it was—a corpse. Breathing hard, he stood over it and tried to comprehend what had happened. Next he peered down at his own shirt. Brains. He had seen brains before, seen them many times on sidewalks spread out beside dead men, pools of mushroom soup. He grabbed up the gun again.

These physical reactions led to intellectual ones, the first being: you killed him.

I didn't mean to, he told himself. I wasn't trying to kill him. I was trying to scare him.

Then he thought miserably, I don't know what I was trying to do.

There were ways to cover up this crime, or any other, the most obvious being to make it look like what it was not. Joe could turn Lyttle's pockets inside out, making it into a robbery, or shoot him in the head several times more, making it a gangland execution. Or he could plant some drugs—

But Joe thought of none of these things. He found he could not think at all. Overcome by horror at what he had done, he began backing away from the corpse. The rubble was uneven underfoot, and he nearly fell. To leave like this was the equivalent of scrawling his signature across George Lyttle's chest, but he either did not realize it or did not care. He could not believe he had killed a man, did not want to believe it. He was leaving behind evidence that would bring detectives quickly to his door, beginning with the two sandwich bags of credit cards; in addition George Lyttle's attaché case leaning so casually agape against the wall contained Mary's address and phone number, and the papers Joe had strewn about bore his fingerprints. Plus he was covered with gore. As soon as he left the alley he would attract the attention of witnesses.

It was then about four-thirty in the afternoon, and the sun was low. He reached the street and ran. George Lyttle's chrome-plated gun now empty, still flashed in his hand. Within a block there were pedestrians who flattened themselves against walls as he ran by. Black people who had seen guns often enough, though not like this. He realized he must be weeping. His tears were principally for Mary and the children, for he believed he had destroyed their lives as well as his own.

His run did not last long. His chest was heaving, he was unable to breathe, and this forced him to a walk. He shoved the gun down into his side pocket, alongside the other one, his own, and he glanced around trying to determine where he was. As soon as he had found a street sign, he related that particular corner to the nearest station house. He knew the location of every station house in the city, every courthouse too, every hospital, specialized knowledge, the epitome of specialized knowledge, knowledge useless to anyone other than a cop. The nearest station house was the 25th on East 119 Street. He began to walk there, intending to surrender, to make a full confession, and after that to accept whatever anyone wanted to do to him.

When the station house was still three blocks off, his steps slowed and a sense of his own dignity reasserted itself. He would not walk in there like all the other hysterics cops saw, most of whom could not even be understood during their first ten minutes inside the station house door. He was calmer now, and old habits had begun to take hold of him. There were normal police procedures to cover occurrences of nearly every type including this one, and the first of these was to make the proper notifications. A great many offices would have to be notified, the precinct, division, and borough commanders, of course, as well as the chief of detectives, the police commissioner, and public information. Also the medical examiner and the district attorney—there were others too, but these were the ones that came immediately to mind. He had reached a phone booth by then, and he stepped into it determined to make the first of his notifications now, and he dialed the district attorney's number and asked to be put through to Judith Adler.

When she came on the line he said as calmly as he could, "I found the man who raped my wife, and I—and I—"

He was interrupted by a sob. He was trying so hard to control himself that he could not believe that such a convulsive sound had come from his own chest. "And I killed him," he concluded.

Judith said, "Oh, Joe."

"I'm not asking for anything. I'm just notifying you."

"Where are you?" she asked sharply.

"I'm going into the two-five to surrender."

"I'll be right there. Don't say anything to anybody until I get there."

"But I have to," explained Joe patiently. "Don't you see? I have a lot of notifications to make. I better make a list of them. Forensic will have to know too, and—"

Judith cut him off. "I'll get there as fast as I can."

Joe, having hung up the phone, continued his slow walk toward the station house.

26

THOUGH LEANING FORWARD OVER THE FRONT SEAT, Judith was unable to make the cab go faster. The station house when she reached it was deserted except for the switchboard officer and the clerical man, and a single prisoner, she was told, in the cage upstairs. The news had cleaned the place out, said the clerical cop. Everyone was at the crime scene.

"Crime scene?"

"The site of the occurrence," corrected the clerical cop, who was about fifty years old and still a patrolman. He looked at her over the top of his glasses. One did not argue with district attorneys.

"What happened?"

On the other hand, one didn't have to answer their questions. "I wouldn't know," he said blandly.

It made Judith furious, but she could do nothing. There was no person or object on whom to focus her rage. To spend it on persons of low rank was undignified and wasteful. The clerical cop was immune, and he knew it.

Just then the precinct captain came up the stoop and in through the station house door, a big, florid-faced man in a baggy uniform. After eyeing Judith, he ignored her, lumbering forward toward the high muster desk, crossing the boards as heavily as a ship. She had to step in his way to get him to acknowledge her at all. After identifying herself, she requested facts, but the captain avoided giving any.

"It's being investigated now," he said. His name was Mullen.

"Yes, but what happened?"

Mullen was accompanied by his desk lieutenant, a much younger man who stayed two paces back and refused to be drawn into the conversation. "What a mess," Mullen replied, and he turned toward the lieutenant. "Wouldn't you say it was a mess, Tommy?"

"You're right, Captain, a mess."

Mullen took off his cap. He was white-haired, tall, and fat. He was what street cops called a hairbag. He wasn't going any further and was lucky to have got this far. Judith knew the type. The lieutenant was the same. They had recognized the Joe Hearn case at once for what it was— complicated, and therefore dangerous. They were staying as far away from it as possible.

"How is Inspector Hearn?" she asked, and her voice sounded to her more anxious than she wished.

"There's brains all over him," said Captain Mullen.

"He was wiping them off with Kleenexes," added the lieutenant, no doubt trying to shock her. She ignored him. She did not even wince. But she decided to ask no further questions of Mullen, who might have a big mouth to go with his big belly. She feared hardening his perception of whatever he might have seen or heard. Or perhaps she only feared to learn what the facts might be.

She rode to the site in the back of a patrol car called in by radio. Because of stalled traffic the car was unable to approach too closely, so she got out and walked forward through the jam. Other cops were trying to untangle it. The streets were blocked partly by police vehicles, partly by crowds of spectators. Department vehicles were parked on the sidewalk, or double-parked in the street—seven or eight of them. She noted the forensic van too. Its rear doors were spread wide. In front of it was the medical examiner's car. The wooden barriers were up. Spectators pressed against them on all three sides, and there was not a white face that she could see.

"Excuse me," she said trying to push her way through. Most of them were staring at the entrance to the alley, though nothing could be seen there. A cop moved the barrier to let her through. The crowd was watching her now. Concentration had shifted, along with eyes. She was conscious of people ogling her, wondering who she was.

Wearing high heels, she went down the three steps into

the alley. To step over the rubble was not easy. A biblical image came to mind, together with the word Golgotha— place of stones, place of execution. Golgotha meant Calvary. There were cops down in the alley too. Too many of them, more than were needed. They ought to be back on patrol by now. Somebody ought to get them out of here, she thought. But the hairbag captain was back in his station house, his lieutenant was safe there too, and no one seemed in charge.

Ahead was a floodlit area. She moved toward it, stepping carefully. A final cop moved aside, making room for her, and she stared down at the corpse, which was brilliantly lighted. It was as if the sun were shining straight along the surface of the earth at alley level, straight into his eyes. Part of his skull was gone. He had already been lifted onto the medical examiner's canvas sheet which was about to become a body bag. As Judith watched, the attendants threw the folds over him and zipped the bag shut. Hoisting the stretcher at either end, they began moving it up the alley toward the street.

The medical examiner, holding his bag, watched them go. His name was Dr. Blumberg.

Judith shook hands with him. "Cause of death?"

"An ear-to-ear shot."

"A police bullet?" She was peering farther down the alley looking for Joe Hearn, but did not see him.

"A smaller caliber than that, I believe."

Two detectives were on their knees in the rubble collecting bullet fragments. She watched them find one; it went into a plastic evidence pouch. The rubble near their knees was stained with blood and brains, but there was no viscous pool such as sometimes collected. Judith peered about. She was looking for the police commissioner, and for Chief of Detectives Cirillo. She was looking for faces she knew, for this seemed to her a very big case. The brass ought to be here by now.

She said to Dr. Blumberg, "Who's in charge?"

"Not me."

One of the bystanders detached himself and stepped forward. He was dressed in civilian clothes.

"I'm running the investigation," he said, and gave his name and rank. Judith had expected a captain at least, but he was a detective sergeant. His name was Markey.

"Where are the heavyweights?" inquired Judith.

"I've been told to handle this like any other possible line-of-duty shooting," said Markey stiffly. She noted his use of the word "possible."

"You mean they're not coming?"

"They'd be here by now."

Judith thought it over. Forty or fifty citizens were killed by New York cops each year, usually during the commission of a crime, and usually by uniformed patrolmen or ordinary detectives. It was rare for sergeants to fire their guns on duty, rarer still for lieutenants, and almost unheard of for higher ranks. But Joe Hearn was an inspector; he commanded the Narcotics Division as well. A homicide of this kind ought to have pulled in the top brass from all over the city. Instead it had been dumped into the lap of a sergeant. The brass was not coming. They did not want to risk contamination. Let the sergeant handle it.

When she questioned him, Sergeant Markey did give her certain facts, though not all he knew by any means, she believed. One shot had been fired from the inspector's service revolver. Apparently that bullet was not lodged inside the deceased at this time. All eight shots had been fired from the Saturday night special, one of which had resulted in the deceased's instantaneous demise. It was not clear who had done all this shooting, Markey said. It was possible the deceased had done most of it himself.

"Then it's line of duty," said Judith. "It's self-defense, or maybe even an accident, but line of duty?" Her tone had risen as she spoke, turning her statement into a question. It was a risky question to ask, but she had to ask it.

"Maybe he committed suicide," Markey said, watching Judith carefully. "The only thing is, he seems to have been handcuffed to a pipe at the time."

Her heart seemed to go out through the bottom of her stomach. It was as if it was resting now on her knees. Joe murdered him, she thought. Executed him. To Markey she said sharply, "What point are you trying to make?"

"No point. The investigation isn't closed yet."

Judith tried to read his face, but there was insufficient light and insufficient information. Markey was about thirty-five. Either he was one of the bright ones trying to get ahead, or else one of the stupid ones determined not to make a mistake. It was impossible to tell. Either way he would look to see which way his superiors were leaning before presenting any conclusions of his own. This placed the burden, and any decisions that would have to be made, squarely on her. Markey's own conduct, once she had made them, could not be predicted.

"Apparently Inspector Hearn arrested him in the railroad station," Markey said. "Then he brought him here."

"The station," said Judith sharply, "is two blocks away."

"You always take the perpetrator off the street when you're arresting him," said Markey. "That's standard procedure."

"I know that."

Markey watched her. He said nothing.

"Has Inspector Hearn made any statements?" inquired Judith.

"He said all kinds of things. He was babbling." Markey watched her shrewdly. "A young cop would be cutting notches in his gun, but at his age when you kill someone it shakes you up."

Judith was silent. She waited to hear whatever Markey would say next.

"He didn't make much sense." Markey showed a blank page in his notebook. "When he told me he murdered the perpetrator in cold blood, I didn't even take it down. Admissions like that don't mean anything."

Their eyes met. Another rape case involving a cop, Judith thought bleakly. The usual horror. They do it, and then they are absolutely appalled at what they have done. Their principal emotion after the act is remorse. Total, unappeasable remorse. They desire to pay the full price.

"Where is he?"

"Out back," said Markey, and he gestured over his shoulder toward the daylight at the end of the alley. "I got a uniformed guy watching him. I was afraid he might try to do something to himself."

Judith, stepping carefully, went down the alley toward the courtyard. Though she ignored him, Markey followed. She came out into the daylight and was surrounded by buildings. Every single one of them appeared to have been condemned. Sheets of aluminum had been nailed over the windows all the way up. Joe was on the other side of the courtyard, his hands plunged into his pockets. He was facing the other way, and she did not call out to him.

At her feet the former garden was littered with rubble, with ruined furniture, with broken bathroom fittings, with chunks of plaster still attached to lathes.

Markey pointed toward Joe. "That's him over there."

"Stay here," Judith said, and she made her way across the courtyard. Joe, who had turned, watched her approach. But she stopped two paces away.

Face-to-face with him, she found herself unable to speak. Neither reached out to touch the other.

He said, "Hello, how are you?"

His face was drawn, his eyes were red, and the flesh of his cheeks sagged. He seemed to her to have aged ten years in the few hours since she'd seen him. This aging process was perhaps irreversible. He was a different person now than he had been this morning or would ever be again. He is no longer the man with whom you think you fell in love, she reminded herself, and she felt herself begin to pull away from him.

Although she searched for words adequate to the situation, none came, and she knew perfectly well why: because her role here was not defined. Only two roles were available, and they were mutually exclusive. By trade she was a prosecutor; and prosecuting, it seemed to her, took precedence over loving. Prosecuting had boundaries, whereas loving had none; therefore prosecuting seemed the more serious role. It exerted discipline. It constricted her in a way she was used to. You're not his lover anymore, she told herself. He's made loving him impossible. Your job now is to prosecute him. But a part of her wished to be his lover still, wished it more than ever, wished to comfort him, to hold his head to her bosom.

The conflict made her impatient with him.

"Did anyone read you your rights?"

He nodded. "Sergeant Markey. It wasn't necessary."

"You should have a lawyer."

"I don't need a lawyer."

Her impatience rose up. "If you can't afford a lawyer, one can be provided for you."

"I know that," he said gently. "I can afford a lawyer. There's no need. I went there to kill him and I killed him. I'm not going to hide anything. He raped my wife. I say that to explain my motivation. It's not an alibi. I'm not trying to excuse myself."

And there you have it, Judith thought grimly, a voluntary confession to an officer of the court, myself. An open-and-shut case. Case closed. She said, "If you had a lawyer right now he'd tell you to keep your mouth shut."

Joe only looked at her. He said nothing. He accepted the reprimand without protest.

Judith said, "I'm told you handcuffed him to a pipe."

"Yes."

"With his own handcuffs?"

"I didn't have mine with me, you see."

Judith knew what her next move should be. She should place him in front of a videotape machine and elicit a full confession. It was a job she was very good at. She had done it many times. Suspects often blurted out the whole story. A guilt-ridden cop like Joe Hearn would be easy for her. She could hear her questions in advance: You immobilized him, is that correct? And then you executed him in cold blood, is that correct?

She was as unhappy as ever before in her life. Oh, why did I come here? she asked herself. Why didn't I stay in my office? Why did I imagine I might save him?

You can't save him, she told herself. Besides which, your duty is elsewhere—to the law, and to the people of the State of New York. Your duty is to your oath of office, to your solemn word.

She said, "I think you told Sergeant Markey the same thing, that you went there to kill him, and that you—" Here her voice broke. She was unable to maintain its harsh tone. "—That you intended to kill him all along."

Joe nodded.

"All right," said Judith. "How many other people have you said that to?"

"I don't know."

"Captain Mullen, the precinct commander was here, I believe. Did you tell it to him?"

"No." But Joe seemed unsure of himself. "I don't think I did."

Judith tossed her hair angrily. The situation was impossible. "My advice to you is to get a lawyer before you tell anyone else."

"That's not necessary."

"A lawyer would tell you to plead self-defense, or accident. A lawyer would tell you to claim it was a line-of-duty shooting."

"Well, it wasn't."

"Nobody is going to weep very hard for the deceased, Joe," she said. "Joe, please."

He only shook his head. He was like a child who had run away from home and now refused to return. There was nothing she could do for him. The law would take its course, and no one could stop it.

It made her angry, impatient, and miserable all at once. How could he have committed so foolish an act? He had ruined his own life, and possibly hers as well. Certainly he had ruined whatever they might have had together. She said in a cold voice, "You don't even have proof he was actually the man who raped your wife."

Joe withdrew the packet of photos from his pocket. Wordlessly he handed them over. The one on top showed George Lyttle in the mirror as he raped Mary Hearn.

It had the same effect on Judith as on Joe earlier. It made her blink her eyes. They started blinking of their own accord and for about sixty seconds would not stop.

Presently she was able to say, "I'll keep these if I may." They were evidence and would be used against him in court. No juror, seeing them, was likely to believe that Joe had killed George Lyttle by accident or in self-defense. The argument that this was a line-of-duty shooting would simply not stand up. However much the jury might sympathize with him, he would have to be charged, because that was the law. He was a police inspector, a man of public trust, and from such a man such conduct could not be condoned. She began to consider what this charge should be, murder or manslaughter. One of the degrees of manslaughter, most likely. Which degree? She didn't know. A Class B felony at least, eight to fifteen years in jail. She tried to think like a lawyer, to concentrate on the legal technicalities. But she was unable to force her mind to stay on track.

"You'll go before the grand jury," she said.

"Of course." Every police shooting went before a grand jury which in nearly every instance ruled justifiable homicide and dismissed the case. But barring a miracle, no jury would dismiss this one.

"What will you say?" she asked him.

"The truth."

"What's the truth according to you?"

"I killed him in cold blood."

They'll indict him for sure, she thought. "You're upset," she said. "You might say something completely different tomorrow."

He again shook his head.

Turning away from him she crossed the former garden to the place where Sergeant Markey waited. "See that he gets a lawyer," she told him. "I don't want him interrogated and I especially don't want him signing any statements until one gets here."

She could do no more for him than that, and she went out through the alley. She went out past Dr. Blumberg, the assistant medical examiner, who was still there, though the corpse was gone. She nodded to him and kept moving. She came out onto the sidewalk with its wooden barriers, its crowd of staring black faces. Only when she had passed through them and was making her way toward the nearest subway did she begin to cry.

27

MARY AT THAT TIME STILL WAS PACING THE FLOOR OF her kitchen. She was smoking. Each time she passed it she stared at the telephone. It hung at eye level like an icon that could perhaps perform miracles. All it had to do was ring. But it remained silent.

During the last hour she had dialed the railroad station repeatedly. She did not know it was a railroad station. She had let it ring and ring. Someone, the first time, had picked up. After that, nothing. A telephone deep in the city ringing, so far as she knew, in a void.

She withdrew another cigarette, lit up, took a few drags, stubbed it out, and almost immediately lit another. She paced from the sink to the dinette table, three steps in one direction, three back. On the table stood her pocketbook heavy with money. The ashtray beside it was about to overflow. Mary rarely smoked, but if this went on would need a carton to get through the day.

To dial the number again seemed useless. She was waiting now to be contacted—for her own phone to ring with further instructions. She did not know what else to do. Her life seemed to be closing in on her, together with the walls of this room. Even the day was closing in. Her children would be home any minute, and after that Joe. Then what?

"Hello?" Suddenly the phone had rung. Lunging for it she had knocked the ashtray to the floor.

"What's happening? I have a right to know. You've got to tell me."

Loftus. His voice was full of panic, or outright fear. This

had its usual effect on Mary. It made her angry with him and anger, outwardly at least, made her calm.

"Nothing's happening."

"You promised you'd call."

"When I have something to tell you I'll call, not before. You're tying up the phone. Both our phones."

"Did you talk to him?"

"Whoever answered," Mary said after a moment, "hung up."

"Why did he do that?"

To torture me, Mary thought, why else? "How should I know?"

"Oh, God," said Loftus.

"You're tying up the phone."

"What do we do now?"

"We wait for him to contact us. Now will you please get off the phone?"

"I'm going out of my mind," said Loftus.

Billy had just come in the back door, followed immediately by his sister. Mary stared at her children and wordlessly hung up on Loftus.

They went straight to the refrigerator. She watched them a moment, then shifted her view to the upended ashtray on the floor. She was about to sweep the mess up when the phone rang a second time. Again she lunged for it. There was a moment during which she imagined it would be Loftus calling back, but it wasn't.

"I want you to meet me," said Judith Adler's voice. "How soon can you get here?"

Mary believed she had to stay by the telephone, and she glanced around her frantically. "I have my children home."

"They're old enough to be left alone," said Judith harshly.

Mary was focused on her own problems. Nonetheless, the tone of Judith's voice surprised her. It frightened her too. "I was just about to start dinner," she said. "It's almost dinnertime," she pleaded. "My husband will come home any minute."

Judith said, "Your husband can wait, your children can wait, and dinner can wait. How soon can I expect you?"

"Can you," said Mary after a pause, "tell me what it's about?"

"No, I can't. Take down this address. The sooner you

get here, the sooner you get home. I'll wait for you out front."

Thoroughly rattled, Mary ran upstairs and threw on what she considered "city" clothes. In the kitchen she lifted her heavy handbag off the countertop. "Go watch television," she told her children. "I have to go out for a little while." She debated leaving a message for Joe, or for anyone else who might call, but decided against it. She went out the back door and got into her car.

The assistant medical examiner, Dr. Blumberg, was the last to leave the alley. Once the corpse was gone he had no further business there, yet he stayed. To be inside the police barriers, unlike all those spectators on the sidewalk who were outside, was satisfying to him. In addition, he enjoyed crime scenes. He was a pathologist. He enjoyed pathology of all kinds. Most cops did too, he had noted. Which was probably a good thing since they saw so much of it. Pathology was like any illicit pleasure. Though hooked on it, one rarely admitted this openly. Others would not understand.

Crime scenes were also question marks; Dr. Blumberg was loathe to quit this one until some of his questions were answered. The corpse, now on its way downtown, would wait for him. It was not a very interesting corpse in any event. Some were. Sometimes he could hardly wait to get back to the morgue and dig into them. But this time he had only a cranium to take apart, he believed. The rest of the cadaver had looked in perfect condition, no pathology there. A healthy young animal. Cut and dried.

He watched ballistic detectives on their knees, sifting the moist rubble for bullet fragments. Floodlights shone down on them. One of them had a bald spot in the back of his head. It occurred to Dr. Blumberg that a crime scene was like a wound in the hide of society. Cops swarmed over it like maggots. The blood attracted them. They fed on it. They found the wound and began to gorge themselves.

This alley was still crowded with uniformed cops. They stood like tourists on an old battlefield, and brooded about the traumatic events that had taken place here, events that were already receding swiftly into the past; once the blood had dried, once the cops had gone away, it would be impossible to conjure them up very well ever again. If one liked to brood, it was now or never.

The police photographer had finished and was packing his gear. He took away most of the floodlights and went out of the alley. The uniformed cops began drifting away. The detective sergeant who had the case came into the alley from the courtyard, accompanied by the shaken inspector who had done the shooting. They were talking about lawyers. The inspector said he didn't want one. The sergeant seemed to consider this awhile. Finally he said to him, "In that case, sir, you're free to go."

Dr. Blumberg had to step aside for them.

"You still here, Doc?" the sergeant said to him as he passed.

Dr. Blumberg decided it was time to leave. Already it was difficult to conjure anything up. The corpse must have reached the morgue by now—was probably already being prepared for him. It would be stripped, measured, weighed, photographed, arranged for him on the slab. His assistant would be laying out his tools. That cranium might be interesting after all, once he had taken it apart—scalpel first, then the Skilsaw.

As he went out of the alley, he was deciding which blade he wanted in it. He went out through the crowd to his car and drove downtown.

Judith had perceived Mary's agitation over the phone but had misread its cause. She doesn't want to see me, she thought. She's trying to cling to domestic normalcy. Her hold on normalcy is fragile, and I am a threat to it. It is the threat she is responding to, not me personally. Now, waiting outside on the sidewalk, she watched Mary come up on foot. It was beginning to get dark. Mary was wearing a skirt and a suede jacket belted at the waist.

"I had to park two blocks away," she said, and pretended to give a lighthearted laugh. Her true emotion, Judith saw, was fear.

"So what's so mysterious?" Mary asked.

Judith watched her glance up at the wall of the building and give a start to read the sign there: OFFICE OF THE CHIEF MEDICAL EXAMINER.

"Joe?" Mary said, almost in a whisper.

"No, not Joe," responded Judith crossly. "Come on." And she led the way inside.

They entered a reception room. There were rugs on the floor and magazines on a coffee table. The receptionist smiled and spoke into a telephone on their behalf. It was like a dentist's waiting room, though corpses were being cut up all over the building; it was the only work done there. Mary, as they waited, seemed increasingly fearful. From time to time she gave Judith a nervous smile, and she could not keep her hands still, but she asked no further questions.

Judith saw all this but kept silent. She refused to take pity on her.

An attendant came and led them downstairs. They walked along a corridor. There were viewing windows in the wall. Through the windows could be seen rows and rows of refrigerated lockers, and also corpses that lay under shrouds on gurneys that had been parked here and there against walls, because presumably all the lockers were full. Side by side the two women followed the attendant down the corridor. They passed a family group peering through a window at a corpse on a trolley. The attendant beside it had just peeled back the shroud revealing a bloated blue face, and the family group had begun solemnly nodding. Judith watched Mary, who quickly turned her face away. They passed still more windows, more lockers. Behind all those locker doors lay real corpses naked on pull-out trays, nearly all of them dead of unnatural causes. It was a scene one witnessed often enough in movies, Judith thought. Mary would recognize it. Movies could not prepare a person for the reality, however. The reality was the plenitude of death, its ubiquity, its multitudinous numbers. So many lockers. The dead were as commonplace as newspapers, a throwaway item to be discarded tomorrow and forgotten soon after. Mary walked with her eyes on the floor.

When the attendant stopped them at the final window, Mary turned and faced the opposite wall, while Judith peered into the dissection room: rows of stone tables bearing naked corpses, over whom leaned teams of men in white coats. The doctors were working hard as if trying to resuscitate them. But resuscitation was not the game here. Stainless-steel tools rose and fell regularly, catching the light, and from time to time the central figure at each tableau spoke into the microphone that hung over the center of the table.

Dr. Blumberg saw Judith and waved. He came out through a door in the wall and stood beside them.

He seemed very cheerful. "I'm having him brought over now."

An attendant wheeled a gurney up to the window and peeled the shroud back as far as the naked chest.

Mary was still studying the opposite wall. Judith spoke to her sharply: "Take a look at this, please."

After a moment Mary turned around. She said nothing. She peered down at the late George Lyttle.

A towel had been wrapped around the top part of his head. "I prettied him up a bit," explained Dr. Blumberg with a chuckle. "We didn't want to shock anybody too much."

To Mary, Judith said coldly, "Someone you know?"

Mary nodded.

"Is it him?"

Mary nodded again.

"If you're sure, please say so."

Mary had to swallow before she could speak. "Yes."

"Your office reached me just in time," commented Dr. Blumberg. "I was just about to get into him."

The words seemed almost sexual in their import, and Judith was aware of this. "Thank you, Dr. Blumberg." She led Mary back down the hall. "Now you don't have to worry about him anymore," she said, "isn't that nice? Best therapy in the world, wouldn't you say?"

It was an identification that served no legal purpose whatsoever, as Judith had known all along, and her anger disappeared, to be replaced by a sudden rush of shame. Why did I bring this woman here? she asked herself. Why did I put her through this? I have begun acting as irrationally as her husband.

The two women went upstairs and out onto the sidewalk where they stood in silence watching the traffic move up First Avenue. At last Mary said, "What happened?"

"A cop shot him."

Mary's head nodded up and down several times. It was as if she knew the answer to the next question, but had to ask it anyway. "My husband?"

Judith was feeling as dispirited as a woman spurned. She answered, "Your husband, yes."

"Is he all right?"

"Sure. I saw him awhile ago. He's fine."

Mary's voice broke. "Can I see him?"

"He got into his car and drove away, or so I'm told. No one seems to know where he went."

From the look of her, Mary was trying to keep from crying. She said, "That man back there, what was his name?"

"George Lyttle."

"Was he carrying anything on him that—anything of mine?"

"I don't know," said Judith, and the desire to hurt Mary had returned. "You better ask your husband."

After a pause, Mary said, "What will happen to Joe?"

"That's for the grand jury to decide." Why did I tell her that? Judith asked herself. Now all three of us are suffering. Two wasn't enough?

Mary said, "I'll go home and wait for him. He's sure to come home. I'm certain of it." She paused. "Or at least call," she said in a whisper. "At least he'll call. Don't you think?"

But Judith did not answer.

Mary moved off from her down the street, eyes fixed on the ground, head nodding up and down. Watching her, Judith understood for the first time why she had brought Mary here, why she had marched her through that awful morgue, why she had forced her to make the useless identification, why she had inflicted this grisly experience on them both. It was because she had wanted another look at the woman Joe Hearn loved enough to kill for.

28

IN RUSH-HOUR TRAFFIC JOE HEARN HAD MOVED UP the West Side Drive. To one side of the road was the park. There passed row after row of dwarf cherry trees and dogwoods, all of them in flower in this season, cherry-vanilla ice-cream cones rising up out of spring green grass. He did not see them as such. He did not see them at all. On his other side flowed the wide deep Hudson, its surface brushed by wind. A freighter stood at anchor in midcurrent, prow pointed upstream. In the wind in the late afternoon light the edges of the ship were clear and sharply defined. Across on the Jersey side, also in sharp relief, rose the cliffs of the Palisades. He saw none of this either. He steered up the long steep ramp onto the George Washington Bridge. Now he was above the river, driving west. The towers of the bridge fell behind him. The 25th Precinct was far behind him. He was driving very fast. He was trying to outrun whatever it was that pressed so heavily on his chest, on his life. He was trying to outrun thought.

He crossed the waist of New Jersey into Pennsylvania where he stopped to fill his tank and to buy a bottle in a liquor store. He phoned Mary. This was habit. He didn't think it out. If the news had reached her she would be worried about him, and he dialed the number without knowing what he could say to her, but perhaps it was good-bye. Mary was not home, though it was suppertime. Billy took the call and noted nothing strange about his father's voice or anything else. No, he did not know where Mom had gone, but it was late and there was nothing on the stove. Joe pictured his children. They were alone in the house. He had traumatized their lives too. The innocent would be brought down with the guilty. But he could see no way out.

He got back into the car, onto the turnpike. He was still running. The country became hilly. Each time he topped a rise he could see the Alleghenies ahead, together with the last of the sunset stains of gold that lay upon wooded crowns, that unrolled partway down slopes like carpets. The country was getting bigger, but could not hide him. The towns were farther apart. He was like a boxer who had been hit by a knockout punch. He was still standing, barely; he just could not think what to do next. His mind no longer worked. It tried to focus on those choices that were left. But there were no choices left.

The night got very dark. At times there were no towns, no glow anywhere on the horizon, only endless miles of forest ahead and to either side. He was aware of the immensity of the land, but this immensity was all pressing in on him. The country was pressing down on his chest and he could not breathe. An unending succession of headlights came his way. They came almost at regular intervals, like fixed lampposts along a boulevard, like lights strung between trees. They were there blinding him, then would pass. They were of universal brightness, and would never stop, but they illuminated nothing. The darkness only closed in again. His eyes began to close. He fought against sleep. He wasn't there yet, hadn't done what had to be done. A car crash was no solution. People survived them, even at speeds like this. They lived for years in wheelchairs. He knew a better way.

When he could go no farther he stopped at a motel. By then he was somewhere in Ohio. He registered, paid in advance, and in the room assigned him, switched on the light. The room was empty, of course. It was also cold. He was cold. Moving to the wall thermostat, he turned up the heat. But it was not radiators that warmed hotel rooms, it was people. It was the life one brought into them. It was belongings out of a suitcase, out of a toilet kit. By morning, especially if one were not alone, hotel rooms could be cozy. He remembered waking up beside Mary in the hotel rooms of their honeymoon, rooms strewn with clothing, and the suitcases still unopened on the rack. But tonight he had nothing with him except the bottle, which he set down on top of the television set, and his gun, which he removed from his belt and placed on the bedside table. He stared down at it, even picked it up again in his hand.

The room was as alien as any in which he had ever stood. In the bathroom he found the cardboard ice container. He went out and walked down the corridor to the ice machine. That was habit too. It didn't matter whether the liquor was iced or not. He realized he hadn't eaten. He was not hungry. It was just as well. The anesthetic would work faster and better, and when he felt no more pain it would be time. Back in the room again he poured bourbon over the ice, and drank off half of it. After turning the television on, he stripped down to his underwear and, carrying the bottle and glass, got into bed. His gun was still on the bedside table, next to his hand, next to his head. He picked it up and looked at it. He put his finger inside the trigger guard. How ugly it was, how pure, how absolute. He was surprised he still had it. He had never hurt anybody with a gun until today. The ballistic technicians at the scene should have taken it away from him for tests, he believed. The true badge of his office, and one he did not want to live without. He was glad he still had it. The instant solution. It could solve any problem, and for so many cops it already had. It wasn't even dishonorable. On the contrary it was entirely logical, part of the long tradition. He was far enough away so that strangers would find him. By the time Mary had to see him they would have cleaned him up. He didn't want it to be messy for her.

Television and whiskey were the twin tranquillizers of modern times; formerly there had been only one. A shattered psyche such as his required both, though they were not enough. He stared at the screen, or it stared at him. The programs changed from time to time. He kept refilling his glass.

The sheets were cold on the tops of his thighs, on his knees. But gradually he was becoming numb. All the time he was aware of the gun close beside his ear. Now and then his eyes shifted to it. He was almost, not quite, ready.

In the big bed in the familiar room Mary lay awake, and was desperate with worry about her husband. A killing had taken place. The man who had raped her was dead, but the nightmare went on. She had only the sketchiest details, but she knew Joe. It was not something Joe could do and come away from unmarked. She had no idea where he was. That he had not come home proved he was in anguish. He had fled, disappeared. In such a mood he was in no condition to drive. She imagined him killed in a car crash. Worse, she saw him out of remorse killing himself with his own gun. He had never seemed to her self-destructive in the past, but any man was if pushed far enough, and suicide was the cop's way out. It was one of the occupational hazards of the police world, one of the many, all due to those guns they carried and would not be without. When a cop got in trouble he could unburden himself to no one, not to his best friend, who was probably another cop, not even to his wife. Confidences, to a cop, were not confidences at all, they were admissions, and whoever received them became witnesses, could be subpoenaed and forced to answer questions under oath. Because a cop's confidences could be used against him in court, he got out of the habit of making them. When he needed to talk he couldn't. A cop in trouble had no one to lean on, could seek solace nowhere, or so cops came to think. And so a great many of them in the past, and perhaps Joe tonight, turned to man's best friend. They turned to their guns. They sought solace there. Most put the guns in their mouths. A few shot themselves in the heart. She had known of several cases personally, one a close friend of them both. Even now her husband might be lying dead beside the road, or in a motel room someplace, and the pictures in her mind became so vivid that she heard herself sobbing.

The phone rang beside the bed in the dark. Her lunge was so frantic she knocked the receiver to the floor and had to grope for it. She put it to her ear, praying to hear Joe's voice, terrified she would hear instead the voice of Monsignor Kelly, the police chaplain.

But it was Judith Adler. "I'm sorry to be calling this late," she apologized. "Is Inspector Hearn at home?" she asked formally.

"No, he's not." Mary, having sat up, had turned on the lamp. She peered at the bedside clock but had to wipe her eyes dry to be able to see it. The time was ten after two in the morning.

"Have you heard from him?" The anxiety in Judith's voice almost did not show, but Mary caught it.

She is the one, she thought. The other woman. She is sick with worry too. "Is it something important?" she asked.

"Can you possibly inform me of his whereabouts?"

"I'm sorry, I can't."

The conversation was entirely stilted. It was as if they didn't know each other, had never met.

"I was a bit worried about him," Judith admitted after a silence. This was an understatement. She was as aware of the police tradition as Mary, and had been tormenting herself for hours, but she did not say so. Nor did she describe how, before midnight, she had phoned Ballistics. No, so far as was known, no one had taken away Inspector Hearn's gun. But wasn't it mandatory in a case like this to test-fire his gun? Yes, but—She had been advised to call back in the morning: "The day guys might know something." An hour later she had called Sergeant Markey at home, waking him up. Markey hadn't taken Joe's gun either. "He wasn't charged with anything," Markey said, "—yet."

Judith reported none of this to Mary. "Inspector Hearn did seem a bit upset when I saw him," she said. She had herself under better control now. Perhaps her words sounded a bit precise, but her voice was as casual as she could make it. "I just wanted to check up. I'm sorry I disturbed you."

"I'll have him call you as soon as he contacts me," said Mary. In the silence that followed she thought: This woman is the one he turned to; I should have realized it before. But this was the least of her worries, and she too held herself under restraint, or tried to. I don't care if I can't get him back, she thought. I just want him to be alive. "If you'll give me your number—"

Judith did so, and the connection was broken, and the two women lay in the dark and did not sleep, and the night continued.

At four o'clock the next afternoon Judith Adler, as chief of the trials division, chaired a meeting of the personnel evaluation committee in the conference room next to her office. Present were five other department heads. The elected district attorney of New York County did not attend, for at that hour he was making a speech to the Bar Association in a midtown hotel ballroom. He rarely attended meetings of Judith's committee anyway, being content to approve its decisions. About three hundred young prosecutors worked for him: he could not be expected to know them all.

The meeting had already lasted more than two hours. The conference table was piled high with personnel folders, and yawns were being stifled here and there around her. "Only a few more now," Judith said stubbornly. "Patrick O'Connor," she said paging through the next dossier. "He's had eight trials this year and lost six. Four were murder trials and he blew them all. What do we do with him?"

All day she had moved doggedly through her work. She was continuing to do so. She had talked by phone with Ballistics and with the medical examiner. She had received and studied their written reports. She had talked twice to Sergeant Markey. She had scheduled the grand jury hearing for the following day, but by now she believed there would be no principal to appear before it. No one had yet heard from Inspector Hearn or knew where he was, and her mood was close to desperation.

Work kept her from thinking.

A voice across the table, a department head named Felix Potter, murmured, "Pat O'Connor is a good lawyer."

"Is he?" said Judith. "He's blown six out of eight. Six felons are loose who ought to be in jail, and he's responsible."

This was not necessarily an exaggeration. There were so many arrests, so many cases, that in general no defendant was brought to trial unless the evidence against him was overwhelming.

"Pat's been having marital trouble lately," someone offered.

Judith gave her decision: "I think he should be asked to leave."

She looked at each of the department heads in turn. Most of them studied the tabletop, but one by one they nodded agreement.

She opened the next dossier. "Herman Glazer," she said. "He's another one. His last trial was the armed robbery of a liquor store. He puts the victim on the stand and then forgets even to ask him to identify the defendant as the man who stuck up his store. It was an open-and-shut case and he lost it."

"Judith's in a bad mood," said Felix Potter.

Her mood had nothing to do with it, she told herself. She was doing her job. "I've talked to the judge who had that case," she persisted, "and also to the one who had Glazer's previous case."

"Would you be satisfied," someone suggested, "if we transfer him back to the complaint room?"

"Fine," said Judith. "who's next?" And she opened another dossier.

When the meeting ended, she went back into her office and stood peering out the window. She had had Katz and others phoning all over the city searching for Inspector Hearn. They had not found him. Katz had been under orders to break in on any meeting if he had news, but he had not done so. She herself had phoned Mary Hearn twice. Each time Judith had had to try to calm her down, even though by then she needed calming herself. Mary had not heard from him either. When I first met him, Judith thought, he seemed so competent, so tough. It was part of what I found so attractive. I misread him. He wasn't tough at all. She believed that the next phone call she received would announce that Hearn's body had been found. I could have saved him, she thought, and began to cry.

Just then she heard her door open. Wiping her eyes, she turned from the window.

Mr. Katz had stuck his head into her room. He was smiling. "Inspector Hearn is on line two," he said.

The first emotion that came over Judith was relief. It was accompanied by a flood of tears so that she had to turn back to the window again. But she got her voice under control. "Where is he?"

"I don't know. We didn't find him, he just called in."

With this information Judith's emotion transformed itself into anger. She became furious both with Hearn and with herself. That he could have been so thoughtless. That she could have been so foolish as to worry. Turning from the window, she gave Katz his instructions. "Tell him I'm in conference." Her tone was curt, and Katz looked surprised. "Tell him he goes into the grand jury at two P M. tomorrow afternoon." And a few minutes after that, she thought, he'll be under indictment. Under the law no other result was possible. She stayed at the window until Katz returned a few minutes later.

"He'll be there," Katz said.

Immediately Judith wished she had taken the call. "How is he?"

"Fine, I guess. He asked me to inform his wife that he was okay."

"Inform her, then," snapped Judith. "What are you waiting for?"

Abruptly she began to gather up the papers on her desk: the reports from Ballistics, and the medical examiner, her notes on her conversations with Sergeant Markey. Shoving everything into her briefcase, she went home, took her usual hot shower, padded around in bathrobe and slippers preparing supper for herself, and finished off as usual with a cup of tea in the other room in front of the TV. Trying not to think about Hearn, she watched the seven o'clock network news—stories about arms sales approved to one country, terrorist attacks in another—separate stories told as if they were unrelated. Why did no one make the connection between guns and killing? Why was such a connection ignored? But international carnage could not hold her interest, and although she left the screen burning she saw nothing, heard nothing further. She had more personal violence on her mind, and she concentrated on it. In the darkened room she remembered George Lyttle on the alley floor with half the head gone. The screen images flickered and changed. She turned her attention to the man who had killed him, while the screen painted her face in lurid colors that blended one into the other, bleached her pale as a corpse, then a moment later set fire to her lips, her chin, her hair. Having tuned it all out she concentrated on her appearance—and Joe's—before the grand jury tomorrow. The Inspector Hearn case—no first names please. She would present four witnesses, the last of them Joe. She would read the jurors the relevant law, and explain it. The entire procedure would take less than half an hour, after which twenty-three of his fellow citizens would indict Joe Hearn. The charge would be murder, or else murder's imposter, manslaughter. He would be bound over for trial. There was nothing she could do about it. The time for sentiment was over. She would be governed now by principle. She had taken an oath of office just as Joe had, and would abide by it, as he had not. The grand jury would indict him, not her. She would merely present the case.

Given the personal relationship between her and the defendant, it was absolutely unethical that she go into that courtroom tomorrow, and she knew this, however fiercely she denied it to herself. But no one suspected the personal relationship. They had been too careful. And she would never tell. She struggled with this problem again now. She wanted to go with Joe to the end, could not give the case up. And Joe would never tell either—would he?

It was not true that a prosecutor could control a grand jury, she told herself. Although sometimes they did. Or thought they did. But she did not intend to try.

She got up and made herself another cup of tea, then returned to her chair. The room was still illuminated only by the television, by the gaudy colors that its screen continued to splash onto the walls. She would stand in the grand jury room as so often in the past and examine her witnesses. It was not her job to judge Joe Hearn, only to present the facts of the case clearly so that the grand jury's vote, when taken, would be an enlightened one.

This was an awesome power over defendants' lives, power that had troubled Judith often enough in the past, though never as much as now, as she tried to ignore its existence. She would obey her oath of office. It was all a question of love, she told herself. Betray love and you are lost. Judith's first love, she told herself, was the law. She has loved the law long before she ever heard of Joe Hearn. She was not in love with Joe Hearn now, never had been. It had only seemed like love, as had the romantic attachments of her adolescence, and romantic love was only a dream. She was too old now to be taken in by it.

But suppose Joe, once indicted, chose to make public the intimacy of their prior relationship? If he did, she'd be in trouble. She might be disbarred. It was a risk, but one that she willingly, almost eagerly, accepted. It was as if she wished to put her life and career in his hands in order to prove to him in the only way left to her—prove to him what?

She went to bed. She would have no further contact with him until he entered the grand jury room. It was almost like an old-style wedding—the bride would not see the groom until the ceremony began.

29

Joe recrossed the George Washington Bridge. He sailed high above the river. From the water far below came bursts of sunlight, the brightness exploding up at him. He came down into city streets and knew that he was home. This tumultuous city was home to him in a way that the various Long Island suburbs where he and Mary had lived could never be.

In two hours he would go before the grand jury.

He had awakened in his Ohio motel room at noon the next day, his gun still on the bedside table beside his head. At first he was surprised to be still alive. I drank myself into a stupor, he thought. I fell asleep. He was disgusted with himself. He dressed, put the gun in his pocket, and walked across to a diner where he ordered coffee. It came in a thick mug and he poured sugar in. He sat over it a long time. He had the worst headache of his life which, before an hour had passed, made him wish that he had shot himself before it got this bad.

He began to replay yesterday. He went through it physically step by step from the moment he intercepted the phone call until the moment George Lyttle lay dead on the rubble. He tried to consider each step clearly by pushing all emotion to one side, but this was hard to do. However much he may have wanted to murder George Lyttle, he had not done so. He had not been able to do it. George Lyttle had in fact killed himself by diving into the bullet. The killing was a terrible accident neither more nor less. Morally speaking he was innocent of the man's death. He had every moral right to remain a cop, he told himself, and for a time believed it. It was what he wanted to believe. But others would decide, not him.

He drove to a nearby shopping center, bought a razor, and came back and shaved. He brushed his teeth with soap and a washcloth wrapped around his forefinger. He drove downtown and bought a new shirt and tie, then waited two hours in a hotel coffee shop while his suit coat was dry-cleaned. He had bought the New York newspapers in the lobby. Waiting, he read them. The stories were in a minor key. There were no civil rights protests, at least so far. ARMED RAPE SUSPECT KILLED RESISTING ARREST. Perhaps this time the civil rights leaders would remain silent. He stood up and paid his check. If so, it might help his case.

After that he had phoned Judith Adler, for he had questions to ask her, the principal one being: Do I have a chance? When she refused to take his call, this question seemed to him answered, along with most of his others, and he had asked simply that his wife be informed that he was safe. He did not want to talk to Mary yet. What was there to say except that his future, and therefore hers, did not look good?

He had brooded about the grand jury for most of the 500-mile drive. It was not necessary for him to compose a statement, or even imagine what testimony he might give. Once sworn he would answer each question. The questions, or more accurately the questioner, the prosecutor, would determine the future course of his life. He did not know who this prosecutor would be, and was hoping for some inexperienced young man who knew little about the events in question, who had no personal interest in him or the case. If instead the prosecutor were Judith herself, if she had not withdrawn, this would mean, he believed, that she had cut herself off from him, that she represented now that great amorphous mass, The People of the State of New York. The People did not care what happened to him, and her object would be to indict him.

He drove through the streets of the city, slowly, as if for the last time. He believed he had never loved New York as much as now, only an hour or two before its machinery would destroy him.

He parked in the lot opposite the Criminal Courts Building and went upstairs, where he was told that Assistant

District Attorney Adler herself would present the case. They put him in a small room and told him to wait.

Inside the grand jury room Judith stood in the well and glanced up into the faces of the fourteen men and nine women who sat in tiers in a semicircle above her. The power, she told herself, was up there. Her role would be minimal, a ritual function only.

The first of the four witnesses was to be Captain Lauder, the ballistics expert and head of the police lab, who took his place on the chair in the well and was sworn.

Judith had climbed the steps to the topmost tier. She knew Lauder from past cases and did not like him. As a ballistics technician he was a true expert, and in court his testimony had never successfully been shaken. But he was also an obsequious little man and the department's number one gossip monger, and he looked eager to pick up more juicy tidbits today. This was still a case about which very little had been made public. Judith herself had clamped a lid on it. She had ordered Sergeant Markey to say nothing even to his superiors, much less to the press, until after the grand jury hearing. And he appeared to have obeyed her. She herself had refused to comment, and Inspector Hearn had not been available at all. Even Police Headquarters, though obviously agog about the case, as yet knew little.

And now Lauder sat in the well looking smug, awaiting her first question. When today's hearing ended he would rush out like a newsboy hawking extras in the street. He would know more than Chief of Detectives Cirillo, who would no doubt be pleased to take his call.

From her position on the topmost tier she said, "Please state your name and rank for the record."

Lauder did so.

"And by whom are you now employed and in what capacity?"

Lauder answered these questions also. He seemed quite pleased with himself.

"And on a certain day"—Judith did not give the date—"did Inspector Hearn come to you with certain evidence to be analyzed?"

"Yes, he did. According to my report, the date was—" It was Lauder's intention, Judith knew from her phone conversation with him, to testify to this date, for it proved how long Joe had been tracking George Lyttle—it tended to prove premeditation.

"Please confine your answers to yes or no until your opinion is asked for."

With satisfying promptness the smirk disappeared. The report, half out of his pocket, did not advance farther.

"Now, Captain Lauder, was part of this evidence an empty roll of adhesive tape from which your technicians lifted a single partial fingerprint?"

It was Lyttle's print. Judith let Lauder testify to this. She let him identify and describe Lyttle's gun. It did not take much to make Lauder swell with self-importance. Judith had seen him do this on the witness stand before, for he had testified in about half the murder cases that she had tried to verdict.

"All right," she said. "Let's move now to your examination of the bullet fragments recovered by detectives in the alley in Harlem on Tuesday last."

The smirk was back on Lauder's face. "My report shows—by the way, it's dated—"

But Judith cut him off. "Captain Lauder, may I ask you to confine yourself to answering the questions, please."

When he had subsided, she asked a number of questions related to the recovered bullet fragments, but his testimony even on these subjects, his admitted area of expertise, did not please her either, and she found herself trying to undermine it.

"But you have no proof that all eight shots were fired in that alley."

"No, but—"

"Just answer the question, please."

Presently she excused him. She sent him out of the room like a schoolboy. She had had enough of Captain Lauder.

But he had left the twenty-three jurors mystified, or she had, and several turned around to stare at her quizzically. They still did not know what kind of case this was, nor what bearing, if any, Lauder's testimony might have.

The ballistics expert was followed by the assistant medical examiner, Dr. Blumberg, another pompous little man whom Judith had dealt with frequently in past trials, her ally in all of them. Always she had treated him with respect, but today he annoyed her on sight. Apparently he had lingered in the alley until long after she had gone, and now he began to describe not only the cause of death and the appearance of the corpse, but also the appearance of the alley, of the investigating detectives, of Inspector Hearn.

Judith brought him back sharply to the testimony he was there to give. He was like the worst type of journalist, she thought. He didn't take part. The suffering meant nothing to him, except that he came in afterward and in his fashion recorded it. He was a voyeur, a peeping Tom.

"The powder remnants on the head of the deceased," said Judith crisply, "prove that the fatal shot was fired at extremely close range, is that correct?"

Obviously it was the kind of testimony he most liked to give—specific physical facts colored by his own specialized experience, meaning colored by his opinions.

"Extremely close range," he concurred.

"And would this be consistent with a struggle between the police officer and his prisoner over the weapon?"

Blumberg hesitated.

"Please answer yes or no."

"It's possible."

"Thank you, Dr. Blumberg."

Blumberg seemed disappointed to find his turn in the limelight cut so short. As he shambled out the door, the jurors in their tiers began to shift position slightly and to cough. But when several of them glanced around at Judith, she chose not to meet their eyes. Instead she studied her notes which were affixed to a clipboard.

The next witness, Sergeant Markey, was shown in. After being sworn he described how Inspector Hearn had led him into the alley of the condemned building on the rubble of which lay the deceased perpetrator, George Lyttle.

"Was Inspector Hearn attempting to hide or cover up any facts or details in connection with the case?"

"No, he wasn't. In fact—"

"A yes or no answer is sufficient, Sergeant Markey," said Judith. "This is not a trial. Now, did Inspector Hearn explain to you how he happened to arrest the deceased?"

"He said the deceased had previously raped his wife. The deceased was trying to extort money from his wife in exchange for the return of her credit cards and some photos taken of her at the time of the rape."

"And did you find any of these items in that alley?"

"Yes, I did."

Markey only knew about the terrible photographs, now locked in her desk; he had not seen them. He could not even imagine the effect they might have had on an already distraught Joe Hearn.

"Would you describe the appearance of Inspector Hearn when you first saw him, please."

"His suit was covered with brains and blood."

Judith stared down at her notes. Below her one of the jurors sighed. Another shifted position noisily. This was the first Judith realized how absolutely motionless, how totally silent, the jurors had become.

She said, "And would this be consistent with a struggle over a gun?"

Markey watched her carefully. After a moment, he said, "Yes, it would be."

"Describe his appearance further, if you please."

"Well, he was extremely broken up," said Markey. "He was babbling, you might say."

Yes, thought Judith, and she felt such a rush of sympathy for Joe Hearn that for a moment she thought she was going to have to ask for a recess. Instead, she gripped her clipboard tighter. There was no place for emotion in a courtroom. It was up to her to maintain her professionalism, to concentrate on honor, duty, her sacred oath—exclusively male concerns in the past, hers now; concerns that had controlled men's acts for centuries but that now in these modern times had begun to control everybody's.

"And did Inspector Hearn make certain admissions to you?" There—now it was done. Markey would give his testimony and Joe as a result would be indicted. It was out of her hands.

"Yes, he did." Markey was still watching her.

"And what were those admissions, Sergeant Markey?"

"May I consult my notes?"

Judith looked down at her clipboard. When she glanced up again, Sergeant Markey was watching her with the same calculating scrutiny as before. Alone among today's witnesses, Markey was unknown to her. Her only previous contacts with him were the few minutes in the alley, plus a few phone calls. Nonetheless, she believed she understood his type. The Police Department was full of men whose only thought was to curry favor with superiors, men who would do and say whatever these superiors demanded, believing this the one sure route to advancement.

I went there to kill him, and I killed him.

Sergeant Markey, looking up from his notes, said only, "He said that he handcuffed the deceased perpetrator to the pipe." Markey then fell silent. He watched Judith and he waited. He was waiting, she realized, for cues from her. How did she want him to proceed? Did she want him to give testimony that would indict Hearn, or didn't she?

But Judith waited too and attempted to keep her face blank. She would not coach him or lead him. She would give him no direction, no hint of which answers she was hoping for. Let him say whatever he wanted to say. Let him say the truth—whatever this truth might bring.

"He didn't have any handcuffs with him," Sergeant Markey continued at last. "So he used the perpetrator's own handcuffs. I believe they might have been the same handcuffs the perpetrator had used to handcuff Inspector Hearn's wife so as to rape her."

Below Judith there was again movement from the jurors. Apparently this startled Markey, for he became almost loquacious. "He had to immobilize the perpetrator so he could search the briefcase for evidence, so he could know what he had."

"You say you took his admissions down in your notebook," said Judith. "Does your notebook contain any other admissions besides those you have already revealed?" But the admissions are not in his notebook, she admonished herself. He told you he never wrote them down.

Markey, watching her, shook his head. "No, it does not," he said, and he gave her a slight smile.

The smile said to her: you can rely on my discretion. The smile made her ashamed. She seemed to be trying to save Joe Hearn's life despite herself. And why? Did she hope he would feel such gratitude that he would mistake it for love? And if he came rushing into her arms, would she mistake this for love also, and accept him? She could not have him back. She had once thought it possible to love Joe and the law both. But no one could have two loves because what did you do when forced to choose between them? If she saved Joe now, she betrayed the law. She had betrayed it already by being here at all. If she saved Joe, she saved him for another woman, not for herself. And the cost was to betray her oath. If she saved Joe she would lose both her loves.

It was all too confusing to be resolved in an instant.

"Thank you, Sergeant Markey," she said. "No further questions."

She needed more time. She would put the decision off a moment longer; there was still one witness to go.

Inspector Hearn was led in. He was wearing the same brown suit he had worn in the alley. He must have had it cleaned. The tie was new. He was freshly shaven, and his hair was combed, and he looked, Judith thought numbly, very nice. He walked toward the chair recently occupied by Captain Lauder, purveyor of malicious gossip, and by Dr. Blumberg, the professional ghoul, and by Sergeant Markey whose practice it was, whether through stupidity or cool appraisal of his own best interests, to pander to the real or imagined whim of any superior, any superior at all, including now herself; so that she thought, Joe Hearn, you're worth more than all of them put together.

He sat down. She watched him look over the jurors. His eyes moved from face to face. These were the faces of his judges. Because if they indicted him today, bound him over to be tried, then he was, as a cop, finished. He did not smile, but his gaze was not hostile either. It was calm appraisal. In front of his judges, she noted with an emotion very like pride, Joe Hearn did not flinch.

When he had been sworn she studied her notes a moment, as if preparing her lines of questioning, but the only thought in her head revolved around the word intercourse— the old English word one never heard anymore—our last intercourse together, she thought, is to be a legal procedure, the equivalent in our case of a divorce.

And so she began her examination of him; the formal, legal questions came first.

She said briskly: "Have you been promised immunity from prosecution in exchange for your testimony here today?"

"No, I have not."

"You specifically waived your right to immunity?"

"Yes, I did."

"You signed a waiver to that effect?"

"Yes, I did."

"And were you advised to seek legal counsel before so doing?"

"Yes, I was."

"And did you seek such legal counsel?"

"No, I did not."

He's helpless, Judith thought. Helpless. I can do with him whatever I choose.

"Inspector Hearn," she said, "you are here because whenever a police officer kills a citizen, even if in the line of duty, a grand jury hearing is mandatory. Do you understand that?"

"Yes, I do." He looked at her impersonally. He looked at her, she thought, as if he had never seen her before, as if he cared nothing for her now and never had.

"Tell us please how you happened to arrest the deceased two days ago."

"I intercepted a telephone call from him to my wife, and—"

All I have to do is let him ramble, Judith thought, and he'll be indicted. He'll indict himself. She interrupted: "He had raped your wife and was now trying to extort money from her, is that correct?"

Joe's voice dropped, and he stared at the floor. "Ten thousand dollars," he said.

"Your wife had been given a phone number to call, and you tracked down the location of this number, and when her call came in you were waiting there to arrest whoever answered, is that correct?"

"That is correct," said Joe. His eyes were still fixed on the floor. He's reliving it now, Judith thought watching him. She wanted to comfort him, take him in her arms. He's going to relive it many times over the next few years—perhaps for the rest of his life. She said, "And you moved your prisoner down into that alley in order to handcuff and search him, is that correct?"

His gaze came up. "That is correct."

"And did there come a time when you handcuffed him to a pipe fixed to the wall?"

"Yes, there did."

"And did you find evidence in his attaché case that this was indeed the man who raped your wife?"

"Yes, I did."

"And at a certain point in time did the deceased break loose from the handcuffs and the water pipe, and did he try to harm you?"

"I don't know how it happened," said Joe. His voice had become choked with emotion, and he stared again at the floor. "I wish it hadn't happened."

Judith was aware that all twenty-three jurors again leaned forward in their chairs, and she thought she could feel from them a great outpouring of sympathy that reached down from the tiers toward Joe Hearn.

"You had discovered the unregistered gun in his attaché case, is that correct?"

"Yes, and I—"

"You were holding the unregistered gun in your hand, and at that moment the deceased broke loose from the wall, and leaped upon you, is that correct?"

"They were his handcuffs," mumbled Joe. "They were practically toy handcuffs. I never should have trusted those handcuffs. But I didn't have any with me, don't you see?"

"Inspectors rarely make street arrests, is that correct?"

Joe appeared not to hear the question. "I haven't carried handcuffs since I was a lieutenant." It was as if this fact alone explained the entire series of events. And for him perhaps it did. "I should never have trusted those handcuffs."

"When he leaped upon you, did you believe your life was in danger?"

Joe, staring at the floor, shook his head in a bewildered way.

"There was a struggle for the gun, is that correct?"

"I don't know how it happened. It all happened so fast."

"You pulled the trigger, and killed the deceased, George Lyttle, is that correct?"

"I—yes, I killed him."

"You killed the man who raped your wife, who was attempting to extort money from your wife, with his own unregistered gun, is that correct?"

Joe looked up. His eyes scanned the tiers of jurors. "That is correct," he said, and waited.

"No further questions," Judith said. "Thank you, Inspector Hearn."

Joe left the grand jury room. He did not look in her direction again. He walked out with his eyes on his shoes.

When the door had closed behind him, Judith descended into the well. She stood beside the chair in which the witnesses had sat, and addressed the jurors. She asked if any of them had any questions. Did they wish to question any of the witnesses again? She looked all around, but no juror spoke up.

Did anyone have any questions to put to her? she next asked, and again she waited, her eyes moving from face to face, but this elicited no response either. Now she explained to them their options. They could indict Inspector Hearn for homicide on any one of the following counts, and she enumerated them, explaining the law in each case, and the range was rather broad. Or else, she concluded, they could rule this a justifiable homicide by a police officer in the performance of his duty.

"Talk it over among yourselves," she said, "and come to a decision. I'll be waiting outside."

In the antechamber Joe Hearn stood staring out the window. She did not go to him. The warden sat at his desk. There were several rows of benches there, all empty. Judith took a seat and peered down at the clipboard in her lap. She did not know where the other three witnesses might be. She had ordered them all kept apart, and presently she would give the order to dismiss them.

The wait was not a long one. After several minutes the buzzer sounded above the warden's desk, and he got up and went into the grand jury room. When he came out a moment later, he was carrying in his hand the long narrow form, and he was grinning. His thumb was jutting up into the air. "Case dismissed," he said to Joe Hearn. "Congratulations."

Joe had turned from the window. Now he came over to where Judith was sitting. She stood up, and they faced each other most likely for the last time.

Joe took both her hands and said, "What a nice lady."

Judith had two impulses. One was to say, "Oh, Joe," and fall into his arms. The other was to rage at him. She wanted to say, "You made me betray the law, and now I have to resign." But she did not say this to him either, for it constituted an intimacy and she knew there were not going to be any more intimacies between them.

She was very close to bursting into tears, but she managed a smile and a handshake. "Inspector," she said, "I suggest you go home and tell your wife. She should be very relieved to hear the news."

With that she turned abruptly away from him. She walked out of the room. Outside she had the whole long marble corridor to negotiate, for the elevators were at the far end. Her heels rang on the marble floor. She could hear Joe Hearn coming after her, and so walked even faster. About halfway along the corridor he gave up. His footsteps stopped. Her own slowed somewhat, but she did not turn around, and she kept walking. When the elevator doors opened, she stepped inside without looking back. The doors closed, and she descended alone.

News of the verdict swept through the courthouse. Within minutes, like a high-voltage charge of electricity, it had jumped the gap and reached Police Headquarters. Chief Cirillo was informed. His head nodded several times, then he reached for his telephone. His first call was to the police commissioner. After that he made others.

30

AS HE WALKED OUT THE BACK DOOR OF THE CRIMI-
nal Courts Building, Joe's emotions were in turmoil. He
crossed the street and was in Chinatown. It was there the
reaction hit him. He stood on Mott Street, its sidewalks
crowded with Chinese people and its stalls banked high
with Chinese produce. He was like a man who had avoided
a car crash at the last millisecond. The terror came only
now, when it was over. The stalls were pushed out almost
to the curb. The crowds had to detour around them and
around him, for his chest was heaving and he could not
catch his breath. Hot lacquered ducks hung in steamy
windows, but he could barely see them. He was so weak
he could barely stand.

These sensations passed, and were followed by others
that were less visceral, more complicated. Thoughts of
Mary, of Judith, of his own future fought for space in his
head. What about his honor as a policeman? Had justice
been cheated just now? The Police Department would
review the case, he knew. His superiors might still decide
to bring him up on departmental charges—which could
result in his dismissal. But he did not believe this would
happen. He was so sure of it that he became euphoric.
The system had exonerated him. He was not going to
stand trial for killing George Lyttle. The grand jury had so
ruled. It had heard witnesses and had reached its verdict.
He was still a cop and had only to acquiesce in that verdict
to remain one. He was free. His head swam with freedom.
He became aware of individuals around him, of Chinese
faces and voices. He saw the stalls now, noted the piles of

fruits and vegetables, some of which were Chinese also and so foreign to him he could not even give them names. All this in his own city that he had been born in, had known intimately since he was a boy. The sun was shining and the breeze carried the odors of strange cooking into his face, strange garbage also, and he began to suck in drafts of air, savoring all this strangeness. Strangest of all was life itself, which had never seemed so precious.

Next his emotions fixed on Judith. As he strode along he was filled with gratitude. He could never repay her. She had given him so much, at who knew what terrible cost to herself, and he had nothing to offer in return. How could he give her something back? Something big. What should it be? These questions were too much right now. He would solve them tomorrow. Whatever it was should make her believe how much she had meant to him, that he would be in her debt forever.

Finally he allowed himself to think about Mary. Before leaving the Criminal Courts Building he had recovered certain evidence from the case. His hand in his side pocket opened and closed around it, and he walked along brooding. He could not be sure what his reception from her would be. And having admitted this uncertainty to himself his elation went away, and he became troubled. After a moment he stepped into a booth and tried to phone her. He would relieve her mind if she was worried about him, share the good news if she was receptive to it. But there was no answer.

He had crossed Canal Street into Little Italy by then. In two blocks the city had changed. Old Italian women in black sat at open windows and they gazed down at him as he walked by. He remembered how close his marriage had been at first, and how casual in recent years. He had taken Mary for granted—that was the best he could say for himself. There were street-level social clubs with open doors and men sitting in them with their hats on. It was his fault, all of it. The marriage would be different in the future, he promised. If there were a future. He passed Italian restaurants; he could see through into gardens out back. Suppose Mary left him? To her trauma of the past weeks he had only added more trauma. Perhaps she despised him. Perhaps she would not want to live with him anymore. He passed a coffeehouse with gleaming espresso machines behind the bar. She might already have gone away from him for good. The odor of coffee overlaid that part of the street. Realizing he was famished, he went in and drank a cappucino and ate a pastry and brooded some more. After that he walked back to the lot where he had left his car and drove home.

But when he had parked in his driveway and gone inside, he found that his house was empty. It was one thing to accept intellectually the idea that Mary might leave him. It was another to find evidence of it.

He rushed through all the rooms, but his wife was not there. The kitchen was spotless, nothing on the stove, not a spoon in sight. Upstairs their bed was made. Only sunlight lay upon it, not her. Any stray articles of clothing had been put away—or taken away. It was like a room that was to be shown to strangers. Nothing of her was left in it. He went outside. This was her garden, her flower beds. There were no tools visible, or bags of mulch or baskets for her cuttings. It was as if she wasn't coming back. He stood in the driveway, his head darting around, looking for her in every direction. He became convinced she had run off with Loftus after all, that he had driven her to it.

Only a few minutes passed before Mary's car turned in onto the gravel. She stopped it and got out. She was wearing pants and a sweater and her hair was tied back at the nape of her neck. She was carrying a package.

She came up and kissed him on the cheek, but her smile vanished quickly, and the kiss, under the circumstances, was insufficient. He became very tense.

"I didn't know where you were," he mumbled.

She walked toward the house.

"Everything," she said, "worked out well, I hear." In the kitchen she put her package down on the counter.

His emotions, as he watched her, were no different from those of their courtship, adoration mixed with fear. A creature as precious as this was indeed in his presence, but he was not certain she meant to stay there. She was not giving him any signs.

"I was out buying champagne," she said. She was fishing the bottle out of the bag.

"Chief Cirillo called," she explained.

Joe lacked the confidence to approach her. "What did he say?"

"That everything was okay." Her head was nodding up and down but she was avoiding his eyes. "According to him there was never anything to worry about."

"According to him." Joe tried a smile. So there would be no department charges. Joe had guessed right—it was over. But he was amazed at how little this news meant to him right now.

"He wants to drive you to work tomorrow. You're to wait out front."

She glanced at him briefly, but he still had no way of telling what she was thinking.

She found an ice bucket and stood the champagne bottle in it. From the fridge she took an ice tray which she broke open. He waited, but she did not turn around. She poured the ice in around the bottle. She turned on the kitchen faucet. Over her shoulder she said, "Would you like some champagne?" She was watching the ice float up around the bottle.

Joe's arms enveloped her from behind. He held her tight, breathed the scent of her, but at first she did not react. Only when she pressed the back of her head against him did he realize she was crying.

"I was afraid you wouldn't come home," she sobbed.

"If you'll stay with me I'll quit the Police Department."

"I was afraid you'd go to her. When you were missing she was suffering too. As much as I was."

"Don't cry. Please don't cry."

"I hadn't heard from you. I went out to buy the champagne. I thought if it was waiting here for you—if you wouldn't come back to me, maybe you would come back for the champagne."

"I have nowhere to go. There is noplace else I want to go."

"I went to that hotel with someone."

"If you'll stay with me I'll do anything for you."

"I don't know how or why. I changed my mind as soon as I got there."

"I know all that."

She turned in his arms, wiping her eyes. "I already had the door open. I was already leaving when—"

"I want to make love to you."

Pulling back, she wiped her eyes. "You mean right

now?" She tried to give him a smirk. "What about the champagne?"

They went up the stairs arm in arm, stopping every few steps to kiss, just as they used to do in the very beginning.

In the bedroom the sun was streaming in the window. The act seemed as significant as going to bed together for the first time. As a result no clouds collided in the sky, the earth did not stand still in its orbit. Their mutual apprehension did not abate until it was over. But there was something miraculous about it nonetheless, just as there had been twenty years previously, awe that such a momentous event—not sexual delirium but the coming together of lives—had actually taken place.

Afterward, as she lay against him, half on top of him, they began to talk to each other about their children, about themselves, about important matters and silly ones. They talked with an intimacy and a freedom that had been lacking between them for months, if not years.

Finally Joe said, "I meant it before. I'm going to resign from the department."

"No, you're not."

He did mean it. The Police Department was his life, but in his heart he said good-bye to it. "I'm going to call up Bill Buchanan." It was an offering he wished to make her. His head nodded up and down several times. "If it's still available, I'm going to take that job he mentioned."

"I don't want you to resign," said Mary, her offering to him.

They began to argue about it—the gentle argument of lovers, each speaking the other's lines.

"I want you to have the extra money."

"I can wait for that."

"We'll take an apartment in New York, close to the galleries you like best."

"Bill's job or another job will still be available next year, or the year after."

"We'll keep this house, or buy a bigger one. You'll be able to buy all the clothes—"

"This is my house, and I don't need any clothes."

"You should have a fur coat, and—"

"I want you to stay a cop."

"Mink, I guess. I don't know how much they cost, but with my new job—"

"Being a cop is a holy calling, you said once. Don't you still believe that?"

"I've put you through so much."

"I was so worried about you."

Her hand lay on his chest. "And I want to be the wife of a two- or three-star chief. Or the wife of the PC himself—I'd be so proud. Make me proud, Joe."

"I just want to make you happy."

"I am happy. Being together is all I need."

A little later in the kitchen Joe pulled the cork on the champagne bottle and poured out two glasses. They sat down at the table in the dinette and interlocked their arms so that their faces and champagne glasses were only inches apart. They grinned at each other, distorted big-eyed grins that swam in and out of focus.

"To you."

"No, to you."

"Well then, to us."

There was the clink of glasses, and they sipped. "The trick now," said Mary, "is to disengage without spilling the rest of it."

"Or breaking the glasses."

It made them laugh.

"Oh, I almost forgot," said Joe, digging into his side pocket. "I brought home your keys and credit cards." He put them on the table. The cards were bound by a rubber band. From the key ring still hung the plastic elephant that Susie had given her mother as a present last Christmas.

"Keys that don't fit the locks anymore." Mary stared at them. "Credit cards that have been replaced." She frowned. One other thing had to be settled. "He took some photos of me, too."

"The district attorney's office has them." Joe put his hand over hers.

"Did you—"

"No, I didn't."

After a moment Joe added, "They have been or will be destroyed. We have nothing further to worry about."

"It's nice to hear you say we," she said.

Joe dug into his pocket a second time. "I brought this home too," he said. It was her wedding ring. He took her hand and for the second time in their lives he slipped it onto her finger.

"Oh, Joe," she said. But he only nodded, unable to speak at all.

31

JUDITH HAD SAT IN HER OFFICE THE REST OF THE afternoon with the door closed. She received no visitors, accepted no calls. But her eyes remained dry. I can't even cry, she told herself.

About five o'clock she wrote out a letter of resignation—after so many years, two lines—and carried it across the hall. I have acted improperly, she told herself. I have no choice. She realized the district attorney would question her. The strains of her job had become too much, she would tell him. No, she had no other job to go to; she was going to take a long vacation and then see. A prosecutor's work being in some ways unrelievedly morbid, it took considerable resilience to live such a life for long, the DA would comment. Judith had lasted longer than most. Resilience wore out after a time, like a boxer's ability to absorb pain. The DA would ask her to change her mind, then thank her, saying yes, he understood.

And so she entered his anteroom and spoke to his secretary; but the boss, she learned, was gone for the day. Furthermore, he planned to take the rest of the week off.

So there was no one to resign to.

"I can reach him up at his country place. Was it anything special?"

Judith could not resign to the secretary and did not wish to resign by telephone. Her letter went back into her pocketbook. It did not have to be done today after all. Although her resolve remained intact, she found she was grateful for the reprieve.

The next morning she phoned Mr. Katz and announced

she had decided to go away on vacation. Young Brian Crawford was to run the office in her absence.

"How long will you be gone?" inquired Mr. Katz.

She snapped at him. "Until I come back."

Katz only laughed. "A few days will be good for you. You looked like you needed it."

She flew to the Caribbean. Her hotel was on one side of the island. The town and most of the restaurants were on the other. She took pleasure in being isolated. Around the hotel, on the beach, she smiled if someone greeted her. Otherwise she spoke to no one. The hotel was a long, low building that crouched under palm trees at the head of a U-shaped lagoon. About a mile out the sea crashed against the reef that closed off the lagoon. The water in the lagoon was clear and bathtub warm.

The hotel was surrounded by gardens, by arbors of bougainvillea and poinsettias. The paths were lined with hibiscus, geraniums, flowering cactus, and other tropical plants. The paths were in the shade all day and in the early morning they were always damp from the gardeners' hoses. There was a tennis court behind the hotel and the thunk of balls punctuated the silence as each day she walked to and from the breakfast room.

On the beach she wore a modest one-piece bathing suit and big dark sunglasses. She sat on her reclining chair under a palm tree and gazed out to sea. A novel lay in her lap, but she seldom read. I haven't known where to draw the line between my life and my work, she told herself. When she returned to New York she would hand in the letter that was still in her pocketbook—at which time she would have no life and no work either.

Hazy islands populated the horizon. Inside the lagoon there were anchored yachts, and the sails of the windsurfers moved back and forth. Sometimes she watched the bronzed young man who had the windsurfing concession and who gave lessons all day, principally to giggling young women. Since this was a French island, most such girls were topless. So were many of the women on the beach, even older women who no longer had the shape for it.

Judith had read this about French beaches somewhere; even so the sight of females flaunting themselves at first shocked her. But she must have got used to the idea, for one day in the hotel boutique she bought herself a bikini.

She went in there to buy a kind of muumuu, and a wide floppy straw hat such as other women on the beach were wearing. As an afterthought, she bought the bikini, the first in her life. A white one. But in her room when she put it on she felt naked and brazen, though she seemed to hold it up well enough. Nonetheless, it was some time before she could make herself go out and onto the beach. It was nearly noon by then. She walked up and down the sand in front of all the sunbathers, getting used to the bikini, getting used to her new self. I'm still fairly young, she thought. I'm not some old hag, I'm in better shape than most of them. The sand was so hot it burned the soles of her feet. She was trying to concentrate, for almost the first time in her adult life, on her own thoughts, needs, reactions, rather than on those of others. But this required attitudes that were unfamiliar to her. I'm not the conscience of the world, she told herself. Other people put themselves first, why shouldn't I?

She decided to take windsurfing lessons. The young man's name turned out to be Pierre, and this made her smile. For a Frenchman the name seemed so perfect. He had a cute French accent to match his cute little bottom—a thought that made her frown even as it crossed her mind. Pierre led her through dry runs on dry land, then took her into water only two feet deep. Standing beside the board, he held it steady while she climbed up on to it. She had to balance herself on all fours before trying to stand, a position that felt to her provocative, or perhaps even obscene, and quickly she pushed herself upright. I'm a repressed woman, she told herself. But knowing it and doing something about it were two different things. Pierre was placing her feet for her. He was handling the lower parts of her legs. There had been a great deal of touching so far—too much, she believed. He has an eye for vulnerable women, she thought.

Windsurfing proved more difficult than it had looked, and once as she fell off, she landed half on top of Pierre and the crash nearly skinned her white bikini off her. There were only strings holding it on to begin with. It gave her an extremely insecure feeling.

Pierre was about twenty-five, very good at his job, very sure of himself. He reminded her of young Benjy Goldberg. He was a natural on the water as Benjy was a natural in court. They had the same dark good looks, the same physical energy. The difference was that Benjy wore three-piece suits whereas Pierre's uniform was a pair of those tight, oh so tight, French briefs.

Her hour ended, and she went back to her book, but it seemed to her that the imprint of Pierre's fingers remained on her body.

She watched him give lessons to a bare-breasted twenty-year-old she hadn't noticed previously. She felt a pang of jealousy and laughed at herself.

That afternoon as she tried to read she was interrupted by Pierre.

"Time for another lesson, I think," he said.

She studied him a moment. "I think I've had enough for one day."

"I see you do not have a car."

How did he know that? Judith wondered. I haven't even told him my name.

He was grinning at her. "Soon I drive into town," he said. "In one hour. Perhaps you like to come with me, maybe?"

He is a very good looking young man, she thought. Accent on the "young."

In the car driving toward the town he said, "I cannot continue calling you mademoiselle, I think."

Judith gave her name.

He said, "I will call you Judy."

No one had called her Judy in years, except Joe Hearn.

He told her he was from Cannes on the French Riviera. He was moving around the world from resort to resort teaching windsurfing and scuba. He had been gone from home only ten months and had reached this far already. Next stop Acapulco, or Tahiti. An airhead, Judith thought.

That night when she came out of the dining room he was waiting for her in the bar. He wanted to buy her an after-dinner drink. He called it a "digestif." She told him she had a headache, and refused.

She had been there by then five days. The next morning after breakfast she rubbed oil not only onto her shoulders, face and thighs but onto her bare breasts as well. Then she put on the bikini and went out. It was already very hot, and the glare off the water was blinding.

After watching the windsurfers for a while she got up

and walked down the beach away from the hotel. Though not very wide, the beach was extremely long, extending around the lagoon from the hotel almost as far as the headlands in both directions. A long curved rim of sand. Judith walked along looking for interesting shells, studying odd pieces of driftwood. Soon she was so far from the hotel that, when she looked back, she could barely make out the swimmers and sunbathers in front of it—people who seemed to be focused one and all on their tans. She herself was running from violence apparently—from violence as much as duty. It was violence to which they were oblivious. She envied them. They had never seen it. They didn't know it existed.

She peered around her. There was no one else down here at all. A bit farther on the headland rose up in a series of jagged boulders. She was certainly out of sight of everyone now, and after a moment's hesitation she removed her bra. No one can see me, she told herself. She sauntered back and forth carrying the bra by its string, and this seemed daring to her. Although perhaps half a mile from the hotel, people might guess that she was not wearing it. She walked farther out to the headland, stepping carefully on bare feet. Standing on a large flat rock she removed the bottom of the bikini too. She stood stark naked in the sunlight looking out to sea, and the warm trade winds bathed her entire body. Turning this way and that, she basked in total nudity.

When at last she glanced back toward the hotel, she noted that a tiny figure on a windsurfer was headed her way. Whoever it was could not possibly see that she was naked. Nonetheless, Judith hurriedly stepped into the bikini bottom. But, feeling stubborn, she refused to put the top back on, and instead left it dangling from one hand. The distant figure was still advancing. She decided to ignore it, and so stood staring out to sea watching a great white cruise liner, half invisible in the glare, pass the island far offshore.

When she turned around this time, the figure was much closer, and she recognized it as Pierre. Her instinct was to tie her bra back on—and quickly. She had been resisting this instinct with great difficulty for some time already. But other emotions intervened. She was tired of being proper and correct. She stepped down into the water and began to wade toward Pierre, her chest outthrust, though every inner voice shrieked at her to cover up. This was more than modesty. A good deal of instinctive fear was mixed with it. Did she imagine he was going to rape her? Did she imagine he would be overcome with lust? Naked breasts did not have that power anymore, at least not here. Rape was not on everybody's mind, only hers. She stood in thigh-deep water, gazed straight at Pierre and said, "How come you're not giving lessons?"

A banal remark, though for her this was not a banal moment.

"Shall I give you a ride back?"

"I can walk, thank you."

"Do you want to see the most beautiful beach on this island?"

The next afternoon he took her to it, a secluded crescent of sand at the bottom of a cliff. They had parked on top and were descending via a ledge cut into the cliff face, and suddenly the beach came into view. It was tiny, an exquisite jewel, and at first glance she loved it. But then she noticed something else. There were about thirty people down there, men, women, and even children all swimming or standing or sunning themselves, and they were all stark naked. Pierre, who was carrying towels, a foam rubber mattress, and snorkeling gear in a straw basket, did not seem surprised. He set his things down on the sand, and at once stripped to the buff. He seemed to do it with lightning speed, so fast Judith could hardly believe her eyes. She was as uncomfortable as she had ever been.

She was wearing her muumuu over her bikini. As she stood somewhat stunned, the nude Pierre stripped it off her. A moment later his hands were at her bra strings. She felt the hot wind against her flesh.

Pierre lifted swimfins, masks and a snorkel out of his basket and started toward the water. "Come on," he said over his shoulder. "I show you the beautiful fish." Judith glanced around her. No one was paying any attention to Pierre, or to her either. No one even looked in her direction. Presently she stepped out of her bikini bottom, and picked up the other mask, snorkel, and fins.

Standing in water up to his knees, Pierre watched her come toward him. He was smiling. His head was nodding up and down approvingly. She forced a smile. As he fitted the mask to her face, his elbow encountered a breast. He was not in any way aroused, and she wondered about this. Did he come to this place so often that it no longer affected him? Did he manage it perhaps by concentrating on baseball, or whatever might be the French equivalent? Or did he in fact have no sexual interest in her at all? This last seemed the most likely. She supposed he must find her quite old.

Putting her face in the water, she swam out over the reef, and the fish were as beautiful as Pierre had promised.

That night after supper he was again waiting for her in the bar. This time he did not offer her a drink. He said only, "Would you like to come to my room?"

He is inviting me to have sexual intercourse with him, thought Judith—a young man she scarcely knew, did not particularly like, and would never see again. He only wants what is known as a "quick lay," thought Judith.

She nodded, and followed him out of the bar. She followed him down dark paths through the garden. There were trees and vines overhead. The sweet-smelling flowers perfumed the night all around her. It occurred to her that this was why she had come to this island, to break out in some way, to be like other unattached young women, to have done with terrible crimes and broken victims, to lose herself in a meaningless adventure—and what was sex under circumstances such as this except a substitute for adventure?

With this realization came an onrush of self-disgust, together with anger. They had progressed some yards along the newest dark path, when suddenly Judith said: "No."

She had stopped in her tracks.

Pierre stopped also, and turned around and stared at her in the darkness.

"I'm terribly sorry," she said. "I've made a mistake."

She offered no other explanation and did not wait to note his reaction. Turning on her heel, she strode back in the direction of her room. Once she got there, she locked herself in and lay on the bed in the dark and stared at the ceiling.

The next day she flew back to New York.

The plane landed at 4:00 PM. and she was at the courthouse carrying her suitcase an hour later. She stepped into an elevator full of young cops she didn't know, and for the first time in days felt comfortable inside her skin. She felt this was where she belonged. She was home. Nonetheless she began saying good-bye to it. The letter was about to come out of her handbag. She had come here to resign.

She set her suitcase down beside her desk and listened to Mr. Katz complimenting her on her tan.

"See if the district attorney can see me now," she said.

He could not; it would be about thirty minutes, Katz reported back. So Judith told him to gather her immediate staff together—those who were in the building at this time. They had a right to know she was resigning. She would tell them first.

One by one her young assistants drifted in. She heard many more compliments about her tan. She looked at them and thought, I wish you could have seen me yesterday running naked on the beach. But she did not wish this at all.

She decided to wait until all had gathered before she announced her resignation. In the interim young Benjy Goldberg dropped a flyer on her desk, saying, "We have a new pressure group to cope with. You better read this."

In law enforcement, pressure groups were a serious problem and it was with a feeling of dread—as if all this still concerned her—that Judith picked up the flyer.

The new "pressure group" was called Females for Felons, a privately funded organization, Judith read, dedicated to the proposition that denying incarcerated men heterosexual gratification was cruel, barbaric, and nonrehabilitating.

Judith glanced up at Benjy, who was smirking.

Females for Felons had been founded, she read, by a Dr. Leo Ferguson—doctor of what? Judith wondered—who had formerly served two years in a state prison for armed robbery. Since his parole he had successfully recruited "sixty-seven outstanding young women for therapeutic assignments at nearby institutions," or so the flyer said. In addition, he claimed to have an overload of six hundred volunteer applicants between the ages of eighteen and thirty-eight for this "dynamic rehabilitation program."

Her assembled staff members, watching Judith read, had begun to laugh. She was finding it difficult not to laugh herself. Attached to the flyer was a "confidential application" for potential volunteers. Which ages did they prefer for sexual intercourse, and which positions? What about cunnilingus and fellatio? Would they have any objections to making love with a deformed person, or as part of a ménage à trois?

"Dr. Ferguson was in here," said Benjy. "He was looking for you. He wanted you to endorse his program. It would mean everything to him if you would."

Everyone was laughing. Judith's gloom momentarily lifted, and she found herself giggling.

"I told him you weren't here," Benjy said. "He said he'd be back. I told him you'd be glad to see him."

She looked at the young man fondly. How he's grown, she thought. A month ago he wouldn't have dared make jokes like this in front of me. She looked at all of them while the laughter died down, nine young lawyers sitting in a rough semicircle, some with briefcases beside their chairs, all with case folders on their laps.

Although she had brought them together to inform them of her decision, this proved harder to do than she had thought. In fact she could not do it at all. A silence began to build up.

"What's come through the intake room in my absence?" she said, and she watched the case folders open.

"Who goes first?" inquired Brian Crawford. "Shall I tell her about the spanker?" He glanced around the room for approval. Heads began nodding, and Judith noted this. "Well—" began Crawford, and he told of a man whose habit it was to hang "casting call" notices on college bulletin boards. He would lure girls to a series of one-room offices where he had videotape equipment set up.

Judith grimaced. Another videotape case. She expected to hear next about dismembered corpses.

Once alone in the office with the girl, the man would make her get into a frilly little costume. He would then hand her the "script," according to which she was a college student who had got an F on her exam. As a result her professor, to be played by none other than the casting director himself, was obliged to spank her. He laid each girl out across his lap and spanked her soundly in front of his camera.

"He spanked every aspiring actress in every college dramatic department in the metropolitan area, I think," said Brian. "The colleges were completely taken in. One of them hired a bus to take the girls to his office. He must have spanked two hundred and fifty girls before one of them complained."

Everybody was laughing.

"That's all he did," continued Brian. "He spanked them. He promised each girl he would send the film to Hollywood for the producer's consideration, and he sent the girl home to await the producer's phone call."

Even Judith was laughing now.

"You know the movies," Brian said, "don't call us, we'll call you."

Brian was shaking his head in wonderment. "He's the president of a major insurance company, and legally speaking, we have a problem."

Judith said, "What do we charge him with?"

"Right. The girls consented, after all."

The laughter died out and the legal problem was discussed. It would have to come under one of the fraud statutes, probably.

The next case—David Reidy began to describe it—presented legal problems also. A prostitute had got raped with a thermos bottle.

This created an image in everybody's mind, one so bizarre that all the grins came on again.

"Did it kill her?" inquired Judith.

"No, no." Reidy said. "The worst thing about this case is that it fit fine. Easy as pie."

Everyone began giggling, Judith included.

"That's where the legal problem comes in," said Reidy. "Usually in such cases the medical evidence is conclusive. But in this one it isn't, if you know what I mean. No abrasions or lacerations. Nothing."

"Sounds like she enjoyed it," said Benjy.

More laughter. In the face of such grotesque events one had either to laugh or cry, Judith thought. And one couldn't cry all the time.

The laughter was interrupted by Marcy Miller. "Here's a case you're not going to believe."

"I don't believe any of them so far," said Judith. But she did. She was again in contact with the extremes of human behavior, was again experiencing the normal range of her working day's emotions: bewilderment, wonder, awe.

"The victim is a female patient in a hospital room," said Marcy. "She's sedated. The male defendant has sneaked into her bathroom where he's putting on a dress. He comes out of the bathroom wearing makeup and a dress. She's in traction. He jumps on the bed and caresses her. She comes to and starts screaming, and he runs out." Marcy's head was nodding up and down. "The defendant had lost a testicle in an automobile accident," she explained. "I guess he had an identity complex."

Everyone was laughing.

"I can top that," said Benjy Goldberg.

Judith thought, This is like a vaudeville act—and it's the same every week, every day.

"The victim," said Benjy, "was a man, a woman, a lesbian, and a transsexual."

"How many victims is that?" inquired Judith, puzzled.

"One. It's all the same guy, or woman, or whatever he was."

"Was?"

"He was this fag who did nightclub shows in drag. His stage name was Dottie Fuck-fuck. I mean, he didn't work in your better nightclubs. Finally he had a sex change operation. This altered his stage act a bit. From now on the climax of his act every night is when he hoists his skirts and shows himself off."

Brian Crawford exploded with laughter.

"He throws over his homosexual lover and marries a guy," continued Benjy. "The morning after the wedding night he calls up the homosexual lover and says to him, 'My husband's an animal. I think he broke it.'"

The room broke into gales of laughter. Judith was laughing as hard as anyone.

Benjy said, "The homosexual lover is wild with jealousy. So is the husband's former girlfriend, who is a lesbian by the way—wait till you see the witnesses in this case—and they persuade the husband to help them kill Dottie Fuck-fuck."

Benjy himself was laughing now. Judith had tears of laughter in her eyes. Finally she said, "It's really just an ordinary murder, isn't it? It's not ours."

"The victim," said Benjy, "had a mouthful of semen."

"So it's ours," said Judith.

And the laughter stopped.

Mr. Katz stuck his head in the door. "The district attorney is ready to see you now," he said to Judith.

Having told them nothing of her decision, Judith dismissed her young assistants. I'll tell them tomorrow, she thought, and she walked across the hall.

The district attorney was sitting behind his desk eating an apple. "Sit down," he said, "that's a great tan you have there." Reaching into a paper bag, he threw her an apple, and she caught it.

"You have a pretty nice tan yourself," she said.

What was it now that so weakened her resolve? Was it seeing her young assistants again, and laughing with them so hard over such terrible crimes? I can't help wanting to help, she thought. Was it the warmth in this old man's eyes? Was it something as ordinary as catching his apple on the fly?

They sat munching their apples, and the old man gazed at her affectionately. "It's nice to get away for a few days, isn't it?"

"It's nice to get back, too."

"Was there something special you wanted to talk to me about?"

She wanted to say: I have come in here to resign. But she couldn't do it.

She had made some mistakes, but would not make those particular mistakes again. She was needed here, and she wanted to stay.

"Something special?" she said. "No, nothing special."

27 million Americans can't read a bedtime story to a child.

It's because 27 million adults in this country simply can't read.

Functional illiteracy has reached one out of five Americans. It robs them of even the simplest of human pleasures, like reading a fairy tale to a child.

You can change all this by joining the fight against illiteracy.

Call the Coalition for Literacy at toll-free **1-800-228-8813** and volunteer.

Volunteer Against Illiteracy. The only degree you need is a degree of caring.